LADY EVE'S INDISCRETION

GRACE BURROWES

sourcebooks
casablanca

Published by Sourcebooks Casablanca, an imprint of Sourcebooks,
Inc.
P.O. Box 4410, Naperville, Illinois 60567-4410
(630) 961-3900
FAX: (630) 961-2168
www.sourcebooks.com

Printed and bound in the United States of America
VP 10 9 8 7 6 5 4 3 2 1

This book is dedicated to my beloved daughter, who has taught me more about love, and more about getting back on the horse, than anyone else in my life. Heather, being your mom is and ever shall be my greatest privilege and my greatest joy.

Windham Family Tree

KATHLEEN ST. JUST

- - - - - - - - - -

PERCIVAL WINDHAM, *DUKE OF MORELAND*

m.

ESTHER, *DUCHESS OF MORELAND*

CECILY O'DONNELL

- - - - - - - - - -

MAGDALENE WINDHAM
Book Five, *Lady Maggie's Secret Scandal*

m.

BENJAMIN PORTMAINE, *EARL OF HAZELTON*

DEVLIN ST. JUST, *EARL OF ROSECROFT*
Book Two, *The Soldier*

m.

EMMALINE FARNUM

COLONEL BARTHOLOMEW WINDHAM, *MARQUIS OF PEMBROKE* (deceased)

GAYLE WINDHAM, *EARL OF WESTHAVEN*
Book One, *The Heir*

m.

ANNA SEATON
JAMES

VICTOR WINDHAM (deceased)

VALENTINE WINDHAM
Book Four, *The Virtuoso*

m.

ELLEN FITZENGLE MARKHAM, BARONESS ROXBURY

SOPHIE WINDHAM
Book Three, *Lady Sophie's Christmas Wish*

m.

WILHELM CHARPENTIER, *BARON SINDAL*

LOUISA WINDHAM
Book Six, *Lady Louisa's Christmas Knight*

m.

JOSEPH CARRINGTON, *EARL OF KESMORE*

JENNY WINDHAM
Book Eight

EVE WINDHAM
Book Seven, *Lady Eve's Indiscretion*

One

"WHAT YOU SEEK TO ACCOMPLISH, MY LORD, IS ARGU-ably impossible."

Earnest Hooker shuffled files while he sat in judgment of the Marquis of Deene's aspirations. When the ensuing silence stretched more than a few moments, the solicitor readjusted his neck cloth, cleared his throat, and shifted his inkwell one inch closer to the edge of the blotter centered on his gargantuan desk.

Two of his minions watched the client—whom they no doubt expected to rant and throw things in the grand family tradition—from a careful distance.

Lucas Denning, newly minted Marquis of Deene, took out the gold watch Marie had given him when he'd come down from university. The thing had stopped for lack of timely winding, but Deene made it a point to stare at his timepiece before speaking.

"Impossible, Hooker? I'm curious as to the motivation for such hyperbole from a man of the law."

One clerk glanced nervously at the other when Hooker stopped fussing with his files.

"My lord, you cannot mean to deprive a man of

the company of his legitimate offspring." Hooker's pudgy, lily-white hands continued to fiddle with the accoutrements of his trade. "We're discussing a girl child, true, but one in her father's possession in even the simplest sense. The courts do not exist to satisfy anybody's whims, and you can't expect them to pluck that child from her father's care and place her in… in *yours*. You have no children of your own, my lord, no wife, no experience raising children, and you've yet to see to your own succession. Even were the man demented, the courts would likely consider other possibilities before placing the girl in your care."

Deene snapped the watch shut. "I heard her mother's dying wishes. That should count for something. Wellington wrote me up in the dispatches often enough."

One of the other men came forward, a prissier, desiccated version of Hooker, with fewer chins and less hair.

"My lord, do you proceed on dying declarations alone, that will land you in Chancery, where you'll be lucky to have the case heard before the girl reaches her majority. And endorsements of a man's wartime abilities by the Iron Duke are all well and good, but consider that raising children, most especially young girl children, should not have much in common with battling the Corsican."

An insult lurked in that soft reply, but truth as well. Every street sweeper in London knew the futility of resorting to the Court of Chancery. The clerk had not exaggerated about the delays and idiosyncrasies of that institution.

"I'm sorry, my lord." Hooker rose, while Deene

remained seated. "We look forward to serving the marquessate in all of its legal undertakings, but in this, I'm afraid, we cannot honestly advise you to proceed."

Deene got to his feet, taking small satisfaction from being able to look down his nose, quite literally, at the useless ciphers whose families he kept housed and fed. "Draw up the pleadings anyway."

He stalked out of the room, the urge to destroy something, to pitch Hooker's idiot files into the fire, to snatch up the fireplace poker and lay about with it, nigh overcoming his self-discipline.

"My lord?"

The third man had the temerity to follow Deene from the room, which was going to serve as a wonderful excuse for Deene's long-denied display of frustration—a marquis did *not* have tantrums—when Deene realized the man was carrying a pair of well-made leather gloves.

"My thanks." Deene snatched the gloves from the man's hand, but to his consternation, the fellow held onto the gloves for a bit, making for a short tug-of-war.

"If your lordship has one more moment?"

The clerk let the gloves go. The exchange had been bizarre enough to penetrate Deene's ire, mostly because, between Hooker & Sons and the Marquis of Deene, obsequies were the order of the day and had been for generations.

"Speak." Deene pulled on a glove. "You're obviously ready to burst with some crumb of legal wisdom your confreres were not inclined to share."

"Not legal wisdom, my lord." The man glanced over his shoulder at the closed door behind them.

"Simple common sense. You'll not be able to wrest the girl from her father through litigious means, but there are other ways."

Yes, there were. Most of them illegal, dangerous, and unethical—but tempting.

Deene yanked on the second glove. "If I provoke him to a duel, Dolan stands an even chance of putting out my lights, sir, a consummation my cousin and sole heir claims would serve him very ill. I doubt I'd enjoy it myself."

This fellow was considerably younger than the other two, with an underfed, scholarly air about him and a pair of wire-rimmed glasses gracing his nose. The man drew himself up as if preparing for oral argument.

"I do not advocate murder, my lord, but every man, every person, has considerations motivating them. The girl's father is noted to be mindful of his social standing and his wealth."

Vulgarly so. "Your point?"

"If you offer him something he wants more than he wants to torment you over the girl, he might part with her. The problem isn't legal. The solution might not be legal either."

If there was sense in what the young man was saying, Deene was too angry to parse it out.

"My thanks. I will consider the *not legal* alternatives, as you suggest. Good day."

"My lord, that wasn't what I meant—"

Deene was down the stairs and out the door before the idiot could finish his sentence. Fortunately for all in Deene's path, his coachman was just bringing the horses around the corner at a sedate walk. Deene climbed in before the vehicle even stopped moving.

Anthony Denning folded down his edition of the *Times*, his expression impassive. "Any luck with your pet weasels?"

Deene appropriated the spot beside him, since Anthony was on the forward-facing seat. "They were waiting for me to lay waste to the office from the moment I arrived."

"Uncle once said that was the best way to get their attention."

Deene stared out the window, knowing Anthony was simply trying to make conversation. "His tempers were just another way for him to feel powerful while incurring ridiculous costs and earning a reputation as a dangerous lunatic."

Anthony set the paper aside as Deene banged twice on the roof quite stoutly. The horses moved up to the trot only to come back to the walk two blocks later.

"I should have ridden."

"You should have let me accompany you," Anthony said. He had the knack of sounding not like he was scolding, which he was, but like he was saddened to have been denied an opportunity to serve.

"You'll make a lousy marquis when Dolan douses my lights, Anthony. I appreciate the support, but my problems with Dolan are personal."

Anthony bore the same Denning family features as his cousin: blue eyes, wavy blond hair, a lanky build, and decent features. He'd *look* like a Marquis of Deene, but he'd never be able to carry out the displays of temper, incontinent drinking, and excesses of sexual indulgence Polite Society expected of the titleholder.

Anthony did, however, make a fine supervisor to the myriad Deene land stewards, for which Deene was shamelessly grateful.

"I'll take Beast out this afternoon prior to the fashionable hour. Perhaps some carousing tonight will improve my humor as well."

Anthony picked up his newspaper, a bland smile on his face. "A man newly out of mourning cannot neglect his carousing. Once the Season starts, you'll be waltzing the night away. Then there's every house party and shooting party in the land to attend while each ambitious mama in the realm tries to put you on a leash for her darling daughter."

"If you're trying to cheer me up, Cousin, you are failing spectacularly."

Though the solicitors had mentioned that a man with a wife might stand a better chance in the courts than one without.

What a dolorous, uncomfortable thought.

⌗

Lady Eve Windham's great fall had happened on her sixteenth birthday. In the eyes of Polite Society, it was a bad fall from a fast horse.

Eve's family knew it to be a fall from grace, while Eve understood it to be a fall of even more disastrous dimensions than that. A long, hard fall, involving injury to her heart—not just her left wrist and hip— and requiring years of convalescence. Seven years later—she found something ominously biblical about the length of time—she still hadn't gotten back on a horse.

Nor entirely mended her heart.

Neither situation merited much notice though, because she'd been born the youngest daughter of Their Graces, the Duke and Duchess of Moreland. The Windham family's consequence was such that the exact nature of this youthful indiscretion was never allowed to reach the ears of the gossips, sparing Eve that most inconvenient and troublesome Windham family tradition—Great Scandal.

Great Scandal might as well have the status of a great-aunt, so frequently did it come to call upon the Windhams. His Grace's offspring included two by-blows, both fortunately conceived prior to his acquisition of the title, and also—God be thanked—before his acquisition of a duchess.

When Windhams married, the firstborn was typically not a nine-months babe. In fact, nobody could recall when a Windham firstborn *had* been a nine-months babe, not even back to the present duke's late grandfather. And yet, Windham infants were notoriously healthy from birth.

The Windham sisters had by a narrow margin evaded what amounted to the family curse. With Maggie and Sophie wed, that margin was so narrow as to suggest Windham brides conceived on their very wedding nights. The third Windham sister to marry, Louisa, Countess of Kesmore, was being closely watched to see if she too was going to present her earl with an heir in such spanking time.

Eve Windham, by contrast, had no intention of allowing herself to encounter those circumstances conducive to the subsequent appearance of a baby.

Not now, not ever.

And therein lay a problem of disastrous—even scandalous—proportions, for no less a person than Esther, Her Grace, the Duchess of Moreland, had lately taken a notion to see her two remaining unwed daughters escorted up the aisle.

Locked in wed, as Eve's brothers used to say.

All three brothers were married now, and saying very different things indeed.

"Smile, Evie. Trottenham is on his way over."

Eve pasted the requisite smile on her face and glanced around the ballroom. "Be still my tender heart." The tone of her words was at variance with their content, which caused Eve's sister Genevieve to smile as well.

"He's not so bad, or you wouldn't have given him a minuet."

Eve said nothing as her latest admiring swain wove ever closer through the crowd. Jenny was right: he wasn't so bad, or so good. He'd serve as one of this Season's decoys if need be.

Eve kept her smile in place, though the thought of another entire Season—months!—of social prevarication made her oppressively tired.

"My lady." Trottenham bowed over her hand, bringing his heels together like some stuffy Prussian officer.

"Mr. Trottenham, a pleasure." Though it wasn't.

"I believe the sets are forming for my dance." He wiggled his blond eyebrows, probably his attempt at flirtation. Jenny took a whiff of her wrist corsage, though Eve thought her sister might be hiding a smirk.

Eve placed her gloved fingers over his hand, and for the thousandth time, prepared to tread that fine line between reeling a man in and casting him away. In the course of the dance, she batted her eyes, though twice she forgot the name of Mr. Trottenham's estate. She let him hold her a trifle too close—as she tittered. The grating titter was a rarefied art form.

"Lady Eve, has my conversation grown tiresome?" Trottenham twirled her gently under his arm while he spoke, and the slight resulting vertigo was Eve's first clue she was in trouble.

"Nonsense, Mr. Trottenham. I'm merely concentrating a bit on the steps of the dance." She treated him to her most fatuous simper, while sounds around her altered as if from far away, including the sound of Eve's own voice. Each sound became both clearer—more detached from other noises—and less real.

"One can't expect such a pretty little lady to dance and follow a conversation." Trottenham beamed an indulgent smile at her. "Though my sisters tell me…"

He prattled on, while Eve dealt with the peculiar sense that her head was three feet wide and that she could feel sensations with her hair. By the time the dance concluded, the visual distortions had begun.

"Jenny, I must leave." Eve kept her voice down. The next afflictions would be nausea and much-worse vertigo, and there was no way on earth Eve could afford talk to circulate that she had been unwell or dizzy at a social function.

Jenny's perpetual smile dimmed. "Is it a megrim, dearest?"

"A bad one." Though there was no such thing as a good megrim. "There must have been red wine in the punch."

"Mama's playing cards with Aunt Gladys. I can fetch her and have the coach brought around."

"There's not time." Before Eve's eyes, odd lights began to pulse around Jenny's head.

"Deene is here. He can see you home."

Eve made no protest, which was surely a measure of abject misery. "Fetch him."

Jenny moved off while Eve sidled closer to the French doors letting in fresh air from the terrace. The Season was still a few weeks off, so the night was brisk. The darkness beckoned, as did the quiet.

Quiet and darkness were her only friends when a headache struck. Laudanum was a last resort, lest she become dependent on it.

"Lady Eve." Deene stood before her, tall and strikingly handsome in his evening finery. He bowed over her hand, doing a credible impersonation of a proper gentleman. "You don't look well."

How perceptive. At least he'd spoken quietly.

She managed to bat her eyes at him. "Get me out of here without causing talk. *Please.*"

His gaze traveled over her quickly, assessingly. Eve would have hated that, except it was a completely impersonal inventory. "A breath of fresh air is in order."

"Deene, nobody is going to believe—"

He tucked her hand over his arm, beamed a brilliant smile at her, and led her out to the terrace. As soon as they'd gained the edge of the illumination cast by the torches, he paused and took off his jacket. "Unless you start squawking, nobody remarked our departure."

He settled his jacket over Eve's shoulders and gave

the lapels a little tug to bring it close around her. Eve's first impression was of blessed warmth.

"Thank you."

"My pleasure." He didn't exactly sneer the words, but neither were they sincere. No matter. If he could get Eve home without further embarrassment, she'd suspend their skirmishing for one evening and be grateful.

He offered his arm again. "There's a gate this way we can use."

Eve hadn't meant to hesitate, but it was difficult even to think when that ominous ache started up at the base of her skull.

"For God's sake, Eve Windham, it was just a kiss under the mistletoe, probably inspired by your papa's wassail more than anything else."

She had to put her hand on his arm while the feeling of the ground shifting beneath her feet swept over her. "My brothers said it was white rum."

"The occasional tot makes the holiday socializing less tedious. You really do not look well."

The last observation was grudging, almost worried.

"I did not mean to swill from your glass, Deene. You should have stopped me." They had to get to the coach. The night felt like it was closing in, and Deene's voice—a perfect example of male aristo-cratic euphony—was swelling and shrinking in the oddest way.

"I might have stopped you, except you downed the whole drink before I realized what was afoot, and then you were accosting me in the most passionate—"

Eve clutched his arm and swayed into him,

breathing shallowly through her mouth. "If you insist on arguing with me, my lord, I will be ill all over these bushes."

"Why didn't you say so?" He slipped an arm around her waist and promenaded her down the steps. By the time they got to the garden gate, the nausea was subsiding, though Eve was leaning heavily on her escort. She had the notion that the scents of cedar and lavender coming from Deene's jacket might have helped quiet her stomach.

Deene ushered her through the gate, which put them on a quiet, mercifully dark side street.

"How often do these headaches befall you?"

"Too often. Sometimes I go for months between attacks, sometimes only days. The worst is when it hits on one side, subsides for a day, then strikes on the other."

Deene pulled one of his gloves off with his teeth, then used two fingers to give a piercing, three-blast whistle. "Sorry."

All the while he kept his arm around Eve's waist, a solid, warm—and quite unexpected—bulwark against complete disability. "The coach will here in moments. Is there anything that helps?"

"Absolute quiet, absolute dark, time." Though her mother used to rub her neck, and that had helped the most.

He said nothing more—Deene wasn't stupid—and Eve just leaned on him. Her grandmother had apparently suffered from these same headaches, though neither Eve's parents nor her siblings were afflicted.

The clip-clop of hooves sounded like so much gunfire in Eve's head, but it was the sound of privacy, so Eve tried to welcome it. Deene gave the coachy directions to the Windham mansion and climbed in after Eve.

"Shall I sit beside you, my lady?"

An odd little courtesy, that he would even ask.

"Please. The less I move, the less uncomfortable I am."

He settled beside her and looped an arm around her shoulders. Without a single thought for dignity, skirmishes, or propriety, Eve laid her head on his shoulder, closed her eyes, and was grateful.

❧

To see Eve Windham brought low ought to have been satisfying in some private, ungentlemanly regard. Instead Deene felt unwelcome inclinations toward protectiveness and—it was hard to admit such a thing even to himself—helplessness.

And if there was one feeling he resented with a passion, it was helplessness where a female was concerned.

Small, silent, and miserable beside him, Lady Eve was obviously suffering with every bump over the cobbles and turn on the streets.

"Evie, is there anything I can do?" The name had slipped out, harking back to a time when he'd been more an older-brother-by-association to his fellow officers' sisters. "Evie?"

She cuddled closer, like a suffering animal looking for relief. "My mama used to rub my neck. I hate this."

She was helpless too, he realized, and equally unhappy about it. How strange, that after growing increasingly quarrelsome with each other, they'd find pride as their common ground. This temporary truce put him in mind of the way the French and British armies would declare an unspoken détente regarding the use of rivers and streams flowing between their respective warring camps on the Peninsula.

"Let's try something." He pulled a lap rug from under the padded bench and spread it over his knees. "Down you go."

With him braced against a corner of the coach, he eased Eve facedown over the makeshift pillow on his knees. When she made no protest, he found her nape with his bare hand and started a slow massage. "Does that help?"

"Heavenly."

He could feel her ease somewhat, though in deference to her condition, the horses were moving only at a walk. "Shall I take your pins out?"

"Please, God. I can feel them. My hair hurts."

He might have smiled, but her torment was obvious in her voice. Carefully, so carefully, he eased the pins from her coiffure, until her hair hung down in a long, golden braid. She was unmoving against him while he alternated between gently squeezing the sides of her neck and rubbing her nape.

They would not speak of this peculiar interlude, and Deene had been a fool to bring up their one stupid kiss at Christmas past. Eve had been adorably tipsy, having swiped his glass of thoroughly spiked punch, and he'd enjoyed the effects of the alcohol on her demeanor. Enjoyed her passionate, artless, determined kisses much more—and much longer—than he should have.

She'd been a cheerful, even mischievous girl, dear

and sweet and easy to tease. With her brother Bart's death, something had changed and not for the better. When Deene had made some courtesy calls after selling his commission, he'd found Eve Windham to be punctiliously proper, stiff, and even chilly toward him, though Bart had more than intimated that the lady had her reasons.

She wasn't chilly now. She was utterly undone. It pleased him not at all to see it.

He had, though, been pleased to find himself accosted in the coat closet out at Morelands over the holidays. The old Eve had been there in that kiss—wicked, sweet, playful, but also all grown-up in the best places.

"Eve, we're here. Shall I carry you?"

She sat up slowly, her hand going to her forehead. "I can walk."

Or she'd crawl, or expire of pride in the filth of the mews before she'd allow him to assist her where others might notice. He handed her out of the carriage, and any fool could see she was none too steady on her feet. "You can ring a peal over my head later, my lady."

"Deene, no." Such a weak protest wasn't going to deter him from scooping her up against his chest and proceeding toward the house.

"For once in your stubborn life, hush. Your brothers would expect this much of me."

The reference to her brothers was intended as a sop to her pride and a warning—it was also the truth. In addition to the late Lord Bart, Deene had also served with Devlin St. Just, now Earl of Rosecroft. If Rosecroft got wind Evie had received cavalier treatment when in distress, a friendship Deene valued greatly would falter. To say nothing of what the lady's father would do to Deene should Moreland learn his daughter had been allowed to suffer needlessly.

"Where are you taking me?"

"Inside." He'd run tame in this house for years, so he was able to clarify. "To your room."

He managed the service door off the kitchen, it being the family practice not to lock it until everyone was in for the night. Two flights up had him in the family wing, where he himself had been an occasional guest.

"Which door, Evie?"

"Don't call me that. Next one on the right."

The listlessness of her scold rankled, and when Eve's lady's maid came scampering out of the dressing room, Deene felt a reluctance to surrender his burden.

"Lady Eve is suffering a megrim. You'll want to fetch the lavender water and perhaps a tot of the poppy. You're not to brush out her hair or do anything other than exactly as she directs."

The woman's expression suggested she'd never beheld her lady in a strange gentleman's arms, much less in the confines of the lady's own apartments. "I'll take good care of her, my lord."

"See that you do." He wanted to deposit Evie on the bed, but her dignity would not thank him. Carefully, he set her on her feet, keeping an arm around her shoulders.

"Turn down the bed, Hammet." Eve's voice was a weary thread of sound. "Please."

The maid bustled off to put coals in the bed warmer, leaving Deene to peer down at the woman half-leaning on him. "Shall I alert anybody?"

"Hammet is used to this. Good night, Deene, and thank you." She went up on her toes, blinked her pretty green eyes at him once, then kissed his cheek and subsided on a sigh.

After that, there was nothing for Deene to do but bow courteously over her hand and take his leave.

⌘

"Papa?"

"*Oui, mon coeur?*"

Mischievous blue eyes peered up at Jonathan Patrick Francis Dolan. "Why don't you speak the Irish anymore? I hear it only if you sing to me."

Dolan smiled down at the prettiest female he'd ever beheld. "Because a proper lady knows her French." He turned a page in a worn copy of *Robinson Crusoe*. "Shall I read about poor Crusoe in French?"

Translating as he went would be a challenge for a man who'd picked up his French on the docks of Calais, but for her he'd muddle along.

"Please don't." Georgina shifted on the sofa beside him. "Miss Ingraham makes me recite in French every morning. Will you sing to me tonight?"

Eight years old and already she was learning to wheedle. He didn't know whether to be proud or dismayed. "Will you apply yourself to your French, *acushla mo chroí?*"

She pursed her lips while Dolan ran his hand over a tidy golden braid. Thank a merciful God she'd gotten her mother's English blond locks and not Dolan's unruly auburn hair.

He'd stopped up in the nursery suite when he should have been down in his office, reviewing the accounts of any number of lazy subcontractors, thieving factors, and useless suppliers. The next thing he knew, he'd been cozened into reading just a few pages of an old favorite, and an hour had gone by.

Not a wasted hour, but a precious hour stolen from a press of business that never left him enough time with his only child.

"Tell you what," he said, setting the book aside. "If Miss Ingraham gives a good account of your French, I'll sing to you tomorrow night."

"Why not tonight?"

"I'm going out, my heart, and you are going to mind Miss Ingraham, say your prayers, and dream sweet dreams."

She reached for the book and laid it open on her lap. "I'll dream of a pony."

"Learn your French, and I'll get a pony for you to keep at Whitley."

The look she gave him was curiously adult. "We won't go to Whitley until it's summer, and it's not even completely spring yet."

Before she could start needling him, Dolan kissed her crown and rose. "Learn your French, Georgina dearest, and then you'll be in a stronger bargaining position."

"You'll start on my needlepoint, next. I'll never get a pony." Fortunately, she was grinning.

"Who wants a pony when there are magical unicorns to be had?" He tapped her nose with one callused finger and took himself off, before she could tell him there were no unicorns. The first time she'd informed her father of this truth, Dolan had permitted himself a wee drop of medicinal whiskey despite it being broad daylight.

He'd recognized it as the beginning of a slippery slide away from the innocence and ease of parenting a very young child, toward the utterly bewildering prospect of shepherding a wealthy young Englishwoman into a happy and pampered adulthood.

"A caller for you, sir."

Every time he heard Brampton's voice, Dolan felt a little satisfaction. His butler had been lured away from nothing less than a duke's household, and was the embodiment of English dignity and propriety.

Brampton held out a little silver salver—gold, Dolan had learned, was too ostentatious—and Dolan peered at the card thereon.

"Tell the marquis neither I nor Miss Georgina are at home, and don't expect to be for quite—" No, let the sodding beggar keep coming around and being turned away. "Just tell him we're out for the day."

"Very good, sir."

Brampton withdrew, having the knack of moving silently and at just such a speed as to convey determination on an important errand, but not quickly enough to suggest urgency. Dolan watched him processing down the paneled corridor.

Someday, Jonathan Dolan would visit his daughter's household and see just such a butler, except that fellow would address the lady of the house as "my lady." Dolan let himself into his office and went back to dealing with the thieves, rogues, and charlatans with whom he did business every day.

❧

"You look like you could spit nails. Hardly encouraging to all the sweet young things twittering about the ballroom."

Deene knew that slightly ironic bass-baritone, and turned to see Joseph Carrington, Lord Kesmore, sipping champagne at his elbow.

"Evening, Kesmore. What has lured you from the wilds of Kent so early in the year?"

Kesmore's dark brows twitched down. "Raising hogs is vulgarly profitable. I say this to you in strictest confidence as your neighbor and friend, and as a man who has seen you so drunk you sing odes to the barmaid's feminine attributes. There is, however, a certain hardship upon the man—particularly a man newly married—who undertakes such a commercial endeavor when the weather moderates and the hog pens must be cleaned of several months' worth of pig shit."

Despite the cloying heat of the ballroom, despite the gauntlet forming for him as the orchestra warmed up, Deene's lips quirked up. "You came to Town to avoid the smell of pig shit?"

"Pig shit wafting in my bedroom window at night, pig shit scenting my linen, pig shit… but I am whining, and thank all the gods it's not me the mamas are trolling for this year."

Deene snagged a glass of champagne from a passing footman, lest he look over and see pity lurking in Kesmore's typically impassive gaze.

"My cousin Anthony, who is much more socially astute than I am, says I must accept all of the invitations now that I'm done with mourning, and leave the tedious business of the marquessate to him as my second-in-command. I suspect him of something less than selfless devotion in his advice."

"Let's head for the card room then. In my company, fewer of the sweet young things are likely to approach you directly."

A generous offer, except in the card room one gambled—an undertaking best reserved for those with ample disposable income.

"I'll bide here among the potted palms." Deene paused for a fortifying sip of his wine. "The mamas patrol out here in the ballroom, but the aunts and grandmamas are in the card room, and those dragons I am not yet drunk enough to deal with."

Kesmore did shoot him a look of pity, or perhaps simple commiseration, since the earl was himself newly married. "I'm off then, and I'll leave you to your fate. You could always say your old war injury is acting up and the dancing is beyond you."

As Kesmore stalked away, Deene lifted his flute to salute that helpful notion, and went back to leaning on a shadowed pillar as unobtrusively as he could. Given that he was several inches over six feet, his hair was golden blond perfectly hued to gleam by candlelight, and his title the highest available on the marriage mart in three years, he suspected his evening—and likely he, himself—were doomed.

Two hours later the suspicion was a patented, sealed conclusion.

"My lord, you really must lead my darling Mildred out." Lady Staines affected a simper that came off more like a glower. "She's ever so shy, and yet quite the most graceful thing on two feet."

The ever-so-shy Miss Mildred Staines was the selfsame young lady who'd not fifteen minutes ago tried to accost Deene on his way to the men's retiring room. She had claws where her fingernails should be, and if Kesmore hadn't come along at an opportune moment—

"Oh, Deene! There you are!" Eve Windham swanned up to him, a blond, green-eyed confection in a pale blue ball gown that showed only a hint of cleavage. Though why would he allow himself to remark such a thing when he was about to be dragged by the hair into holy matrimony by Lady Staines and her familiar?

"Lady Eve." He bowed over her hand, which bore a slight, pleasing scent of mock orange.

Eve greeted the ladies with voluble good cheer then beamed a smile up at Deene. "Come along, my lord. The sets are forming."

For just one moment, just the merest blink-and-he'd-miss-it instant, Eve looked him directly in the eye. She was trying to tell him...

Bless the woman. And it was the supper waltz, too.

"My apologies, Lady Eve. I was distracted by the charm of my companions. Lady Staines, Miss Staines, if you'll excuse me?"

He led Eve to the dance floor and bowed as protocol required. "You have my thanks."

She curtsied gracefully. "Repaying a favor owed."

She came up smiling, a different smile from that brilliant, cheerful—and, he suspected, false—smile she'd dispensed before the Staines women.

The introduction sounded, and he took her in his arms to the extent called for by the dance. "Have we waltzed before, my lady?"

"You have not had that pleasure since I put my hair up. The last time was at a Christmas gathering at Morelands. You were on leave with Bart and Devlin."

The music began, and as they moved off, Deene cast his memory back. He'd danced with several of the Windham sisters, even Maggie, who had been accounted the family recluse until she'd married Hazelton.

He had danced with Eve on the last leave Lord Bart had taken before his death. When Deene glanced down at his partner, he saw a shadow of that recollection in her eyes, which would not do. He pulled her a trifle closer on the next turn.

"Deene." She made his title, just five letters, sound like an entire sermon on impropriety.

"If you're going to rescue me, you have to do a proper job of it." He aimed a smile at her, pleased to see the shadows had fled from her eyes. "If I'm not seen to flirt with you, the Lady Staineses of the world will think I am still quite at large, maritally speaking."

"You are at large, maritally speaking. Just because I appropriated your company for one dance doesn't mean I'll be your decoy indefinitely."

"Decoy." He considered the notion. "The idea has a great deal of merit. And you're bound to me for supper as well, you know."

He saw by her slight grimace that she hadn't intended

this result. Her generosity had been spontaneous, then, which meant she hadn't watched him being hounded and chased and harried the livelong evening.

"A waltz and supper." She paused while they twirled through another turn, and this time Deene pulled her a shade closer still then let her ease away. "Lucas Denning, behave, or I shall put it about you have a fondness for leeks."

He danced her down the room—she was very light on her feet—realizing that his taunt had backfired. In that one moment when she'd been against his body, he'd felt an unmistakable flare of arousal.

"Just for show, my dear. You must tell me how you've managed all these years to avoid wedded bliss. I will pay you handsomely for such a secret."

Her gaze flicked up from where she'd been staring determinedly at his shoulder. "You need a wife, Deene. You've only the one cousin to manage the succession, and he's not married. Besides, I'm not avoiding anything. I simply haven't taken."

"Haven't taken?" He'd heard her brothers grumbling about having to beat Evie's swains away with muttered threats and thunderous scowls.

"I'm short. A proper English beauty is willowy, like Jenny." She gave him the false smile again.

"You fit me well enough." The words were out, grumbled but honest, and Eve went back to staring at his shoulder.

And they had yet to get through supper. He cast around for a harmless topic.

"What do you hear from St. Just?" As conversational gambits went, that one was creditable. Eve's oldest brother had served with Deene, then two years after Waterloo, been awarded a Yorkshire earldom.

"He's thriving up in the West Riding. We saw him at Christmas, and I think the dales agree with him—or marriage and fatherhood does."

Did she sound wistful, or was she merely missing her brother?

"Perhaps I should pay him a visit." Though it was probably still winter on the dales.

Eve was silent a minute, then she cast her gaze over him again in that assessing, female way. "Lucas, they're just girls. They've been brought up to want nothing more than a man who can provide for them and give them babies. Your title, your fabulous good looks, your estates, they are so much gilt on the lily. Find a woman with whom you can be affectionate friends and propose to her."

Affectionate friends. She described a sophisticated, practical version of marriage, such as the beau monde expected, and such as Eve likely expected, but to Deene it loomed like an extra-chilly circle of hell crafted just for titled English lords.

Though many more evenings like this one, and the choice was going to be taken from him.

❧

By the time the music came to a close and Eve's partner had led her off the dance floor, she was regretting the impulse that made her pluck the man from the jaws of Lady Staines's ambitions. He was a former cavalry officer, titled, and blessedly good-looking. Surely the prospect of a few tittering ninnies wasn't putting that haunted look in his sky-blue eyes?

"Shall I fix you a plate, my lady?"

He was smiling down at her, his expression genial.

She'd forgotten this about him—he was a gentleman. A significant contretemps involving Maggie's past had been resolved directly before her marriage, but only with Deene's willing, adroit, and very discreet assistance. A damsel in distress, or a damsel in need of sustenance, would both loom as an inescapable duty to him.

"Please, but avoid the aged cheeses and anything bearing a resemblance to red wine." She moved along the buffet line with him while he piled a single plate high with various delicacies.

"Let's find a quiet corner, shall we?" Her escort leaned down to nearly whisper in her ear. "The less conspicuous I am, the less I'm likely to attract a wife."

She did not snort, but the man could hardly help but attract notice. Were she anything less than the daughter of a duke—the theoretically *eligible* daughter of a duke—he would be swarmed even in the buffet line.

"Perhaps in the gallery?" Eve suggested. She led him across the hall to the long, high-ceilinged space that opened onto the terraces. A few of the doors were propped open, making the place both quieter and cooler.

"Down there." Deene gestured with the hand holding the plate. His other arm had been offered to Eve for escort, as if by her very presence she could ward off encroaching mamas.

Which, if it came to that, she could.

They found a small table beneath an arch, a blessed oasis of privacy in an otherwise dauntingly public evening.

"I believe I owe you an apology," Eve said when they were seated.

He lounged back in his chair, a delicate little wrought iron piece that barely looked capable of holding his weight. "For?"

"Perhaps not an apology." Eve picked up a forced strawberry and considered it. "I love strawberries, but I have this notion they taste better when they're allowed to develop according to their own natures." She popped it in her mouth and watched while Deene did likewise with a smaller berry.

He had a lovely mouth. She hadn't forgotten that for a moment, blast the man.

"What would you be apologizing for?" He picked up another strawberry, drawing Eve's attention to his hands. Without his gloves, their strength was obvious. Those hands had been on her person, they'd offered her relief from misery, and at Christmas...

She frowned at a section of orange. "You haven't tattled, so to speak. You have my thanks for that."

"Tattled." He sat forward, a predator catching a scent. The strawberry had disappeared, Eve knew not where. "Tattled, regarding your headache? What kind of gentleman would I be if I bruited a lady's distress all around the clubs? How would that—?"

Eve shook her head. Men were obtuse. Her brothers claimed that women were too indirect and subtle, but it was a bona fide fact men were thickheaded about certain important matters.

"At Christmas," she said very quietly. The walls had ears, after all. "You didn't"—she stared at another section of orange—"kiss and tell. I appreciate that."

She felt compelled to state her thanks for his discretion. The words put something right between them that Eve had been allowing to drift in the wrong direction. The spatting and skirmishing was all well and good, but this needed to be said too.

"Now this is interesting." He addressed a luscious strawberry, red-ripe all over, the exact shape and size a strawberry ought to be, but when had his chair shifted so close? "I am trying to do the pretty without being caught in parson's mousetrap, I suffer a small lapse of propriety while under the influence with a lady whom all esteem, and you think it's *your* name I'm protecting?"

He popped the strawberry into his mouth and considered her in a lazy-lidded way that had Eve's insides pitching in odd directions.

"Why are you bristling, Deene? I'm offering my thanks."

He finished chewing the strawberry, though his blue eyes had bored into hers as he'd consumed it. "Did you enjoy our kiss, Evie?"

Evie. Only her family called her that—and him. He said it with a particular intimate inflection her family never used though.

She sat up very straight. "Your question has no proper answer. If I say no, then I am dishonest—I flew at you, after all, and you had to peel me off of you—and if I say yes, then I am wicked."

"Because if you *did* enjoy that kiss," he went on as if she hadn't spoken, "for I certainly enjoyed it, then perhaps you might be thanking me for the kiss and not for keeping the silence any man with sense or manners would have kept."

With him staring at her like that, it was hard to grasp the sense of his words, but Eve made the effort.

He was offended that she'd thanked him.

Any man admitted under her parents' roof would have been discreet about such a moment.

He had enjoyed that kiss.

He leaned forward, so close Eve could catch the scent of his lavender-and-cedar soap, so close she could…

Feel his lips, soft and knowing, against her cheek. Oh, she should turn away. There was no convenient tankard of spiked punch to blame, no holiday cheer, no reckless sense of yet another sibling slipping away into marriage.

His hand came up to cradle her jaw, then to shift her head slightly so she faced him. Those soft, knowing lips teased their way to her mouth, gently, inexorably. He did not use force or even anything approximating force. He *supported* her into the kiss.

That other kiss had been different. They'd started off observing a silly holiday tradition and ended up breathless and—she hoped—mutually surprised.

This kiss was—God help her, it was *tender*, deliberate, as delicious as the strawberries she could taste when Deene's tongue seamed her lips. Her hand cradled his jaw, too, not to keep him close but to complement the sensation of his tongue easing into her mouth.

"Deene, I don't know what to do."

He said nothing, just covered her mouth with his again, openmouthed, and then his tongue came calling, teasing her to taste him in return. When she did, she felt a shudder go through him, felt him hitch

closer physically, and felt her own sense of balance
desert her.

Now she kept her hand on him as a point of reference, a way to keep the concepts of up, down, north,
and south—his body and hers—all in an understandable relationship. He'd shaven recently, and—

He took her lower lip between his teeth and didn't
exactly bite, but closed his teeth over her flesh. The
sensation was not of being trapped but of being held.
Eve felt his other hand, large and warm, settle on her
neck. The contact was lovely, comforting, intimate,
and reassuring, while the kiss was anything but.

Maybe he sensed she was reaching her limit,
because he took his mouth away and rested his forehead against hers instead. "Tell me you enjoyed that,
Evie. One kiss doesn't have to mean anything. It isn't
a great scandal. It's just a small pleasure between two
people who likely have little enough pleasure to call
their own."

His hand moved around to cover her nape, as if
to encourage her to remain in this forehead-kiss until
he'd had her answer, while she wanted to hide her face
against his shoulder. "I enjoyed it. I should not have,
but I did. The other, too. At Christmas. I enjoyed that."

Such an admission was stupid, but in the privacy of
their odd embrace—her other hand had come up to
grasp his lapel—honesty felt safe. Honesty with him.

He eased away but kept his one hand on her jaw for
a last, fleeting caress. The loss of him left Eve chilled
and bewildered. What had she just permitted?

What had she just admitted?

"Have the last strawberry." He pushed the plate

closer to her, his expression inscrutable. He'd tasted like strawberries.

"Perhaps a bit of ham and melon," she said, helping herself. Was this how sophisticated people conducted their kisses? Between bites of fruit while half the beau monde chattered itself insensate a few rooms away?

She was saved from having to scrounge up some credible inanity to serve as conversation by the approach of Jenny and Louisa. Her sisters should have been a welcome sight, a source of relief.

Amid all the other emotions rioting through her, Eve could not identify either relief or welcome.

❦

Deene knew for a fact Eve Windham had been out at least a good five years. She'd had beaus, followers, and admirers, and even several offers, but she kissed like... like an innocent.

At Christmas, she'd flung herself into a kiss with such abandon, Deene had wondered who was holding onto whom under that sprig of mistletoe. When he should have stepped back and turned the moment into a holiday superficiality, she'd cupped a hand around his neck and made a sound of longing and pleasure in the back of her throat, and that—more than the rum, more than the holidays, more than too many months of celibacy—had him diving right back into the kiss.

Burgeoning lust alone had made him step back.

It was no better now. She sat across from him, eating daintily, as if all the fire and wonder shared a few moments before had never happened.

"You two are hiding." Lady Genevieve Windham

smiled as she advanced down the gallery, her expression confirming that she was teasing more than accusing. Lady Louisa's—Lady Kesmore's—expression was far less congenial.

Which, in fairness, was not unusual for the fair Louisa.

Deene rose. "Ladies, welcome. Shall I fetch more chairs?"

"No need for that." Louisa still did not smile. "We've come to retrieve Evie. Mama has a breakfast to attend tomorrow, and we're taking our leave."

Eve rose, looking neither relieved nor upset to be going. When had the little hoyden he'd known turned into such a composed woman?

"Deene, good evening." She cocked her head to meet his gaze. "My thanks for a lovely waltz, and for... everything." She smiled slightly, a very different smile from any he'd seen her give out previously. This smile was sweet and a trifle mysterious. "I hope the rest of your evening is as pleasant as mine has been."

She linked arms with her sisters and departed, a petite blond bookended by taller siblings, and yet Deene had the sense Eve was the one establishing the direction of their progress.

He did not dare linger here alone in the shadows, not with the likes of Lady Staines ready to unleash their daughters on him in any unguarded moment. He picked up his plate and headed directly for the card room.

❧

"I fear I'm going to be next."

Eve waited to make this prediction until the footmen

had left and the tea trays were on the low table before the sofa.

Louisa looked up from her book—Louisa's nose was always in a book—and frowned. "Next? Next as in what? We're supposed to divine the context without any further clues, Evie?" She set the book aside and leaned forward in her chair. "Food is next, and about time too."

"What did you mean, dearest?" Jenny was sitting at the other end of the sofa, slippers off, back resting against the arm and her knees drawn up before her.

"Next to get married."

Eve's sisters were silent for a few moments, but they exchanged the most maddening of older-sister looks before Jenny leapt into the breach.

"Is Mr. Trottenham your choice then? He's a very pleasant fellow, I must agree."

"Not Trit-Trot," Louisa said, picking up a chocolate tea cake. "He's a ninnyhammer."

"He is a ninnyhammer." Eve's best decoys were always ninnyhammers. "I don't know who. I just have a feeling I'd better choose someone, or Her Grace and His Grace will start nosing about, and then all is lost."

"Lost how?" Louisa put three more cakes on her plate. "If being married means all is lost, then I'm finding it a rather agreeable end."

"Louisa, you're supposed to eat some sandwiches first," Eve observed.

"And hope there are some cakes left by then, when you two will have had at them first? I intend to eat a deal of sandwiches. What do you mean, all is lost?"

Jenny swung her feet off the sofa and set aside her

copy of *La Belle Assemblée*. "Their Graces want only to see us happy. Maggie had offer after offer, and Papa turned every one of them down."

"Maggie's situation is different," Eve said. "She made it to thirty. She was safe. Sophie has gone and married her baron too, though, and Louisa's led Joseph up the aisle. We two are all our parents have to focus on."

"Not all." Louisa frowned at her only remaining cake. "Papa has the Lords to run. Mama has Polite Society. Then, too, they've grandchildren to consider."

"But they still have us too." Eve made a little production of pouring tea all around: plain for Jenny, sugar for herself, cream and sugar in quantity for Louisa, which was an injustice of the first order. Louisa never gained weight and never seemed to stop eating.

Eve sat sipping tea, but the sense of impending marital doom gathered like a pressure in her chest. An inkling of a solution had come to her only last night, when she'd been coming home from the ball with her mother and sisters.

A white marriage.

They were not as fashionable as they'd been in old King George's day, but Eve suspected they weren't entirely unheard of anymore either. Lord and Lady Esteridge had such an arrangement, and his lordship's brother was tending to the succession.

"Shall we help you look for prospects?" Jenny asked. "Kesmore wasn't a likely prospect, but Louisa is thoroughly besotted with him."

Louisa shot Jenny an excuse-my-poor-daft-sister look. "Kesmore is a grouch, his children are complete hellions, he can hardly dance because of his perishing limp, and the man raises pigs."

"And you adore him," Jenny reiterated sweetly. "What about that nice Mr. Perrington?" Gentle persistence was Jenny's forte, one learned at the knee of Her Grace, whose gentle persistence had been known to overcome the objections of Wellington himself.

"Mr. Perrington has lost half his teeth, and the other half are not long for his mouth," Louisa observed as she moved on to the sandwiches. "Thank God he hides behind his hand when he laughs, but it gives him a slightly girlish air. I rather fancy Deene for Evie."

"Deene?" Eve and Jenny gaped in unison.

"You fancy Lucas Denning as my husband?" Eve clarified.

Louisa sat back, a sandwich poised in her hand. "He'd behave because our brothers would take it amiss were he a disappointing husband. Then too, he'd never do anything to make Their Graces think ill of him, and yet he wouldn't bring any troublesome in-laws into the bargain. He needs somebody with a fat dowry, and he's quite competent on the dance floor. He'd leave you alone for the most part. I think you could manage him very well."

Jenny's lips pursed. "You want a husband you can manage?"

Eve answered, feeling a rare sympathy for Louisa, "One hardly wants a husband one *can't* manage, does one?"

"Suppose not." Jenny blinked at the tea tray. "You left us one cake each, Lou. Not well done of you."

Louisa turned guileless green eyes on her sister. "You left me only four sandwiches, Jen."

They all started laughing at the same time, then ordered more sandwiches and more cakes, while Eve wondered if she had the courage—and determination—to find herself a man who'd be a husband in name only.

❧

"It's like this." Anthony lounged back in the chair behind the estate desk and steepled his fingers. "You aren't poor, exactly, but you haven't a great deal of cash."

Deene paced the room, wondering if his own father had felt a similar gnawing frustration. "Give me figures, Anthony. The marquessate holds at least sixty thousand acres, and I have another ten thousand in my own name. There's a soap factory in Manchester, a distillery on some Scottish island. How can I be poor?"

"Not poor, but that sixty thousand acres includes some thirty thousand bound with the entail. You can't sell it, but you have to maintain it. You must tend to the land, the cottages, the woods, even the ditches."

Deene peered at his cousin and stopped perusing a library stacked twelve feet high with books nobody read. "How does one tend to a ditch, for God's sake?"

"If it's a ditch that channels storm water, you have to keep it clear, else you'll have standing water, and that seems to lead to cholera and other nuisances."

Deene knew that. Anybody raised in expectation of holding property knew that. He pinched the bridge of his nose as a headache threatened to take up residence behind his eyes.

"Forgive me my exasperation. I should have spent

the last year gathering up the reins of my estate, not rusticating in Kent under the guise of mourning." More like a year and a half, truth be told.

Anthony's smile was sympathetic. "I've been stewarding the properties for more than a decade, Cousin, and I can tell you, his late lordship had no more gathered up the reins after thirty years than you have after less than two. We'll manage, just don't take to extravagant gambling."

"Do I need to marry for money?"

The question had to be asked. Deene could see the runners in the upper floors were worn, the carriages in his mews were out of date, and sconces in more than just the servants' quarter of the house were burning tallow candles.

Sometimes, though, a man needed to hear his sentence pronounced in the King's English.

"Marry for money?" Anthony's finely arched blond brows rose then settled again. "I didn't know you were thinking of marrying at all."

"And yet"—Deene settled into a chair facing the desk—"you constantly remind me you have no desire to inherit the title. Do we let the crown have the estate then? You've certainly shown no signs of marrying."

Too late, Deene realized the words weren't going to sound like the good-natured ribbing they were meant to be. With a carefully blank expression, Anthony closed a few of the ledgers lying on the desk, rose, and tugged on his gloves.

"Don't stick your neck in parson's mousetrap just yet," Anthony said. "Your father tried to right the marquessate's fortune in just such a manner, if you'll recall."

Tit for tat. The conversation needed to move on. "You'll get me figures, then?"

Anthony gestured to the ledgers. "Here are your figures. It's a moving target, you see. We sell a few thousand spring lambs, but in the next month, we must hire a dozen crews for shearing. Until you've had a few years—a few decades—to get a sense of the problem, the figures you see can be very misleading. A place to start would be the household ledgers. They're fairly straightforward."

Straightforward. Straightforward was a quality that seemed to have fled Deene's existence on all fronts.

"Anthony, have you ever bitten lengthwise into a fat, juicy, perfectly ripe strawberry?"

Anthony tapped his top hat onto this head, his smile returning in its most patient variation. "I'm sure I have. Are we to raise strawberries?"

"Not immediately. Thanks for your time. I'll look forward to seeing what the present cash reserves are, though, regardless of how fluid the number."

Anthony took his leave. Deene sat at the desk and opened the most recent ledger for household expenses at the London residence, which Deene would use for his abode over the next few months.

God help him.

Several hours later, his eyes were crossing, his temples were throbbing, and he had no idea how he'd make sense of the expenses listed on page after page of the damned accounting book. He'd been top wrangler in math at Cambridge his final year, and he could determine nothing from looking at the columns and columns of orderly, perfectly legible entries.

Though as he sat back and tossed the pen on the desk, he suspected part of the problem was the shocking resemblance of a strawberry split lengthwise to a particularly lovely and intimate part of the female anatomy.

Two

"HAVING FAMILY IN YOUR EMPLOY IS ALWAYS A mixed blessing."

His Grace, the Duke of Moreland, made this observation while Deene ambled along at his side in the gardens behind the Moreland mansion. "You want to provide for your dependents, and you expect they'll be somewhat more loyal than strangers would be, but it can also get complicated."

"Anthony has done a magnificent job," Deene countered. "He's never once by word or deed indicated he has designs on the title."

His Grace paused to sniff a white rose. "Then you are fortunate indeed, since he's all the family you've got."

"Not all."

His Grace straightened. "There is the girl. I'd forgotten, but you likely haven't. How does she go on?"

Upon the death of Deene's father, Percival, Duke of Moreland, had come calling with his duchess as part of the usual round of condolence visits. The Moreland estates neighbored with the seat of the

Deene marquessate, and if nothing else, His Grace and his late lordship had ridden to hounds together countless times.

What had begun as a neighborly gesture had turned into something unprecedented in Deene's experience: a mentorship of sorts on Moreland's part.

"The girl isn't in poor health, from what I can tell. Dolan does not permit me to call."

"He wouldn't turn your wife away."

Deene didn't flatter himself that he was any particular friend of Moreland's—he was a vote, perhaps, on some of the duke's pet bills—but Moreland had been generous with advice at a time when Deene was without much wisdom of his own.

"Except I have no wife."

This provoked a surprisingly sweet smile from His Grace. "Then you should rectify that poverty posthaste. Because I am the lone male in my household at present, I am more privy to the ladies' views on your situation than I would be otherwise. I understand you are being stalked by the debutantes and their mamas."

"Of course I am being stalked." Lest this conversation continue on into the Moreland home itself, Deene gestured to a bench and waited for Moreland to seat himself before doing the same. "I am the highest available title, unless you count some septuagenarian dukes with ample progeny, and I am in need of an heir. When I am riding to hounds, I will never pursue Reynard with quite the same lack of sympathy I have in the past."

"The fox most often escapes the hounds, because

he's running for his life. The wrong wife can make you entirely resent yours."

How honest could one be with a man twice one's age?

"I cannot say my parents' union escaped such a characterization."

His Grace stretched out long legs and leaned his head back, closing his eyes. "Times were different then. Matches were usually arranged by the parents for dynastic reasons, and expectations of the institution were different. Here is my advice to you, young man, which you may discard or heed at your pleasure: do not marry until you meet that person whom you cannot imagine living the rest of your life without. Call it love, call it affection, call it a fine understanding. Put whatever label you want on it. You will be wed for the rest of your life or perhaps for hers, and that can be a long, long time."

His Grace sat up and speared Deene with a look. "Take your cousin about with you socially. Have him shadow your moves so you're not waylaid in the rose arbor by some scheming minx. I know of what I speak, young Deene, having climbed out of more than one window in my heedless youth. If it hadn't been for my brother Tony, there's no telling what my fate might have been."

The confidence was surprising and... endearing. Moreland was tall, with the ramrod straight posture of the former cavalry officer and a head of distinguished white hair to go with blue eyes that could turn arctic when his will was opposed.

Just now though, the man did not look so much

like a duke as he did like a husband, a papa, a hale old fellow who valued his family above anything else.

"And here comes my duchess now to make sure I'm not lecturing you into a stupor." His Grace rose smoothly to his feet and met his duchess on the graveled walk. "My dear, I was just coming to fetch you."

She greeted Deene genially then gave His Grace her hand, which he tucked onto his arm.

"Deene, you will excuse us? Her Grace has requested my escort on a visit to Westhaven's household, and this is a privilege I would not forego even to ensure I have your vote on the shipping amendments."

Deene bowed to the duchess, who very likely fit Eve's definition of an English beauty even in the woman's sixth decade of life: tall, willowy, kind green eyes, and hair shading from gold to wheat around a face still lovely and unlined.

"Your Graces, I bid you good day, and of course you have my vote, Moreland."

"Run along into the house, then. I'm sure the girls will be sitting down to lunch. You can ask them who's most desperate for a husband and avoid the traps accordingly." His Grace winked, patted his duchess's hand, and led her off in the direction of the mews.

They had a peace about them, a sense of effortless communion Deene found fascinating, even as it made his chest feel a trifle queer.

He would not be joining the ladies for lunch—the lunching hour had passed—but he let himself in the French doors leading to the Moreland library, thinking to head straight for the front door.

"Why, Lord Deene. A pleasure." Louisa, Lady

Kesmore, smiled at him, a somewhat unnerving prospect involving a number of straight, white teeth. Lady Jenny's smile was sweeter, and Eve's smile was forced. They sat on the sofa, to Deene's eye a trio of lovely women showing graduated degrees of disgruntlement.

"I beg your pardon, my ladies, Mr. Trottenham. I did not realize I'd be intruding unannounced."

"Deene, good day." Trottenham rose and bowed, smacking his heels together audibly. "The more the merrier, I say, what? Saw your colt beat Islington's by two lengths. Well done, jolly good and all that. Islington's made a bit too much blunt off that animal in my opinion."

Trottenham apparently had a nervous affliction of the eyebrows, for they bounced up and down as he spoke, suggesting either a severe tic or an attempt to indicate some sort of shared confidence.

"Perhaps the ladies would rather we save the race talk for the clubs?"

"The ladies would indeed," Louisa said. "Sit you down, Deene, and do the pretty. Mr. Trottenham was just leaving." She gave a pointed look at the clock, while Eve, who had said nothing, busied herself pouring tea, which Deene most assuredly did not want.

"Leaving?" Trottenham's eyebrows jiggled around. "Suppose I ought, but first I must ask Lady Eve to join me at the fashionable hour for a drive around The Ring. It's a beautiful day, and I've a spanking pair of bays to show off."

Deene accepted his cup of tea with good grace. "Afraid she's not in a position to oblige, Trottenham, at least not today." He smiled over at Eve, who blinked once then smiled back.

Looking just a bit like Louisa when she did.

"Sorry, Mr. Trottenham." She did not sound sorry to Deene. "His lordship has spoken for my time today."

Trottenham's smile dimmed then regained its strength. "Tomorrow, then?"

Jenny spoke up. "We're supposed to attend that Venetian breakfast with Her Grace tomorrow."

"And the next day is His Grace's birthday. Couldn't possibly wander off on such an occasion as that," Louisa volunteered. "Why don't I see you out, Mr. Trottenham, and you can tell me where you found these bays."

She rose and took him by the arm, leaving a small silence after her departure, in which Deene spared a moment to pity poor Trottenham.

"I have an appointment at the modiste," Lady Jenny said, getting to her feet. "Lucas, I'm sure you'll excuse me."

She swanned off, leaving Eve sitting before the tea tray and Deene wondering what had just happened. "Did you tell them I've a preference for leeks?"

"I did not, but I cannot vouch for the queer starts my sisters take. Does this mean we must drive out?"

He studied her, noting slight shadows under her eyes and a pallor beneath the peaches and cream of her complexion. He hadn't truly intended the offer, but neither was he exactly unwilling to make good on it.

"Not if you don't want to. My horse can develop a loose shoe. You can come down with another megrim."

She grimaced. "I never pretend I have one if I don't—it's tempting fate too badly. Are you going to drink your tea?"

"No." He set the cup and saucer down, feeling vaguely irritated to see her looking pale and peaked. "What's troubling you, Eve Windham?"

She was silent for a moment, while Deene became aware the library door was closed and there were strawberries on the tray before her. He lifted his gaze from the damned fruit on the tray and clapped his eyes on the lady, which did not do much to stem the useless thoughts proximity to Eve Windham seemed to arouse… provoke, rather.

"I don't believe in dissembling on general principles." She glanced out the window to the gardens struggling to advance against a season when the nights were still chilly. "I suppose I can drive out with you."

"As flattering as your enthusiasm for my company is, I will still oblige you with a turn in the park. Do you need to change?"

He certainly had not intended to spend an hour or two tooling around Hyde Park with Eve Windham, except His Grace's words echoed in Deene's head: ask the Windham sisters about the social scene. Any former cavalry officer understood the benefit of sound intelligence.

Eve would know all the debutantes and the climbers, the ambitious mamas and the young girls politely described as high-strung. Abruptly, this little turn in the park loomed like a fine idea, despite any wayward notions Deene's male parts might be taking.

"I can go as I am, but I must fetch a wrap." As

she rose, she picked up a strawberry and bit into it, leaving Deene to realize that no matter what they discussed, this little trip around The Ring would be a long drive indeed.

Probably for them both.

❦

As her husband settled onto the coach seat beside her, Esther, Duchess of Moreland, tucked her hand into his.

"Husband, I must ask you something."

His smile was the embodiment of patience. "If you're going to quiz me on my habits at the club, I can tell you I've been very circumspect in my drinking. There's nothing more pathetic than some old lord passed out in his chair, droplets of wine staining his linen, yesterday's copy of the *Times* crumpled in his lap. You'd think such an example would scare the young fellows into sobriety."

"It's about the young fellows I wanted to ask you."

Beside her, Esther could feel her husband waiting. The patience they had with each other was only one of the blessings reaped from thirty-odd years of marriage.

"Are you meddling a bit, Percival, by having Deene over to the house as often as you do?"

He didn't immediately break into remonstrations and protests, which suggested the question had been timely.

"He'd do, Esther. Evie bristles when he's about, but Jenny might suit him."

"She *bristles*?"

They shared a look, part humor, part despair, before His Grace spoke. "I've not had Deene's finances looked into yet, if that's what you're asking. I like the man, and I recall all too well what it was like when the title befell us."

He always referred to it like that: the title befell *us*, not just him. Our duchy, not simply his dukedom. He was not an arrogant husband, though he could be a very arrogant duke—which Esther did not regard in any way as a fault.

"You think Deene needs a wife, then?"

He patted her hand, a slow stroking gesture that likely soothed him as much as it did her. "The fellow in need of a wife is probably the last fellow to realize his predicament, to wit, your dear and adoring husband in a younger incarnation. Deene's antecedents did not set a sanguine example in this regard. I've encouraged him to choose wisely."

"You refer to our sons when you allude to fellows not knowing they needed wives."

This merited her another smile, one hinting of mischief. "With regard to wise choices, of course I do. They take after their papa in this. If Deene were to seek to join our family, Esther, would *you* approve the match?"

She needed a moment to consider her answer. To better facilitate her cogitation, she laid her head on His Grace's shoulder.

"He was very kind to Evie when she needed help the other night."

"Ahh."

In that simple expostulation, Esther understood that her husband divined the direction of her thoughts.

"Our perpetual darling." His Grace sighed and put

an arm around Her Grace's shoulders. "The proposals have slowed to a trickle, but I'm thinking Tridelphius Trottenham is coming to the sticking point."

"He will not do."

"Of course not. Evie always engages the affections of fellows who are perfectly acceptable in any role save that of husband. She has a genius for it."

They didn't need to say more on that topic. Eve had her reasons, of which they were all too aware.

Esther again took her husband's hand in hers. "She'll get her courage back, Husband. She's a Windham. She just hasn't met the right fellow yet."

His Grace maintained a diplomatic silence, which Esther was wise enough—married enough—to comprehend did not signal agreement.

The day wasn't exactly warm, but it was sunny. Still, with a stiff breeze resulting from Deene's horses being at the trot, Eve felt chilled.

And this had to be the reason why she sat a little closer to Deene than was strictly, absolutely proper.

"If you're cold, there's a blanket under the seat for your lap."

"I'm fine."

He glanced over at her. "You're pale, Eve. Has another megrim been afflicting you?"

The shops and stately homes of Mayfair sped by, though in a couple of hours the streets would likely be too crowded to proceed at such a lively pace. "A gentleman would not remark such a thing."

He leaned a little closer, as if imparting a confidence.

"A lady would not be gripping the handrail as if her driver were about to capsize the vehicle."

Dratted man. She relaxed her grip.

"Take a breath and make yourself let it out slowly." He said this quietly too, still in that conspiratorial tone. Eve wanted to elbow him in his ribs. Out of deference to the welfare of her elbow, she took a breath.

Which did help, double drat him.

"We have two perfect gentlemen in the traces," Deene said. "I traded your brother Devlin for them and got the better of the bargain."

"How old are they?" Another breath.

"Rising six, and the most sensible fellows you'd ever want in harness."

Eve considered the horses, a pair of shiny chestnuts, each with white socks on both forelegs. "Why didn't Devlin want them?"

"They're quite good size for riding mounts, but I think mostly he wasn't looking to add to his training responsibilities."

There was nothing in Deene's tone to suggest he was being snide, yet Eve bristled. "You saw Devlin at Christmas. He's doing much better now that he's married."

Deene drove along in silence, turning the horses through Cumberland Gate and onto The Ring. Eve kept breathing but realized part of the reason she was in such difficulties.

Since the accident, she'd driven out only with family. She didn't know if this eccentricity had been remarked by Polite Society, but given the level of scrutiny any ducal family merited, it very likely had.

Her brothers hadn't been on hand to drive her anywhere for ages. In recent memory, she'd driven out only with her mama. While Her Grace was a very competent whip, even a noted whip among the ladies, Deene at the ribbons was a very different proposition.

A more confident proposition, in some regards. For one thing, he was a great deal larger and more muscular than any duchess; for another, he was former cavalry; and on top of that, he was just... Deene.

"I did not mean to scold," Eve said. "Devlin had us worried when he came back from Waterloo."

Deene kept his gaze on the horses. "He had us *all* worried, Lady Eve."

She wanted to ask him, as she'd never asked her own brother, what it was that made a man shift from a clear-eyed, doting brother with great good humor and a way with the ladies, to a haunted shell, jumping at loud noises and searching out the decanters in every parlor in the house.

Except she knew.

She must have moved closer to Deene, because he started in with the small talk.

"The leader is Duke, the off gelding is Marquis. They're cousins on the dam side."

"There must be some draft in them somewhere," Eve remarked. Quarters like that didn't result from breeding the racing lines exclusively. "They've good shoulder angles too. Have you ever put them over fences?"

This earned her a different glance. "You're right, they do. I suppose the next time I take them out to Kent, I'll have the lads set up a few jumps. Is His Grace still riding to hounds?"

"In moderation. I think you do have a loose shoe on the… on Marquis. Up front."

"How can you tell?"

"The sound. That hoof sounds different when it strikes the ground. Listen, you'll pick it up."

They clippety-clopped along, though to Eve the sound of a tenuous shoe was clear as day.

"Your brothers said your seat was the envy of your sisters," Deene remarked a few moments later. "When they talked about you taking His Grace's stallion out against orders, they sounded nothing less than awed."

"I was twelve, and I wanted to go to Spain to look after my brother. Proving I could ride Meteor seemed a logical way to do that."

"I gather your plan did not succeed."

She hadn't thought about this stunt in ages. Meteor had been a good sort, if in need of reassurance. He was in the pensioner paddocks at Morelands now, his muzzle gray, his face showing the passage of years more than his magnificent body. Eve brought him apples from time to time.

"I had a great ride, though." It *had* been a great ride. Her first real steeplechase, from Morelands to the village and back across the countryside, with grooms bellowing behind her, her brother Bart giving chase as well, and all hell breaking loose when she'd eventually brought the horse back to the stables.

"I bet it got you a stout birching, though."

She had to smile. "Not a birching. His Grace stormed and fumed and shouted at me for an age—not about riding the horse, but about taking him without permission—then condemned me to mucking stalls for a month. Mama was in favor of bread and water and switching my backside until I couldn't sit a horse anymore."

"I gather you were sad when the punishment ended?"

He was a perceptive man, and he'd also known her before.

And there it was again, the great divide in Eve's life: Before the Accident versus After the Accident. She forced herself not to drop the thread of the conversation, because that divide was private, known only to her.

She hoped.

"I learned a very great deal in that month from watching the horses, listening to the lads, and seeing them working the horses in the schooling ring. I learned how to care for my tack, how to properly groom a beast and not just fuss about with the brushes, how to tack up and untack, when a horse was cool enough to put away, what to do with an abscess or a hot tendon."

She fell silent. In some ways that had been the happiest month of her childhood.

Of her life.

Beside her, Deene went abruptly alert. Eve followed his gaze to where a little girl was playing fetch with a spaniel. The governess or nanny was on a bench nearby, reading a book.

"Take the reins, Evie."

Before Eve could protest that she *couldn't* take the reins, she did not *want* to take the reins, and she *would* not take the reins, Deene had thrust them into her hands.

He hopped out of the still-moving vehicle and approached the child.

"Uncle Lucas!" The girl squealed her greeting and pelted toward Deene, arms outstretched. The horses shifted a bit at the commotion, making Eve's insides shift more than a bit.

"Steady, gentlemen." Thankfully, she still had the equestrian skill of sounding more relaxed than she felt. While Deene swept the child up in a hug, Eve also made her hands and arms relax, then her middle, lest the horses pick up on her tension and decide to leave the park at a dead gallop.

She exerted the same discipline over her thoughts as she had her body.

"And, ho." Obediently, both geldings shuffled to a halt. "Stand, gentlemen." She gave a little slack in the reins, and thank God, and perhaps Deene's ability to train a team, the horses stood like statutes.

"Shall I hold 'em, miss?"

The tiger—whose existence Eve had completely forgotten—scrambled off the coach and stood blinking up at her.

"That won't be necessary. I don't think his lordship will be long."

The nanny was speaking to Deene in low tones, her hand plucking at her collar. Deene kept the girl perched on his hip but reached out with one hand and snatched the ball from the woman's hands. He pitched it quite hard, then set the girl down while the dog ran off after the ball.

While Eve watched, Deene took the girl's hand and led her over to the curricle.

"Lady Eve, there's somebody I'd like to introduce you to. This is my niece, Miss Georgina Dolan. Georgie, Lady Eve is my friend, so please make your curtsy."

The girl dipped a perfect curtsy. "Pleased to meet you, my lady."

She came up grinning, as if she knew she'd done it exactly as instructed.

Eve smiled down at a pair of dancing blue eyes framed by fat, golden sausage curls.

"Miss Georgina." Eve inclined her head on a smile. "A pleasure. Is that your dog?"

"Charles. He's the best. My papa got him for me when I turned seven. Are these your horses?"

"They belong to your uncle." Who remained at the child's side, holding her hand. "Their names are Duke and Marquis. I'm sure your uncle would let you pet them."

"Uncle?" She turned a wheedling smile on Deene. "I don't want to pet them, I want to *ride* them."

"Which would get horsehair all over your pretty dress, my dear, and render your nanny apoplectic."

The governess, a prim blond, was looking nervous enough, standing just a few feet off, the ball at her feet, the dog sitting nearby and panting mightily.

"You took me up before you a long time ago," the child said. "When I was just a baby."

"You were not a baby, but it was a long time ago," Deene replied, his smile tight. "I'm sure your papa would ride out with you if you asked him."

A mulish expression blighted otherwise angelic features, giving the girl a resemblance to her uncle. "He will not. Papa is too busy, and he says I can't have a pony until I speak French and we're in the country, which won't be until forever, because the roses aren't even blooming yet."

Deene's lips flattened, which was a curious reaction to a child's predictable griping.

"I'll bet you can draw a very pretty pony, though," Eve suggested. "One with bows in his mane and even one in his tail."

The child shot Eve a frown. "I thought a bow in the tail meant the horse kicked."

"At the hunt meet, it can mean that. In your drawing, you can make it just for decoration."

The nanny had approached a few feet closer, her expression almost tormented. Clearly, the woman wasn't used to having her charge plucked from her care. Deene's glance at the governess was positively venomous, but thankfully aimed over the child's head.

"Can you play some fetch with me and Charles, Uncle?"

"Eve, would you mind?"

"May I play too?" For some reason, she did not want to leave Deene, the child, and the woman to their own devices.

"Oh, please!" Georgina shrieked and clapped her hands together. Marquis took a single step in reaction, which should have sent Eve into a blind panic.

"Settle, Marquis." The beast flicked an ear at Eve's voice and held still.

Deene had only to glance at his tiger, and the boy was up at the horses' heads while Deene himself helped Eve from the vehicle.

"We can play catch, all of us," Georgina caroled, grabbing Eve and Deene by the hand, "and Charles will run mad between us. He loves to run and loves to come to the park. I love to come to the park too, and I think Miss Ingraham does also. She reads lurid novels, though I would never tell Papa."

Children were like this. Eve used to volunteer to watch the little ones in the nursery at church, and this startling honesty was something she'd forgotten. She'd been this honest once: *I don't want to pet them, I want to ride them.*

She played catch, berating Deene sorely when he threw the ball too high over her head, tossing it gently to the girl, and keeping an eye on the fretful governess. When even the dog was too tired to play anymore, Deene went down on one knee.

"Give me a hug, Georgie. I must take Lady Eve home now, and if we play any longer, you'll have to carry Charles back to your house."

The girl bundled in close and wrapped her arms around her uncle's neck. While they embraced, Deene's hand stroked over the little blond head, the expression in his eyes... bleak.

He kissed the girl's cheek, stood, and led the child over to her caretaker. "My thanks for your patience, miss."

The woman muttered something too low for Eve to hear, and then Deene was handing Eve up into the curricle. The tiger climbed up behind, and Deene just sat there.

He did not take up the reins.

He did not speak.

"Deene?" His face was set in a expression Eve hadn't seen before—angry and determined, for all she couldn't say exactly which handsome feature portrayed which emotion, or how.

"Lucas?"

"You'll have to drive, Evie."

She didn't question him. He was clearly in no state to take the reins. She unwrapped them, took up the contact with each horse's mouth, glanced back to make sure the tiger was holding on, and gave the command to walk on.

"Is there a reason why you're off balance, Deene?"

He snorted. "Off balance? A fair term for it, and yes, there are many reasons, the most recent being that the climbing Irish bastard who sired my niece had to go and give the damned dog my father's Christian name. Dolan's disrespect is about as subtle as a runaway ale wagon."

❦

As Eve sat beside him and drove the horses along at a relaxed trot, Deene became aware that he was grinding his teeth, which was hardly proper conduct in the presence of a lady.

"I beg your pardon for my language, Lady Eve."

She didn't take her gaze from the horses, just sat serenely on the bench. "I didn't know you had a niece."

He should have realized the child might be in the park at an odd hour. He'd set his spies loose in the mornings, when most nursemaids took children for an outing. Now he'd know to keep watch at all hours.

"I am barely allowed the appearance of being her uncle."

"Her father is protective?"

Deene counted to ten; he counted to ten in Latin and then in French. "He is barely deserving of the name Father. The child is kept virtually prisoner in her own home, and she has no friends. I am not permitted to call on her, though I am permitted to send her presents, and she sends the occasional carefully worded note of thanks. Dolan would never look askance at material goods, but he treats that girl…"

He was nigh to ranting, but Eve did not appear at all discommoded by his words.

"He raises protectiveness to a vulgar art," Deene concluded. Georgie was a possession to Dolan, just as Marie had been a possession, a prize.

Eve turned the horses onto Park Lane while Deene counted to twenty in Italian.

"What was that comment Mr. Trottenham made about your colt beating Islington's?" Eve asked.

Ah, she was Changing the Subject, bless her. Deene seized on the new topic gratefully.

"I got tired of hearing the old man brag on his colt and decided to turn King William loose for once."

She clucked to the horses, who picked up the pace a touch. "King William is a horse?"

Deene propped his foot on the fender. "King William is a force of nature in the form of a colt rising four. He's going to be the making of my racing stud, if only I can find the right balance of conditioning and competing for him."

Eve smiled at the horses before them. "He has the heart of a champion, then. He wants to run even when he needs to laze about for a day or two, am I right?"

"You are exactly right. He doesn't want to run, he *needs* to run, needs to show the other boys who's fastest. Put him against a filly, and he's greased lightning."

She feathered the horses through a turn made tight by an empty dray near the curb. "I'd forgotten Devlin's stud farm was originally one of your parcels. Do you spend much time there?"

Without Deene realizing exactly when or how, his ire at Georgie's father, his towering frustration, and even—a man did not admit this outside his own thoughts—his sense of helplessness faded into any horseman's enthusiasm for his sport. And Eve did not merely humor him with a pained smile on her features; she participated in the conversation with equal enthusiasm as Deene waxed eloquent about his stud colt.

"I've never met a stallion with quite as much personality as Wee Willy. The lads dote on him and cosset him as if he were their firstborn son."

"Is he permitted apples?"

"In moderation. He's a fiend for sugar or anything sweet, though."

"Typical male." She gave him such a smile then, it was as if somebody had put a lump of sugar on Deene's own tongue. That smile said she was pleased with him, with herself, with life and all it beheld—and all he had done was talk horses with her.

When they turned onto the square before the Moreland mansion, Deene was almost sorry to see the outing end. He helped Eve down from the vehicle, then paused for a moment, his hands at her waist.

"We never did broach the topic I'd intended to bring up."

She had her hands braced on his arms, making him realize again how diminutive she was.

"What topic was that?"

He let her go and signaled to the tiger to walk the horses while he offered Eve his arm. "I'll walk you in, but let's go by way of the gardens, shall we?"

She took the hint and trundled along beside him quietly until they were away from the street.

"My original agenda for requesting your company this afternoon was not to talk your ear off about King William."

She took a bench behind a privet hedge and patted the place beside her. "Your agenda was rescuing me from Mr. Trit-Trot, though I fear you're too late. He has that blindly determined look in his eye."

"Trit-Trot?" While he took the place beside her, Eve took off her bonnet and set it aside, then smoothed her hand over her hair.

When that little delaying tactic was at an end, she grimaced. "Louisa finds these appellations and applies them indiscriminately to the poor gentlemen who come to call. She's gotten worse since she married. Tridelphius Trottenham, ergo Trit-Trot, and it suits him."

"Dear Trit-Trot has a gambling problem."

One did not share such a thing with the ladies, generally, but if the idiot was thinking to offer for a Windham daughter, somebody needed to sound a warning.

And as to that, the idea of Trit-Trot—the man was now doomed to wear the unfortunate moniker forev-ermore in Deene's mind—kissing any of Moreland's young ladies, much less kissing Eve, made Deene's sanguine mood... sink a trifle.

"He also clicks his heels in the most aggravating manner," Eve said, her gaze fixed on a bed of cheery yellow tulips. "And he doesn't hold a conversation, he chirps. He licks his fingers when he's eaten tea cakes, though he's a passable dancer and has a kind heart."

Bright yellow tulips meant something in the language of flowers: *I am hopelessly in love.* In his idiot youth, Deene had sent a few such bouquets to some opera dancers and merry widows.

Rather than ponder those follies, Deene considered the woman beside him. "I never gave a great deal of thought to how much you ladies must simply endure the company of your callers. Is it so very bad?"

She shifted her focus up, to where a stately oak was sporting a reddish cast to its branches in anticipation of leafing out. "It's worse now that Sophie, Maggie, and Louisa are married. One heard of the infantry squares at Waterloo, closing ranks again and again as the French cavalry charged them. I expect we two youngest sisters share a little of that same sense."

Oak leaves for bravery.

He spoke slowly, the words dragged past his pride by the mental plough horse of practicality. "I might be able to help, Eve, and you could do me a considerable service in return."

Now she studied a lilac bush about a week away from blooming. *First emotions of love.*

"You already rendered me a considerable service, Lucas." She spoke very quietly, and hunched in on herself, bracing her hands on the bench beneath them.

She'd called him Lucas. He'd been Lucas to the entire Windham family as a youth, and now he was

Lucas to no one save Georgie. He wasn't sure if he liked this presumption on Eve's part, or resented it.

"I can have a word with Trit-Trot if you want me to run him off."

She waved a hand. "I'll mention the fact that I have only two dozen pairs of shoes, and the Season is soon upon us. In the alternative, I can suggest I'm never up before noon because I must have my drops every night without fail just to sleep. The tittering has slowed him down some, and if that doesn't serve, I'll turn up pious."

So casual, and yet as she sat there on the bench, scuffing one slipper over the gravel, she was a battle-weary woman.

On impulse, he reached over and plucked her a yellow daffodil.

"What's this?" She accepted the flower in a gloved hand, bringing it to her nose for a whiff.

Yellow daffodils for chivalry.

"You look in need of cheering up, but I see my offer was arrogant."

"What offer was that?"

"I was going to assist you to assess the prospects of the various swains orbiting around you, and you were going to keep me informed regarding the ladies circling me."

Now that he put the scheme into words, it sounded ungentlemanly, but Eve was not taking offense. She sat straighter and put the flower carefully to the side on the bench.

"You've been traveling off and on for the past few years," she said. "This can put a man behindhand when in Polite Society."

Egypt, the Americas, anywhere to escape his father and the man's scathing tirades.

"I'll be keeping to home territory for the foreseeable future, and you're right: I have no idea who is overusing her laudanum, who owes far too much to the modistes, and whose mama plays too deep in unmentionable places."

Now that he enumerated a few of them, the pitfalls for an unwary suitor seemed numerous and fraught.

Eve regarded her slippered toes. "Before the boys married, we used to gossip among ourselves terribly. They never told us *everything*, I'm sure, but they told us enough. We did the same for them, my sisters and I."

And this was likely part of the reason no Windham son had been caught in any publicly compromising position, nor had any Windham daughters. And now the Windham infantry had been deserted by both cavalry and cannon.

While he had ever marched alone, which was a dangerous approach to any battle. "What do you know of the Staines ladies? They're very determined, almost too determined."

He asked the question because he genuinely wanted to know and had no one to ask whom he could trust. He also asked because he sensed—hoped, maybe—that Eve missed providing this sort of intelligence to her brothers.

"Lady Staines has a sister," she said, dragging one toe through the gravel. "She chronically rusticates in Northumbria, but it's said she's quite high-strung."

"Ah. And the daughter?"

Eve bit her lip then picked up her daffodil. "She did not make a come out until she was nineteen. Nobody knows precisely why, and Lady Staines does not permit the girl to socialize at all without her mama hovering almost literally at her elbow. We tend to feel sorry for Mildred, but she ignores all friendly overtures unless her mother approves them."

And here he'd been half-considering offering for the girl just to trade the misery of the unknown for the misery of the known. He spent another half hour on that bench, listening to Eve Windham delicately indicate which young ladies might hold up well in a highly visible marriage, and which would not.

"Your recitation is unnerving, my lady." In fact, what she'd had to say, and the fact that she was privy to so much unflattering information, left him daunted.

"Unnerved you in what regard?"

"I would never have suspected these polite, graceful young darlings of society are coping with everything from violent papas, to brothers who leave bastards all over the shire, to high-strung aunts. It puts a rather bleak face on what I thought was an empty social whirl."

She did not argue. She sniffed her little daffodil. "Has this been helpful?"

She was entitled to extract her pound of flesh, so he was honest, up to a point. "You have been extremely helpful, and to show my gratitude, will you come with me to Surrey next week to make King William's acquaintance?"

He put it purposely in the posture of compensation

for services rendered, as if that particular exchange was the only one they managed civilly.

Her brows rose while she batted her lips with the flower.

They were pretty lips, finely curved, a luscious pink that put him in mind of a ripe—

The spring air was obviously affecting his male humors.

"I will come with you, provided you're willing to take Jenny and Louisa as well, if Kesmore can spare her. They'd enjoy such an outing, and I'm sure King William would enjoy the company."

"We have an appointment, then."

He rose and bowed over her gloved hand, feeling a vague discontent with their exchange. As he made his way back out to the street, he turned and gave her a wave. She waved back, but the sight of her there on the bench, clutching her lone flower, left a queer ache in his chest.

Thank God, she wasn't his type. He liked women with dramatic coloring and dramatic passions. Women with whom a man always knew exactly where he stood, and how much the trinket would cost that would allow him to stand a great deal closer.

But Eve Windham could talk horses, she was proving a sensible ally, and he did like to kiss her. She also drove a team like she was born to hold the reins.

What an odd combination of attributes.

❧

"What did Deene say to Miss Georgina?"

Dolan kept his voice even when he wanted to thunder the question to the rafters. Miss Amy Ingraham was not a timid soul, but neither did she deserve bullying. She stood before him on the other side of his massive desk, back straight as a pike, expression that particular cross between blank and deferential only a lady fallen on hard times could evidence to her employer.

"His lordship said very little, sir. He played catch with the child and introduced her to Lady Eve Windham."

Windham?

"One of Moreland's girls?" The duchess herself would have been "Her Grace"—never "lady" this or that. Dolan knew that much, though the entire order of precedence with its rules of address left an Irish stonemason's son ready to kick something repeatedly.

"I believe Lady Eve is the youngest, sir."

This was the value of employing a genteel sort of English governess, granddaughter of a viscount, no less. She'd stay up late on summer nights and pore over *Debrett's* by the meager light of her oil lamp, and she'd recall exactly which family whelped which titled pups.

"How young is this Lady Eve?"

"She's been out several years, sir, from what I understand."

"Did she say anything to Georgina?"

Miss Ingraham took a substantial breath, which drew attention to her feminine attributes. The day he'd hired her, Dolan had noted the woman had a good figure to go with her pretty face and pale blond hair. He knew of no rule that said governesses couldn't be lovely for their employers to behold, though knowing the English, such a rule no doubt existed.

"Her ladyship complimented Miss Georgina on

her curtsy, praised the dog, chided his lordship for throwing the ball too high, and thanked Miss Georgina for giving the horses a chance to rest."

Lady Eve had *chided* his lordship. Dolan gave the lady a grudging mental nod, duke's daughter or not. Deene was in need of a good deal of chiding, though he was no worse than the rest of his arrogant, presuming...

"Was there something more, Miss Ingraham?"

If anything, her spine got straighter.

"Speak plainly, woman. I don't punish my employees for being honest, though I take a dim view of dishonesty."

"Miss Georgina seemed to enjoy her uncle's company very much, as well as that of Lady Eve."

He peered at Miss Ingraham a little more closely. She had fine gray eyes that were aimed directly at him, and a wide, generous mouth held in a flat, disapproving line.

"How much do I pay you, Miss Ingraham?"

She named a figure that would have kept Dolan's entire family of twelve in potatoes for a year, which was more a measure of their poverty than the generosity of her salary.

"Effective today, your salary is doubled. Start taking Miss Georgina to St. James's Park for her outings. That will be all."

❧

"Are you attending one of Papa's political meetings, or did Anna shoo you out from underfoot?"

Gayle Windham, the Earl of Westhaven, smiled at his sister's blunt question.

"Hello to you as well, Louisa." He passed the reins of his horse off to a groom and glanced from Jenny to Louisa. "You two are up to something."

Standing there arm in arm, the flower of genteel English womanhood, they exchanged a sororal look. That look spoke volumes, about who would say what to whom, in what order, and how the other sister would respond. Westhaven's sisters had been exchanging such looks as long as he could recall, and he still had no insight into their specific meanings.

His only consolation was that Maggie had once admitted there were fraternal looks that caused the same degree of consternation among the distaff.

"Walk with us." Jenny slipped an arm through his, while Louisa strode along on his other side, a two-sister press gang intent on dragooning him into the mansion's back gardens.

"Don't mind if I do. I trust all is well with both of you?"

Jenny smiled at him, her usual gentle smile, which did not fool Westhaven for one moment. Genevieve Windham got away with a great deal on the strength of her unassuming demeanor, almost as much as Louisa got away with on the basis of sheer brass. He kept his peace, though. They'd reveal whatever mischief they were up to when they jolly well pleased to—and wheedling never worked anyway.

"What do we know of Lucas Denning's marital prospects?" Louisa fired her broadside without warning.

Westhaven stopped walking and shrugged off Jenny's arm. "Why do *we* want to know anything at all about such a topic? Among the five of you sisters, I'm fairly certain you could tell me how many teeth, how much blunt, and what type of cattle are associated with every titled bachelor in Polite Society."

And how they knew such things was enough to unnerve even a very happily married man.

"He has all his teeth," Jenny observed, linking her arm with Westhaven's again. "We understand the family coffers are a trifle… reduced, due to the late marquis's spending habits, and we know Deene owns a racing stud and keeps a nice stable here in Town. We want to know about his *prospects*."

Westhaven took the liberty of seating himself on a bench near a patch of yellow tulips. "Haven't a clue, my dears."

They were his sisters. Sometimes a little deliberate rudeness was necessary in pursuit of proper sibling relations.

Louisa put her hands on her hips and glared at him. "We aren't asking out of idle curiosity, you dolt. We *need* to know, and if you don't spill, I will simply ask Kesmore. Lucas was racketing about before the old marquis died, and then he went off ruralizing for his mourning, so our usual sources know very little. Is he looking to run in double harness?"

Every prospective duke ought occasionally to be referred to as a dolt, and it was apparently the sworn duty of the man's sisters to see to the matter.

"He has a title, Lou, and only the one second cousin to inherit. I'm fairly certain he'll be looking for a filly to run with him in double harness, as you so delicately refer to the state of holy matrimony."

Another look passed from Jenny to Louisa—a smug, satisfied, so-there sort of look.

"What do you two think you know?"

Jenny sat beside him. "We know, Brother, that we saw Evie driving out with Deene, which would have been remarkable enough."

He did not ask, for Louisa's expression confirmed she was dying to shock him further.

She took the remaining end of the bench. "We also know that when they came tooling back, there was Deene, reclining against the seat like the Caliph of Mayfair, and Evie handling the ribbons."

Evie. Handling. The ribbons... *News, indeed.* Westhaven rose and turned to glower at them. "You will not remark this to Eve, and you will not tattle to Their Graces."

"Too late." Jenny looked worried now, and Louisa looked annoyed, which was her version of what others would call anxiety. "Mama came to the door to see us off on our perambulation, and she saw Evie driving Deene's team too."

Bloody hell.

"We need to warn Evie," Westhaven muttered. This was what came from making purely social calls on one's parents, from heeding a wife's gentle admonitions to spend more time with his siblings.

Now the damned look was directed at him, and he knew very well what it meant. Jenny—ever anxious to be helpful—spelled it out for him anyway. "Yes, Brother, *we* do need to warn Evie."

He left them there on the bench, no doubt hatching up more awkwardness for him to deal with. When it suited his family, he was the *heir*, the duke-in-training, and therefore called upon to handle whatever odd business nobody else wanted to handle.

He desperately hoped Their Graces lived to biblical ages to forestall the day when he graduated to the title altogether. While he was offering up a short prayer to that effect, he found Eve in the music room.

"Greetings, Sister." She was sitting at the piano, the instrument dwarfing her petite presence.

"Gayle!" She hurried off the bench and hugged him tightly.

A man with five sisters did not dare admit to having favorites. He appreciated each of them for their various attributes: Maggie for her courage and brains; Sophie for her quiet competence and practicality; Louisa for her independence and well-hidden tender heart; Jenny for her determination and kindness.

But Evie… Evie was just plain lovable. Where Jenny smiled and dragged him about by the arm, or Louisa called him a dolt, Evie hugged him and called him by his name.

"Were you thinking to play an étude?" he asked, leading her to a settee against the wall.

"I was thinking to have some privacy. Shall I ring for a tray?"

"No, thank you. As soon as His Grace catches wind of my presence, I'll no doubt be sequestered in the ducal study with several trays, a decanter, and such a lengthy lecture on whatever damned bill is plaguing our sire at the moment that my appetite will desert me. You're in good looks, Evie."

She was. Eve was an exquisite woman in a diminutive

package, but today there was something a little rosier about her complexion, a little more animated in her bearing.

"I got some air, which on a spring day is never a bad idea. How is Anna?"

He was ever willing to expound on the topic of his countess, but he couldn't let Eve prevaricate that easily.

"You were out driving with Deene."

Some of the life went out of her. "Are you going to castigate me for this? I know Lucas has a certain reputation among his fellows."

"Every unmarried man of means at his age has a certain reputation among his fellows, whether it's deserved or not." Though she had a point—at least before his travels, Deene had been somewhat profligate in his appetites.

Somewhat profligate? Was there such a thing?

"He can be decent company." Eve didn't seem to be defending the man so much as justifying her actions to herself.

"He has been a firm friend to this family, Evie. I do not raise the subject of your outing to criticize you in any way. I'm asking, rather, because I want to know what the man did that got you to take up the reins when, for seven years, everything your entire family has done in that direction has been unavailing, hmm?"

❧

Gayle was going to be a superb duke. He had a kind of quiet perspicacity about him that fit well with the obligations of both an exalted title and being head of a large family. But he hadn't yet learned to hide from his eyes the hurt and puzzlement Eve saw virtually every time she caught her brother regarding her.

"I'm not sure what Deene did." She rose from the sofa, and being a good brother, Gayle allowed her space by remaining seated. "I suppose it was what he didn't do."

"I should also like to *not* do it, then, whatever it was, as would Louisa, Jenny, and—I regret to inform you—Her Grace."

"Merciful heavens."

He did rise, but ambled over to the piano bench, sat, closed the cover, and rested an elbow on it. "It's just a ride in the park, Evie. If you want my advice, go on as if it didn't happen."

"Stare them down. One of Her Grace's favorite tactics."

She settled beside him on the piano bench, realizing that she wanted to talk to somebody about this outing with Deene.

"He simply put the reins in my hands and jumped out of the vehicle before the horses had even come to a halt." Recalling the moment brought a frisson of anxiety to her middle but also a sense of blooming wonder.

"He assumed you were capable of handling a team, which you are."

Gayle was frowning, as if he, too, were puzzled.

"I am not." She got to her feet. "I *was* not." Again he let her wander the room while he watched her out of curious green eyes. Deene shared Westhaven's build—tall, a shade more muscular than lanky—but Westhaven had hair of a dark chestnut in contrast to Deene's blond, blue-eyed good looks.

"I assumed I wasn't capable," she eventually clarified. "He proved me wrong, and I have never been happier to be wrong, it's just… why him?"

"Does it matter? You enjoyed an outing and learned something wonderful about yourself."

As usual, the man's logic was unassailable.

"They're a lovely team, his geldings. Marquis and Duke. His stud colt is King William." She felt sheepish recounting these details, almost as if she were confessing to Deene taking her hand or kissing her cheek.

"I've met His Highness, and if he's brought along properly, I agree with Deene he's a one-in-a-million horse. St. Just was quite taken with him as well."

"Devlin is taken with anything sporting a mane and a tail."

And then, with breathtaking precision, Westhaven made his point. "You were once too."

Rotten man. Rotten, honest, brilliant, brave man. How did Anna stand being married to such a fellow?

Eve sank onto the settee but did not meet her brother's gaze for some time. His four little true words were underscoring something Eve had long since stopped allowing herself to acknowledge: by eschewing her passion for all things equestrian, she'd firmly closed an unfortunate chapter of her life and minimized the possibility of any more severe injuries to her person.

She'd also given up one of her greatest joys and told herself it was for the best.

"I made a small misstep in my enthusiasm to take the reins," she said.

Gayle waited. He was an infernally patient man.

"I did not want to be in Deene's debt, so I agreed

to assist him in separating the sheep and goats among the Season's offerings on the marriage market. He has no sisters…" She fell silent rather than further justify her actions. She wasn't sure they *could* be justified, except on the odd abacus that had taken up residence between her and the Marquis of Deene.

"I'm sure he'll appreciate your aid in this regard, Evie."

There was something ironic in Westhaven's comment, but not mean. Westhaven would never be mean to his siblings—probably not to anybody—but he could be quite stern and serious.

He got up, crossed the room, and paused to kiss Eve's forehead before he left for his appointment with the duke.

A good man, a wonderful brother, and even a dear friend.

And still, Eve hadn't told him she'd agreed to another outing with Deene. Hadn't told her sisters either.

⟡

Deene bit into a pastry only to pull the thing from his mouth and stare at it.

Stale as hardtack, not just inadvertently left sitting out for an hour.

"Something amiss, Cousin?" Anthony lounged at the foot of the table, the *Times* at his elbow and a steaming plate of eggs, kippers, and toast before him.

"Nothing that a few helpings of omelet won't set to rights." Deene dug in, wondering vaguely why the *Times* wasn't sitting at his own elbow.

Anthony glanced up from the paper. "You're off to Surrey today?"

"I am, and in the company of three lovely ladies. Envy me."

"Three? I'd heard you occasionally entertained two at once, but three is ambitious even for you." Anthony topped off his teacup from the pot near his other elbow.

"My record is four, if you must know, Denning pride being what it is. And they all four had red hair. Pass the pot, would you?"

What an asinine waste of a night that had been, too. Five people hardly fit in a very large bed, for God's sake, even when stacked in various gymnastic combinations.

"Why ever would you attempt to please four women at once?" Anthony sounded genuinely intrigued as he slid the pot down the table.

"The idea was for them to please me—which they rather did—and to prove false a certain allegation regarding that dread condition known as whiskey dick in relation to a certain courtesy earl in the Deene succession."

"I am agog at the lengths you've been forced to go to defend the family honor, Lucas."

Anthony went back to his paper, in case his ironic tone hadn't underscored the point clearly enough. Just when Deene might have helped himself to more eggs, Anthony looked up again. "Which three ladies will you entertain today?"

"Louisa, Countess of Kesmore, as well as Genevieve and Eve Windham. We're paying a call on King William, and I am escorting them, not entertaining them."

"A pretty trio, but two of them are perilously unmarried, need I remind you."

"As am I, need I remind you. When do you think you can have some figures ready for me, Anthony?"

Anthony peered at the paper and turned the pages over. "Which figures would those be?"

"The ones relating to our cash, our blunt, our coin of the realm."

Anthony went still in a way that indicated he was not even trying to look like he was reading, but was instead merely staring at the paper while he formulated a polite reply. He sat back and frowned at his empty plate.

"You're determined on this? You really want to wade through years' worth of musty ledgers and obscure accountings? I'd commend you for your zeal, but it's a complicated, lengthy undertaking, and it truly won't yield you any better sense of things than you have now."

"I want to know where I stand, Anthony."

He needed to know, in fact, though he was hardly going to admit that to Anthony, cousin or not.

"Don't worry." Anthony's smile was sardonic. "We've the blunt to keep you in red-haired whores for as long as you're able to enjoy them four at a time."

Deene dispatched the last of his eggs and rose. "Perhaps we can start on that accounting after breakfast tomorrow." He'd phrased it as a suggestion between cousins, though Anthony ought to have heard it as something closer to an order from his employer.

Anthony lifted his teacup in a little salute. "Your servant. Enjoy the ladies—but not too much."

Whatever that meant.

The day was fair, though not quite warm. In a fit

of optimism, Deene had the horses put to the landau. The vehicle had been imported just before the old marquis's death and was the best appointed of the town coaches. Deene elected to drive the thing rather than endure unnecessary miles sitting backward and trying to make small talk with the Windham sisters.

When he got to the Windham townhouse, he found Lady Eve waiting for him in the family parlor, dressed for an outing but sporting a mulish expression.

"You're here."

Her inauspicious greeting indicated they were about to spar. He kept his expression politely neutral, despite the temptation to smile. "Was I supposed to be somewhere else?"

"No, you were not." She crossed the room in a swish of skirts. "My sisters are supposed to be here as well, ready to depart with us, but no, Louisa has begged off, and Jenny just sent Hammet to tell me she is also utterly, immediately, and incurably indisposed for the day."

Eve was piqued. It was on the tip of Deene's tongue to say they could simply reschedule—or better still, cancel altogether—but something in her expression stopped him.

"Would you be disappointed to miss this outing, Lady Eve?"

She swished over to the window and stood facing the back gardens. "Disappointed? Merely to miss a few hours in the country, stepping around the odoriferous evidence of livestock? Of course not."

She was an endearingly bad liar. He came up behind her and put both hands on her shoulders to prevent any more of this swishing about, and spoke very quietly near her ear.

"You would so be disappointed." He could feel it quivering through her, an indignation that her siblings would desert her like this.

She turned, forcing him to drop his hands. He did not step back.

"The weather bids fair to be a lovely day, my lord. I haven't seen the countryside since we spent the holidays at Morelands, and I have every confidence Mr. Trottenham intends to speak to Papa this very afternoon."

She was not about to admit she'd been panting to make the acquaintance of his horse, but Deene was almost certain this was her true motive. By the end of the day, he vowed he would make her admit her objective honestly.

"Come with me anyway, Lady Eve. I brought the landau, the staff at The Downs is expecting our party, and once the Season gets underway, we'll neither of us have time for an outing."

She was wavering. He could see her wavering in the way she almost worried a nail between her teeth but recalled at the last moment she was wearing gloves.

"Or don't come with me." He slapped his gloves against his thigh. "I'll get a great deal more accomplished if I'm not forced to play host to somebody reluctant to make even such an innocuous outing with an old family friend."

Her fists went to her hips. "*Forced*, Deene? Did I force this invitation from you? Did I force you to boast about the capabilities of a mere colt such as I might see on any of a dozen racecourses? Did I tell you to bring an open carriage when the weather this time of year is anything but certain?"

He stepped closer but kept his voice down in contrast to Eve's rising tones. "You will *never* see the like of this colt on any racecourse, unless King William is in the field. Never. This horse has more heart, more bottom, and more sheer, blazing—"

"Excuse me." Esther, Duchess of Moreland, stood in the doorway, her expression puzzled. "Eve, I thought you would have left by now. One doesn't get days this promising very often so early in spring. Deene, good morning."

"Your Grace." He bowed to the appropriate depth and wondered if Her Grace had heard him exchanging *pleasantries* with Eve.

"I am not inclined to go without Jenny and Louisa, Mama. They would be disappointed to miss such an excursion."

Her Grace's expression shifted to a smile more determined than gracious. "Nonsense. If they want to indulge in some extra rest, that's no reason to deprive yourself of fresh air, or of the company of such an amiable gentleman as Deene. He's practically family. Be off with you both, and, Deene, bring her home at a reasonable hour, or you will deal with me."

Said in perfectly cordial tones, but Deene did not mistake the warning.

"Of course, Your Grace." He winged his elbow at Eve—arguing before the duchess was *not* in his schedule—and was relieved when Eve wrapped a gloved hand around his arm.

"Have a pleasant time, my dears."

As Deene ushered Eve through the door, he caught
the duchess giving him a look. When their gazes
collided, she must have gotten something in her eye,
because it appeared for all the world as if Her Grace
had winked at him.

Three

DAMN AND BLAST LUCAS DENNING FOR NEEDLING HER, for that's exactly what he'd done. Eve drew up sharply in the mews and dropped her escort's arm.

"Deene, where are your footmen, where is your driver?"

"Probably enjoying a merry pint or two despite the hour of the day."

He started toward the landau while Eve resisted the urge to clobber him with her parasol. When he turned back to her a few paces away, he wore a smile that could only be described as taunting.

"Eve Windham, I am competent to drive you the less than two hours it will take to get to The Downs. For that matter, you are competent to drive me as well. You know this team, they're perfect gentlemen, and it's a calm day. Get into the carriage."

The gleam in his blue eyes suggested he knew exactly what manner of challenge he'd just posed, both in referring to her driving skill and in *ordering* her into the carriage.

She walked up to Duke. "Good morning, Your Grace. You're looking very handsome today." She took a bag of sliced apples from her reticule and fed the beast a treat. This was bad manners on her part—one never fed another's cattle treats without permission. The horse's bit would be particularly sticky and slimy now too.

She moved around to Marquis and offered him the same attention, taking an extra moment to scratch the gelding's neck.

"Loosen the check reins, Lucas. These horses are going to stretch their legs when we leave Town, and your grooms have fitted the harness with a greater eye toward appearances than the animals' comfort."

He blinked, which was a supremely satisfying response to the use of the imperative on a man too handsome and self-assured for his own good.

While Deene tended to the harness, Eve climbed onto the driver's bench at the front of the vehicle. She was not going to sit back in the passengers' seats all by herself, shouting at Deene to make conversation for the next two hours.

Though apparently, that would not have been his intent. Eve had been telling herself for some miles that it was exhilarating to be behind such a spanking—and not the least bit frightening—team when Deene finally spoke.

"Did you or did you not wear a very fetching brown ensemble just so you might also wear brown gloves, the better to be petting horses?"

She had. That he would divine such a thing was disconcerting.

"The ensemble, as you note, my lord, is attractive, and the skirt cut for a walking length so I might move about your stables without concern for my hems. Then too, I've been told brown flatters my blond hair."

He glanced over at her with such a fulminating look that Eve realized she'd brought them to the point of departure for another argument, which had *not* been her intent. She was driving out for the second time in a week with somebody besides family, and it was a pretty day.

"Tell me about The Downs, Lucas. St. Just said you inherited the property when you were a boy."

"I did. What would you like to know about it?"

He was going to make her work for it, but she was a duke's daughter. If she couldn't make polite conversation with a familiar acquaintance, she didn't deserve her title.

"What draws you to it? You've many properties, and yet this is the one you take the greatest interest in."

He looked for a moment like he'd quibble with even that, but then his shoulders relaxed. "My cousin Anthony is the Deene estate steward for all intents and purposes, and he does a marvelous job at a large and thankless task. Each property has a steward, some have both house and land stewards, and they all answer to him. The Downs is my own…"

He fell silent while the horses clip-clopped along.

"I have a little property," Eve said, not wanting the silence to stretch any further. "It's a dear little place not three miles from Morelands, part of Mama's settlements."

"Is this Lavender Corner?"

"It is. I've fitted out the household to my taste, and some days I just go there to enjoy the place."

"To be alone?"

He was aiming another look at her while she tried to formulate an answer that was honest but not combative, when something—a hare, a shadow, a deer moving in the woods to the side of the road—gave the horses a fright.

Between one moment and the next, Eve went from a relatively innocuous chat with her escort to blind panic. As the vehicle surged forward, she clutched the rail and resisted the urge to jump to safety.

Except it *wasn't* safety, not when the horses could bolt off at a dead gallop over uneven terrain. As the trees flew by in a blur, she was reminded yet again that nowhere in the vicinity of a horse could she *ever* be truly safe.

"Ho, you silly buggers." Deene's voice was calm over the clatter of the carriage. "That's enough of this. It was a damned rabbit, you idiots, and you're not getting any more treats if this is how you comport yourselves before a lady."

His scold was lazy, almost affectionate, and to Eve's vast, enormous, *profound* relief, the horses slowed to a canter, then a trot.

"Lucas, I'm going to be sick." When had she gotten her hand wrapped around his arm?

"You are not going to be sick. If I pull them over now, they'll understand that a queer start earns them a rest and possibly a snack. We'll let them blow in another mile or two when their little horsey brains have forgotten all about this frolic and detour."

Eve closed her eyes, and in sheer misery, rested her forehead on Deene's muscular shoulder. A mile was forever, and yet what he said made perfect sense—to a competent horseman.

"I want to walk back to Town, Lucas. Right now, I want to walk back to Town."

She felt him chuckle, damn and blast him. If he hadn't been the one holding the reins, she would have walloped him.

"I've seen you ride through much worse misbehavior than that little contretemps, Eve Windham, and you did it with a smile. There's a pretty view coming up. I typically let the team rest there."

While Eve breathed in the lavender and cedar scent of Deene's jacket—a cure-all for not just megrims, apparently, but a nervous stomach as well—she considered that she might possibly, in some very small regard, be overreacting.

She raised her head but kept her arm linked with Deene's.

"You were going to tell me about The Downs."

"You were going to tell me about Lavender Corner."

Or they could argue about who was going to tell whom about which property. Despite her lingering upset, despite the looming challenge of the drive back to Town, Eve smiled.

Though she still did not turn loose of Deene's arm.

❧

From time immemorial, the horses who stayed alive were the ones who galloped off at the first sign of possible danger, and then, two miles later, paused to consider the wisdom of their flight—or to get back to swishing their tails at flies and grazing.

Deene wasn't upset with his team for having a lively sense of self-preservation, though he was out of charity with them for scaring Eve Windham. He forgave them their lapse of composure when he realized Eve's unease was keeping her glued to his side, a petite, warm, female bundle of nerves, trying to decide whether to resume arguing with him or treat him to another round of polite discourse.

She opted for discourse—a small disappointment.

"I do go to Lavender Corner to be alone," she said. "I always make some excuse, that I'm meeting with my housekeeper, that I want to see how the gardens are coming, but mostly…"

Her words trailed off, and Deene stepped into the breach, even as he wondered what she wasn't saying.

"I grew up with only the one sibling, and as a child, a five-year age difference made Marie seem like an adult. I always thought a lot of brothers and sisters would be wonderful, but I suppose it has drawbacks too."

Her grip on his arm eased fractionally. "It is wonderful, unless they go off to war and don't come back, or have to spend years expiring of blasted consumption. Even then, I would not exchange the people I love for anything in the world."

What could he say to that? The people he loved encompassed his niece, whom he was barely permitted to see, and Anthony, though Deene would never mistake his cousin for a friend.

"One can tell you love each other," he said, it not being an appropriate moment for a disagreement. "It's there in your humor with each other, your protectiveness, your honesty. We've reached our pull off."

For which he was grateful. Talk of love was for

women among themselves, where it could safely stray off to that most inane subject, being *in* love. He pulled up the team, set the brake, wrapped the reins, and jumped down.

"Let's stretch our legs, shall we?"

He didn't really mean it as a question. Eve's face was still pale and she would fare better for using her legs.

"You'll let them graze?" she asked from her perch on the bench.

"They don't deserve it, but yes, if you prefer." He held up his arms to assist her to the ground, and she hesitated. In the instant when he would have remonstrated her for her rudeness, he understood that forcing herself to move at all when there was no driver at the reins was... difficult for her. "Evie, come here."

He plucked her bodily from the carriage—he was tall enough to do that—and let her slide down his body until her feet were planted on terra firma. When he would have stepped back, she dropped her forehead to his chest.

"I'm an idiot."

"If so, you're a wonderfully fragrant idiot." Also lithe, warm, and a surprisingly agreeable armful of woman. He kept his arms around her as he catalogued these appealing attributes and helped himself to a pleasing whiff of mock orange.

"I panicked back there when the horses startled."

She sounded miserable over this admission. He took a liberty and turned her under his arm, keeping his arm across her shoulders while they walked a few paces away.

"I know you took a bad fall before your come out, Eve. There's no shame in a lingering distaste for injury. I still get irritable whenever I hear cannon firing, even if it's just a harbor sounding its signals."

And for the longest time, thunder had had the same effect, as had the sound of a herd of horses galloping en masse. She moved away from his side, and he let her go while he released the check reins so the horses could graze.

"Being rattled from years at war is not the same thing at all as letting one fall—one, single fall—turn me into a ninnyhammer seven years and two months later."

She probably knew the exact number of days as well, which made him hurt for her.

"I beg to differ with you, my lady—though I realize it has become an ungentlemanly habit. Tooling around the park, nobody's team is going to spook at anything, except perhaps Lady Dandridge's bonnets. If this is the first startled team you've been behind in years, then I'd be surprised if you weren't a little discommoded. Walk with me." He held out a hand to her. "There's a patch of lily of the valley that is not to be missed over by those trees."

She shot a wary glance at the horses, who were placidly grazing on the verge.

The look she gave his bare hand was equally cautious.

In that moment, he experienced a profound insight regarding Eve Windham, the things that spooked her, and *why* they spooked her. He ambled along in silence with her, hand in hand, resenting the insight mightily.

He found it much easier to consider Eve a well-bred young lady with ample self-confidence borne of a ducal upbringing, a very appealing feminine appearance, and no small amount of poise. He did not want to think of her as... wounded or in any way vulnerable.

"Have a seat," he said some moments later, shrugging out of his jacket and spreading it on the ground for her.

Another woman would have argued over this rather than the silly things he debated with Eve—argued over the impropriety of being just out of sight of the road, of sharing a coat with a lone gentleman—but Eve sank gracefully to the ground, tugged off her gloves, and drew her knees up before her.

He sat beside her for a few moments in silence, letting the burbling of a nearby stream underscore what he hoped was a soothing silence. The air was redolent with the scent of lily of the valley, but beneath that he could still catch a little note of mock orange.

And Eve.

❧

Now would be a fine time for Lucas Denning to share a few of his lovely kisses, but no, he had to sit beside Eve in the grass, all solemn and gentlemanly.

She wanted to scream and lay about with her parasol.

At the ninnyhammer horses and her ninnyhammer self. Also at the ninnyhammer *man* beside her, gone all proper, when what she could have really used, what she would have appreciated *greatly* was the heat and distraction of his mouth on hers, the feel of all that fine muscle and man right next to her, his body so close—

A thought popped into her head all at once. A novel, startling thought she'd never had before: if the man was such a blockhead as not to realize this was a kissing moment, then the woman could certainly be astute enough, bold enough—

She rounded on him and swung a leg across his middle before her mind articulated the rest of this brilliant idea. The element of surprise allowed her to push him flat to his back, and perhaps some element of misplaced gentlemanly restraint meant she could get her mouth on his before he reacted.

Though it was *such* a wonderful reaction. He growled into her mouth, lashed his arms around her, and rolled with her, so she was beneath him amid the lilies of the valley, his kisses mixing with the lush fragrance of the flowers, the scent of crushed green grass, and the feel of the cool earth at Eve's back.

Then he went still, and the disappointment Eve felt was so keen she was tempted to punch his shoulder... until his mouth came back to hers, sweetly, slowly, like a sigh feathering across her cheek, easing its way to her lips.

She relaxed, in her body and in her mind. He wasn't going to deny her, and this was really a much nicer approach. She winnowed her hands through his hair, marveling at the softness of it, like light embodied beneath her fingers.

His tongue was soft too, and hot and tempting against her lips. Lovely appendage, a man's tongue. She hadn't always thought so and probably *wouldn't* think so, but for—

Her articulate mind ground to a halt as Lucas gave her a little more of his weight, right *there*, where for seven years, a kind of loneliness and shame had mixed together to create an unnameable heaviness. As he pressed his body to hers, the weight inside her shifted, becoming somehow lighter and lovelier.

"Evie."

He sighed her name against her throat in a voice she'd not heard from him before, one imbued with longing and passion.

Ah, God, the pleasure of his open mouth on her skin. It was like horses galloping for joy inside her, like…

She arched up into him, knowing full well what that rising column of flesh was. To hold him to her and glory in his desire for her should have been unthinkable, but when his hand settled over her breast, she buried her nose against his throat and rejoiced.

It had been so terribly long, and this was what a spring day was for. This was what youth and life were for.

He closed his fingers gently around her breast, and lightning shot from her nipple to her womb. Lovely, sweet, piercingly pleasurable lightning that made her *squirm* for more.

And then, when she would have started tearing at his clothing, a sound intruded. A rude, wrong sound that had Lucas going still above her and shifting himself up onto his knees and forearms so he crouched over her.

The wheels of a large conveyance lumbered past on the other side of the swale. Over the clatter of the vehicle, Eve heard a man's voice.

"…Probably off in the trees taking a piss. Pass me yon flask, Jordie…"

Above her, Deene let out a held breath.

There were men with pretty manners, and then

there were men who were not always gallant, and yet they were truly chivalrous. Eve accounted Deene some points in the chivalry department when he didn't immediately roll away from her but stayed for a moment tucked close to her, his hand brushing her hair back from her temple.

His caress soothed her and helped her settle. It kept inchoate shame from gaining a toehold over the warmth still pooling in her middle.

She might have initiated the kiss, but Deene was showing her that he'd participated in it willingly. When she turned her face into his palm, he sighed and kissed her cheek, then drew back.

"Evie, tell me you're all right."

"I am fine." When he took himself away, she'd be bereft, but to hear honest concern in his voice made even that eventuality bearable.

He rested his forehead against hers then shifted away, leaving Eve lying on her back amid the lilies of the valley, mourning his loss but also consoled by his rueful smile.

"You pack quite a wallop, my lady."

Wallop. She smiled back at him, for she *had* walloped him without even using her parasol.

"I was either going to kiss you or give in to some other kind of upset." She liked lying there amid the flowers, despite what it was probably doing to her fashionable brown ensemble. "And your kisses are lovely, Lucas."

In the spirit of chivalry, she had to tell him that much.

"As are yours. But, Eve, we've had a narrow escape."

And with that one solemn comment, Eve felt not

the lovely, fragrant breeze of a joyous spring day, but that she was lying in the dirt, looking a fright, very likely having destroyed whatever grudging respect Deene had felt for her.

"Don't poker up on me." Deene used one finger to trace her hairline, then took her hand in his and drew her to a sitting position. "I'm not displaying the crests on the landau today, and that was hardly a fashionable conveyance that just passed."

But his warning was clear: but for those two happenstances, she'd be ruined. A party from Town who recognized the Denning family crest would have remarked to one and all that the Marquis of Deene had been off in the bushes all alone with Lady Eve Windham. A little digging might have been necessary to find out with whom he'd driven out, but somebody—many, gleefully helpful somebodies, more likely—would have seen Eve leaving Mayfair up on the bench with Deene.

"Merciful heavens." Eve dropped her forehead to her knees. "I'm sorry, Lucas. I did not think. I wasn't—"

"Hush." He stayed beside her, apparently in no hurry to rise. "A near miss is by definition not a disaster, and I could never regret such a pleasurable interlude, except that it does rather contradict the trust your family has placed in us both."

She nodded and liked that he didn't start fumbling around, blaming himself, when she'd been the one to accost him. If he'd taken that away from her, she would have *had* to use her parasol.

"It was just a kiss," Eve said. "We've kissed before."

"And it has been a delight on each occasion." He

sounded puzzled and pleased, if a little begrudging, which made Eve smile despite the rest of the thought he was too kind to say:

And *this* occasion must be the last.

He needed to marry, and she needed to avoid marriage. If they kept up with the kisses, sooner or later their near misses and narrow escapes would yield to the inescapable forces of Polite Society.

And that she could not allow.

❧

To be thirty years of age, an experienced man of the world, and yet utterly flummoxed by the kiss of a proper Mayfair lady was… not lowering, exactly, but astonishing—and little had astonished Lucas Denning since his first pitched battle on the Peninsula.

If he'd had sisters to ask, he might have put it to them: Was it usual for a woman well past her come out to shift from composedly sitting beside him on the driver's bench, making conversation, to flat panic, to scorching passion in a matter of moments?

Except the insight of genteel womenfolk probably had less to do with Eve's behaviors than did the sieges he'd witnessed in Spain. When the walls were finally breached, mayhem of the worst kind ensued. Decorated veterans became animals, their most primitive natures ruling all their finer inclinations.

To think Eve Windham was besieged by fear was not comforting at all.

What *was* comforting—also unnerving—was to see how King William reacted to the woman.

"If I'd taught him to bow, he'd be on both knees

before you, Eve Windham. That cannot be good for a horse who's destined to compete for a living."

"But he's such a magnificent fellow. How could I not be smitten?"

The smile she gave the colt was dazzling, so purely beneficent Deene could not look away from the picture she made billing and cooing with the big chestnut horse. Willy was shamelessly flirting right back, batting his big, pretty eyes at her, wuffling into her palm, and wiggling his idiot lips in her hair. It wasn't to be borne.

"Would you like to hack out with me, Eve?"

The smile disappeared. "I'm not dressed appropriately. Thank you for the invitation, nonetheless."

He hadn't expected her to accept, though he had wanted to hear her reply. He shifted closer to her in the stall, close enough that he could stretch out a hand to his horse and not be overheard by the lads.

"I'd put you up on Willy here. He's gentle as a lamb under saddle."

"You'd let me ride your prize racing stud?" The longing in her voice was palpable.

"I don't think he's going to hear, see, or obey anybody else when you're in the vicinity. Willy's in love."

The blighted beast nickered deep in its chest as if in agreement.

"What a charming fellow." Eve's bare hand scratched right behind Willy's ear, and if he'd been a dog, the stallion's back leg would have twitched with pleasure.

What was wrong with a man when he wanted to tell his horse: *She petted me first, so don't get any ideas*?

"I'd love to see you on him, Lucas. I'll bet he

has marvelous paces." Now the smile was aimed at Deene, and even the horse seemed to be looking at him beseechingly.

"I cannot disappoint a guest. We'll have some luncheon up at the house, and the lads can saddle him up."

As Deene escorted the lady from the loose box, Willy managed to look crestfallen before he went back to desultorily lipping at his hay.

"Some horses just have the certain spark, you know," Eve said as they wound through the gardens. "They have a sense of themselves. The breeding stock have it more often, but my sister Sophie has a pair of draft horses…"

She nattered on, a woman enthralled with horses, while Deene speculated about just one more kiss, this one in the greening rose arbor. Rose arbors were intended to facilitate kissing—his own reprobate father had explained this to him not long after Deene had gone to university.

Except… Deene recalled the duchess, waving them on their way just a few hours prior, recalled the fear he'd seen on Eve's face when the horses had startled… and recalled how long it had taken him to get his unruly parts under control after kissing Eve—being kissed *by* Eve—amid the lilies of the valley.

There was nothing wrong with kisses shared between knowledgeable adults, but *that* kiss had threatened to escalate far beyond what Deene felt was acceptable when neither party had intentions toward the other. Nonetheless, the scent that was supposed to evoke return of happiness would forever after bring to his mind a walloping passionate interlude with a lovely woman—who was enamored of his horse.

"So if we were to come back out here, say, next week, might you be willing to hack out with me then, Lady Eve?"

She paused midreach toward her tea—she preferred Darjeeling—and pursed her lips. "I want to."

"Then, Evie, what's stopping you?"

Now she glowered at the teacup. "Nothing."

She was lying again, though he had to allow her the fiction. She alone knew the worst of the specifics, but it was common knowledge she hadn't been on a horse for years.

"Tell me about your accident."

She glanced up. "You aren't going to taunt me by snatching away the invitation to hack out, dangling it just out of my reach, pretending it's a matter of indifference to you?"

It was Deene's turn to glower, for she'd just listed his best tactics when sparring with her. "Would that help?"

She sat back. "Sometimes it has helped. When you had me drive home from the park... I hadn't even taken the reins in years, Lucas. To find myself driving a team right in the middle of Town put me quite at sixes and sevens."

This was not an admission; it was a confidence. A puzzle she was sharing with him *and only him*, as intimate as a kiss and in its own way even more exquisite.

"I have faith in you, Eve Windham. You were a bruising rider, a thoroughgoing equestrienne in the making. I'd like to see you on a horse again, if that would make you happy."

She did not beam a dazzling smile at him, which was the intended effect of such a pretty speech. She instead looked like—God help them both—she might tear up and start bawling right here on the sunny, sheltered back terrace of his country retreat.

This would necessitate that he comfort her, which might not be a bad thing if he'd had the first clue how to go about it.

"Beg pardon, my lord."

Aelfreth Green stood, cap in hand, at the edge of the terrace.

"Aelfreth?" The lads had been as smitten with Eve as the damned stallion. Aelfreth would not have intruded on the lady's meal for anything less than fire, loose horses, or other acts of God.

"Sorry to interrupt, milady, your lordship, but Bannister says you'd best come."

Foreboding congealed in Deene's chest. "Eve, you'll excuse me?"

"Of course."

He rose, visions of Willy cast in his stall, with bowed tendons and incipient colic befalling the horse.

"It's Franny, your lordship," Aelfreth muttered as they strode away. "She's not passing the foal."

Behind him, Deene heard a chair scrape back.

"Come along, Lucas." Eve seized his arm and started towing him forward. "If it's a foaling gone sour, there's no time to waste."

He extricated his arm from her grip. "Eve, it isn't in the least proper for you to be in the vicinity when a mare's giving birth."

"Hang proper. I've assisted at foalings before. We

raise plenty of horses at Morelands, you know, and just because I no longer ride or drive or… any of that, doesn't mean we have time to argue."

She was right, blast her. An animal that historically gave birth where all manner of predators could interfere developed the ability to get the process over with quickly—and did *not* develop any ability to deal with protracted labor.

"Miss might be a help," Aelfreth added. "The mares sometimes want for another female when things go amiss."

"For God's sake, this isn't a lying-in party."

Nobody graced that expostulation with a reply, and when Deene got to the foaling barn, the situation was grim indeed. Bannister, the grizzled trainer and head lad, was outside the foaling stall, his expression glum.

"The foal willna come, your lordship. She'll soon stop trying."

A black mare lay in the deep straw, her enormous belly distended, her neck damp with sweat.

Deene started stripping off his coat. "What's the problem?"

"The foal…" Bannister glanced at Aelfreth.

"Won't come, I know. Have you had a look?"

Another glance—at Aelfreth, at Deene, at the mare, everywhere but at Lady Eve Windham.

She laid a hand on the man's hairy forearm, as if they were great friends. "Speak freely, Mr. Bannister. Is it a red bag? A breech?"

"I dunno, mum. But she shoulda dropped that foal nigh thirty minutes ago."

Deene did not swear aloud, but in his mind, he

bitterly railed against a staff that had let him eat tea and crumpets for half an hour while a mare was in distress.

"Bring me soap and water," Deene said, passing his coat to Eve and starting on the buttons of his waistcoat. "Strong soap and some towels. Eve, I urge you to get back to the house. Frankincense is a maiden mare, she's small, and this is not going to end well."

"Sometimes it just takes them longer their first time, Lucas. We mustn't panic."

She was studying the mare while Deene passed her his waistcoat and stripped off his shirt.

"And sometimes, panic is the only thing that will carry the day. Bring me the damned bucket." He did not raise his voice in deference to the horse groaning and thrashing her way through another contraction.

Eve set his clothing on a saddle rack and started undoing the buttons of her jacket. "She's a very petite mare, Lucas. You'd best let me do this."

Deene stopped in the process of shoving his shirt at her. "Let *you*? Let *you* put your hand… No."

"Yes, let me. I've done this before, and I'm good at it, Lucas. For once being petite is an advantage. Compare your arm to mine and think of the mare."

She thrust out a pale, slender arm—an appendage perhaps half the diameter of his.

While Deene stood there, bare to the waist, anxiety for the horse nigh choking him, Eve dropped her arm and pointed at the stall.

"There's your problem, Deene. You've got a leg back, at least."

While the mare grunted, a single small hoof emerged beneath her tail.

"Milady is right," Bannister said. "Foals is supposed to dive into the world, their noses atween their knees. That one's hung up a leg."

He shot Deene a look and turned to head down the shed row—to where the guns were stored in a cabinet in the saddle room.

"Lucas, don't try to stop me." Eve was down to a very pretty camisole and chemise, both of which left her arms bare below midbicep.

"I will allow you to try," Deene said. "But only because there is no time to make you see reason."

Aelfreth appeared with the bucket, and Eve started scrubbing her arm. "The contraction is passing, and now's the time to investigate. Talk to the mare, Lucas, she has to be terrified and exhausted."

That Eve would enlist his aid was a small consolation, but he hadn't been about to leave her to her own devices in a stall with an animal half out of its small store of wits with pain. He moved to the horse's stall, approached the mare's head, and crouched down.

"Help has arrived, Franny. We'll get you free of this little blighter in no time. You and Willy can admire him all you want then and boast of him to the other mares…"

He pattered on like that, stroking the horse's neck in what he hoped was a soothing rhythm. Behind the horse, Eve was on her side, right down in the straw, her expression calm as she petted the horse's quarters.

"No surprises," Eve said to the horse. "Just another lady back here, and Deene is correct. We'll have this nonsense over with soon, and I promise you—on my mother's solemn assurances—the first one is the worst."

Deene took up the patter while Eve examined the mare internally. When the mare began to grunt again, his heart about stopped.

"Eve?"

"I'm fine, and it's a leg back." Her voice was strained, and Deene knew all too well what the tremendous pressure of a contraction did to a human appendage intruding into the birth canal. Bannister—who was a fine man to run a racing stable—swore it could break a man's arm.

Which Deene hoped was the exaggeration of the uninitiated.

"Eve, do you think you can bring it around?"

"I can, I just need—" The mare heaved a great sigh and went still. "I need purchase to push the foal back."

She needed strength to do that, to use the time between contractions to shove the foal back into the womb where it could get its feet untangled enough for a proper presentation.

"Hold on." He left the mare with a pat to the neck and came around to the back of the horse. "Just give me a moment."

For a moment was all they'd have.

⁓

She'd been a girl of fourteen the last time she'd done this, drafted into service in the same situation—a small mare, disaster for both mare and foal looming at hand, a desperate measure permitted only because St. Just had begged His Grace to allow it.

And the mare and foal had lived.

That recollection gave Eve renewed strength, but

scrabbling in the straw, she had nothing to brace herself against until a hard male chest blanketed her from behind, and a strong male hand settled on her shoulder.

"You've got the foal, Eve?"

"I do, I just need a little… more…" Just a few inches, just an inch. With Deene applying a steady brace to her shoulder and Eve hilting her arm inside the mare, she managed—just barely—to aid the foal in slipping back into the womb from the birth canal.

"Can you find the knee or the elbow, anything to ease the leg forward with?"

Another contraction was going to hit, and any second, while Eve tried sight unseen to sort one slippery foal-part from another.

"An elbow." She hoped.

"Pull forward gently until you've got the foot coming along."

The mare was small, but the distance was at the limit of Eve's reach, and the room to maneuver nonexistent.

"Push harder, Lucas. I can't get any purchase."

He applied a painful pressure to Eve's shoulder, all but shoving her face into the mare's sweaty rump, but it gave her the fraction of an inch she needed. The leg was slippery and the space confined. She tugged, she pulled, she yanked, and with a sudden give, the foot slid forward.

"Done." She slumped back against Deene's chest and slipped her arm from the mare's body, only to find herself summarily hauled to her feet.

"Then let's get you out of here, because any moment now Franny is going to start thrashing again."

Eve let Deene lead her from the stall as the mare

began to strain and groan again. "I've seen foals born before, Lucas."

This remonstrance came out weakly, for a sudden light-headedness was afflicting her—no doubt the result of being plucked from the straw after such an exertion.

"You've probably been kicked before too, which would not excuse me did I allow it to happen again." Deene spoke briskly, and he swabbed briskly at her arm, from fingers to shoulder, with a clean, damp towel.

He needed to scold her about something; the realization made Eve curiously happy. "I'm sure you're right, Lucas."

When he had scrubbed her arm thoroughly, he set the towel aside, grasped her by her wrist, and tugged her across the barn aisle, stopping only long enough to retrieve his coat.

"*I've* never done what you just did." He settled his coat over her shoulders, the scent of him bringing as much comfort as the warmth. "I've handled cows—a *single* cow, one time, and sheep, but they hardly need any help—not horses, for God's sake. You could have been kicked, or the mare might have rolled. If your parents find out I permitted this, I will never be allowed to so much as—"

She put two fingers to his lips, lest he raise his voice and disturb the mare. "My papa has permitted me to provide the same aid at Morelands, but it was only the once, years ago. Now, hush."

He was bare from the waist up, upset, and in some sort of male tantrum. Eve put her forehead on his sternum and her arms around his waist. She remained like that until she felt Deene's arms come around her, slowly, carefully, enfolding her in warmth.

She felt his chin resting on her crown. "I keep underestimating you, Eve Windham."

Eve turned her face so she could listen to his heart—a marvelous benefit to hugging a man without his shirt. "I underestimate me too."

They remained like that, embracing, giving Eve the sense they were settling each other's nerves as they did. Deene didn't let her go until Bannister called softly from across the aisle.

"A right proper stud colt, we've got, but he be a big bugger, begging milady's pardon."

Deene leaned down to whisper in her ear. "Thank you. It's Willy's first colt, and I... just thank you."

He slipped away and started giving orders, while Eve stood there wearing his coat and wondering which was better: kissing the Marquis of Deene or foaling out his mare.

❧

The damned horse was showing off, adding that extra little fillip of élan to his strides, the smallest spark of additional grace, and as every lad on the property gathered on the rail, Deene had the sure conviction Willy knew Eve was watching him show off his equine wares.

But what a ride... Never had the stallion been more supple and willing, never had he flowed over the ground with quite such ease. When Deene brought the animal to a perfectly square halt before Eve where she perched on a top rail, her eyes were sparkling.

"Lucas, you were not boasting. He's magnificent. A gentleman-scholar-poet-athlete-artist of a horse, and so very, very handsome."

"Do you want to cool him out?"

The horse had hardly broken a sweat, but the highest standards of care dictated that he be walked after his exertions at least for a few minutes.

"Yes, I most certainly do." She climbed down and scrambled between the rails while Deene ran up the irons and loosened the girth. When he stepped back, Eve took the reins and led the beast away on a circuit of the schooling ring.

"That's the best he's done, your lordship." Bannister's gaze followed Eve and the horse. "All that trotting about, he ain't never looked that fine before."

"He's growing into himself."

Bannister eyed Deene up and down. "Her ladyship has a way about her, more like. You should bring her by again soon."

Bannister walked off with the rolling, bowlegged gait of the veteran equestrian, leaving Deene to watch as woman and horse ambled around the arena. Eve was talking to the horse in low, earnest tones, and the horse gave every appearance of listening raptly.

An image of Mildred Staines flashed in Deene's mind. He'd seen her riding in the park on a pretty bay mare just a few days previous. Mildred sat a horse competently, but there was nothing *pretty* about the picture. Her habit was fashionable, her horse tidily turned out, her appointments all coordinated for a smart impression, but...

Eve was still wearing Deene's coat, her skirts were

rumpled, her boots dusty, and she sported a few wisps of straw in her hair. She stopped to turn the horse the other direction, pausing to pet the beast on his solid shoulder.

I could marry her.

The thought appeared in Deene's brain between one instant and the next, complete and compelling. It rapidly began sprouting roots into his common sense.

She was wellborn enough.

She was pretty enough.

She was passionate enough.

She was—he forced himself to list this consideration—well dowered enough.

And she charmed King William effortlessly.

Why not? Little leaves of possibility began twining upward into Deene's imagination.

He knew her family thoroughly and wouldn't have to deal with any aunts secreted away in Cumbria.

He was friends with her brothers, who did not leave bastards all over the shire.

The Windham hadn't been born who lost control when gambling.

And Eve Windham was a delightful kisser.

Why the hell not? The longer he thought about it, the more patently right the idea became.

Eve was grinning openly as she brought King William back over to the rail. "I've found my perfect companion, Deene. He doesn't make idle conversation, doesn't click his heels annoyingly, doesn't reek of leeks or cigars, and would never drink to excess. I suppose you'll make me turn him over to the lads for his grooming?"

"You suppose correctly." He fell in beside her as she led her charge to the gate. "I hadn't intended to stay this late in the day, and now it looks to be clouding up."

"I don't care." She gave the horse one last pat. "I made a new friend today. The entire outing has been worth it."

Smitten, the two of them. It gave a man pause when he had to consider that his horse's charms might be interfering with the ideal moment for a proposal of marriage. Deene ushered Eve up to the house so she might repair her toilet, and waited on the terrace while she was within.

By the time she emerged from the house, Eve was a slightly rumpled version of the picture she'd presented first thing of the day, but to Deene's eye, also more relaxed.

"I've had the tops put up on the landau, Lady Eve. Aelfreth will drive us."

Her brows knit as Deene shrugged into the jacket she'd borrowed for the past couple of hours. "That isn't quite…" She fell silent. "I suppose it will be dark before we reach Town, and I do not relish a soaking."

"My thinking exactly." Though if she had insisted, he'd also been prepared to ride up on the damned box if necessary to appease the proprieties. When he climbed in beside her, she made no comment.

When he took the seat next to her, she still made no comment, confirming his sense that Eve Windham was indeed, very solid wife material. He rested against the squabs, inhaled a pleasant whiff of mock orange, and contemplated marriage to the woman beside him.

❧

The day had been *wonderful*. Eve settled into the coach with a sense of contentment she hadn't experienced in ages.

Deene lowered himself beside her—right beside her—and that was wonderful too. In the course of the day, he'd become subtly affectionate with her. He plucked wisps of straw from her hair, took her hand in his, stood a little too close…

She doubted he was even aware of such small gestures, but they left her feeling a precious sense of being cared for, however fleetingly.

"Are you nervous, Eve?" He slid an arm across her shoulders, no doubt meaning to bolster her courage.

She was feeling quite brave, in truth, though she made no protest at his familiarity. "You think I'm nervous to be in a closed carriage with dirty weather closing in, and us miles from Town?"

"I was trying to be delicate."

She relaxed against him. "The horses are not fresh, a little rain isn't likely to unsettle them, and…" And what? And Deene was right there beside her? There was more to it than that, though his presence was certainly reassuring.

"And?"

"And something about this day has been good for me. I ought to be nervous, though I've never been in a coaching accident, per se, but I am no more than a touch uneasy."

He did not tell her to put her fears aside; he did not talk her out of them; he did not do anything other than take her hand. "So you were impressed with Wee Willy?"

Ah, horse talk.

"I am enthralled with him. When will you next compete him?"

"Quite possibly at the local meet before Epsom in June, though Bannister would have me believe such decisions are a function of reading chicken entrails and tea leaves."

"You need to work your stallion on the opposing lead in canter, Deene. Sheer speed is impressive, but he needs strength and suppleness to go with it, or he'll end up blown before he's eight."

As the miles rolled by, they conducted a discussion—*not* a debate—regarding the merits of working the horse on hills, over fences, and on the flat. Eve found herself wishing London were twenty miles farther, and that pleased her too.

Deene still had her hand in his when he shifted the topic slightly. "What will you name the colt?"

The lads decreed she should have the naming of Franny's foal; Deene had loudly approved the notion, and that had been that: she was godmother to a baby horse.

And *that* had been what put the day to rights. Being allowed to be useful, to pitch in despite the proprieties, was what had allowed Eve to climb into a carriage behind a pair of horses who had already given her a good fright.

"I haven't named a horse in ages." Though she used to name all the fillies at Morelands. "A stud's firstborn son needs a substantial name, something that resounds with virtue. My sisters and I used to debate what to name our children as we practiced putting up our hair."

That last had slipped out, a function of approaching nightfall and the pleasurable warmth of Deene beside her.

"So you want children?"

Inane question—every woman wanted children and a home of her own. The inane question put a small puncture in Eve's sense of wellbeing.

"We don't always get what we want, Lucas. Some things are beyond human control." She resisted the impulse to slip her hand from his. An argument was drawing closer, one she did not want to have with him.

Not now, not ever.

"I would like the opportunity to try to provide you with children, Eve Windham. We could raise them up in Kent, not far from your parents. I have enough land that I can move the stables there if you prefer. I think we'd suit wonderfully."

"You think we'd suit?" Her voice did not shake with the impossibility of his offer—she was the daughter of a duchess, and knew well how to maintain her composure, but, God help her, she had *not* seen this coming.

He was going to ruin this wonderful day, ruin it thoroughly, and all Eve could think was that she'd misplaced her parasol.

"We would manage well enough. We're each of appropriate station, we know one another's families, the lands all but march, and it would spare you from the importuning of the Trit-Trots of the world."

Drat him for his common sense. Were he speaking from the heart rather than his pragmatic male brain, she might have considered what he was saying for a few moments before rejecting him.

"It would also spare you from the Mildred Staineses of the world."

"With the Season looming, that is not a small consideration. We have something else weighing in favor of a marital union."

He was proposing without asking her to marry him. His aplomb was impressive, also... *heartbreaking*. Deene was, to her surprise, a man she would enjoy being married to in some regards, and he was bringing his addresses to her first, not to His Grace—and still, his proposal must be rejected just like all the others.

"What is this something else, my lord?" His politics no doubt all but marched with His Grace's; he'd charged the French with Devlin and Bart; he wasn't afraid of Louisa or muddled by Jenny's sweet good loo—

Her only warning was Deene's bare hand on her chin, gently turning her face up to receive his kiss, the most beguilingly gentle kiss so far. His lips pressed softly against hers, and his hand cupped her jaw then slid back into her hair to cradle the back of her head.

Not this again. Not this lovely, spreading warmth rising from her middle and obliterating all reason; not the raging desire to shift herself beneath him and taste his skin and breathe his scents.

Bodily loneliness swamped her as Deene's mouth moved on hers. Nobody was intimate with her the way Deene could be; nobody *touched* her except for the fleeting contact permitted by Society's rules or familial affection. She opened for him, fisted her hands in his hair, and dragged him closer.

And when she was aching for him to give her one last taste of pleasure and passion, he eased away, resting his forehead on hers.

"We have passion, Eve Windham. That is no small consideration either."

Passionate kisses did not always tell the tale. Eve knew this from bitter experience. A man, even a very young man, could kiss like a dream and make a girl lose every shred of common sense and still, the man's most intimate attentions could be… distasteful. Painful even.

Deene, by contrast, would be a sumptuous lover, generous, skilled, beautiful…

She cut the thought off and made herself speak in brisk, ruthless tones. "I appreciate the honor you do me, Lucas, but I am no more interested in your proposal than I am in Trit—in Mr. Trottenham's. We would not suit."

He pulled away, straightening beside her. To suffer the loss of him with indifference was necessary if Eve was to make her point.

"Eve Windham, if the way we kiss is your idea of *not* suiting, then God help the man you do suit. He'll go up in flames the moment you bat your eyes at him."

"There will be no such man."

An argument would help a great deal, but no, Deene sat beside her, his arm around her shoulders, his thumb idly stroking the side of her neck. Eventually, she allowed herself to yield to the temptation he offered and rested her head on his shoulder. Soon enough they'd reach Town, she'd climb out of the carriage, and the day that had gone from hell to heaven back to hell would be over.

There was time enough to cry later.

⁓

"Where in the hell is Lord Andermere?"

Deene used Anthony's courtesy title before the staff routinely, though he seldom adopted such an impatient tone of voice, much less profanity.

"His lordship was called down to Kent, my lord." Gower spoke with the studied calm of a butler who'd spent forty years in service to the Denning family.

"When was he called down to Kent?"

"Yesterday morning, I believe, my lord. He said he received a note from Mr. Bassingstoke."

Bassingstoke was the land steward at Denning Hall. It made sense that Anthony might be called away on a property matter, but it made no sense whatsoever that he'd leave without a word to Deene, when they were supposed to spend the morning poring over ledgers.

"Send a note around to Hooker. I'll be paying a call on him before noon."

Gower bowed. "Very good, my lord. Will that be all, my lord?"

"No, it will not." If Deene couldn't start on the ledgers, he'd tackle the matter from another angle. "Send Mrs. Hitchings to me in the library in twenty minutes."

Gower withdrew quietly—Gower did everything quietly—leaving Deene to pour himself another cup of tea, finish reading the financial article he'd started when he sat down to breakfast, and polish off the rest of his eggs and toast. Mrs. Hitchings was waiting for him when he arrived to the library.

"Ma'am, good morning." Deene took a seat behind the estate desk, hazarding that the housekeeper would be more nervous if he instead paced the room. "You are welcome to sit, Mrs. Hitchings."

Relief crossed her tired features as she perched at the very edge of a chair, her back ramrod straight, her gaze fixed on some point beyond Deene's left shoulder.

"How long have you been housekeeper here?" In her white caps and drab dresses, she'd been a fixture in the townhouse as far back as Deene could recall.

"Nigh twenty years, your lordship."

An answer, and not one word beyond the question she'd been asked. They hadn't been easy years.

"And how many housemaids do we have?"

"Twenty at the moment, your lordship, though they tend to turn over."

"How many footmen?"

She frowned slightly. "The footmen answer to Mr. Gower, your lordship. I would put their number at about the same as the maids."

"And their wages?"

At that question—and only that question—her gaze flickered across Deene's face, her eyes betraying a wary consternation. "I wouldn't know for certain, your lordship. Lord Andermere sees to the paying of the wages."

"What about the marketing, do you keep an account of that?"

"I hand in the sum to Lord Andermere at the end of

each month, your lordship. If he's not in Town, then I give it to Mr. Gower."

There was no house steward for the townhouse—except Anthony, apparently.

"I would appreciate it if in future, Mrs. Hitchings, you apprise me of the sum expended as well. That will be all. Please send Gower to me directly."

Gower's litany was the same, though he of course remained standing while Deene interrogated him. Neither servant knew much of the household finances other than the single sum they reported to Anthony.

As Deene called for his horse to be saddled, he concluded such an arrangement was likely in the interest of domestic harmony, it being the province of the lower orders to grouse about wages, working conditions, and the tightfistedness of employers generally.

The ride into the City gave Deene an opportunity to consider yesterday's developments with Lady Eve Windham—to further consider them, just as he'd been awake considering them for half the night.

She was attracted to him; of that there could be no doubt.

Nonetheless, she'd also unhesitatingly rejected a proposal from a very eligible catch, when her own tenure on the marriage market was growing woefully long. Her rejection stung more than it should have, but it also puzzled, which was annoying as hell.

Solicitors were annoying as hell too, but in a way that allowed Deene to vent and posture away some of his irritation.

"This is very short notice, my lord." Hooker came up from his bow and took hold of a velvet coat lapel in each hand. "Very short notice indeed. May I inquire as to the nature of your lordship's errand?"

Why was it the legal profession excelled in planting a sense of shame in a paying client?

Deene remained standing, requiring that Hooker do likewise. The skinny, younger associate was hovering near the fire, which Deene noted was burning cheerily on a temperate day.

And how much was that costing the already strained Deene coffers?

"My errand, as you put it, is to accept from you a status report regarding the pleadings I asked to have drawn up well over a week ago."

Hooker pursed his lips. He turned loose of his lapels and stared for a moment at the floor. When Hooker had studied the floor long enough to make Deene's jaw clench, the solicitor looked up and turned to his associate. "Bring me his lordship's file."

The associate fairly scampered out of the room while Deene let a silence extend.

"Perhaps your lordship would like some tea?"

"No, thank you."

"Do you take coffee, then? Some sustenance? What we have on hand is modest, your lordship, but certainly available for your comfort and convenience."

From his own father, Deene had learned that the best rebukes were offered in the most civil tones. "This is not a social call, Hooker."

"Of course not, your lordship. Might I inquire if we'll be looking at any marriage settlement documents in the near future?"

An attempt at cross-examination and surprise, both.

If the old windbag was half as good at the law as he was at conducting himself like a lawyer, then—with a half-decent barrister added to the payroll—Deene should soon have custody of his niece.

"Have you seen any announcements in the *Times*, Hooker?"

"Announce—? I have not, your lordship."

Deene turned to survey the narrow street below, allowing Hooker to conclude for himself that solicitors would no more be privy to Deene's personal attachments than would the general public.

After a soft tap, the door opened to reveal the scholarly associate. "The file, Mr. Hooker."

A fat, beribboned folder was passed over to Hooker with a ceremony befitting High Church on a solemn holiday.

So much theatre, when all Deene wanted was to hug his niece. To know she was happy and thriving, to see her occasionally and have all of Polite Society know she was, unfortunate paternal antecedents notwithstanding, a *Denning*.

"Ah, yes. Here we are." Hooker bent over the folder, setting papers in various piles on his desk. "We are making quite good progress on the pleadings, your lordship. Bitters here is taking the lead."

"I'd like to see the draft documents."

Hooker straightened, his expression all benevolent concern. "My lord, you must understand, such an undertaking requires a command of arcane legal language, law Norman, knowledge of appropriate precedents, and a great deal of preparation."

"Nigh two weeks have gone by since I indicated

these papers were to be drawn up, sir. Show me the draft."

Hooker's look of long-suffering should have been studied on Drury Lane. He passed over a single sheet of foolscap, which Deene took in at a glance.

"This is a list of cases." And no date. The list might have been hastily tucked into the file in the past five minutes.

"One starts with the relevant precedents, my lord, and a good deal of research into how those cases bear on the present circumstances. As I said, this is an arcane and complicated legal undertaking. Allow me to say to you we are honored to ensure it will be handled in the most thorough and competent fashion possible."

Deene unclenched his jaw and set the single piece of paper on the desk.

"Allow me to say, Hooker, that you will not be paid for all this painstaking research—which I do appreciate, of course—until such time as I have pleadings in my hand, suitable for submission to a court of appropriate jurisdiction. I bid you good day."

He had the satisfaction of seeing Hooker's brows crash down.

"And, Hooker? One more thing. I dipped my toe in the law at university, at least to the extent a man likely some day to serve as magistrate ought to. Those cases listed on your precious paper relate to trade agreements and civil contracts. While not a lawyer, I'm hard put to understand how custody of a girl child involves those aspects of the law."

For Deene to close the door softly on the way out was a small triumph and short lived. The truth of it was

Hooker and his imps had been sitting on their back-sides, swilling tea—or coffee—eating cakes, and doing exactly nothing to pry Georgie loose from the clutches of the climbing cit who called himself her father.

As Deene made his way to his horse, he found his mind turning to the nonlegal means of extricating Georgie from Dolan's custody. A concocted duel, a rigged card game, a flat-out kidnapping... each dishonorable, dangerous alternative was becoming increasingly tempting.

Four

"IF THIS ISN'T A PROVIDENTIAL BLIGHT ON AN OTHER-wise fair spring day." Dolan offered his brother-in-law a cheeky smile calculated to irritate his Royal Importance-ship no end. "Deene, good day to you."

The marquis's rapid progress down the sidewalk halted. "Dolan, good day. I want to see my niece."

Some burr had gotten under the saddle of Love's Young Dream—one of Marie's terms for her younger brother. His blue eyes were spitting fire, and his lean form was bristling with indignation.

"We don't always get what we want, your lordship."

Deene was hanging onto his composure by a grati-fyingly obvious thread, and yet a rousing set-to on the street—though mightily entertaining—would serve no one, least of all Georgina.

"Perhaps your lordship might explain to me why you want to see your niece?" Dolan turned and ambled along in the direction of Deene's travel. "Grown men don't typically associate voluntarily with small girls."

Deene at least comprehended the need to avoid a

scene—the English were predictable in this regard—for he fell in step beside Dolan.

"I do not have to explain my motives for seeking the occasional company of my sister's only offspring."

It was an effective hit, but the wrong answer.

"Perhaps you need not explain your motives to God Almighty, your lordship, but I am the girl's father." Oh, the pleasure of being able to say that so gently and implacably. Dolan considered brightening his future perambulations about Town with more frequent collisions with his benighted Lord Brother-In-Law.

Marie's wit was not the least of the attributes Dolan missed about his late wife.

"Let me put it this way, Dolan. Either I see her with your permission, or I will take any means necessary to see her without."

"I'm quaking in my muddy bogtrottin' boots, your lordship." Dolan let his brogue broaden perceptibly, then noticed no less a person than the Duchess of Moreland making a brisk progress down the street. "Heard your colt finally put that braying ass Islington in his place. One would hate to miss the rare opportunity to offer you a sincere compliment, Deene, particularly when the compliment can be rendered in public."

"And my thanks for your kind observation is rendered just as publicly. At least tell me how Georgie goes on."

Marie had always sworn her brother wasn't cut from the same cloth as the previous marquis and marchioness, but Marie was—had been—blind when it came to the people she loved. Dolan silently apologized

to his wife's sainted memory, but allowed himself to
doubt the sincerity of Deene's query.

"Georgina, as always, thrives in my care, Deene,
and you'd better hope your colt never comes up
against my Goblin."

Deene's expression had become that bland, handsome mask of impassivity Dolan could only envy.
The English were arrogant, ungrateful, and not to be
trusted, and they could not be relied upon to turn up
stupid at times that suited any but themselves.

"Your Grace." Deene made a lovely little bow to the
duchess, who bestowed a dazzling smile on the idiot.

"Deene, good day." She turned, that smile still on her
lips, and waited for Deene to handle the introductions.

A sweet moment, to be introduced to a duchess,
and by no less than his own seething brother-in-law
in view of all and sundry.

"Your Grace, may I make known to you my
brother-in-law, Mr. Jonathan Dolan? Dolan, Esther,
Duchess of Moreland."

And abruptly, the sweet moment turned...
tainted. For one instant, Dolan forgot how a man—a
gentleman—behaved upon introduction to a duchess.

Deene had bowed. Dolan bowed to the same
depth and came up with his best charming smile in
place—Her Grace was an easy woman to smile at,
pretty even at fifteen years Dolan's senior, with a
palpable graciousness about her not typical of her kind.

Not that Dolan had been introduced to so very
many duchesses.

"Mr. Dolan, a pleasure. My daughter was compli-
menting your Georgina just the other day. If raising

my five girls is any indication, your daughter will soon be turning your hair gray and breaking hearts. Deene, I'll be expecting you for supper Tuesday next. The numbers won't balance if you decline."

She murmured her good days in such dulcet, cultured tones Dolan could almost forgive her for being a damned duchess.

"I'd heard you were driving out with the woman's daughter. I wouldn't mind having the daughter of a duke for Georgina's aunt."

Deene had recovered himself thoroughly. He aimed a stare at Dolan that felt uncomfortably pitying. "Dolan, there is more to choosing a wife than the benefit she brings you and your *bogtrotting* relations."

"And do you number your sister's only child among those bogtrotting relations, Deene?"

They'd descended to insults that hit dangerously close to tender places, and lowered their voices accordingly. As Dolan watched his brother-in-law's handsome face, he reflected that learning to trade insults like a true English gentleman was not an accomplishment to be proud of.

"You had best hope your Goblin never finds himself running against King William. I would not want to have to explain to my niece why English bloodlines are superior to all others, even as they relate to lower species."

Dolan smiled, so English was that insult.

"Perhaps you're right, my lord, at least when it comes to running fast. Shall we part on this cordial note between enthusiastic horsemen, or go another three rounds?"

For one disturbing moment, something bleak flickered through Deene's eyes.

"Good day, Dolan. Please give my compliments to Georgie and tell her I asked after her. You have my thanks as well for the flowers you keep on Marie's grave."

"Good day, Deene."

On that civil—and puzzling—note, they did part, though Dolan felt the need for a quiet place to sit and reflect on the entire conversation before administering the week's verbal beating to his solicitors.

Marie had loved her brother. It was probably accurate to say that upon being forced to marry Dolan, her brother was the *only* person she'd loved. Dolan could acknowledge that he and Deene had both loved Marie in return, though of course in quite different ways.

And yet, for the one moment when bleakness had flickered through Deene's eyes, Dolan would have sworn that they also shared another emotion where Marie was concerned, an emotion more burdensome than love.

Dolan had to wonder on what grounds the marquis might be entitled to feel guilt where his sister was concerned—if indeed that had been guilt Dolan had seen flickering in Deene's handsome blue eyes.

❧

"Eve Windham, what on earth can you be poring over in here when any sane creature is outside on such a glorious day?"

Louisa sat herself—uninvited and unwelcome—right beside Eve on the small sofa.

"I'm making a list, if you must know." Eve set the list aside, though she'd hardly kept her aims secret from her sisters.

"Of?" Louisa, having the advantage of greater reach, helped herself to Eve's scribblings. "These are names of men."

"My sister is a genius."

This provoked a grin as Louisa perused the admittedly short list. "These are single men, but what a group you've gathered on your paper, Eve. Trit-Trot; Sir Cleaveridge Oldman, better known as Old Sir Cleavage; Harold Enderbend, known to his familiars as Harold Elbowbend." Louisa continued to study the list, her grin fading. "These are your white marriage knights, as it were?"

"They are a start." Though it had taken Eve all morning to come up with even a half-dozen names.

"Scratch Trit-Trot off your list. Joseph says he gambles excessively."

Eve took up the paper and did as Louisa suggested, but it was no great loss. Trit-Trot would bow and blather her witless in a week.

Cleaveridge would not keep his hands to himself.

Enderbend was a sot whose drunken wagering would bankrupt them in a year.

Eve nibbled her pencil. "Can you think of anybody else? Mind you, this is strictly in the way of contingency planning."

"We should ask Jenny. She notices things. This discussion will require sustenance."

That Louisa wasn't laughing at Eve's project was both reassuring and unnerving. While Lou rang for trays—plural—another footman was sent off to retrieve Jenny from the gardens.

"We're trying to find Eve a white knight husband, but it's rather difficult going," Louisa explained to their sister. "We need a fellow who will leave her in peace but be attentive and civil. He must be good-looking enough to be credible and have all his teeth."

Jenny took a seat in the rocker and frowned at the list. "He must be able to keep Eve in the style to which she has become accustomed."

Before the tea trays had arrived, Eve's sisters had concocted a list not of eligible husbands, but of the characteristics such a man must possess.

He must like to travel—preferably to foreign parts for extended periods.

He must be mild mannered, but a man of his word.

He must be affectionate *enough*, but not *too* affectionate.

It wouldn't hurt if he already had an heir.

Nor if he were devoid of relatives who would be curious about the nature of the marriage.

Such an effort her sisters put forth to secure Eve a list of appropriate possibilities, and yet nowhere on their list were the things that might have made a white marriage bearable:

He must be kind.

He must be that rare man who could befriend an adult woman.

He must be loyal—faithful was a ridiculous notion under the circumstances.

And it really, truly would not hurt matters if he loved horses, either.

"Eve has left us." Jenny made this observation

when Louisa had laid siege to the sandwiches and cakes an hour later.

"I'm thinking," Eve said, which was not a lie. She was thinking of never seeing Franny's foal grow up, never bestowing a name on the little fellow, or petting Willy's velvety nose ever again. Never again kissing the only man to make her insides rise up and sing the glories of being a healthy young female…

"Jenny has come up with a capital notion. You must marry this portrait painter everybody is raving about. I forget his name, though he and Joseph are cordial."

Eve forced herself to attend the topic, more because her sisters left unsupervised would have her betrothed to the fellow without her even being introduced to him.

"Elijah Harrison. He has a title," Jenny said, "but he doesn't use it. He's mannerly and quiet, also very talented and an associate member of the Royal Academy, one of the youngest so far."

Louisa got up to brace her back against the mantel and cross her arms. "He's also mostly to be found dozing among the ferns at the fashionable entertainments."

Jenny set the list aside, her chin coming up. "He must work during daylight hours and has not the luxury of sleeping until noon every day; moreover, he's a marvelous dancer."

Oh-ho. Louisa's lips quirked up, as did Eve's. "Jenny is smitten," Lou pronounced. "S-m-i-t-t-e-n. We must strike his name from your list, Evie. Alas for you and My Lord Artist."

Eve resisted the urge to join in the teasing. Jenny showed her hand so rarely that Louisa was probably right in her surmise.

Louisa was right a maddening proportion of the time. But drunks and painters?

Eve looked at the list again. "Perhaps we should ring for a fresh pot."

Jenny looked relieved, Louisa determined, and though the list of requirements grew longer, the list of names did not.

❧

"Are you suffering a bilious stomach, Deene, or have you taken to glowering the matchmakers into submission?"

Kesmore's question caused Deene a start, for the man had given no warning of his presence.

"And when did you take to lurking among the ferns, Kesmore?"

"Perhaps I'm lurking among the shy, retiring bachelors. It isn't like you to be demonstrably out of sorts, Deene, particularly not in company with the fair flowers of Polite Society."

No, it was not, which sorry state of affairs Deene laid directly at Lady Eve Windham's dainty feet. "Cleaveridge is all but drooling on his partner's bosom."

"What a lovely bosom it is, too. Moreland's women are a pretty bunch."

This casual observation from a man who appeared to have no interest whatsoever in bosoms pretty or otherwise—save for that of his countess—made Deene want to stomp across the dance floor and pluck Eve from Cleaveridge's arms.

"She's up to something."

"The ladies usually are. We adore them for it, and in polite company refer to it as a mysterious feminine quality."

Deene turned to study Kesmore amid the shadows under the ballroom's minstrel's gallery. "With the exception of your recently acquired countess, I've yet to see you adoring a human female since you mustered out, Kesmore. One hears rumors about you and your livestock, however."

"My livestock are lining the Kesmore coffers sufficiently to launch my daughters in style when the time comes. You insult the beasts at your peril."

Though Kesmore's voice was mild, Deene had the sense the man was genuinely protective of his pigs. This ought to be a point of departure for much raillery between former officers who'd served together under Wellington, but it was instead an odd comfort.

A man could apparently do worse than be protective of the woman who'd rejected his very first marital proposal... though Deene doubted Kesmore was actually jealous of the boar hogs courting his breeding sows.

"Cleaveridge does have an unfortunate tendency to stare at the wrong parts of a lady's person, doesn't he?" Kesmore kept his voice down, though as Deene watched Eve's progress through the concluding bars of the dance, he wanted to shout at Cleaveridge to turn loose of Lady Eve.

At her final curtsy, Cleaveridge bowed to precisely that angle most convenient for ogling and even sniffing at Eve's breasts.

"Deene." Kesmore's hand on Deene's arm prevented him from starting across the ballroom. "Enderbend is making a charge from the punch bowl."

"All of his charges start and end at the punch bowl."

"Perhaps Lady Eve is on a charity mission to dance

with all the hopefuls who will never graduate to the status of eligibles."

She was on a mission to part Deene from his few remaining wits, making a strategic retreat the only sane course. "I'm off to play a hand of cards. Care to join me?"

Kesmore gave him an unreadable look. He had Deene's height, though Kesmore's coloring was dark, his build heavier, and somewhere in the middle of Spain his features had lost the knack of smiling.

"Take this." Kesmore shoved an empty glass against Deene's middle and limped away. Deene could only watch in consternation as the crowd parted before Kesmore with the hasty manners shown a man condemned to limp for the rest of his life.

Consternation turned to outright surprise when Kesmore offered his arm to Lady Eve and left Enderbend looking like a besotted fool at the edge of the dance floor.

Lest Deene be caught wearing the same expression in public, he did withdraw to the card room.

✌

Eve could not have been more surprised when her most recently acquired brother-in-law, Joseph, the Earl of Kesmore, informed her she'd agreed to take some air with him at the conclusion of the quadrille.

She should have refused, particularly with Mr. Enderbend looking so eager for his dance—and flushed, and red, and savoring quite noxiously of spirits. Eve caught a whiff of Enderbend's breath and accepted Kesmore's unexpected offer.

In addition to being Louisa's spouse, Kesmore was a neighbor. In the settled countryside of Kent, this meant that even prior to his marriage he could be accounted a family friend. He rode to hounds with His Grace at the local meets. He attended the assemblies and balls. He made calls and returned them, particularly at the holidays.

Eve would not have said he was *her* friend, however.

"I am capable of dancing, you know."

"I beg your lordship's pardon?"

He glanced down at her, his expression amused without anything approaching a smile lightening his saturnine features. "If you're making some sort of penance for yourself out of dancing with the dregs, Lady Eve, you must include me on your card. Waltzing with a cripple has to rank with partnering the sots and lechers among the company."

He was gruff. Widowers, even widowers who did not limp, might be gruff, but this was... needling.

"If I refuse a gentleman a dance without cause, then I must sit out the rest of the evening, my lord. What purpose is there in attending such a gathering, if not to dance?"

Another glance, somewhat measuring. "What purpose, indeed?"

Eve realized her rudeness too late. "I apologize, my lord, but do I surmise you choose not to dance rather than that you cannot dance?"

His expression softened, making him look for a moment almost wistful. "With the right woman, I dance well enough, as your sister can attest. Shall we avail ourselves of the terrace?"

The ballroom was stifling, the noise oppressive, and supper had only just been served. "Thank you. That would be lovely."

He paused by the punch bowls to fetch them each a drink, then led Eve from the ballroom to the torch-lit terrace where two other couples were in desultory conversation by the balustrade.

"Shall we sit, Lady Eve?"

"Nothing would be more welcome."

She chose a bench against the wall of the building, one more in shadow than torchlight. Kesmore held their drinks while Eve arranged her skirts, then came down beside her with a sigh.

"I am not an adept dancer, mind you, but prior to my marriage I was damned if I'd sit about with the dowagers as if longing for my Bath chair. So I learned to stand and aggravate my deuced knee and grow blasted irascible as a result. Apologies for my language."

"His Grace can be much more colorful than that."

Kesmore peered at their drinks. "Suppose he can. Would you like the spiked version or the unspiked one? I warn you, I'll poison the nearest hedge with the unspiked one if that's the one you leave me."

Eve resisted the urge to study him more closely but found his lack of pretense a relief. This was the man who'd captured Louisa's heart, though nobody had quite figured out how.

"May I have one sip of the spiked variety? A lady grows curious, after all."

This earned her another of those amused, unsmiling expressions. He passed over a glass, which allowed Eve to note the earl's hands were bare. "Slowly, my lady. Our hosts are gracious with their offerings."

She slipped off her gloves and took a drink from the proffered glass.

"Merciful… My *goodness*. How do you gentlemen remain standing?"

He passed her the other glass, though she just held it while the burn in her vitals muted to a rosy glow.

"Some of us don't remain standing, at least not much past midnight. One has to wonder what you were about, Lady Eve, to stand up with Enderbend this late in the evening."

He sounded almost as if he were scolding her, which was a considerable margin beyond a passing spate of gruffness.

"My choice of dance partners should be no concern of yours, my lord." She spoke as gently as she could, telling herself Kesmore's leg was hurting him, and he'd very likely been dragged to the evening's gathering as a function of Louisa's continuing loyalty to her unmarried sisters.

"I am not concerned, exactly. One more sip?" He held up his glass of punch.

"Perhaps one more." It was a lovely, fruity concoction, and his lordship had spoken nothing but the truth regarding their host's hospitality, for the punch was cold, even at this advanced hour.

And yet it warmed nicely, in small sips.

Eve pondered that contradiction while she took yet another sip.

"I apologize if it seems I chide you for your choice of partner, Lady Eve, but I have little to do at these

engagements save observe the company in all its folly.
I cannot think you harbor any serious attachment to
these buffoons you stand up with, and yet you are
comely, well dowered, and of marriageable age. Also
very consistent in your behaviors."

He was leading up to something, so Eve let him
natter on. If she was going to be subjected to some
avuncular lecture, she might at least enjoy his punch
while she did.

"I note you allow I'm comely."

"Quite, though you hardly use it to your advantage,
which I also note to be part of your pattern. Though
I am loathe to pry, I am a gentleman, and I account
myself at least on friendly terms with Their Graces, so I
will be blunt: Are you in need of a friend, Lady Eve?"

She stared at her drink—his drink, what remained
of it—and tried to puzzle out what he was asking.
"Everybody needs friends."

Did Kesmore have friends? She'd never had occasion
to wonder. She suspected Louisa was his friend—an
odd and vaguely disquieting notion.

Did *Deene* have friends? As the punch brought
a little sense of relaxation to go with the warmth
coursing through her veins, Eve tried to recall if she'd
ever seen Lucas out among his fellows, riding in a
group in the park or sharing the top of a coach with a
few other men at some race meet.

Kesmore took the drink from her hand. "I will
regard your answer as a ladylike affirmative and
presume to offer myself in that humble capacity. Let's
sit a few more minutes before we subject ourselves to
the company inside once more."

While the couples ten yards away continued to chatter, and the throng in the ballroom started up a waltz, Eve wrinkled her nose at her unspiked drink and tried to fathom what on earth could have prompted Kesmore's peculiar offer.

Then it occurred to her: on her list—on her private list—of attributes a husband of convenience ought to have, the most important characteristic was that he should be capable of befriending an adult woman.

What an unlikely coincidence that Louisa's taciturn spouse should possess this very trait.

Her companion broke the silence. "Will you be attending the Andersons' soiree on Friday, my lady?"

Eve didn't know what interest her new, self-appointed friend might have in her schedule but saw no reason to dissemble.

"I am not. Jenny and I are taking a two-week repairing lease at Morelands before the Season starts up in earnest. We miss our sister Sophie."

"I have never understood why the social Season must start up just as spring is getting her mitts on the countryside. It's quite the most glorious time of year, and we spend it here in Town, sleeping the days away, sweating en masse in stuffy ballrooms by night."

In the presence of a lady, a gentleman did not typically refer to anybody sweating, except perhaps an equine. Eve did not point this out to Kesmore.

She patted his muscular arm. "Louisa says you miss your piggies. Perhaps you need a repairing lease as well."

His brows shot up, and then the man *did* smile. He looked positively charming, almost dear, so softly did a simple change in expression illuminate his features. His eyes lost their anthracite quality and developed crows' feet at the corners, while his mouth, which Eve might have honestly described as grim, became merry.

"I do miss my piggies. Lady Louisa is correct."

"She very often is. One gets used to it."

The smile did not entirely fade; it lingered in Kesmore's eyes as he rose and offered Eve his arm. They left their empty glasses on the bench, and Eve had to admit a short interval in the company of a friend—even such an unlikely friend—had done much to restore her spirits.

And still, when Kesmore had bowed over her hand and taken himself off to ache for another hour at the edge of the room, Eve found herself visually searching the ballroom again for just a glimpse of the Marquis of Deene.

❧

"Come along, Deene."

Deene nearly stumbled as Kesmore snagged him by the arm and pulled him toward a staircase at the corner of the ballroom.

"Taking English peers prisoner went out of fashion several years ago, Kesmore, even among the French."

"I'm not taking you prisoner, but if we're to get a fresh start in the morning, we can't be dawdling about here until all hours."

"So now I'm taken prisoner and kidnapped?" Though leaving was a capital notion indeed. Mildred Staines had been positively ogling Deene's crotch at the supper buffet. It gave a man some sympathy for the suckling pig in the middle of all the other offerings.

"You're due for a repairing lease in the country, a final inspection of the home farm and so forth before planting begins. Then you may take yourself back to Town to be chosen by your bride."

Deene paused at the top of the steps. "The fellow still does the proposing, as I recall, not the other way around."

"Comfort yourself with that illusion if you must, but as of tomorrow, we're going to Kent for a couple of weeks."

Deene's retort died on his lips.

Another two weeks of watching Eve Windham be drooled on, leered at, stumbled over, and danced down the room, and Deene would be left witless indeed.

"I'll catch up with my steward and show the colors before the tenants. A fine idea indeed." He couldn't get out of the ballroom soon enough, though by rights, they ought to say good night to their hostess first.

"Shall I make our farewells, Kesmore?"

Kesmore didn't answer immediately. Deene studied the man and saw that his gaze was fixed on Lady Louisa twirling around the dance floor as graceful as a sylph in the arms of some dashing young swain.

"You fetch the coaches. I must retrieve my lady wife and put that poor devil dancing with her out of his misery."

Deene watched as Kesmore all but swaggered down the stairs, and wondered if Lady Louisa would protest—even for form's sake—over the early end to her social evening.

❧

Evie had long ago concluded that some edict had gone forth from Their Graces that no Windham coach was ever to stop or even pause to water horses in the hamlet of Bascoomb Ford. She'd been complicit in this ducal fiat by making certain she always had a book with her on the journeys to and from Town, always had knitting, or—failing all else—a nap she absolutely had to take.

And in a nice, comfortable traveling coach shared with her sisters, there was no reason to suspect the day's trip to Morelands would be any different.

Which meant once again Eve put aside the nagging thought that *someday*, someday when she had the time and the privacy, she was going to come back to Bascoomb Ford and revisit the scene of her worst memories.

"I'm thinking of dodging the Season." Louisa lobbed this cannonball into the middle of a perfectly amiable silence.

Jenny looked up from her knitting. "The notion always has a forbidden sort of appeal, doesn't it? I couldn't imagine leaving Mama to make the explanations though. *We* might have given up, but *she* has not."

Such a forthright reply from Jenny was not to be brushed aside. "Papa hasn't given up either," Eve pointed out. "His darling girls must find their true loves."

Louisa's smile was subdued. "Or their convenient husbands. You were certainly trolling the ballroom diligently last night, Eve. Make any progress?"

There was understanding in Louisa's eyes, no taunting, not a hint of teasing.

Eve let her gaze go to the window. Bascoomb Ford was just over the rise and down a long, gentle declivity. The approaches to the town she knew well, but the inn, the green, the little church... they were hazy in her mind and sharp at the same time.

"I need a longer list. I'm thinking a couple dozen names, and we should start with the men known to have left-handed preferences."

Jenny's needles ceased their soft clicking. "Such preferences can get a man hung, dearest. If he has a title, it could be attainted, his wealth confiscated. Why would you marry into such a possibility?"

Yes, why would she? And who would have thought such direct counsel would come from Jenny?

"It's my best hope of finding a situation where my willingness to accept a white marriage is viewed as an asset to the fellow. My alternatives are the men seeking my fortune, and that leaves me no guarantee my spouse would honor the terms of the bargain."

"An unenforceable bargain at law," Louisa agreed.

Eve had given up her innocence to learn that a man intent on exploiting her as a means of wealth was no bargain on any terms—her innocence, her ability to trust, and for months, her ability even to stand without excruciating pain.

"Ladies," Jenny said, putting her knitting back into her workbasket, "I find I must ask you to permit me a short delay here at the next inn. Nature calls in a rather urgent fashion."

Louisa did not react with anything more telling than a yawn. "I could tolerate stretching my legs. The horses will appreciate a rest and some water."

With no more ado than that, after seven years of seeing the place only in her nightmares, Eve Windham was once again at the modest posting inn of Bascoomb Ford.

"I'll be along in a minute," Eve said as the coach carrying the ladies' maids and extra footmen came rumbling up before the inn. "I want to move around a bit as well."

They did not even exchange a glance. Jenny slipped her arm through Louisa's, and they disappeared into The Coursing Hound. Eve got as far as the bench on the green across from the inn, though even that was a struggle. Her legs felt a peculiar weakness; her breath fought its way into her lungs. When she sat, it was of necessity.

The little inn stood across the rutted street—spring was a time for ruts and treacherous footing—looking shabby and cozy at once. A white glazed pot of pansies graced the front door, just as it had seven years ago— purple and yellow flowers with one orange rebel in the center of the pot.

The orange pansy was different; not much else had changed.

The white glaze on the pot was still smudged with dirt, the boot scrape was still rusty and encrusted with mud, and in the middle of the inn yard, an enormous oak promised shade in summer.

Just a humble country inn, and yet… Eve saw not the inn, but what had transpired there, just there in that upstairs bedroom. Canby hadn't even pulled the curtains shut, hadn't gotten them a quiet room at the back. He'd jammed a chair under the door, muttering something about not being able to trust the locks in these old places.

She'd forgotten that. Forgotten the sight of him hauling the chair across the room, and the excitement and dread of knowing what would come next.

Though she *hadn't* known. She hadn't had the first clue that a man could profess his love and show her only tender regard for weeks, then turn up crude and businesslike about enjoying his intimacies. She hadn't known he might backhand her and tell her to be quiet lest somebody be concerned and all her lovely money slip through his greedy hands.

His lovely money, and not even the dowry she might have brought him, but money her family would pay him to keep quiet about ruining her. When he'd finished with her and gone back to his celebratory drinking, she'd pretended to sleep until he'd passed out beside her on the bed. She'd spent hours afraid he'd come at her again, until she'd realized she had another option.

Her slight stature had allowed her to slip out the window at the first sign the sky was lightening. She'd crossed the roof of the porte cochere and dropped to a pile of dirty straw raked into a corner of the inn yard, dreading each rustle and squeak as she'd made her way to the stables.

The same dread she'd felt all those years ago—no giddy anticipation about it—welled up from her middle in a hot, choking ball of emotion. She forced herself to breathe, in… out… in… out, and the ball only grew larger.

As if she were watching a horse race where she

held no stake, Eve tried to observe this monstrous, long-unacknowledged feeling, but it had turned to sheer pain, to oppression of every function she possessed—heartbeat, thought, breath—and she might have fainted right there on that worn bench except a sound penetrated her awareness.

Hoofbeats, regular, rhythmic, more than one horse. Not the dead-gallop hoofbeats of her brothers coming at last to rescue her, but a tidy, rocking canter.

Even to turn her head was an effort, but one well rewarded.

Two men approached riding a pair of smart, substantial mounts. The chestnut on the left looked particularly familiar.

Her heart, her instincts, some lower sense recognized the animal before her brain did. "Beast."

The awful emotion subsided, not into the near oblivion she'd been able to keep it at before, but enough for Eve to realize there was no other horse she'd have been more grateful to see.

Save perhaps one gray mare, of whose fate Eve had allowed herself to be kept in ignorance for more than seven years.

❧

"As I live and breathe, that's the Windham crest on those coaches. My lady is making good time."

Deene was too disturbed by the journey's earlier revelations to wonder why Louisa would be traveling in a Windham coach rather than Kesmore's own conveyance. Though it occurred to him Louisa might be traveling with her sisters, and what Deene would do when next he and Eve Windham crossed paths again, he did not know. Throttle the woman.

Or kiss her—or both, though not in that order.

And there she sat, serene and lovely, on a bench across the way.

Kesmore flicked his hand in an impatient motion. "Give me your reins, Deene, and I'll see the horses tended to and some luncheon procured."

"My—?"

"Or you can stand here gawping like the village idiot for a few moments longer. I'm sure Lady Eve is admiring the sight of you in all your dirt."

Kesmore snatched the reins from Deene's hand, and nodded at Eve on her bench. She lifted a hand but did not rise, of course, her being the lady, and Deene being… the gentleman.

He sauntered over and offered her a bow. "Lady Eve, good day. Might I join you?"

"Deene, good day. Of course you may."

She pulled her skirts aside in that little maneuver women made that suggested a man mustn't even touch their hems, despite any words of welcome.

"I gather your mother and sisters are within?" His Grace would be riding, of course. Not even a duke could be expected to have the fortitude to ride in the same coach with four women on anything less than an occasion of state.

"Louisa and Jenny, along with the three Fates."

"Beg pardon?" There was something off about Eve's voice. Something distant and subdued.

"Our lady's maids."

She said nothing more, and when Deene studied

her, she looked a trifle pale. There was an uncharac-teristic grimness to her mouth, as if she'd just taken a scolding or would dearly like to deliver one.

Perhaps being leered at and drooled upon was exhausting.

"Kesmore is ordering up some luncheon in what-ever passes for a private parlor at yonder hostelry. We'll make a party of it, I'm sure."

"The inn boasts a private dining parlor and four rooms upstairs. Two at the back, two at the front. The front rooms should be cheaper, because they're noisier and dustier, but the innkeeper claims they have a pretty view of the green, so the difference in cost is slight."

She did not offer these lines as conversation so much as she recited them. The subtle detachment in her voice was mirrored in her green eyes. And how would she—a lady through and through—have reason to know the cost of the rooms at such an unprepos-sessing establishment?

He studied her a moment longer, and any thought of teasing her over her choice of dance partners—her choices in any regard—fled Deene's mind.

"Shall we go in to lunch, Eve?" He rose and offered her his hand. She stared at it—a well-made, slightly worn and very comfortable riding glove on a man's hand—then put her palm to his.

Deene was mildly alarmed to find it wasn't merely a courtesy. Eve borrowed momentarily from his strength to get to her feet. When she rose, she stood next to him, making no effort to move away, their hands still joined.

He shifted her grasp so he could assume the posture of an escort, but kept his hand over hers on his arm. "Eve, are you feeling well? Is a headache trying to descend?"

"Not a headache. Let's join the others."

Not a headache, but something. Something almost as bad, if not worse. At lunch, she said little and ate less, and seemed oblivious to her sisters' looks of concern. Kesmore proved a surprisingly apt conversationalist, able to tease even the demure Lady Jenny with his agrarian innuendos.

When lunch was over, Deene offered to see Eve out to the coaches.

She paused at the bottom of the stairs in the common. "Deene, will you indulge me in a whim?"

"Of course." Though whatever she was about, it wasn't going to be a whim.

"I'd like to see one of the front rooms."

He followed her up the stairs, dread mounting with each step. This whim was not happy, it was not well advised, and yet he did not stop her.

The guest room doors stood ajar, two at the front of the building and, very likely, two at the back, just as she'd said. She moved away from him to stand motionless in the doorway on the right-hand side.

Over her shoulder, he saw plain appointments: a sagging bed that might accommodate two people if they were friendly with each other and diminutive; a wash stand; a scarred desk gone dark with age; and one of those old, elaborately carved heavy chairs that would be uncomfortable as hell and absolutely indestructible. Curtains gone thin from many washings, a white counterpane that might once have sported some sort of pattern.

Just a room, like a thousand others along the byways of Merry Olde England.

And yet... He rested a hand on Eve's shoulder when what he wanted was to pull her back against his body, or better still—take her from this place altogether, never to return.

For an interminable moment while he could only guess her thoughts, Eve looked about the room. Her gaze lingered on the bed then went to the window.

"Thank God for the window." She spoke quietly but with a particular ferocity. And yet she stood there until Deene felt her hand cover his own.

Her fingers were ice cold.

"Thank you, Deene. We can leave."

She made no move to return below stairs, so Deene turned her into his embrace. "We'll stay right here until you're ready to leave, Eve Windham."

All of her was cold and stiff. Whoever this woman was, she could bear no relation to the warm, lithe bundle of Eve with whom he'd stolen so many delightful moments. A shudder went through her, and she drew back. "Take me to the coach, Lucas."

And still, her voice had that awful, brittle quality.

He took her to the coach, and when he wanted to bundle her directly inside, shut the door, and tell the driver to make all haste to Morelands, the inevitable delays associated with a party of women ensued.

Lady Jenny decided to travel with the maids so she might have somebody to hold the yarn while she wound it into a ball. Lady Louisa's maid had yet to take a stroll around back—to the jakes, of course.

Kesmore bore it all with surprising patience, but

then, the man had likely traveled with small children, which was trial by fire indeed.

At Deene's side, Eve stood silent and unmoving.

"Shall we walk a bit, Eve?"

A pause, and then, "Yes, we shall. That direction."

She pointed down the road toward what was likely unenclosed common ground, a gently rolling expanse of green bordered by a woods no doubt prized by every local with a fowling piece.

When Eve moved off, she did so with purpose, while behind them, Deene heard Lady Jenny mutter to Lady Louisa, "Let her go, dearest. It's better this way."

If he'd had doubts about the significance of the locale before, the concern in Lady Jenny's voice obliterated them. Eve kept walking in the overland direction of the main road, until the rise and fall of the land obscured them from the view of the others.

At some point in their progress, she'd dropped his arm and marched ahead, her intent unquestionably to put distance between them.

"I just need a moment, Lucas."

"You want me to leave you here?" The notion was insupportable. She'd gone as pale as a winding sheet, and her breathing had taken on an odd, wheezy quality. She didn't answer, other than to turn her back, so Deene ambled off a few yards and sat on a boulder.

He was not going to marry this woman—she'd made that plain—but fate or the well-intended offices of certain meddlesome individuals had put Deene here with her at this precise moment, and here he would stay until her use for him was done.

She stood in profile, as still as a statue, her arms

wrapped around her middle, the breeze teasing at stray wisps of her blond hair.

And something was clearly very wrong. "Eve?"

Her shoulders jerked. "I can't breathe. Don't come any closer."

He hadn't heard that hysterical note in a woman's voice since his sister had learned she was to be sold in marriage to a brute of a stranger. The same cold chill shot down his spine as he went to Eve.

"Go away, Lucas." She held a hand straight out, as if she could stop him so easily. "This is—"

The breath she drew in was loud, rasping, and heart wrenching. He got his arms around her, the only alternative to tackling her if she tried to run off.

"Eve, it's all right."

"Go away, damn you. Just leave me alone. It will *never* be all right." A hint of tears—tears were far preferable to this cold silence.

"I'm not going anywhere."

"I can't breathe... Lucas, I can't—"

He cradled the back of her head, tucking her against his chest. "Then don't breathe, but for the love of God, *cry*, Evie."

He held her close, close enough to feel the cataclysm building in her body, to feel not a simple storm but a great tempest breaking loose from long imprisonment.

Her sobs were more terrible for being silent, and had he not been holding her, Deene knew she'd have collapsed to the ground under the weight of her upset. Where she'd been cold and stiff before, she was giving off a tremendous heat now, her body boneless as she clung to him.

She did not quiet exactly—her tears had been far deeper than a mere noisy outburst—but she shuddered at greater and greater intervals. Deene scooped her up and carried her to the boulder he'd recently vacated. What he wanted was to cradle her in his lap; what he did was sit her beside him and keep an arm around her shoulders.

"This is where you fell."

She lifted her forehead from where she'd pressed it to his shoulder.

"This is indeed where I fell. Have you a handkerchief?"

He passed her the requisite monogrammed linen, knowing he must not look at her while she used it.

"The scent of you is calming, Lucas, at least to me."

"Then you must keep my handkerchiefs near at hand. I gather you hadn't been back here in some while."

She sighed out a big, noisy sigh. "Not in seven years. The place—the memory—sneaked up on me today, and I thought I was brave enough."

No count of the months this time. That had to be progress. "You *are* brave enough."

He recalled the bleakness in her eyes as she'd stared at the miserable sagging bed, and he wanted to howl and shake his fist at God.

"I'm not so sure. I hadn't expected to feel such rage."

If he let her say more, she'd regret it. And he wasn't certain he was brave enough to *hear* more.

Repairing lease, indeed.

"You were bedridden for months, Eve. Of course you're entitled to be angry."

Her head came up, and though her eyes were red and glistening with the aftermath of her tears, Deene was relieved to have her meeting his gaze.

"What? I can't divine your thoughts, Evie."

"You say that so easily, *of course I'm entitled to be angry.*"

"Your horse tripped and went down in the damn sloppy, spring footing—horses trip every day, but this horse tripping left you having to relearn how to walk, and despite how cheery the letters you wrote to your brothers made it sound, that process was hell."

"It was hell." She spoke as if trying the words on and then said them again. "It *was* hell." More confidently. "It was awful, in fact. Bloody miserable, and not just for me."

He knew what she was recalling, because he'd heard her brothers fill in the missing parts: the indignity of bodily functions when one was bedridden, the forbearance necessary when loved ones offered to read yet again a novel that had once been a favorite, the tedium so oppressive it made the pain almost a diversion.

Eve Windham had courage, of that Lucas Denning would never be in doubt.

"Can you walk now, Eve?"

She pulled her lower lip under her top teeth, her expression thoughtful. "Do you mean, can I walk to the coach?"

"Can you *walk*?"

The thoughtful expression became a frown. "I can walk."

"Then be as angry as you need to be, for as long as you need to rage, but applaud yourself for the fact that while other women would have taken permanently to their beds, you have given to yourself the great gift of once again walking. This is no small thing."

She didn't argue, didn't diminish her own accomplishment, which was fortunate, because he would have argued at her right back.

"I have always wondered about something, Lucas." She tried to return his wrinkled, damp handkerchief, but he closed her fingers around it and pushed her fist back to her lap.

"What have you wondered?"

"Did Papa shoot my mare?"

Ah, the guilt. Of course, constraining all the anger she'd been entitled to, all the hurt and bewilderment, would be the guilt. It was all Deene could do not to kiss her temple.

"Your brothers talked him out of it, possibly abetted by your mother."

"How do you know this?"

"Sieges are the very worst way to conduct a military campaign, in one sense. The effort is tedious beyond belief." He fell silent, memories resonating with other associations in his mind. "Your men spend days, even weeks, digging trenches while the sappers dig their tunnels and the artillery batters the walls, and pretty soon, morale goes to hell—pardon my language. The drinking and brawling pick up, nobody sleeps, and by the time you're ready to breach the walls, men will volunteer for even the suicide details just to end the siege."

"What has this to do with my mare?"

"When sleep wouldn't come, and Old Hooky wasn't inclined to permit inebriation among his staff, we'd lie awake and talk, or sit around a campfire and talk. Your brother St. Just was profoundly comforted to have gotten your mare out of His Grace's gun sights before reporting back to Spain with Lord Bart."

Eve hunched in on herself, becoming smaller against Deene's side. "Her name was Sweetness, but she had tremendous grit. I know both her front tendons were bowed. As I lay on the ground, she could barely stand beside me, but she would not leave me. I told myself if Papa shot her, it would have been out of kindness."

Deene sat beside her and tried not to react. That passing comment about shooting a horse was not just about a horse: Eve had considered taking her own life. Right there, sitting on that cold, miserably hard boulder, Deene made a silent promise to the woman beside him that had nothing to do with marriage proposals and everything to do with being a gentleman.

"Bowed tendons can heal. All it takes is lengthy rest and proper care."

Eve was not placated. "A horse who's gone through such an injury can never be as good as new, Lucas."

"We're none of us as good as new." He rose lest he wrap her in his arms and never let her go. "I expect your sisters have gotten themselves sorted out by now."

He did not offer his hand. She stood on her own.

"I expect they have. Would that I could say the same for myself."

Deene did not pounce on the lure of that comment; he instead walked beside her, not touching her, until they returned to the coaching inn.

"A fine day for a constitutional," Kesmore remarked briskly. "Lady Jenny and Lady Louisa went ahead with the maids, and Deene, your nag is tied to the back of the coach. If you will both pardon me, I'll go on ahead lest I eat your dust for the rest of the afternoon."

He bowed to Eve and swung up onto his black horse, cantering off with a salute of his riding crop.

"Will you keep me company, Lucas?"

He did not want to. He *wanted* to put as much distance between himself and Eve Windham's tribulation as he could. She had borne too much for too long with too little real support, though, and he knew what marching on alone entailed all too well.

He climbed into the coach and sat beside her, but that was as far as he could go. He did not put his arm around her.

In fact, the sensible part of him—the part that would be heading back to Town in two weeks—hoped never to put his arms around her again.

❧

Eve's thoughts bounced around like skittles in her head:

Her sisters had taken off, probably without a second thought—or had they?

Deene was so wonderfully warm next to her, but how was she to face him after such a display?

She was hungry.

What had Kesmore made of this situation?

And when all that effluvia had been borne away by the passing miles: *Why was I so bitterly angry?*

At some juncture, she'd taken Deene's arm and put it about her shoulders, the better to use him for a bolster. He was being delicate, as he'd call it. Keeping his silence out of deference to her feelings. Dratted man.

She wished he'd kiss her—not a wicked, naughty

kiss, but a comforting kiss, a kiss to anchor her back in her body, to steady her courage. Such a wish was foolish, allowable only because she and Deene were bound to become nothing more than cordial acquaintances. On that list of possible convenient husbands, she'd have to put the contenders with family seats in Kent toward the bottom of the pile.

That would cut down on chance encounters with Deene... and his future marchioness.

"Why was Mildred Staines ogling you like you'd hidden the entire table of desserts in your smalls, Lucas?"

To prevent him from removing his arm, Eve laced her fingers with his.

"Why, indeed? Kesmore informs me there are rumors going around regarding my past, among other things."

"You're the catch of the Season, of course there will be rumors."

"These are nasty rumors."

Damn him and his delicacy. "Do these rumors involve red-haired beauties of dubious reputation?"

She felt him tense up, then relax.

"You've heard them too?"

"No. Westhaven, duke-in-training that he is, won't tell us, and if he tells Anna, she doesn't pass along the best gossip either. We've hardly seen Maggie since she married Hazelton—and I know you had a hand in that, Lucas, so get your prevarications ready for the day I inquire about it. But as to your rumors, I thought men strutted about the gaming hells, twitting one another over such things where the decent women couldn't hear them."

"They do."

He said nothing more, but rather than return to her own brown study, Eve decided to further investigate his.

"Are the rumors untrue?"

"They are... exaggerations and inaccuracies, also very ill timed."

"Then they're very likely started by those fellows who want to knock you out of contention for the best marital prospects. It's ruthless business, acquiring the right spouse. I wish you the joy of it."

He did remove his arm. "Are you enjoying your own endeavors in this regard? Having turned down my suit, Evie, are you now recruiting more appropriate candidates?"

He apparently wanted a nice, rousing argument, but Eve was too wrung out to oblige him.

"I was taking pity on the unfortunate, like a gentleman dances with the wallflowers. Would you be very offended if I attempted a nap, Lucas?"

Under no circumstances was she going to allow him an opportunity to interrogate her about all that drama back at Bascoomb Ford. She needed to interrogate herself first, and at some length.

"Nap if you can."

She lifted his arm across her shoulders again, needing the comfort of it. Today had been an exceptional day, and Eve permitted herself the indulgence of Deene's proximity on that basis alone.

For once the Season started and they were off hunting their respective spouses, who knew when they might ever be private again?

Five

EVE WINDHAM DID NOT SNORE, AND SHE HAD THE knack of being pretty even in sleep. Deene tormented himself with these guilty secrets—secrets only a husband ought to know. Better by far that he suffer to know them, however, than that he hear any explicit confidences from her.

He knew there was a great deal more to her bad fall than either of them had acknowledged, and for the sake of his peace of mind, he wanted it kept that way.

Let her tell her sisters, or her mama. Let her write letters to her brother Devlin in the North; let her learn what she could from the family who'd loved her since birth. For if Deene were to accept her most intimate confidences now, he would be unable—flat *helpless*, in fact—to let any other man assume responsibility for her.

Any situation involving him, helplessness, and a woman was to be avoided at any cost.

He instead turned his mind to the gossip Kesmore had passed long, for even the weight of Eve's head resting against his thigh was insufficient to distract him from that bit of news. According to the talk in the clubs, Deene's profligate raking on three continents—or was it four, considering that Turkey was part of Asia?—had left him with unfortunate health consequences that could potentially disfigure or even end the life of any marchioness of Deene.

The effects of disease—nobody used the specific word "syphilis"—had been evident in the late Lord Deene, too, hadn't they? A wicked temper, unfettered spending, intemperate drink...

That such characteristics were common to many an aging peer was apparently beyond the grasp of the average gossip, and in truth, such rumors were only bothersome in passing.

The ones intimating Deene was close to financial ruin were the more difficult to bear. Coming as they did upon the very opening of the Season in which Deene sought to take a wife, there could be only one possible source of such malice.

And before too much more time had passed, Deene intended to make Jonathan Dolan pay for every nasty, sly, vulgar lie ever to pass the man's lips.

❧

Jenny stared at the apple in her hand. "I am disloyal for saying so, but I am enjoying this respite without Mama and Papa. With just us and Aunt Gladys here, it's peaceful."

Eve paused halfway through paring the skin from another piece of fruit. "You aren't disloyal, you're honest. Mama is probably saying the very same thing to Papa about us as we speak."

Louisa was demolishing her apple in audible bites. "Eve's right, and this way, I get to spend another couple of weeks rusticating with my dear Joseph. Do we have enough for the last pie?"

Eve eyed the pile of peeled and sliced apples before her. She generally avoided association with apples, but the Windham daughters enjoyed a secret fondness for cooking, and her sisters' choice today had been pies. "Do we really need seven pies?"

"Five will do if the bounty is limited to us and the senior house staff." Jenny set her apple down. "Six allows us to spare one for Kesmore."

"So our heathen offspring can smear it in one another's hair." Louisa got off her stool and started untying her apron. "Eve, why don't you take the remaining slices down to the stables? Jenny can come with me to surrender the pie to the Vandal horde in my nursery."

Which horde, Eve simply lacked the fortitude to deal with cheerfully today. "I'll clean up here, in any case."

They didn't argue with her, which was a mercy. Kesmore had seen Eve's face splotchy and pink. He'd all but galloped off to avoid the awkwardness of her loss of composure—or perhaps he'd meant to spare her feelings.

It hardly mattered. Since arriving to Morelands several days ago, Eve had slept a great deal, stared off into space almost as much, and taken a few long walks.

And when she walked, she remembered to be grateful for the ability, but she also found her peace punctuated by odd thoughts.

Canby had referred to her repeatedly as "Eve, the

temptress." At the time, she'd thought it made her sound grown-up, alluring, and mysterious. In hindsight, the implication that she was responsible for his behavior, that she'd *caused* him to violate every rule of decency was... infuriating.

Apples could be infuriating by association.

At services, Eve had volunteered to attend the children in the nursery, and this time—this time—she'd looked at all those boisterous, healthy children with their clean faces and broad smiles, and considered that her life would be devoid of the blessings of motherhood. For the rest of her life, while her sisters were raising up children, and her brothers were raising up children, and her cousins were raising up children, she would be... childless.

That was infuriating too.

And now, Louisa and Jenny would hop into the gig and tool over to Kesmore's without a backward thought for their safety, their nerves, their ability to cope with a darting hare or approaching storm.

Eve loved her family, but still, there was much to be angry about.

She scooped up the apple slices that hadn't gone into a pie and wrapped them in a cloth. The day was a pretty day. She was in good health and had the afternoon to herself—she'd try not to be angry about that too.

Meteor was in his paddock, one shared by an aging pony named Grendel. They paused in their grazing as Eve approached, but only Meteor sidled over to the fence.

"Hello, old friend."

Between his cheekbones, at the throat latch where his neck and his head joined, Meteor had a sweet spot, a place he couldn't reach himself that he loved to have scratched. Eve's ritual with this horse started with attending to that spot for him, and Meteor's ritual with her with allowing the familiarity.

"Have you ever been so angry you're sick with it?"

The pony flicked an ear, but being a pony, did not abandon his grass merely to watch another horse being cosseted.

"Deene said, *of course* I'm angry. What does he know? Would you like an apple?"

The horse did not answer, except by ingesting the proffered slice and turning big, brown, beseeching eyes on Eve.

"You are such a gentleman, my friend."

Deene had been a gentleman. Eve was going to have to thank him, and that would rankle, but not thanking him rankled more.

Everything rankled. "I can hardly think. I'm so overset these days. If I were a girl, I'd saddle up and go for a gallop, leave the grooms behind, and let the wind blow the cobwebs from my soul. Another slice? Grendel will soon come to investigate."

Grendel did not investigate, exactly, but he turned his grazing in the direction of Eve's tête-à-tête with Meteor.

"I keep recalling things, things that make no sense. We had an early spring that year, and then an onion snow, so as I lay there in the mud, I smelled both green grass and snow. Snow has no scent, but it did that day."

She fed the stallion another slice. "I did not call for help because I was afraid Canby would find me."

And oh, the shame of that, to lie in the cold mud not just helpless and hurting, but terrified—and afraid she'd wet herself from fear if nothing else. Grendel lifted his head as if considering the probability of cadging an apple slice and took a step closer to the stallion.

"All I could think was I would never be able to face my family, though if I hadn't been in such a tearing hurry to get back to them, I might not have overfaced my mare on bad ground, and lamed us both for the duration. Thank God my brother Devlin found me first. I had been such a fool. I did not know the half of it then."

Meteor had another sweet spot, just below his withers. As a girl, Eve had scratched that spot for him until her arm had ached. She pushed the cloth full of apples near the fence and climbed between the boards.

"I don't have to marry. I know this." When she applied her fingernails to the horse's shaggy spring coat, a shower of coarse dark hairs cascaded to the ground. "But where would that leave me? Papa's little charmer, the doting maiden aunt who isn't a maiden."

Who will never be a maiden again.

Who threw away her greatest treasure on a worthless, scheming, lying, manipulative, *evil* man.

The anger hit her then like the initial staggering gust of wind announcing a brutal tempest, had her leaning into Meteor's neck just to stay on her feet. *Yes,* she was angry. She was infuriated, enraged, magnificently wroth over a past she could not change and a future with too few choices.

Deene had been right about that, but as Grendel sidled close enough to poke his nose under the fence and help himself to an apple, Eve identified the emotion fueling all her anger, and maybe some of her shame as well.

As the tears came down again, what Eve felt was bitter, heartrending sorrow.

❧

"Where the hell have you been?"

Anthony stopped short at Deene's tone, and from the surprise on his cousin's face, Deene surmised nobody had warned Anthony that Deene was in residence at Denning Hall.

"Good morning to you, too, Cousin." In a blink, Anthony's features had composed themselves into a slight smile.

"I beg to differ." Deene aimed a look at the footmen stationed at either end of the breakfast buffet, and they silently left the room. "I thought you were summoned here from Town, Anthony. I come down on your heels and find my cousin is nowhere to be found."

"I'm to report all my comings and goings to you now?" His tone was mild as he helped himself to a full plate.

"Since you are my only adult family, my heir, and what keeps my senior stewards in line, yes, I think that would be both courteous and prudent. Tea?"

"Please."

Deene moved the pot that had been sitting by his left elbow to Anthony's place on his right. "I came out here in part to find you, Anthony, and instead spent more than a few minutes wondering what had become of you. They were not comfortable minutes."

"I'm touched. Pass the cream, if you please."

The alternative to bracing his cousin on sight would have been an interview in the library, with Deene seated at the estate desk and Anthony called onto the carpet like a truant schoolboy awaiting a birching.

That would not serve. They were family first, employer and employee second—or so Deene hoped. Deene passed the cream and the sugar.

"I was in Surrey, and congratulations are in order. I've become a papa again. Where's the salt?"

Deene passed the salt cellar too, but took a moment forming his reply. "A papa, *again*? Did I miss a wedding, Anthony?"

"Of course not. There is cheese in this omelet."

"I prefer cheese in my omelets, and because the kitchen had no notion you'd be gracing us with your presence, my preferences carried the day. Anthony, explain yourself."

"There's little to explain." Anthony put a spoonful of egg on a toast point and took a bite. "I maintain a household in Surrey for my domestic comfort, and as happens in the usual course, the household includes children. I have two girls and now a boy. There was a stillbirth too, so the children's mother was a trifle worried this time around."

Deene looked at the fellow munching on toast and eggs beside him and saw a familiar figure: blond hair, blue eyes, a lanky, elegant build, and the Deene family features on his face.

And yet he saw a stranger. "One can understand

why you would detour to greet your son upon his arrival into the world. I gather mother and child—children—are doing well?"

"She's from peasant stock. Mary Jane knows how to look after herself, and I provide amply for her and the children. Do I take it you also like cinnamon on your toast?"

Deene's gaze fell on the little container sitting near the butter. "Occasionally, and in my coffee."

"Bit of an extravagance, don't you think?"

A casual question, but it might also be an attempt to shift the interrogation away from Anthony's bastard children and to put Deene on the defensive.

Or were the rumors in Town just taking a greater toll on Deene's composure than he'd realized?

"I have larger problems than whether I can afford to stock my spice rack, Anthony, or perhaps I should say, we have greater problems."

Anthony frowned at him. "If you're going to harangue me about the ledgers, old boy, I haven't had a decent night's sleep in nigh a week, and much of what you want is kept in Town."

"Anthony, while you have the luxury of maintaining a casual establishment with a female, I am very publicly soon to be in the market for a wife."

Anthony topped off his teacup and stared at his plate. "I know you feel you must marry, Deene, but you're hardly at your last prayers, and if need be, I can stick my neck in the marital noose. If nothing else, we know I can get children. Mary Jane will raise ten kinds of hell, but sometimes a little liveliness has enjoyable results."

"You'd marry to spare me the effort?"

Anthony's gaze when he met Deene's eyes was hard to read. "I *am* your heir. I *am* your only adult family. I *am* your cousin. Yes, I would marry if you asked it of me. I don't like to think I've spent most of my life laboring in the Denning vineyards so Prinny can get his fat fingers on all our wealth should the title go into escheat."

Something eased in Deene's chest, a doubt, a worry, something he was relieved not to have to name.

"You cannot know how grateful I am to hear it, Anthony, because our situation might come to such a pass."

They spent more than an hour in the breakfast parlor, dissecting each rumor, tracing its likely impact.

"Kesmore isn't a gossip, but he lurks in the usual places—at the clubs, in the card rooms, and at Tatt's. I trust his information."

Anthony's expression was thoughtful. "What about his motives?"

"In what sense?" While it was good to have a sounding board, Deene could not like the direction of Anthony's thoughts.

"He's married to a Windham, and there are at least two of those yet available for marriage. If he's not in favor of your courting his countess's sisters, he'll want to discredit you—all's fair in love and war, right?"

Eve had brought up the same point. "I served with him in Spain, Anthony, and as far as I can see, the man would simply tell me to take my business elsewhere. He does not lack for courage or suffer an excess of delicate sensibilities. Moreover, it makes no sense he'd start a number of rumors and then be the first to inform me of them. I say we're back to Dolan."

Anthony winced and rearranged his cutlery on his empty plate. "What's his motive?"

"Spite. The same motive he has for keeping Georgina from us."

When there was no reply, Deene lifted the pot to refresh their tea, only to find it empty.

"What aren't you saying, Anthony?"

"I, of all men, have a reason to hate Dolan. Marie and I…" Anthony looked away, out the windows toward the pastures rolling beyond the gardens. "That is ancient history, but I cannot help but wonder from time to time about what might have been. I should know better, but memory is not always the slave of common sense."

This was tricky ground. Deene did not interrupt.

"But even I, who cannot stand to hear Dolan's name, am not entirely comfortable ascribing this behavior to him. For one thing, if there is a scandal to be brewed regarding unsound health or finances, the scandal will eventually devolve to Georgina's discredit. Whatever else he is, Dolan is not stupid."

Valid point—an aggravatingly valid point, and yet Deene did not want to acquit Dolan of mischief he'd clearly delight in.

"Dolan is cunning, I'll grant you, but he's an upstart. He will not know that ten years is nothing when it comes to Polite Society's recall of scandal and gossip. He might very well think he can topple my expectations now, and when Georgie makes her come out, there will be no association between my ruin and her fortunes. It makes one worry for the girl."

"Worry for the girl will not redress the reality that insufficient worry was devoted to her mother, though to the extent that I can, Deene, I appreciate your sentiments regarding Georgina's welfare."

On that sad note, Anthony took his leave while Deene remained at the table for another half hour, staring at the empty pot.

❧

Her Grace, the Duchess of Moreland, was looking adorable. Her husband of more than thirty years closed the door to his private study and took a moment to appreciate the privilege of seeing her thus.

She was curled on the end of the sofa closest to the windows, her feet tucked under her, a lurid novel in her hand, and a pair of His Grace's reading spectacles on her elegant nose. As the door clicked shut behind him, she looked up and smiled at her spouse.

When he'd suffered a heart seizure two years past, His Grace had lain amid all the ducal splendor of his household, praying with abject fervor to be allowed to live for a just few more years—even a few more months—basking in the warmth of that smile.

"Percival Windham, you shouldn't have."

He glanced down at the yellow tulips in his hand. "I spared the roses, and it's my own damned garden. I can pick a few posies for a pretty girl when I jolly well please to."

He crossed to the sideboard, poured some water in a glass, and stuck the flowers on the windowsill. His wife would pass by the bouquet, move a couple of blooms about and rearrange the greenery, and instead of looking ridiculous in a ducal study, the flowers would look exactly right.

He adored this about her as well.

She set her novel aside—reading one by daylight was a sure sign none of the children were in residence—and patted the place beside her on the sofa. "What's the occasion?"

"Does love need an occasion?"

She cocked her head and studied him. "Give me a hint."

"It is the anniversary of our third kiss."

The smile blossomed again, a trifle naughtier to a doting husband's eye.

"The Scorcher."

She had named many of their earliest romantic encounters.

The Scorcher. The Ambush. The Ravishment of My Reason. The Obliteration of My Resistance.

He particularly enjoyed recalling that last one and thought she did too. Nothing had pleased a young husband more than to hear a catalogue of his wooing as categorized in Her Grace's intimate lexicon.

"Yes, the Scorcher." He took a seat beside her, and when he reached for her hand, she was already reaching for his. "Such an occasion is not to pass without a token of my esteem."

"And we have the day to ourselves."

"My love, though I know you enjoy my company without reservation, you do not sound particularly happy to find us home alone without a single child underfoot."

She blew out a breath, her expression suggesting

His Grace's marital intuition had scored a lucky hit. "I worry about the girls."

She worried about all the children, their spouses, the grandchildren. *Her husband.*

"They'll look after one another. How much trouble can they get into with the entire Morelands staff ready to peach on them should they get up to mischief, and Kesmore close at hand?"

"Peaching is all well and good, but better yet they should be prevented from getting up to mischief in the first place."

His Grace did not entirely agree with his wife on this point. Children needed to err and stumble and right themselves early and often, in theory. In practice, he knew he had the luxury of assuming such a posture—for it was a posture—only because Her Grace was indulging a rare spate of fretting.

They took turns at it, truth be known.

"You are concerned for our Evie," His Grace observed. "Or am I mistaken?"

"Mostly for her. The Season hasn't even started, and the proposals have already begun, haven't they?"

How *did* she know these things? "Trottenham asked for a private audience last week. I'm hearing noises at the club from some other directions as well."

"Trottenham." Her Grace heaved out a sigh that spoke volumes of maternal frustration. "Percy, she's begun the year riding with the third flight. What if one of them takes advantage? Another mishap would be her undoing."

The third flight. An apt term referring to the riders at the back of the hunt, the cautious, the unskilled, or—in His Grace's experience—the ones too drunk and uncaring of the sport to keep up with the real hunting.

As for Her Grace's reference to Eve's *mishap*… It must go unremarked. "Evie has acquired wisdom since her come out, my love. I have faith in her."

"My faith in her has never wavered. It's my faith in the company she's keeping that fails to inspire."

Trottenham was above reproach, but those other fellows… "I think her sisters will chaperone her more effectively than anyone else. They're very protective of our Evie and recruit their husbands in the same cause."

They all were—now, when it mattered a great deal less than it would have seven years ago.

"Maggie told me something."

He patted her hand. Her Grace and Maggie had become thick as thieves since Maggie had married the Earl of Hazelton—and about damned time.

"Don't keep me in suspense. Hazelton would never betray the girl's confidences." Well, hardly ever. Women apparently thought gentlemen's clubs were only for cards, beefsteak, and reading the newspapers.

"She said having her own establishment was the only thing that kept her sane in recent years because of the privacy it afforded, the sense of control over her domain. I think Eve needs that too."

This was Her Grace, easing into one of her radical notions. Her radical notions had a way of working around to occupying spaces near to common sense by the time she was done with them, but still…

"Evie is far too young to have her own establish-ment, my love. If we allowed that, it would be like,

like… giving up. On her. Or casting her aside. You cannot ask that of me." The idea of Evie, their baby girl, all alone and growing older without family around her—it was enough to provoke something almost as bad as a heart seizure.

Her Grace patted his hand, which was coming to resemble the calloused paw of an old soldier, while hers remained as pretty as the rest of her.

"I agree. It isn't time, and it may never be time, but I was thinking I might see Lavender Corner put a little more to rights."

"You are speaking Female on me, Esther. Does this mean you want to double the size of the place or send the servants over to dust?"

"The servants already keep it in good order. I was thinking perhaps I'd make sure the flower gardens were getting proper attention, the linen aired, the sachets kept fresh. A mother sees things a housekeeper cannot."

He grasped the agenda now. Dense of him not to see it earlier.

"This will require that you jaunt off to Kent posthaste, won't it?"

"The Season hasn't started. There's no time like the present, and I wouldn't be gone long enough for you to miss me."

She carried off airy unconcern quite credibly. His Grace wasn't fooled, but he also wasn't the only one capable of dissembling in the interests of parental pride.

"I have another idea." He brought her knuckles to his mouth for a warm kiss. "How about we get a leisurely start tomorrow and break our journey at The Queen's Harebell?"

He had the satisfaction of seeing her eyes widen and that special smile bloom on her lips.

"Oh, Percy." She cradled his jaw with her hand and kissed his cheek. "The Queen's Harebell in spring, the scene of no less an occasion than Chocolate at Midnight. That is a splendid idea."

Yes, it was, if he did say so himself. Esther rested her head on his shoulder, and the moment became one of a countless number His Grace would hoard up in his heart to treasure at his leisure.

Esther's smile became a little satisfied—not smug; Her Grace was never smug—and His Grace recognized that once again, she'd achieved her ends without ever having to ask for them.

That she could—and that he *almost* always spotted it when she did—was just one more thing to adore about her.

༒

Being an upstart, bogtrotting, climbing cit of a quarry nabob was hard work, which Jonathan Dolan minded not one bit.

He thrived on it, in fact, or he did when hard work meant long hours at the quarries, the building sites, and the supply yards. When it meant longer hours, haggling at the negotiation table, poring over ledgers, and hanging about in smoke-filled card rooms, the prospect was much less appealing.

Much, much less.

"If you can't get your lazy damned crews to put in a full day's work, that is not my affair. Damages will be assessed per the clause *you* negotiated, Sloane."

Sloane paced the spacious confines of the Dolan offices, running a hand through thinning sandy hair while Dolan watched from behind a desk free of clutter.

"The damages will put me under, Dolan. I told you, it isn't that the crews *won't* move your stone, it's that they *can't* move your stone. The rain in Dorset this spring has been unbelievable. This is not bad faith. It's commercial impossibility."

The blather coming out of the idiot's mouth was not to be borne.

"Is that so? The weather is responsible? So we've moved from liquidated damages to the commercial impossibility clause?" Dolan kept his tone thoughtful, though even posturing to that extent was distasteful.

Relief shone in Sloane's squinty brown eyes. "Yes! An act of God, exactly. Torrential rain and no one able to manage. I knew you'd see reason. Hard but fair, that's what they say about you."

"Pleased to hear it. Do they also say I'm able to read and write in English?"

They probably speculated to the contrary, but Dolan took satisfaction in seeing Sloane's gaze grow wary. "I beg your pardon?"

"I can read, Mr. Sloane. I'm sure you'll be pleased for my sake to learn I can read in several languages. One of them English, though it's by no means my favorite. And because I own the quarry in Dorset, I also maintain a subscription to the local paper nearest that quarry. Shall I read the weather reports to you?"

Dolan opened a drawer at the side of his desk and pulled out a single folded broadsheet dated about ten days past. "Plowing, planting, and grazing being of central import to much of the shire, the editor is assiduous in his record keeping and prognostication."

Sloane had sense enough to stop babbling.

"Mr. Sloane, sit down." Not an invitation, which also should have been a source of satisfaction, considering the man was English to his gloved, uncallused, manicured fingertips.

He dropped into a chair. "I just need a little more time."

A little more time, a few more potatoes, a little more daylight… The laments were old and sincere, but useless.

"You are late on the deliveries because you do not pay a wage sufficient to attract men who can be relied upon. Because you skimp on wages, your wagons and teams are not properly maintained, and they break down. Knowing you are under scheduling constraints, the smiths, wainwrights, and jobbers take excessive advantage of you when their services are needed on an emergency basis, and once again, to save money, you turn to the most opportunistic and questionably skilled among them."

He did not add: you are an idiot. He did not need to.

"I have a family." This was said with quiet desperation, which was probably the very worst aspect of being a quarry nabob. Watching grown men literally sweat while their dignity was sacrificed to their shortsighted greed.

"You also have a mistress, who is likely more for show than anything else. You have too many hunters that you never ride, and you have daughters to launch upward lest your wife have unending revenge on you for your failures."

Sloane nodded, and Dolan wondered if this was how the priests felt in the confessional: tired, disgusted, and… trapped in their ornate robes and elaborately carved little boxes.

And still Sloane sat there, quivering like a fat, beautifully attired hare waiting for the fox to pounce.

"Lie to me again, Sloane, and I will have your vowels. I will use them to discredit you from one end of the kingdom to the other. You will have no mistress, no stable at all, no fancy clothes, and very likely no family worth the name. You have two weeks before the damages will start to toll. Get out."

Sloane's relief was a rank, rancid thing. The odds of the man making a delivery in the next two weeks were not good, but Dolan built slack into every schedule he negotiated, then added more slack, because most of the time, it did rain like hell in Dorset in the spring.

When Dolan was sure Sloane had vacated the entire premises, he grabbed hat, gloves, and cane and left the office, locking the door behind him.

A clerk glanced up from his desk as Dolan passed. "I'm away until tomorrow's meeting with Ruthven, Standish. Have the files on my desk first thing, send out for crumpets, and dust the damn place before I get here."

"Yes, sir, Mr. Dolan."

The day was glorious, almost warm, and brilliantly sunny because the trees weren't leafed out yet. Dolan strode along in the direction of Mayfair, when what he wanted was to enjoy the day amid the graciousness and privacy of Whitley.

At home more work awaited, a short interlude with Georgina to tuck her in, then more work over a solitary dinner. How was it a quarry nabob felt just as much a slave as if he were still a five-year-old boy, his fingers perpetually cold and muddy from tending the tatties?

The memory was never far from his awareness, which explained in part why he almost plowed over a slight woman carrying some small parcels down the street in the oncoming direction. The parcels scattered, the woman stumbled, and Dolan grasped her by both of her upper arms as she pitched against him.

She righted herself with his assistance, and Dolan found himself looking into a pair of fine gray eyes. "Miss Ingraham. I beg your pardon."

"Mr. Dolan. My apologies."

She tried to draw away, but he held her steady. "The fault is mine. I wasn't watching where I was going."

Her slightly frayed collar and less-than-pristine gloves added to her usual air of constrained dignity. He let her go and bent to pick up her packages. "I gather today is your half day?"

"Yes, sir. If you'll just pass me those boxes, I'll be on my way."

"Nonsense. Where are you going?"

Her ingrained manners wouldn't allow her to entirely withhold the information, but she was a female. She could prevaricate, and he couldn't stop her. Instead, she did the most peculiar thing: she blushed, *and* she smiled. "I was going to the park."

The park, a monument to England's democratic leanings, a place where anybody could enjoy fresh air and sunshine. Dolan cast back and could not recall seeing that quiet smile on any previous occasion. That smile went well with her fine gray eyes and exceptional figure. "Then we've a bit of a walk ahead of us."

He tucked her packages under one arm and winged the opposite elbow at her, and damned if the infernal woman's smile didn't fade to be replaced by a look of reproach.

"Mother of God, it's simply a courtesy, Miss Ingraham. It isn't as if you're the scullery maid."

Her spine straightened, she wrapped her hand around his arm, and they moved off, leaving Dolan with a rare opportunity to observe his daughter's governess outside the child's presence.

"Have you been shopping?" Inane question, of course she had. Dolan wished again his late wife might have spent more time teaching him the difference between interrogation and small talk, for he'd yet to grasp the distinction.

"Just a few personal things. This really isn't necessary, sir."

He did not reply—let her be the one to demonstrate some conversational skills. He was sure she had them, though whether she'd take pity—

"I like the French soaps." She said this very quietly, glancing about as she did. "They're very dear, but the scents are such a pleasure. And there's a particular tea at the Twinings shop. Everybody should have a favorite tea."

She had fine gray eyes, a lovely smile, an excellent figure, *and* she could make small talk.

"I quite agree, Miss Ingraham. My preference is Darjeeling. What's yours?"

❧

For an entire day, Eve tried to study the welter of thoughts and emotions roiling through her.

At breakfast she listened to Aunt Gladys prattle on about how pretty the gardens were—while Eve contemplated ripping up every tulip on the property.

She endured a social call from Louisa and Kesmore, trying not to see the concern in either of their gazes or to allow them to see in her own eyes the nigh overwhelming desire to smash the teapot on the hearthstones.

She held Jenny's yarn and considered strangling her sister the very next time the word "dearest" was uttered aloud.

After tossing away half the night, Eve overslept and woke up ready to discharge the entire senior staff for allowing it. She was eyeing all the pretty, proper demure clothing in her wardrobe with a view toward burning the lot of it when her gaze fell on an old outfit she'd had for years.

It would still fit her.

While she studied the ensemble, an insight—dear God, at long last, an insight—struck her: what was wanted was not destruction per se, but *action*.

No more weeping, wondering, and wandering the house. She yanked the dress out of the wardrobe and tossed it on the bed, then pulled her chemise over her head and regarded her naked body in the mirror.

She bore no visible scars, deformities, or disfigurements as a legacy of her fall. She could walk, she was healthy, and by heaven it was time to start acting that way too.

Her hair went into a practical braid that she coiled up into a bun at her nape. From under the bed, she pulled a pair of boots she hadn't worn in seven years. She dressed without assistance, dodged the breakfast parlor and headed for the kitchen, there to cut up some apples.

She left the kitchen, realizing for all she'd had an insight, it had been only a limited insight: it was time for action, yes, but *what* action?

"I don't suppose you have any answers?" She fed Meteor an apple slice without receiving a reply.

While Grendel sidled closer, she scrambled over the fence to give Meteor's withers a scratching. "I feel like I am going to explode with indignation, horse. Like having a tantrum nobody will be able to ignore, like starting a fire in the formal parlor..."

Like *what*?

She fed him another apple slice then attended to the spot behind his chin that had him stretching out his neck. "You are no help. I come here for wisdom, and I get horsehair all over my outfit."

Grendel came within a few steps, and Eve realized the pony wasn't going to allow her to entirely ignore him. She held out an apple slice to him.

Ponies were not prone to insights. They usually lived a scrappy life among larger animals and inconsiderate children, or casually negligent former owners. A pony was generally left to manage as best it could, and the average pony managed quite well.

Grendel did not take the treat. He regarded Eve out of eyes that seemed at once knowing and blank.

"Eat your apple, you idiot. Meteor won't stand for it to go to waste."

Grendel took a step closer while Eve held the apple slice a few inches from his fuzzy, whiskered muzzle.

"You are no kind of pony if you can't see a perfectly lovely treat—oof!"

He'd butted her middle with his head, once. Stoutly.

"That was rude." She passed the apple slice over her shoulder to Meteor and stood there, hands on hips, feeling as if the pony were glaring right back at her. It was enough to drive an already overset woman—

Yes.

Yes, yes, and *yes.*

"You." She grabbed Grendel's thick forelock. "You come with me, and don't even think of giving me any trouble, or I shall deal with you accordingly."

The little beast came along. He did not give her *any* trouble.

❧

Deene climbed into the saddle, patted his gelding on the neck, and turned the horse down the drive. Anthony had departed a couple of days ago, the plan being for him to go on reconnaissance in the clubs and ballrooms and unearth whatever intelligence there was to be found.

While Deene… buried himself in ledgers that made little sense, rode out to visit tenants who were wary and carefully polite when enduring his calls, made lists of eligible women of good fortune and reasonable disposition… and did not call on the Windham sisters or even on Kesmore.

A clear focus was called for, and proximity to Eve Windham created rather the opposite.

He worried about her. He worried about Georgie. He worried about his finances. He worried about Anthony, so newly a father and trying to appear casual about it.

"I do not worry about you."

Beast flipped an ear back, then forward.

Beast, being a gelding, seldom evidenced worry unless his ration of oats did not timely appear in his bucket. Deene let his unworried mount canter over much of the Denning Hall home farm, then down the track that separated the Hall from the Moreland home-wood.

The land was in the last stages of coming back to life after winter's sleep. The trees were still a gauzy, soft green, the earth had the fresh, cool scent of spring, and daffodils winked from the hedgerows. Deene crossed onto Eve's property, Lavender Something, and crested a rise to see the little manor house, a picture of Tudor repose snug at the bottom of the hill.

As he studied the scene, he had a tickling sense of something being out of order. There were pansies here and there, the windows sparkled in the midday sun, the drive was neatly raked but for—

A groom was leading a pony trap away toward the stables, a fat little pony in the traces.

Beast—or perhaps Deene—decided to amble down and investigate. Eve's property was supposed to be more or less vacant but for staff, which meant nobody had cause to be paying a call.

He hitched Beast to the post in the drive—the

stables likely sported only the one groom—and went up to the house. A knock on the door yielded no response; a slight push on it gained him entry.

The interior upheld the promise of the exterior: pretty, cozy, and warm to the eye in a way having nothing to do with temperature. Eve would be comfortable amid all this light and domesticity.

He spotted her before she detected him. She stood at the window in a second, homey little parlor done up all in gold, cream, and soft hues of brown. Her outfit was brown as well, but sported fetching little details in cream and red—a touch of piping, a dab of lace.

Why did she have to be so damned pretty?

She turned and uncrossed her arms. "Lucas."

As she came toward him, the force of her smile nearly knocked him physically on his arse. She'd never smiled at him like that; he hoped she'd never before smiled at *anybody* like that.

Luminous, radiant, and soft with pleasure and joy. Even as his mind comprehended that she was going to embrace him—and welcomed the idea wholeheartedly—his thinking brain also latched onto one detail: she was wearing a driving ensemble.

For a long, precious moment, he held her while his heart resonated with the happiness and pride he'd seen in her eyes. "You soloed at the ribbons."

She nodded, her hair tickling his chin. "I drove here, Lucas. I drove here *by myself*, and I can't wait to drive myself home. Just saying the words feels good. It feels marvelous."

He clamped his arms around her, lifted her, and

whirled her in circles. "You drove yourself here. You're going to drive yourself home. You're going to drive yourself wherever you damned well please."

Her laughter was a marvelous thing, her body against his every bit as wonderful. He could feel the joy in her, the relief.

"I'm going to drive myself wherever I please, whenever I please, however I please. Nobody will be safe from Eve Windham when she takes a notion to tool about. I might drive up to Yorkshire and call upon St. Just, or out to Oxford to check on Valentine. I shall certainly call upon Westhaven in Surrey, and Sophie and Maggie and… all of them. I can see them anytime I please."

He set her on her feet, letting her slide slowly down his body. "You might nip out to Surrey to see how Franny's foal is getting on. You might take a notion to peek in on the next meet at Epsom."

She stood there, beaming up at him, a woman transfigured by her own courage.

He must kiss her. The moment called for nothing less, and even if it had, he was helpless not to kiss her.

Kissing Eve had been a lovely experience each and every time: tipsy and bold under the mistletoe, surprised but eager in the privacy of shadowed ferns, hesitant but sweet in the confines of a landau…

When she was ebullient, when she was in roaring good spirits with her recent accomplishment, kissing her was… beyond description. Her confidence pulled him in; her joy pulled him under.

Any thought of trouble in London, any thought of the tedium of the Season awaiting him, any *ability* to think deserted Deene between one breath and the next. He registered impressions only:

The buttons of her outfit pressing hard into his sternum.

The slight tug of her fingers where she'd fisted her hand in the hair at his nape.

The way she wasn't the least shy about plastering herself with gratifying snugness against his growing erection.

To hold her this way felt… glorious.

And he registered a small, muted kick of common sense against his conscience: he should close and lock the door.

This last he could approximate. He scooped her up against his chest and backed against the half-open door until it was closed, then advanced with her to lay her down on the sofa. She lay on her back, smiling a secret, pleased smile, giving Deene the sense she was as cast away as he.

"Don't stop kissing me, Lucas. Kissing you is…"

He paused above her, wanting to know exactly what words she'd choose, but instead she held out her arms and gave them an impatient shake. He shrugged out of his coat and came down over her.

"We should take our boots off, Evie. We'll get dust—"

Absurdities. He was spouting absurdities, and even those fled his awareness as Eve fused her mouth to his and curled her two booted feet around his flanks. He pulled back, pleased to find she was panting.

For a procession of instants, she gazed at him, bestowing on him a look that conveyed glee and arousal and… *tenderness*.

The look in her eyes utterly shifted the moment, from one of celebration to one of anticipation. When he lowered his head to rest his cheek against her hair, he understood that for Eve, this was like a soldier needing to pillage after victory in battle, like the necessary carouse after winning a close race or a bet against very long odds.

And it was his privilege to make sure no lasting harm befell her while she indulged in a few moments of heedlessness… no harm whatsoever.

Even if he wanted to bury himself in her heat, wanted to hear her scream his name with pleasure, wanted to feel her desperate with desire.

"Lucas?" The bewilderment in her gaze when he lifted away from her tore at his heart.

"Boots off, Evie. I have an idea. Trust me."

Three complete sentences, one declarative, two imperative. Quite an accomplishment when a man's cock was rioting in his breeches. He tugged her up by one arm and knelt to pull off her boots.

While she sat there looking puzzled and a trifle disgruntled, he untied her stock and eased her jacket from her shoulders, then started unbuttoning her shirt.

"Will I like this idea?"

"You will like it."

"Does it involve my undressing you as well?"

He sat back on his heels, proud of her. "It can."

And then a cloud passed before the sun in her gaze.

"Lucas, there must be a limit—"

Ah, common sense was nipping at her heels too. He put one finger on her lips. "There must. Trust me to see to it. I promise you're safe with me, Eve."

She didn't hesitate for even an instant. She reached

out and started unknotting his cravat. Before Deene could take three steadying breaths, his shirt was open and Eve was drawing a single, incendiary finger down the length of his sternum.

"Back to my idea, Eve…"

Her lips quirked up. "I liked it better when you were kissing me, not just spouting ideas."

Eve, impish and intent on her designs, had Deene counting the pulse beats in his groin. "Then we get back to kissing." He lifted her up and turned, then sat so she straddled his lap. Before she could latch her lips to his, he stared in amazement.

"What on earth are you wearing, Eve Windham?"

Her glance flicked down her front, over an elaborately and very colorfully embroidered set of stays that, thanks to some innovative genius whom Deene would like to genuflect before, laced up the front.

"Jenny makes them. Kiss me."

It took concentration, to kiss her, to loosen those ingenious stays, to not spend in his breeches at the feel of her breasts all silky and warm beneath his fingers.

It took a little contorting too, to get his hand under her skirts while she used her tongue—hot, wet, wicked—on his ear and undulated her spine so her breast pushed against his palm.

And it took persistence, wagonloads of persistence to get her skirts out of the way and find that slit in her drawers, and then kiss her past the bolt of surprise that went through her when he first made contact with the sweet, damp heat of her sex.

"Lucas, what are you—?"

He did not answer with words; he showed her by

repeating a caress of his thumb over the little bud of flesh an aroused man neglected at his peril.

Her breathing changed. She rested her forehead on his shoulder, and he touched her again, more firmly.

"Ohhhh… *Lucas*."

Eve conveyed wonder and surrender with just his name. He relaxed, certain she'd allow him to give her this pleasure, certain she'd take what he offered.

Though not immediately. He had to experiment a little with pressure and speed, had to pause to pleasure her breasts with his mouth, and pause again to gather the reins of his composure.

He could give them both this much, not more. More was for… not for them.

She hitched against him.

"That's it, Evie. Move if it makes you feel better."

She heard him. He knew this because her hips started a slow, languid roll to go with the movement of his thumb. Her pace was voluptuous and savoring, so arousing Deene had to count his breaths to keep from spending.

She did not moan, but he felt it when the shocks of pleasure started to grip her body. She twisted her fingers in his hair, her breathing became harsh, she pushed against his thumb, and then went still while, even with his relevant parts outside her body, Deene could feel her drawing up inside, convulsing for long moments with silent ecstasy.

The need to finish pounded through him even as Eve hung over him, panting against his neck. He got his falls undone on one side, extracted himself from his breeches and was spending all over his belly within half a minute.

Likely less.

And then… more bliss, just to hold her, to hold her and marvel at what had gone before—and mourn that it could not have been more.

❧

Sensations registered with heightened clarity while Eve drowsed on Deene's shoulder:

The scent of lavender and cedar about his person.

The cherishing quality in the way his hand smoothed slowly over her hair.

The feel of his heart, beating in his naked chest against her naked breasts.

The exact temperature of his neck, the weight of his cheek against her hair.

The luminous and novel lightness suffusing her body.

Each impacted her awareness with bell-tone perfection.

And this was just a taste, just a delectable sample of what and whom Eve must give up for the rest of her life. Further intimacies were out of the question, and thank a God in the mood to show some rare mercy, Deene had somehow understood this.

She could not have borne for him to be disappointed in her, could not have borne to see the warmth and approval in his gaze shift to speculation and disdain.

To whom had she surrendered her virtue?

Upon how many had she bestowed her favors?

Was she diseased from all that excess?

Had she borne a child, perhaps, as a consequence of her folly?

But no, Deene had not disappointed her, had not let her down by asking too much or giving too little.

All those promises Canby had made—*glorious pleasure, nothing like it, you'll want it again and again, you'll want* me *again and again*—what lies they'd been.

While Deene had asked nothing and given her true pleasure.

What a goddamned perishing shame they were destined never to share more.

Eve was marshaling her courage to draw back and remove herself from Deene's lap when his hand tightened on the back of her head, and a shocked, very familiar voice sounded from the doorway.

"Good gracious God in heaven."

And then Jenny's voice, urgent, low, and miserable. "Mama, come away. Come away now, please. We must close the door."

Six

EVE TRIED TO SCRAMBLE AWAY FROM THE MAN holding her so gently on the couch, but his embrace became inescapable.

"They've gone, love. Stay a moment more. There's nothing to be gained by haste at this point, and we need to sort this out before we face your family."

Love? Now he called her *love*?

"Let me go. I can't breathe…" She tried to wrestle free, but he had his hand on the back of her head, his arm around her back.

Out in the hallway, the front door didn't close; it banged shut with the impact of a rifle shot ricocheting through the house… and through the rest of Eve's blighted, miserable life.

"Mama slammed that door, Lucas Denning. Her Grace, the Duchess of Moreland, *slammed* a door, because of me, because of my stupid, selfish, useless, greedy, stupid, asinine…"

There were not words to describe the depth of the betrayal she'd just handed her family. She collapsed against Deene's chest, misery a dry, scraping ache in her throat.

"Eve, many couples anticipate their vows, even a few couples closely associated with the Duchess of Moreland."

The reason in his voice had her hands balling to fists.

"I will not marry you." She *could* not, not him of all men. That signal fact gave her scattering wits a rallying point.

Deene did not argue. When an argument was imperative, he did not argue. His hand stroked slowly over her hair, and as the fighting instinct coursing through Eve's body struggled to stand against a swamping despair, some part of Eve's brain made a curious observation:

Deene was breathing in a slow, unhurried rhythm, and as a function of the intimacy of their posture, Eve was breathing in counterpoint to him. The same easy, almost restful tempo, but her exhale matched his inhale.

"We cannot marry, Deene. I won't have it. A white marriage was as far as I was willing to go, and then only to the right sort of man, a man who would never seek to... impose conjugal duties on me."

His arms fell away, when Eve would very much have liked them to stay around her. Better he not see her face, better she not have to see his lovely blue eyes going chill and distant.

"We need to set you to rights."

His hands on her shirt were deft and impersonal, his fingers barely touching her skin. The detachment in his touch was probably meant to be a kindness, but it... hurt.

"Lucas, I cannot think."

"We'll think this through together. I can guarantee

you not a soul will be coming through that door until we decide to pass through it ourselves."

"I hate that you can be so calm."

And—worst thought yet—she loved him for it too, just a little. He wasn't stomping around the room, trying to subtly blame her, cursing his fate while figuring out how to duck away from it. He wasn't thrusting her aside so he could put himself together while he left her floundering to right herself with clumsy fingers and a clumsier mind.

She loved him for his simple gestures of consider-ation, though one could love and hate simultaneously. When she'd been recovering from her accident, this truth had borne down upon her every time Jenny or Louisa offered to read her another hour's worth of bucolic poetry.

"I feel just as if I were lying in that filthy sheep meadow, the scent of sheep dirt all about me, the cold in my bones, the…"

Eve snapped her jaw shut. What on *earth* was she babbling about?

Deene paused in his tucking and buttoning and put a warm hand on either side of her jaw. He kept his hands there until Eve managed to meet his gaze. "If you are in some stinking sheep meadow, I am there with you. Is there tea in this house?"

Tea. Oh, *of course*, tea. "Yes."

And still he did not lift her from his lap. While she watched, he withdrew a handkerchief from a pocket and swabbed at his flat belly.

He had a moderate dusting of chest hair. That she would notice this made Eve doubt her sanity—Canby had had no chest hair—because her impulse was not to look away, it was to touch him. *What would it feel like to run her fingertips over that chest hair?* With self-discipline making far too late an appearance, she denied herself the appeasement of this one small curiosity.

When they were both more or less tidied up, Deene wrapped his hand around the back of Eve's head and once more drew her face down to his shoulder.

"You shall not blame yourself for this, Eve Windham. You are a lady, innocent of any wrong-doing, and I have breached the bounds of gentlemanly behavior altogether."

Not quite *altogether*, though the distinction would make no difference. "Lucas, you have no idea…"

He squeezed the back of her neck, gently, just as he had when Eve had been suffering a megrim weeks ago. "We'll sort this out, Eve. You have nothing to make apology for, not to me, not to Their Graces, not to anybody."

Papa's heart would be broken. She closed her eyes at that realization. Her Grace would be disappointed; she'd get that tight "where did I go wrong?" look about her eyes and mouth, but Papa…

"Come along." Deene patted her hip. "We'll make some tea and get the color back in your cheeks. It won't be so bad, Eve."

He waited for her to extricate herself from his lap, and this took some doing because her hip was stiff—it hardly ever gave her trouble anymore, but of course it would today. When she was on her feet, Deene rose as well, tied her stock around her neck in a neat, graceful bow, saw to his cravat, and offered her his arm.

She took it, a reflex—one she resented even as they arrived to a spotless, empty kitchen.

"May I rummage for some food?" He asked her this as she tossed kindling on the coals in the hearth and took the kettle from the hob.

"There should be bread in the bread box."

Maybe it was a propensity for self-preservation in the adult male, maybe it was the instincts of a former soldier, but as Eve assembled a tea tray, Deene's foraging produced bread, butter, strawberry jam, and cheese. They domesticated in the kitchen in an oddly comfortable quiet, and by the time the tea was steeping in a plain white ceramic pot, Eve realized Deene had been giving her time to settle her nerves.

Or perhaps to settle his own—a cheering thought.

When she lowered herself to a bench at the worktable, Deene came down beside her, meaning she had to scoot a little.

"Don't run off." He poured her tea, buttered her a slice of bread, then spread a liberal portion of strawberry jam on it.

If he tried to feed her, she was going to bite off his hand. "I'm not helpless, Lucas."

The look he gave her was impassive. "Pleased to hear it. Pass the sugar."

So they sat there side by side, swilling tea, and not arguing. As Eve filled her belly—the food was a surprising comfort, as was Deene's bulk beside her— she tried to reconcile herself to her fate while she topped up their cups.

"This is worse than if we'd been happened upon by strangers."

"Your mother and sister will never mention what they saw if you don't want them to, Eve."

Eve studied his profile and saw he believed this made a difference. "They will never mention it in any case, though Her Grace will likely tell Papa. That they know makes a difference, Lucas. To me."

"To me as well. I am formally renewing my proposal for your hand in marriage, Evie. Don't hog the butter."

"I am refusing your suit, though you do me great— don't you hog the jam."

"You want a white marriage. I cannot give you that. The responsibility for the succession lies with me, despite Anthony's willingness to step in, if necessary. I wonder if your father will call me out."

He reached for another slice of bread as he spoke, the observation so casual Eve wanted to slap her hand over his mouth. With no more regard than if he'd asked, "I wonder if Islington will put his colt in the second heat at Epsom?" Deene had heaped terror on top of Eve's dread.

"He wouldn't. Papa *likes* you." The tea in her stomach started to rebel at the image of Lucas, facedown, bleeding his life away in some foggy meadow… Papa, facedown… Or—it had been known to happen—both men, dead or permanently incapacitated over Eve's idiocy.

Oh, merciful, merciful heavens.

"Westhaven might see to it," Deene went on, "given that His Grace should not be involved in such a scandal at this point in his life. All of your brothers are tiresomely good shots. I suspect Lord Val might be pressed into service—time spent in Italy generally improves a man's command of the art of the sword."

He munched away on his bread, while Eve concluded there was never a species, a gender, or a creature on earth as blockheaded as the honorable English male in possession of a pair of dueling pistols—or swords, foils, whatever the proper term was.

Unless it was she, herself, for allowing such folly to be contemplated.

Whatever was she going to do?

They tidied up the kitchen and put the parlor to rights—this involved arranging pillows so the smudges left by Eve's dusty boots were covered up, but as one mundane, simple task followed another, Eve faced the growing realization that the last time she'd fallen so far from sense and proper behavior, the consequences had been disastrous.

This time, if she did marry Lucas Denning, they would be equally disastrous.

And if she did *not* marry him, they could be even worse.

When the groom led Grendel from the stables, the little trap rattling along behind, Deene tied Beast to the back and deposited Eve on the seat. He climbed in and sat beside her, not touching the reins.

She wasn't going to drive. The man was a lunatic if he thought she could manage the reins in her present state. Grendel stomped a small hoof, likely quite aware that this journey would lead homeward and back to his nice grassy paddock.

"Deene, this proves nothing."

"You're not helpless. I have that on the best

authority. It's not two miles by the lanes, and you
know the terrain intimately."

Intimately. To elbow him in the ribs or not to elbow
him in the ribs?

She hated him, no dispute about that now. She
hated him, her life, this day, and herself.

But she took the reins.

❧

Her Grace never paced, never worried a fingernail
between her teeth, never appeared anxious. His Grace
watched while she did all three, until he could bear it
no more.

"Esther, come sit with me. Let me pour you a cup,
and we'll think this through."

She paused at the window to their private sitting
room, arms crossed, spine straight, and yet her posture
testified to despair in the very rigidity of her shoulders.

"Percival, they had been intimate. I could smell it.
Dear God…"

There had been more Dear God-ing going on in the
previous twenty minutes than His Grace could recall in
the past twenty years—and all over young people acting
exactly like young people were slated to behave from
the beginning of time. He took his wife by the hand,
seated her on the sofa, then came down beside her.

"What is it, exactly, my love, that has you so
overset about the situation? Deene is honorable. If Eve
wants him, there's an end to it."

"But Eve…" She laid her head on his shoulder.
"We've raised ten wonderful children, Percival. We've
known heartache and grief."

That she would speak of it was unusual and gave His Grace a pang. After more than three decades, the glances and silences were often articulate enough that painful words need not be spoken. "We've known wonder and abundant joy, too, Esther."

"We've buried two, Percival."

He couldn't argue with that, but thank God it had been only two. Most families somewhere along the way bore the sorrow of an infant taken before the first year, an elder snatched away... as he'd almost been snatched away.

"We still have eight, Esther, and though that cannot compensate for the loss of Victor and Bartholomew, it does console, as do the grandchildren."

She nodded, but His Grace knew she was working up to something, something that might allow her to finally cry, which—as harrowing as it would be for him—was probably necessary before they could sort out Eve's latest contretemps.

"Percy, I will always miss the boys, I will always worry over the others, but Eve..."

He put his arm around her shoulders.

"Tell me, my love."

"Death will come for all of us, and in Victor's case, it was almost a blessing. I am selfish to say so, a bad mother—"

That nonsense required immediate contradiction. "You could not be a bad mother, Esther, not ever."

"But Eve... Our sons were taken from us, and it was awful, but what was taken from Eve... Percy, that broke my heart, over and over. I grieved for our daughter every day she lay in that bed, hurting in body and spirit. And yet, I have never been as angry, either, never been as upset as when I watched our baby girl lose all her spark, all her joy, and all her confidence. That awful, awful man, whom we brought into the household as an employee... I wanted to strangle him with my bare hands. I wanted to aim a pistol at his... directly at him. I wanted to pour oil on him and watch while he was consumed by flames..."

He loved this about her, the ferocity, the soul-deep protectiveness toward those she loved. He hated, however, for her to be distressed.

"Eve was daunted, but she did not lose all her fight, Esther. As long as we love her, she'll never lose the God-given strength to fight. She is a Windham, and one tempered at a young age by vicissitudes her siblings cannot fathom. She'll win through."

Her Grace was on her feet again, pacing to the window. "She will not. She will not see this as an opportunity to seize happiness and the joy she deserves. She'll punish herself, and Deene will be too much a gentleman to force her hand. *She was on top of him*, Percy, in his lap, straddling..."

Not something a father ever wanted to picture, though His Grace allowed a touch of approval that any child of his would take the initiative in such a moment. Young Deene had likely not stood a chance.

"She was not forced, then, Esther. She is well past her come out, and this was her choice."

Her Grace's brows rose, then settled. "That is something."

"It's a very telling something."

Her expression grew thoughtful. "On the occasion

of Your Comeuppance, I believe I made the same point to you."

His Comeuppance. Something had indeed come up on that occasion.

"Just so, my love. Come drink your tea. We must plan our strategy."

⤜❧⤛

To sit beside Eve and not touch her was difficult.

To sit beside her and not argue his case was making Deene clench his jaw and ball his fists and recite the Lord's Prayer in Latin, Greek, French, and German.

Marrying Eve made such *sense*. When last he'd considered the notion, he hadn't been dealing with nasty rumors that had Mildred Staines eyeing his crotch and the clubs going oddly silent when Deene walked into the room. The idea of taking Eve to wife loomed as not just right, but necessary for them both.

The list of arguments in support of their wedding circled through his head faster than the wheels of their conveyance bore them toward a reckoning:

He and Eve were of appropriate rank.

They had shared interests.

Their lands marched.

They were compatible in ways both mundane and intimate.

He needed to marry *well*, and Eve needed to marry a man who'd be a true husband to her if she was to have the children and loving family that was her God-given right. He'd give her all the children she wanted and delight in doing so…

A *white* marriage, for God's sake…

As Eve turned the cart up the Moreland drive, it occurred to Deene that in some convoluted, unfathomable female manner, Eve was probably seeking to relieve her family of worrying over her and punish herself in the bargain with this notion of a white marriage.

Which he could not allow. She deserved so much better. She deserved every happiness a family and home of her own could afford, and more, given... given everything.

She tooled the trap around the circular drive before the house and on to the stables, her driving flawless, as he knew it would be. "You need not come inside, Lucas."

"If I want to live beyond next week, I will not let you face this gauntlet alone."

She winced, a small, gratifying suggestion that the only plan Deene had been able to formulate might bear fruit. He'd never convince her they'd suit wonderfully, but he might be able to scare her into marrying him.

Though the idea made *him* wince. He lifted Eve from the cart as a groom came out to lead the pony away. They stood alone in the stable yard, Deene's hands on Eve's waist to keep her from bolting.

"I will say again, Lady Eve, you have nothing to apologize for, nothing to explain. I took advantage of you, and I will face the consequences."

"Do be quiet. I am cross enough with you and with myself as it is."

She took his arm and stomped along beside him, nearly dragging him up to the house. When she would have slunk in a side entrance, Deene led her around to the front door. This provoked a gale-force sigh.

"We begin as we intend to go on, Eve."

"We won't be going on, Lucas. I will not marry you. Papa would never think of calling you out, and thus you are safe from my brothers. We didn't even…" She waved a hand in circles.

"Her Grace will think we did." Another wince. So he twisted the knife in her conscience. "Lady Jenny will think we did."

Eve paused on the top step before the front door, her expression stricken anew. "Oh, God… Jenny. Poor, sweet…"

A knife once twisted could not be untwisted, and here on the gracious front terrace of one of the most elegant homes in the shire, Deene could not take his intended in his arms.

The front door opened, but it was not a butler who stood there—apparently not even senior staff could be allowed to witness the coming confrontation. His Grace manned the door, blue eyes flashing fire, his face an implacable mask of banked fury.

"Young lady, you will attend your mother in her sitting room at once."

And Deene was supposed to just toddle back down the stairs to await an uncertain fate?

"If Your Grace would allow Lady Eve and me a chance to discuss the events of the—"

"You, sir!" His Grace was not inclined to keep his voice down when discretion might be most appreciated. This was known by all familiar with him, and beside Deene, Eve graduated from wincing to cringing.

"Your Grace, Lady Eve's nerves are not aided by a display of temper, though you have every reason to rail at me."

The ducal eyebrows went up. "I have every reason to kill you, young man. The harm you have done cannot be explained or excused, and no adequate reparation ever made to my daughter."

This was the moment for Eve to step forward and explain that they were betrothed, that the indiscretion was just that, more a slip than a sin. Certainly not a matter of a lady's slighted honor.

His Grace's gaze went to his daughter while a silence stretched, a silence during which Deene wanted to go down on bended knee and beg the blasted woman to marry him.

"Unhand my daughter, Deene."

Eve slipped away from Deene's side and disappeared into the house.

His Grace waited a long moment while Eve's footsteps faded rapidly, and then the older man glanced about. "You, come with me. And get that mulish expression off your face. The last thing Her Grace will do is castigate Eve for a situation that must lie exclusively at your handsome, booted feet."

Was there a softening in His Grace's eyes? Deene was not about to bet his life on it. When the duke led him to a chamber on the first floor, Deene noted an absence of footmen, maids, or other curious ears.

"Your Grace, I think you well might have to call me out."

Moreland opened the door to the ducal study and preceded Deene through it. He closed the door, then turned, and without any warning whatsoever, delivered a walloping backhand across Deene's cheek.

"Perhaps I *shall* have to call you out, Deene. Let's make it a convincing show, then, shall we?"

❧

"Mama, you cannot allow Papa to do anything rash."

Eve stood over at the window, arms crossed at her middle, her shoulders back, and her chin up.

Their baby girl was such a little soldier.

Her Grace took a seat on the sofa, a fresh tea tray on the table before her. "I'd say if there was rash behavior this day, your Papa is not the one to be faulted."

"And neither is Luc—" Eve's jaw snapped shut and remained that way for as long as it took to pour one cup of tea. "Deene is not to be blamed either. There cannot be any duel."

"Am I to felicitate you on your upcoming nuptials then?"

Another silence while the duchess added cream and sugar to the tea.

"You are not. You must know I have no desire to marry."

"Come drink your tea, Eve, and to be honest, I know no such thing. You've had your Seasons. You've had many proposals. It's time you settled down and had some babies to love."

The duchess trusted implicitly in her husband's command of tactics, but this course was difficult for a loving mother to carry off in the face of the bleak determination in Eve's eyes.

"Mama…" Eve sat on the sofa, staring at the empty hearth. "I do not… I cannot…"

Esther passed her the cup of tea, unable to listen

to Eve struggle to bring up things that had remained undiscussed for seven years. "Drink your tea, though if there's to be no wedding, I expect we'll see more than one duel."

Eve set her teacup down on its saucer with a clatter. "More than—!"

"I don't need to tell you His Grace is an old-fashioned man when it comes to a lady's honor. Your brothers are almost more conservative than their papa."

"Mama, how can you sit here, swilling tea and contemplating violence as if, as if—somebody could be hurt, somebody could be killed."

"That would be a pity." Esther took a sip of her tea, sending up a silent prayer that Percy was faring more successfully with Deene.

"I cannot marry Lucas Denning." Eve sat forward and dropped her face into her hands. "Mama, I cannot."

His Grace had patiently pointed out that Eve was not balking at the intimacies of marriage—men could be so blunt!—which had put things in a very different light, indeed.

"If you can ravish the man on a sofa in the broad light of day, Eve Windham, I beg to differ with that conclusion. You *can* marry him, but you don't *wish* to."

The look Eve shot her was not that of a dutiful, troubled, or even confused daughter. It was the look of a full-grown woman bitterly resenting her circumstances. "I can marry him. I do not wish to marry him. Doesn't it count for anything that he's already proposed to me twice and I've rejected him both times?"

Esther considered her teacup. She'd had the sense Deene was more than a little interested, and it was hard not to show satisfaction at being right—though two proposals was admittedly fast work.

"Your rejections count for nothing. Deene should have approached your father before mentioning any intentions toward you."

"I am not a child, Mother, that I can't be spoken to without permission from my father."

"You are not a child, but your position is childish. Your refusal to accept an eminently desirable suit will put at least your father, if not your brothers, at risk, and go a very long way toward ruining any lasting chance Jenny has at a family of her own. You are apparently not shy of your marital obligations, Eve, which reservation I might have understood or been able to address, so you are just being stubborn. It does not become you in the least."

The last statement was downright cruel, implying a disapproval Esther could never feel toward her daughter, but seven years was long enough to punish oneself—and one's parents—for an understandable misstep.

"I hate this day."

"You do not hate Deene."

This remark seemed to double the sorrow in Eve's eyes. "I like him a great deal, I care for him, I—"

The duchess let a beat of silence go by while words were not said that might have surprised even Eve were they spoken aloud. "If you care for him, then I don't think you can jeopardize his welfare simply for a stubborn whim, can you?"

While Esther pretended to sip tea, the fight drained

out of Eve's posture. "Jeopardize Deene's life, Papa's, my brothers'…" She hunched in on herself. "I can't do that, and Deene would never consider dodging off to the Continent for a few years."

"Would *you* take such a course?"

The idea of Eve running and hiding hadn't occurred to Percy, but from the duchess's perspective, it was clearly an option under consideration.

"No, I cannot even be left in peace on some bucolic little French farm, because the idiot men in this family would blame Deene for that, and come after him no matter what I did or said. Everybody would conclude I had left the country to bear Deene's child, and Jenny's fate would be sealed."

"I do believe you're right."

Eve slumped back against the cushions while Esther allowed herself a cautious hint of hope. "We'll obtain a special license, hold the service here if you like. Every debutante making her come out will envy you the match."

"You must do as you please, Your Grace."

Your Grace. The chill in that form of address made Esther doubt the wisdom of Percy's plan. "It's your wedding, Eve, you ought to—"

But Eve was off the sofa and halfway to the door. "Please, excuse me, Your Grace. I find I need some solitude."

She opened the door, and Esther had every intention of letting her go without another word, but there stood His Grace, and Eve's… intended, the latter sporting a right cheek a good deal more pink than the left.

❧

Papa had his tempers, his rants, his perpetual frustrations with the Lords, with Prinny, with the way the old mad king was treated, but nothing Eve had seen before prepared her for the cold-eyed stranger standing next to Deene.

She'd always known His Grace had served in the cavalry, known he'd faced Canadian winters, wolves, and worse, but the look in his eye now…

For the first time in her life, Eve Windham was afraid of her father. Not afraid he would harm her, afraid he would stop at nothing to protect her, even when such protection was hopelessly misguided.

She stepped back as His Grace stormed into the room, Deene following a few paces behind.

The duke had struck him. Such a blow in the context of a duel meant no apology could mend the situation. The beginning of a headache threaded itself into all the other miseries ricocheting around in Eve's body.

"Eve." His Grace turned a glacial stare on her. "Deene has something to say to you. I suggest you give him your entire attention, but mind me: he can apologize to you all he wants. That does not address the disrespect done to me and my house this day. Your Grace." He turned to the duchess and offered his arm. "You have ten minutes, Deene. I suggest you spend them on your knees—in prayer if nothing else."

They swept out, leaving Eve alone with a man who had every reason to think her daft or worse.

"Not here." Deene took her by the hand and led her to the French doors. "They'll post a damned sentry in the corridor, and what we have to say to each other requires privacy."

He took her into the garden, which helped ease a claustrophobic sense gathering in Eve's chest. While they walked along in silence amid beds of tulips and hyacinths, what registered in Eve's benumbed brain was that Deene's hand was warm and dry, not cold and clammy as hers felt.

"Here." He gestured to a bench behind a privet hedge. Roses were leafing out in the nearby beds, but only a few tight buds had yet formed. When Eve took a seat, Deene lowered himself beside her and once again took her hand.

"Well?" It was all she could manage.

"Well." He did a curious thing: he smoothed his fingers over her knuckles and brought her hand to his mouth, pressing his lips to her palm. "A kiss for courage. His Grace has given me three days to notify my seconds—Anthony is in Town, and I suppose Kesmore will serve in addition—while Rothgreb and Sindal are put on notice on His Grace's behalf. We've agreed to recruit Fairly to serve as the surgeon."

Such a cozy family murder they were planning. "Three days?"

"A bit biblical, but His Grace and I agree this needs to be wrapped up before the Season officially starts."

They *agreed*. What they were agreeing to was obscene, but no more obscene than that Eve would allow it to go forward.

"Deene, if I married you, you would be more displeased with your choice than you could possibly know." She hoped and prayed he'd listen to reason.

"Disappointed has a great deal to recommend it over dead, though you must do as you see fit. I cannot promise you your father will delope, Eve, though I assuredly will. Then, too, he has not discounted your brothers issuing their own challenges, and deloping does not seem in character for any of them."

She'd condemn Deene to facing *four* firing squads, then, and what was to stop her three brothers-in-law from joining the fun? She had never known her father to back down, not ever. Her brothers were just as bad.

And she... She was the one being monumentally, murderously stubborn. None of her menfolk would have a chance at Deene if she would just say yes to his proposals.

One glimmer of hope penetrated her misery, a tiny, chimerical possibility: if it came down to a wedding night, Deene might not notice her lack of chastity.

Except he would. He wasn't a stupid man or lacking in perception.

"I can make you a promise, Eve Windham. Several promises, in fact."

"Just not vows, please. I cannot abide the thought of vows."

"If we marry, we will consummate the union for legal purposes and to put the compulsory obligations behind us. Thereafter, I will not press you for your attentions until such time as you indicate you are willing to be intimate with me in a marital sense."

She peered over at him. His cheeks were the same color now. "You would leave me in peace after one night?"

"Not entirely. For appearances, we will live together

as man and wife, share chambers, and go down to breakfast together. We will dote and fawn in public and make calf eyes at each other across the ballrooms, but I will not importune you."

The small, guttering flame of hope burned a trifle brighter. His plan had potential to avoid disaster. She did not know what motivated his foolish generosity, but the plain fact was, after the wedding night, he might not *want* to have anything to do with her.

"And if I never indicate that I'm interested in my conjugal duties?"

"Never is a long time, and I am a very determined man who is quite attracted to you. Also a man in need of heirs, and I am confident you'll not deny me those."

The flame nearly went out. Of course he'd need heirs.

"Unfair, Lucas." Except, he was compromising, while Eve was practically loading four sets of dueling pistols and aiming them at Deene's chest. "You have an heir."

"Who is unmarried, older than me, and for reasons not relevant to the current discussion, not a good candidate for marriage. The succession is my obligation, Eve, and I've avoided it long enough."

She had at least ten childbearing years left, possibly twenty. That was a long time to muddle through with a man who had been nothing but considerate toward her.

And an impossibly long time to mourn him, should the worst occur.

"On the conditions you've stated—that following the wedding night you will not exercise your rights unless and until I'm comfortable with the notion, we can be married, but, Lucas, when you hate the choice you've made—when you hate me—don't say I didn't warn you."

"I will not hate you, I will not hate my choice. *That* I do vow."

His arm came around her. He gently pushed her head to his shoulder, and they sat there amid the thorny roses, officially engaged.

❧

Deene held his intended on the hard bench in the brisk spring sunshine and knew a sense of relief disproportionate to the circumstances. His Grace had proven canny, pragmatic, and ultimately more interested in his daughter's happiness than in any lethal displays of honor.

"You are the first fellow Eve has permitted to do more than sniff her hem since her come out, Deene. If she wants you, then I'll deliver you to her trussed up like a naked goose if I have to."

They'd shared a much-appreciated drink, and Deene had listened to an old soldier plot a campaign remarkable for its cunning and simplicity. Eve's family was rallying around her once more; she simply didn't realize it.

"Shall we go in, Eve? Your father will send an armed searching party for us in another five minutes."

She nodded and rose, keeping his hand in hers. Her complexion was so pale he could see the freckles sprinkled across the bridge of her nose, and her eyes were taking on a pained quality he'd seen in them before.

"This won't be so bad, Eve, I promise."

"This?" Could her expression be any more bleak?

"This discussion with your parents, this engage-ment, this marriage."

Nothing, not a nod, not a grimace. They were back in the parlor, where Her Grace sat on a sofa before the tea service and His Grace lounged against the mantel, glowering fiercely.

Eve took a seat beside her mother, while Deene remained standing. "Your Graces, I am very pleased to inform you that Lady Eve has accepted my suit."

A moment of silence, while Deene suspected His Grace was trying not to let his relief show.

"I'm pleased as well," the duchess said softly. "Very, very pleased. Welcome to the family, Lucas."

His Grace blew out a breath. "I'll send for the special license then, and, Deene, you and Eve go have the obligatory tête-à-tête with the vicar. Duchess, I expect you have invitations to address, and I have every confidence Sophie and her baron will be over here for dinner this very night to celebrate with us. Perhaps they'll bring the children, seeing as the weather's moderating."

Deene watched Eve as her dear papa shifted from outraged patriarch to doting father. She was still pale, and the pinched look behind her eyes was more noticeable. He took a gamble, keeping a close watch on Eve's reaction. "Your Graces, there is no need for a special license."

Her Grace's brows rose, while all good cheer evaporated from His Grace's expression. "What does that mean, Deene, no need?"

"It *means* that despite what Her Grace thinks she

saw, there is no need whatsoever to rush matters. I would prefer—and I expect Eve would prefer—a few weeks to cry the banns, plan a ceremony, and otherwise prepare for the upcoming nuptials. It will kick off the Season with a flourish and give all parties an opportunity to accustom themselves to the circumstances."

He shot the older man a look, willing him to understand that circumstances in a marital context meant settlements, and settlements meant negotiations. Negotiations meant solicitors, and *that* meant at least a few weeks were needed.

"Evie?" His Grace frowned down at his daughter. "What's it to be? Deene has rather a point—we want no hole-in-the-corner associations with your wedding."

"I agree with Deene," Her Grace said. "A few weeks will allow some time to enjoy the preparations."

"I'd rather the banns were called as well," Eve said. "There is no need for haste, as Deene has said."

Their Graces exchanged a look that might have been a little puzzled, though Deene could almost hear them conclude that any baby might come three weeks early with no one the wiser.

"Let's remark this occasion with some decent libation, then," His Grace suggested, good cheer quite back in evidence. "I believe there's some '89 in the cellar worthy of the moment."

"May I defer that generous offer, Your Grace?" Deene crossed the room to offer Eve his hand. "Lady Eve would likely enjoy a moment of privacy, and it would be my pleasure to escort her upstairs."

There was no mistaking the relief in Eve's eyes,

which allowed a fellow to comfort himself that he'd gotten at least one thing right in this otherwise confounding day. Eve was silent as he led her through the house, silent as he stopped outside her bedroom door and took her in his arms.

She sighed, and to his great pleasure, wrapped her arms around his waist.

"Why the sigh, love?"

"This has happened too fast, and I am not at all at peace with it. I like you, Lucas, I like you a very great deal…"

Whatever arguments she was trying to resurrect, they died on another sigh as Deene started massaging her neck. "I like you a very great deal too, and we'll manage, Eve. Trust me on that. I'll call on you tomorrow before I head into Town, and expect to see you there forthwith. No leaving me to face all the good wishes myself, if you please."

The longer he worked at the tense muscles of her neck, the more she rested against him. "Give me a week, Lucas."

"Do something for me."

She was becoming a warm, boneless press of female against him with results as predictable as they were inappropriate. "What?"

"Drive out. Take that little fellow who was in the traces today, hitch up one of your sister Sophie's great beasts, but don't hole up here and fret yourself into a decline. Drive out, Eve Windham. Get into the sunshine, call on the neighbors with your news, let Her Grace show you off a bit, but get the ribbons into your hands again soon."

She pulled away a little to peer up at him. "This is an odd request, but I'll tend to it."

"And my only request until I can squire you about in Town."

She blinked. "My headache feels better."

He'd been able to ease her headache, and she liked him a very great deal. Deene kissed her cheek, waited until she'd disappeared into her room, then strode off to have that drink His Grace had mentioned.

Eve had agreed to drive out. A celebration was, indeed, in order.

❧

To the eye of a devoted and loving baby sister, marriage and motherhood agreed with Maggie Windham Portmaine in every particular. Eve found a softness about her eldest sister, a warmth in her gaze, and a gentleness of manner that hadn't been present before the Earl of Hazelton had taken Maggie to wife.

And yet, the discussion Eve had in mind was likely the most difficult she'd ever undertaken.

"I am so pleased you've brought Deene up to scratch, Evie. He is more than passingly handsome, and I've long suspected he holds you in special esteem." Maggie smiled a smile that had her green eyes sparkling, making a gorgeous counterpoint to a glorious mane of red hair.

"At least you aren't prosing on about the proximity of Denning Hall to Morelands, Deene's friendship with St. Just and Bart, or our ranks being appropriate."

God in heaven, Eve hadn't meant to sound so grumpy. Maggie put her teacup down and surveyed her sister. "Is this marriage to your liking, Eve? You can always join our household. Benjamin has already said so—you or Jenny, any time. You'd love Cumbria, too. I'm sure of it."

Join their household? To be enveloped in the marital bliss of a couple who'd found each other despite daunting odds, settled down, and promptly conceived the requisite heir? At least Deene was sparing Eve that fate.

"I am pleased to be marrying Lucas, but I did not come here exclusively to discuss the nuptials."

Maggie's smile was feline. "Of course not. Who needs to discuss anything when that exquisite ring says it all?"

Eve glanced down at the ring Deene had given her the day after... the day after *it* had happened. She now had two milestones in her life: the accident and *it*.

"This is a Denning family heirloom, not part of the entail." And the ring was quite pretty, green emeralds in a delicate gold setting that did not dwarf Eve's hand. Deene had put it on her finger and whispered something about the rest of the parure being for their wedding night.

Almost as if they were truly...

"If you didn't come here to show off your ring and glory in making a magnificent catch, then what else is there that could possibly merit discussion?"

Eve glanced at the half-open door, and was gathering her courage to get up and close it when Maggie's husband stuck his head past the jamb. "May I interrupt for a moment?"

"Husband." Maggie was on her feet, her arm twined around Hazelton's waist in a move that looked comfortable and natural.

Eve topped up her teacup. "Greetings, Benjamin. You're looking well."

Well, handsome, content, quietly glowing just like his wife.

While Eve was back to wanting to smash teapots.

"And you are looking engaged." Hazelton left his wife's side long enough to kiss Eve's cheek. "I don't need to tell you Deene is a fine prospect, Eve Windham—and I've reason to know."

Deene had had some hand in the matter that had brought Maggie and her Benjamin together, but Eve did not know all of the details. Perhaps when she and Deene were married...

Though likely not.

"He speaks highly of you too, Benjamin. Shall we save you some tea cakes, or are you going out?"

"I'm to meet my cousin Archer at the club for luncheon, so I will decline. Lay waste to the cakes. My love, I will be back in time to drive out with you, if that's your wish."

They exchanged a look suggesting driving out might not be at the top of Maggie's list of wishes. Eve ate two tea cakes in succession while Maggie left for a moment to walk her husband to the door.

"You can close the door," Eve said when her sister returned. "I have a delicate question to ask you on behalf of a friend."

Maggie closed the door and resumed her seat on the sofa. "Ask. If I know the answer, I'll tell you, but if it's about the wedding night, expect it to be lovely. All the idiot notions that circulate among the debutantes are just that."

Lovely? In Eve's mind, an image arose of Canby raising his hand to deliver a stout blow. She recalled the sharp pain of a window sash gouging at her back, and the memory of saddling her mare in the predawn darkness, hands shaking, guts roiling.

Her hands did not shake as she sipped her tea—surely a sign of progress?

"As it happens, this question relates to wedding nights, though certainly not to my own. I'm sure Deene will acquit himself competently."

"Jenny suggested confidence in the same regard when I expressed my concern for you."

Another cake disappeared, while Eve mentally hopped over what Jenny had likely said, and forged on to even more difficult terrain. "My friend is concerned that on her wedding night, her husband might be disappointed to find his bride had suffered a lapse, one lapse, years previous."

"He might…?" Maggie's brows drew down. Eve ate the last cake with chocolate icing. The ones with almond icing started to appeal strongly as well.

Maggie nibbled a fingernail. "She's concerned he could detect her lapse, though it occurred years previous? Afraid the physical evidence of her purity was tangibly destroyed?"

Plain speaking. Even married and besotted with her earl, Maggie was still capable of breathtakingly plain speaking.

"That's it exactly. Will he be able to tell?"

The question lay between Eve and her sister, leaden and ugly, just as it lay between Eve and any hope of a decent future with Deene.

"Might your friend not ask a midwife?" Maggie was studying the teapot as if she'd never seen a teapot before.

"Midwives talk. My friend is watched over by her family very carefully, and even arranging such a meeting would be difficult."

Also beyond daunting.

"Benjamin knew." Maggie said this softly, her eyes taking on a distant quality. "He knew he was my first, though not until…"

"Not until he *was* your first. I see." Not the answer Eve had longed for desperately.

"Can't your friend take her intended aside and have a quiet talk with him?"

"I've asked her this myself many times." Countless times. "She does not want to make any premature or unnecessary disclosures, because if her intended reacts badly, then the choices are to cry off or to go through with a doomed marriage."

"But he might not react badly at all, and then your friend need not worry herself to death over nothing."

Might. Might was quite a word to hang one's entire future on. And if Eve cried off at Deene's insistence, would the idiot men in her family start cleaning their dueling pistols again?

They *might*.

"I will suggest to her again that she have this discussion with her fiancé, but there isn't much time—and if the man can't detect her lack of chastity, not much point, either."

Maggie's lips pursed while a silence stretched, and Eve tried to convince herself again that she should just tell Deene the exact nature of the bargain he was getting.

"Tell your friend something for me." Maggie chose now to spear Eve with a knowing, older-sister look. "Tell her that when she is tired of trying to manage everything on her own all the time, no matter the odds, a fiancé can be a very good sort of fellow to lean on, and a husband even better. I have learned this the hard way, Eve Windham, under circumstances Deene has my leave to acquaint you with. It is sound advice. Shall I ring for more cakes?"

Eve saw the plate was empty. Now, how had that happened?

"Yes, if you please. More of the chocolate, if you have them."

❦

"I want one more opportunity to talk you out of this marriage." Anthony kept his voice down, thank God. He knew as well as Deene did that the primary function of a gentlemen's club, besides providing a refuge from the long reach of female society, was fomenting gossip.

"Not here, Anthony. I'm on foot—perhaps you'd like to accompany me home."

They left amid the usual casual farewells and the occasional comment on Deene's upcoming nuptials.

"It's going to damned rain," Anthony muttered as they gained the streets. "Am I to hold my tongue all the way home, until we're behind a locked door, or might I make my case now?"

"I'm meeting with Westhaven later in the day, so you might as well unburden yourself now."

They paced along in silence, while Deene reflected

on the previous two weeks of being engaged. Were it not for the growing sense that Eve remained reluctant, they would have been two happy weeks. The debutantes and even the merry widows were leaving him in peace, his domestics were happy at the thought of a marchioness on the premises, and marital prospects had a way of improving a man's financial expectations as well—even in the face of Dolan's damned rumors.

And yet, Anthony was determined to piss on the parade.

"Until the moment the vows are spoken, Deene, I will oppose this marriage if for no other reason than that you're being coerced. The lady was in no way importuned, in no way publicly compromised, and this entire farce is unnecessary."

"I say it is necessary."

"I will damned marry, Deene. I've told you this more than once. I have a list of candidates we can select among this evening. She must be well born enough to serve as your hostess, or someday—may God forbid it ever be so—as the Marchioness of Deene."

Deene found himself walking faster. "Choose all you like and hope the candidate of your choice doesn't mind that tidy establishment in Surrey, because she'll find out, Anthony. The ladies always find out."

His mother had devoted much of her miserable marriage to finding out…

"I do not seek a romantic entanglement with any wife of mine, Deene. If she finds out, so be it. Ours will be a practical arrangement. The point is, I can provide you your heir without you having to make this sacrifice."

It was heartening to know Anthony's loyalty truly

ran so deep, and it was also disconcerting to admit Deene had questioned his cousin's integrity to any degree at all.

"So you marry and you even have a son or two, Anthony. Do you know how many sons of titled families I saw fall to the Corsican?"

"Younger sons, of course, the military being their preferred lot. Name me one heir, though, who came to grief in such a fashion."

"Lord Bartholomew Windham."

That shut Anthony up for about half a block, but as they approached the Denning townhouse, Anthony started up again. "I am not sending my offspring to war when the succession is imperiled. Do you think I'm stupid?"

"Of course you aren't stupid. His Grace, the Duke of Moreland, is not a stupid man, either, Anthony, but he lost one son to war and another to consumption. Other families have run through many more heirs than that and turned up without a title to show for it. I can't allow you to meet an obligation that is squarely, properly, and completely my own."

"Fine, then. Stick your foot in parson's mousetrap, but what of the girl?"

"Eve?" Deene glanced at his cousin. This was a new tack, a different argument. "I will make her a doting and devoted husband."

"For about two years at the most. Get some babies on her, and you'll be back to those feats of libidinous excess that have characterized the Marquis of Deene since the title was elevated from an earldom and likely before."

A nasty argument, one Deene would not entertain.

"How is it, Anthony, that you know better than I what sort of husband I shall be? My libidinous excesses, as you call them, date from five, even ten years ago—despite what gossip would inaccurately imply. I could dig into your past or the past of almost any man who came down from university with me and find similar excesses. What is your real objection to this match?"

While Deene waited for Anthony's answer, the first few drops of a drizzling rain pattered onto the cobbled walk. The scent in the air became damp and dusty at the same time—a spring scent, a fragrance almost.

"You want my real objection?" Anthony glanced around, but the threatening weather had apparently cleared the streets. "All right: my real objection is that you're forcing the girl into a union she neither sought nor wants. Bad enough when your sister was treated thus, and it ended tragically for Marie, didn't it? Now you're repeating history with your prospective bride, and that I cannot abide."

Anthony fell silent, while Deene absorbed a significant blow to the conscience.

"I am not forcing Eve Windham to do anything." Except... viewed from a certain angle, not that oblique an angle, perhaps he was.

"If you say so." Oh, the worlds of righteousness the man could put into such a platitude. "Shall I accompany you to this meeting with Westhaven?"

Because it dealt with finances, the question was logical. Because it was a change from a very uncomfortable topic, Deene answered it.

"You shall not. For once, the transaction flows

exclusively to our financial benefit, and that much I think I can handle on my own."

"About the household books…"

In the flurry of wedding preparations, Deene's focus on finances had slipped a bit—but only a bit. "I started on the ones you provided last week, Anthony, but with expenses one place and income another, I don't see how you keep track."

"One learns to, and that way, nobody else can take the measure of your worth with a single peek at the books. When this wedding business is behind you, we'll muddle through it all, I assure you."

This wedding business.

"I shall look forward to that. Don't wait dinner for me. I'll likely be dining with Eve and her family."

"Of course." Anthony looked like he might say more—apologize, perhaps, for his earlier broadside? "I will stand up with you at the wedding, Deene. Have no fear on that score."

"My thanks."

Grudging and belated, but perhaps that was an apology. Deene hurried into the house to change for his meeting with Westhaven—a negotiation Deene looked forward to. Yes, the settlements would benefit him, but they were also the last, necessary step to ensuring that the wedding actually happened.

Then too, it was not a crime for a man to profit from marrying a woman for whom he cared for a great deal. No crime at all. He had myriad uses for the money, not the least of which would be maintaining the kinds of establishments Eve deserved to have for her homes.

And he was *not* forcing Eve to the altar.

Likely thanks to Her Grace's influence with the Deity, the day of the wedding brought the most glorious spring weather London could offer. The Windham family had gathered en masse, including even the Northern contingent, represented by St. Just and his increasing coterie of female dependents—two daughters and one countess, plus a happy gleam in the man's eye that presaged further developments.

As His Grace eyed the packed pews of St. George's on Hanover Square, he reflected that a father better versed in the essential parental art of self-deception might be telling himself he was relieved to be seeing his youngest, smallest daughter off into the keeping of an adoring swain.

The organist took his seat while the crowd in the pews and balconies exchanged their final tidbits of greeting and gossip.

His Grace was not relieved. He himself had been the most adoring of swains once upon a time, and yet Her Grace had had her hands quite full with him, for at least the first ten or twenty years of their union.

Possibly more.

Marriage—a good, loving union such as the Almighty contemplated and sensible people longed for—was a damned lot of work, and much was going to be asked of Evie and her swain before His Grace could aspire to anything approaching relief on his daughter's behalf.

He turned back to the small chamber where Eve stood in her finery, and the sight caused something like a small seizure in his heart. Evie was so petite, but she'd been a fighter since she'd surprised them all by showing up several weeks prior to her expected birth date.

"Daughter, you are the most beautiful sight in the realm today."

She glanced up from her bouquet, an odd little gathering of pink and white heather, orange blossoms, and a few sprigs of hawthorn—for solitude, loveliness, and hope, if His Grace's memory served. Her expression was more anxious than radiant.

"Thank you, Papa. How much longer?"

He turned back toward the nave. "Not long. Your mother has taken her place."

Her Grace had been subdued in the carriage, but the duke suspected he understood why: they'd lost Eve in some sense seven years ago. Losing her again today revived the old aches, old doubts, and guilt. Since that long-ago day, there had been a chasm of bewilderment between Eve and her parents, one they all possessed enough love to want to breach, and yet the chasm remained.

His Grace turned his back on Polite Society in all its spring finery and once again surveyed his daughter. "Tell me something, Evie."

She set the bouquet aside and offered him a painfully brave smile. "Papa?"

"Why are you marrying Deene? Is it because I was wroth with him for trespassing on your... for taking liberties?"

She blinked, looking very like her mother after His Grace had made some inelegant remark before the children. "I was not comforted to think of either you, my brothers, or Deene coming to harm on your idiot field of honor, but that wasn't the entire reason."

His Grace closed the door to the chamber, signaling, he hoped, that he'd have an answer, and Polite Society could go hang until he did. "I should wish regard for your intended played some role. Deene's not a bad fellow."

"Lucas is a good man, and I esteem him greatly."

He crossed his arms, as that little recitation wouldn't fool the most dense of fathers.

"I've seen Deene's racing stables in Surrey, you know." She picked up her bouquet and started fussing the little sprigs of hawthorn. "It's a lovely place, very peaceful. We'll be there for the next few weeks, possibly through the Season."

Which His Grace took for a bit of genius on Deene's part. The newlyweds would get no peace in Kent or in Town. "What has this to do with marrying the man, Evie? And don't think to bamboozle your old papa. I was young once, and I know marriage is a daunting business even when you're entirely besotted with your intended."

She frowned. She did not smile hugely and assure him with a mischievous wink that she and Deene were quite besotted, though His Grace suspected, hoped, and prayed they were.

"When I was with Deene in Surrey last time, I helped birth a foal. The colt had a leg back, and the mare was small. I was best suited to aiding her, and Deene says the foal is thriving."

What this had to do with anything was… His Grace tried not to show his surprise. Eve had recently started driving out. That signal fact had contributed to her being unchaperoned at Lavender Corner, but it had also given Her Grace the first glimmer of hope Eve was "putting that whole sorry business behind her." Hope was a welcome if anxious burden for both of Their Graces.

"You always enjoyed foaling season, always enjoyed the stables." He made the observation cautiously, pretending to make a final inspection of the ducal regalia in the mirror while he instead studied his daughter's reflection.

"If I hadn't been there, Papa, the mare and foal both might have perished, or they'd have lost the mare for sure and tried to save the foal. But I was there, and Lucas allowed me to help her."

Lucas. That Eve thought of her prospective husband as Lucas was encouraging. Only Her Grace called His Grace by name, and likely conversely.

"I'm to name the colt, Papa, but it's as you used to say: you can't just slap a name on an animal willy-nilly, you must first learn who the beast is. I want to learn who that little, bucking, playing, gorgeous beast is."

He cracked open the door and peered into the church, lest he interfere with whatever point Eve was leading up to. "And you needed to marry Deene to do that?"

"Horses can live a long time, thirty years or more with luck and good care. Someday, I want to walk down to that colt's paddock with my granddaughter and feed the old boy some apples. I might tell her tales of his races and his sons, tell her how magnificent he was when he swept across the finish line, or what heart he had in the hunt field."

What on earth was she saying?

"I often enjoyed taking you children to the stables on fine summer evenings. You would talk to me then. I could have you to myself one or two at a time."

He'd forgotten this. It was a dear, dear memory, and he'd forgotten it.

Now she smiled at him, perhaps not radiantly, but genuinely.

"I have not forgotten those fine summer evenings, Papa. And when I take my granddaughter down to see my old friend, I will tell her he had to struggle very hard to come into the world and make his way here. I will tell her... he could have given up, but he didn't—he fought and struggled and eventually prevailed, and I did not give up on him either. Not ever, not for a single moment."

Good... God.

Mercifully for His Grace's composure, the organist chose that moment to begin the fanfare, sparing the duke from any reply. As he led his dear daughter up the aisle, past all the curious smiles and doting acquaintances, all he could think was that on her wedding day, Eve had talked to him of never giving up on a loved one, and of horses.

It had been seven years since she'd spoken to anybody of horses, and she'd chosen to start with her papa—which only made it harder today, of all days, to give her away.

∝∽

No thunderbolt had stopped the ceremony at the last minute; no messenger of God had spoken up to state a reason why the union should not go forward. Eve Windham had been pronounced a wife, though the bishop's voice had sounded as distant to her as the hunting horn blowing "gone away" on a far, windy hill.

"Eat something, Evie."

Deene bent close to her, his smile doting though concern lurked in his blue eyes.

"I couldn't possibly."

His smile slipped, and Eve wondered if they were to have another bad moment. They'd already avoided one when Deene had realized Mr. Dolan had been present at the wedding, little Georgina dutifully turned out in her finest, the governess looking a good deal more spruce at her side than when Eve had met them in the park.

"Perhaps you'd like to leave?" Deene made the offer quietly.

"May we?"

"At some point it's obligatory, if these good people are to truly indulge in the excesses of a ducal wedding breakfast."

"How do we do this?"

She did not want to leave with him, did not want to take any single step closer to the ordeal facing her at the end of the day, but neither could she abide the noise, the good wishes, the concerned looks from her family, and the increasing ribaldry from the guests.

And her wishes became moot, for Deene had apparently colluded with her brothers to choreograph the moment. At some subtle signal, Westhaven stood up and tapped his spoon against a delicate crystal glass.

"Friends, esteemed guests, beloved family—if I might have your attention?"

The long tables filled with guests grew silent as Westhaven went on speaking. "For reasons understandable to any who beholds my baby sister and her adoring groom, we must now bid Deene and his bride farewell. A round of applause to speed them on their way!" Westhaven lifted his glass, and Eve was scooped into her intend—her *husband's* arms. Deene had her out the door and bundled into a waiting carriage before the last guest stumbled onto the terrace, and then she was on her way to Surrey... and God knew what kind of confrontation with her intend—her husband.

"You had the grays put to. Papa likes to save them for special occasions because they look so smart with the black coach and red trim."

Deene gave her an odd smile, and it occurred to Eve that small talk wasn't going to get them very far. Not at this moment, not in this marriage.

"Eve?" He turned on the seat beside her and undid the veil and headpiece she'd worn all day. "This is a very special occasion."

"Oh. Of course."

He withdrew pins from her hair, making Eve realize how uncomfortable that part of her wedding ensemble had been. He had kissed her once outside the church as the reception line was forming, just a little buss to the cheek she'd found both fortifying and alarming.

"Come here, Wife."

Merciful heavens. To *have* a husband was one thing, to *be* a wife quite another. Deene's deft hands

had undone even her bun, so her hair hung down her
back in a braid.

"Husband."

"That would be me." His arm settled around
her shoulders.

"I'm practicing. I have neither had a husband before
nor been a wife. This will take some adjustment."

Now she was babbling. Deene shifted beside her,
so his fingers closed on her nape and gently kneaded
her neck. "We will adjust together. So far, I regard
my station as an improvement over the unwed state."

He wasn't teasing. "In what regard?"

"It's more peaceful, for one thing. I'm not prey to
the matchmakers, the rumors have lost a great deal of
their interest for everybody, and I can look forward
to spending much of the Season in our honey month
rather than being stalked like a sacrificial goat."

Not very romantic of him, but honest. "Did those
rumors trouble you?"

"A bit."

Maybe a decade from now she'd be able to fathom
exactly how much "a bit" was when uttered in just
that tone while Deene glanced out the window with
just that grim expression. Or maybe by then they'd be
entirely estranged.

"You were troubled when you saw Mr. Dolan and
Georgina at the wedding."

He scowled at the lovely spring day, probably
the first nasty expression Eve had seen on her...
husband's face.

"He had no business attending."

Did she pry, or did she back away and start mentally

listing the things they would tacitly agree not to discuss? "I don't think Her Grace gave it a thought when she made up the guest list, Deene. He's raising your niece and thus he's a part of your family. I gather you and he are not cordial?"

Eve would not pry, but she would invite.

"He all but killed my sister after making her endlessly miserable and ashamed. If I hold my father accountable for one thing, it's selling Marie into that grasping, ungrateful, ignorant vulgarian's arms."

The very lack of inflection in Deene's tone was chilling, particularly when Eve herself might be the object of her husband's ire before a few more hours had elapsed.

"He seems a devoted father for all that."

Deene was silent, while the countryside rolled along outside their window for a good portion of a mile. "Anthony had been courting Marie, a match she apparently welcomed. It made sense, they were enamored, and between themselves, I believe they had an understanding."

Eve took Deene's hand in hers. "And then?"

"And then Dolan came strutting along, all trussed up in purchased finery, and offered for her on terms my father didn't even attempt to refuse. Marie was wed to a stranger, one with no family to speak of, no gentility, nothing to recommend him except a growing fortune and a reputation for grasping at any opportunity for financial or social gain."

Something wasn't adding up, though Eve found it difficult to put her finger on the discrepancy. "If Marie was integral to Dolan's plans for betterment, he'd hardly treat her ill."

"She was seventeen years old, Eve. She'd been sheltered all of her life and fully expected to marry into the world she'd been raised in. She tried to talk me into getting her a horse so she could run off the day before the wedding, as if that option were any safer for her."

"How old were you?"

"Nearly thirteen."

What a burden to put on a boy, particularly a boy being raised to fill his papa's titled shoes. "How did she die, Lucas?"

He was silent for so long this time Eve thought he might not answer, and part of her didn't want him to. The tale had to be painful for him, and there would be enough to cope with on their wedding day without adding this recitation to it.

"She lost a child, and they could not stop the bleeding. She faded, and her last request to me was to make sure I took care of Georgie. Dolan will call the child only Georgina—he must ape his betters even in speech—but to Marie, she was Georgie."

Eve let her head rest against her husband's shoulder. "You fault him for getting her with child."

"Georgie's birth was not easy. I have no doubt the accoucheur had cautioned them against having more children, but to Dolan he'd bought and paid for a broodmare, and a broodmare he would make of her."

Many men regarded their wives in this light—many titled men, who would set the broodmare aside if she failed to produce. They'd find a way to nullify the union, strip their wives of any social standing or decent company, and set about procreating merrily with the next candidate, all with the complicity of both church and courts.

"You should know the skeletons in the Deene family closet, Eve, though I'm sorry to bring this up today of all days."

Were she any other bride, she'd like that he felt that way, like that he was confiding in her. "Windhams have their share of skeletons."

This earned her another curious smile, but rather than permit Deene to interrogate her, Eve closed her eyes and leaned her head back. "Weddings are tiring, don't you think?"

Her… husband did not reply.

Seven

DEENE'S WIFE WAS NOT ASLEEP ON HIS SHOULDER AS she'd have him believe, and she was nervous.

Like a procession of sensory still lifes, his memories of the day told him as much:

Eve's hand, slender and cold in his when he'd put the wedding ring on her finger.

Eve's cheek, equally cool when he'd been unable to deny himself the smallest display of dominion outside the church—and she had not kissed him in return.

Eve, clinging in her oldest brother's embrace for a desperately long moment, until St. Just's countess had touched her husband's arm and embraced Eve herself.

A whiff of mock orange coming to Deene's nose and bringing with it a sense of calm until he saw the way Eve gripped her wine glass so tightly he thought the delicate stem might break.

He'd been prepared for bridal nerves. He'd even been prepared for his own nerves—this was the only wedding night he ever intended to have, after all—but he had not been prepared for his wife to be on the verge of strong hysterics.

A change of plans was called for, or neither one of them would be sane by bedtime.

"Evie." He brushed her hair back from her temple. "Time to wake up, love. We must greet our staff."

She straightened and peered out the window. "So many of them, and this is not even your family seat."

Our family seat. He did not emphasize the point.

"Let me pin you up."

She turned on the seat while he fashioned something approximating a bun at her nape. The moment was somehow *marital*, and to Deene, imbued with significance as a result. Deene had laced up, dressed, and undressed any number of ladies, but there was nothing flirtatious in the way Eve presented to him the pale, downy nape of her neck. He kissed her there and felt a shiver go through her.

"You are going to be the sort of husband who is indiscriminate with the placement of his lips on my person, aren't you?"

She did not sound pleased.

"When we are private, probably. You always smell luscious, and I am only a man."

His wife looked surprised, but before she could argue with him, he handed her down and began moving with her along the line of waiting servants standing on the drive. They beamed and bobbed at her. She smiled back with such warmth and graciousness that Deene revised his earlier estimation of her state of mind.

She hadn't been anxious; she'd been terrified of what was to come—and likely still was. As soon as he scooped her up against his chest to carry her over the threshold, all the warmth left her expression, and the corners of her mouth went tight again.

Deene did not set her down when they gained the foyer but addressed the rotund factotum who'd hurried ahead to get the door for them.

"Belt, we'll take a tray in our sitting room, and my lady will be needing a soaking bath as soon as may be. We'll not be disturbed thereafter unless we ring. Understood?"

"Very good, my lord."

"Deene, you may put me down now."

He started up the steps. "Not a chance, Wife. You'll dither and dally and want a tour of the place from top to bottom, or get to talking about menus with the housekeeper. You would leave me to my agitated nerves and no consolation for them but the decanter."

They cleared the first landing. "Agitated nerves? You cannot possibly be serious, Deene."

He was, somewhat to his surprise. "Humor me, in any case."

She went quiet, now when he would have appreciated some chatter, some resistance, some measurable response to distract him from the perfect weight of her cradled in his arms. He reached what was to be their private suite and set Eve down on a blue brocade sofa by the windows.

"You'll have to assist me out of this attire, Wife. I haven't worn such finery since I took my seat in the damned Lords, and even then it was mostly robes…"

She was up off the sofa, wandering around the room. "I haven't seen these chambers before."

She hadn't seen her husband completely naked

before either, but Deene doubted she'd inspect him quite as assiduously as she was peering at the titles of the books on the shelves in the corner. He came up behind her and put his arms around her waist.

"Evie, have mercy upon me and help me get undressed."

She turned, and he did not step back, so they remained in a loose embrace. "Haven't you a valet, Deene?"

"I'm married now. Many married fellows make do with a handy and accommodating wife, the last I recall the arrangements."

"My father…" She paused and started working the sapphire cravat pin loose from all the lace at his throat.

"Your father is old-fashioned in the extreme. I'm not. What was St. Just whispering in your ear about in the receiving line?"

By virtue of one question after another, one article of clothing after another, she eventually got him out of all but his knee breeches. He took pity on her enough to slip into the dressing room between their bedrooms and exchange the last of his wedding finery for a dressing gown and loose trousers, by which time a quantity of food had arrived in the sitting room.

"We are certainly getting the royal treatment," Deene observed. "Belt himself wheeled that cart in, did he not?"

"Belt." Eve shoved a book back onto the shelf. "I will recall his name because butler and Belt both begin with *B*."

This was important to her. Getting out of her wedding dress was apparently not.

"Let me be your lady's maid, Evie." He wanted to take her in his arms and whisper this in her pretty ear, but she was looking quite… prickly.

"I thought my maid came down from Morelands to join this household?"

"And she's no doubt in the kitchen, partaking of the general merriment occasioned by our nuptials. Hold still." He moved around behind her and started divesting her of all the layers of clothing hiding her from his view. When she stood only in a sheer white chemise—with a hem lavishly embroidered in gold, blue, and green—Deene took a step back and shrugged out of his dressing gown.

"Take this. The fires aren't lit yet, and until my naked body is draped over your delectable and satisfied person, it will keep you warm."

She looked like she wanted to say something off-putting, so he kissed her on the mouth—a swift, no-you-don't kiss that worked only because he kept his hands to himself rather than pull her tight against his body.

His lady wife took her revenge by shutting the dressing room door when the bath had been delivered. Deene let the wine breathe while he stared at the door and pictured his naked and curvaceous wife all rosy and delicious in her solitary bath. By the time she emerged an hour later, Deene had lowered the level in the champagne bottle by more than half, and the sun had set.

"Shall we light some candles?" Eve asked—perhaps a shade too cheerfully.

"Let's not. Let's light the fire and enjoy the shadows."

She pulled his dressing gown closer around her, but Deene's lust had been riding him hard, and he could tell she wore nothing beneath the velvet and silk of his clothing.

"My bath revived me," Eve said, still standing in the dressing room doorway. "I'm quite famished."

Deene said nothing. The food was before him on the low table in front of the sofa, and Eve was across the room. Unless he was to toss strawberries at her, she'd have to approach him.

"I've started the first bottle, Wife. Shall you imbibe?"

"Just a bit, if you please."

While she perched on the first three inches of the sofa cushion, Deene held his wine glass up to her mouth. She sipped about as much as would inebriate a small Methodist bird.

For a few minutes, he tried—he honestly did—to feed her. She responded with an increasing number of agitated and unhappy looks, until Deene realized the situation was growing desperate.

And between when a man thinks he needs to say something and when the words start spilling from his idiot mouth, insight befell him: Eve's nerves, her quiet hysteria, whatever she was grappling with, it had to do with her accident.

There would be no teasing her past it, no getting her just tipsy enough, no cajoling or tickling her into more confidence than she honestly possessed. Deene set the wine glass down and rose.

"Come to bed, Evie."

"To... *bed*?"

If she'd been pale before, she was a wraith now.

"Going to bed is a signal part of the wedding-night festivities, unless you'd rather spend a few moments before the fire?"

"I would. I very much would. My hair, you see, is

still damp, and it goes all to a frazzle if I don't…" Her voice trailed off, and Deene kept his hand extended to her. When she put her fingers on his palm, they were again—still—ice cold.

It was time to end this. Not because banked lust was beating a physical pulse in Deene's brain, but because Eve deserved to put these nerves, this lapse of faith in herself—whatever it should be called—behind her. When she came to her feet, he kissed her.

He kissed her the way he'd been longing to kiss her for three weeks, with tenderness and passion and even a little frustration—anger, maybe?—that Eve would bear any lingering burden from a situation she could not have been responsible for.

"Come." He took her by the hand and led her to the hearth, pausing to retrieve a pair of thick quilts from the dressing room before settling beside her before the fire. "You are nervous, Wife. I would have you explain to me the basis for your disquiet."

"Wife."

"That would be you."

She drew her knees up and laid her cheek on them. "I am not nervous."

He had the sense she was being honest, which was not encouraging. If she was not nervous, then she was afraid. "There is not one damned thing to be anxious about, Eve Denning. I am the one who has grounds for worry, for it falls to me to ensure your experiences are wholly pleasurable."

"You do not appear to suffer doubt on this score."

Her voice was calm enough, but he'd seen her start

when he used her married name. "I suffer a proper respect for the challenge before me. Perhaps a kiss for courage won't go amiss."

Her hesitation was minute, but then she went up on her knees and kissed him on the mouth. Deene took her by the shoulders and let himself topple back so she was sprawled on top of him.

"That is not a kiss such as would encourage a horny flea, my love."

"A what?"

"Horny, which indelicate term means a Mister Flea who is hot for his Missus."

"You are being vulgar and ridiculous."

Her tone was prim, but his vulgar ridiculousness was working, because she hadn't moved off him, and her expression bore a hint of curiosity. Deene wrapped his arms around her and started rubbing her back lest she take a notion to retreat.

"Allow me to demonstrate, Marchioness."

He set his mouth to hers and his will to her seduction. By slow degrees, he investigated her mouth and invited her to do likewise with him, to taste and tease, to explore, to indulge. Somewhere in that kiss, he positioned her so she was straddling him, and he arranged their clothing so he was naked beneath her and they were pressed breasts to chest.

"Deene." She pulled back and closed the dressing gown.

"I don't know what you're fretting over, Evie. We've two enormous, fluffy beds to choose from when it comes time to consummate our vows."

"So we're just to indulge in these courageous kisses?" By the firelight, her skepticism was evident.

"Precisely so. Kiss me. I was beginning to feel somewhat encouraged."

She started to smile. He wanted to howl with impatience when he saw caution overtake the curving of her lips. Instead, he palmed her breast through the silk of the dressing gown.

"You're feeling frisky," Eve said, watching his hand on her person.

"I'm feeling married." He levered up by virtue of a dedicated equestrian's abdominal strength, and continued to fondle her while he reinitiated an openmouthed kiss.

Her control slipped a gratifying degree when Deene applied a gentle pressure to one nipple.

"Husband…" She breathed the word, infused it with a touch of surprise, and graced it with a hint of wonder. He repeated the caress, and she went still, as if her body were listening for the sensations a man intent on pleasuring his lady could create with just his thumb and first finger.

Before she could start *thinking* about it, Deene rolled with her, so he was above her and she was on her back beneath him.

"Are all husbands as inclined to move their wives about like so much dry goods?"

"Touch me the way I touched you, Evie. We'll see who's dry goods."

She frowned but ran one palm down his chest. "This hair…" She ruffled it, which had Deene's vitals ruffling as well. He didn't push his erection any more snugly against her, but neither did he make any effort to disguise it.

"Is it to your liking, Lady Deene?"

"It's…" She ran her nose through the dusting of hair on his chest, the oddest, most erotic, endearing touch Deene had ever withstood. "It's peculiar. Soft, but… male. Manly. Even your chest smells good, Deene. I do approve of a fellow who takes his hygiene seriously."

There followed a bit of torture, while Eve—apparently secure in the notion that marriages could not be consummated on the floor—made a scientific study of Deene's chest. She listened to his heart. She tentatively, then more firmly, touched his nipples.

The sizzle of pleasure that set off in places low and reproductive had Deene clenching his jaw.

She sniffed at him, and while submitting to all these experiments and investigations, Deene subtly shifted himself above her, until his cock was nestled against the glorious damp heat that was his wife's sex.

Damp. Thank a merciful God she was damp. Her body was ready for what came next, even if her courage was not. When Eve ran her tongue over Deene's right nipple, he lowered himself more closely to her and got one arm around her shoulders.

"Evie?"

"Husband." She blinked up at him. He saw the moment she realized how close their bodies were to joining. As she drew in a breath—no doubt to start another round of prevarications and peregrinations, Deene eased himself forward between her folds.

"Thank Almighty God in a rosy and joyous heaven, that would be me." He pressed forward one inch, the distance between being a mendicant at the gates of marital bliss and a husband in possession of the key to domestic heaven.

"Lucas?"

He kissed her, a hot, lazy, inflammatory kiss to hide the pleasure and triumph coursing through his blood. "Hmm?"

While Eve fell silent, blinked some more, and lifted a hand only to let it fall beside her head, he eased forward the next blissful inch.

"We are not on the… bed."

"We'll get to the bed, Evie. Are you all right?"

God love the woman, she cocked her head as if to consider her answer. Deene started up a slow, shallow rhythm, easing his way to a fuller joining, listening intently for any sign that Eve's bodily welcome was not as comfortable for her as he'd prayed it would be.

"I am… all right."

"That is quite too bad."

She tensed. "I beg your pardon?"

"All right will never suffice. We are consummating our vows. I would have you in transports. Move with me, Evie."

"Move…?"

He slowed his rhythm more, until she created a sinuous counterpoint to the undulations of his hips, until he was plying her with such focus and purpose it was as if she were inside his body every bit as much as he was inside hers.

"Still all right, Evie?"

"Mmm." She scooted a little, changing the angle to lock her ankles at the small of his back. The shift was slight and devastating.

"God in heaven, Wife…" His breathing grew harsh, and yet he held off. He did not want her in transports, he *needed* her in transports—and ecstasies and delights and entire floods of pleasure—before he could think of spending.

Her legs tightened around him, he felt her finger-nails gripping his buttocks with a sweet, fierce sting.

And yet for a few more interminable moments, he held off.

"Evie… let go."

Her breath came harsh against his throat as she started panting. "I can't get my… I can't…"

"You *shall*…" He anchored a hand under her derriere and held her steady for an onslaught of deep, measured thrusts that sent her over the edge. With her mouth open on his neck, he heard and felt the low, keening moan that slipped from her and felt the way her body seized around his cock in glorious, fisting spasms of gratification.

In the middle of it, as her passion was cresting audibly, she found his free hand, laced her fingers with his, and whispered his name.

He could not have held off at that moment to save his soul.

❧

In the days following her wedding, Eve dwelled in an ever-expanding bubble of emotion characterized predominantly by the joy of one whose hopes and dreams have received not just a stay of execution, but a full, unconditional, royal pardon.

She was married—happily, joyously married—and

not to some mincing, left-handed cipher, or a fortune hunter of dubious motives, but to a man whom she liked and esteemed *greatly*. She had chosen not just well, she had chosen wonderfully and wisely.

Better still, she'd chosen a man who showed her both affection and desire in abundance. That she'd been starving for both was a sobering realization, one that threw into high relief just how contorted she'd allowed her view of herself to become.

Of course she desired her husband—what sane woman would not want Lucas Denning in her bed?

Of course she enjoyed his company. He was charming, devoted, and open with her in a way she hadn't expected but supposed characterized even her parents' marriage behind closed doors.

The desire took her breath away, but the affection... Deene stole her heart with the pleasure he seemed to take in simply touching her and being in her company. They ate every meal together unless Deene was off in Town, meeting with his solicitors, and that was just the start of ways he found to share her company.

"You'll come down to the stables when you've met with Mrs. Belt?"

Deene passed three juicy strawberries from his plate to hers. He'd had strawberries delivered to their rooms last night long after dark, and what he'd done with a mere, unprepossessing fruit... and that was before he'd started with the chocolate sauce.

Eve studied the treat on her plate and mentally reviewed what her husband had asked her. "I'll be down as soon as we've established a schedule for the maids and footmen, worked out next week's menus, arranged for the windows to be cleaned both inside and out, and—"

He put a finger to her lips. "And then you'll come down to see us turn out your foal with his playmates for the first time."

"Yes, Husband." He did not understand that a household would not run itself, and having the maids clean the insides of the windows a month after the footmen cleaned the outsides meant the windows were never truly clean.

He kissed her on the lips and left her in a rosy, happy silence, contemplating the masculine pulchritude of his retreating form. She was still contemplating it when her sister-in-law, Anna, the Countess of Westhaven, came to call at midmorning.

"I was on my way into Town from Willow Bend and thought I'd just peek in. If you weren't yet out of bed, I would have been on my merry way."

Evie linked her arm through Anna's and drew her along a path winding between beds of blooming irises. "You would have reported to the entire family that I was having a lie-in in the first week of my marriage, and Their Graces would have started getting ideas."

Anna's eyes lit with mischief. "Westhaven and I were nearly bedridden the first three months of our marriage. I know he's your brother, but I want you to understand that the term wedded bliss can be grounded in fact, Eve."

"We are not… bedridden." Not when Deene could accost her in the linen closet, the butler's pantry, the saddle room, *and* their bed.

"Are you happy with your choice, Evie?" Anna took a bench in the morning sun, and Eve settled beside her.

"I am quite, quite happy with my husband and with the state of holy"—horny, as Deene termed it—"matrimony. Deene is very considerate."

Doting would have been a more accurate word.

"Considerate, bah." Anna's full mouth flattened. "Considerate, cordial, amicable, civilized. Such words have no place in the vocabulary of those newly wed. Your brothers are worried about you, Eve Denning. They like Deene, but they will cheerfully geld him if he's not being a proper husband to you."

St. Just had vowed as much on Eve's very wedding day. "I should not like my husband gelded."

Anna, blast her, waited while Eve tried to sort out the thoughts she could admit aloud from the ones she'd carry with her to her grave.

"I believe Deene has been lonely."

Anna rearranged her skirts. "Go on."

"He seems to want not just… not just to exercise his marital rights, but to have my company. I'm to join him for all of our meals. I'm to watch the lads with the horses. Deene says I have an instinct for what's needed to make a horse-and-rider combination a partnership and more experience at it than I realize."

She'd been particularly pleased with that compliment.

"One hopes a new husband would comment on his wife's obvious gifts."

Obvious, perhaps, though Eve herself had lost sight of that one. "I had not realized Deene has such an affectionate nature."

"In what regard?"

This was an interrogation, plain and simple, and yet Eve wanted to share the state of her marriage—the wonderful state of her marriage—with somebody. "He likes to touch me and not just... all kinds of touches. He takes my hand. He puts his arm around my waist or my shoulders. When he takes a seat beside me, there's no decorous space between us, even if we're in company or before the servants. He's like... a cat, or a dog. Proximity seems to comfort him."

Brushing her hair comforted him, assisting her to dress and undress comforted him, feeding her, and most wonderful of all—cuddling up the entire night long, not just for a few minutes of postcoital lassitude, comforted him each and every night.

Eve admitted to herself that she took comfort from all these casual generosities on Deene's part too. They nourished her confidence in some way she could not describe and fed some other emotion she wasn't likely to discuss with anybody, ever.

"This is all very encouraging, Evie. Never forget to demonstrate to your husband that you appreciate his trust in this regard."

His *trust*? "Whatever do you mean?"

The smile Anna sported now was diabolically sweet. "I realize Westhaven is a doting and affec- tionate brother devoted to his family, but it might surprise you to know that as a husband, he was initially plagued with a certain reticence."

Reticence ought to have been one of Gayle's several middle names. "I am dumbfounded to hear this."

Anna sailed along, either missing the irony or

choosing to ignore it. "He required reassurances that his small displays of affection and protectiveness were not merely tolerable but welcome."

Westhaven requiring reassurances was an intriguing notion. "Do tell."

"I take my lead from him, of course, but try not to miss an opportunity to reciprocate his advances. If I do not assure him I am charmed by his devotion, he might fall prey to doubt. Doubt is the serpent in the marital garden, Eve. Self-doubt, doubt in one's partner. You must protect your husband from such a torment. Even when he is a ninnyhammer and cannot bring himself to ask you simple questions, you must give Deene the simple answers."

My, my, my. Being married was becoming marvelously complicated. "It shall be my pleasure to offer Deene all the reassurances he could possibly want."

Anna fell silent for one moment while a breeze sprang up and brought the scent of the stables into the garden. "The simple answers too. You tell him you're glad to be his wife. You tell him you desire him. You tell him you care for him. The actions suited to the words have more meaning when you give your husband both... And then..."

"Then?"

"One fine, fine day, you will find him giving you the words too—if he hasn't already."

He had not. This realization was troubling. Not troubling enough to constitute a serpent of doubt, exactly, but a small point to consider.

"Can you stay for tea, Anna?"

"I would not impose. You've been glancing toward

the stables since I arrived. I hazard Deene will find an excuse to seek you out in the next ten minutes if I do not take my leave."

Anna was as good as her word, tooling on her way after more smiles and hugs, leaving Eve to change into attire suitable for the stables and go in search of her husband. As she wandered through the garden, Eve took a minute to savor another darkly potent emotion coloring all her days.

She felt... *vindicated*. Fiercely, unendingly vindicated, for having held her peace for more than seven years, for having carried in her heart the true dimensions of her folly as a much younger woman. For having never told a single soul the exact extent of her heartache and loss.

Never again would the name of her malefactor be allowed to form even in her mind. She had, by virtue of relentless determination and a willingness to bear a load of sheer, nerve-wracking anxiety, been given a fresh start—in her marriage, in her *life*.

She fully intended to grab that fresh start with both hands, and to never let go.

If that meant she continued to bear alone the full measure of her regrets and losses, then she'd gladly bear that lonely burden. She was not foolish enough—innocent enough—to believe a gift the magnitude of her fresh start could be won without some private cost that must, *must* remain forever hers alone.

❧

"My lord, we must continue to advise you against pursuing this course."

Hooker appropriated not the royal "we," not even the pontifical "we," but a new pronoun, the *legal* "we." Deene had been hearing it a lot in the past few weeks, and with each hearing, it grated all the more.

Hooker inhaled audibly, no doubt ready with another sermon about the follies of bringing suit against a father whom nobody could seriously criticize, despite—"albeit, granted, nevertheless, and notwithstanding"—Dolan's deplorable antecedents and regrettable associations with trade.

"Stow it, Hooker." Deene gathered up the papers that had at long last been drafted for submission to the courts. "I will read these in the next several days, make any needed corrections, and expect to have suit joined by this time next week." Deene rose, rolling the bundle into a neat sheaf and holding it out to the thin clerk to be tied with a red ribbon.

"If it is your lordship's wish, we shall proceed with all due, deliberate, and purposeful haste, however there is the small matter of the, um, fees, for the filing and so forth."

In other words, unless Hooker's bill was brought up to date, there would be some delay in the filing of the petition, then another delay involving some redrafting, then a delay to further research some specious detail, all of which would add substantially to the unpaid bill.

"Have you an accounting prepared, Hooker?"

"It so happens I do, your lordship." He snapped his fingers at the clerk, who melted from the room. "Allow me the honor, your lordship, of congratulating you on your recent nuptials. I understand one must act with dispatch sometimes in arranging the ceremony, though might I inquire as to when the settlement negotiations will take place?"

This question, with its unflattering implications toward Deene and his bride, Hooker did not ask before his minion.

Deene tugged on a pair of riding gloves. "The negotiations are concluded. I've reached a private agreement between me and the Windham family, a copy of which is kept with my personal papers, and another given into the keeping of the lady's brother, the Earl of Westhaven. The arrangements did not affect the business of the marquessate."

"That is very unusual, my lord."

"I want control of my situation, Hooker, just as I want control of my niece's future. I should hope you are clear on that point, if no other."

The clerk returned with another sheaf of papers bundled together, this time with a gold ribbon. Such wits, these lawyers.

"I'll bid your lordship good day, then. Again, congratulations, my lord."

Deene did not leave in any particular hurry, but the more time he spent among his solicitors, the more he dreaded the very scent of the place: old books, anxiety, and greed. That he would pollute the early days of his marriage with these trips to Town was a measure of how desperately he wanted to resolve Georgie's situation.

He was unmercifully plagued with the knowledge that he had yet to fully explain the matter to Evie. He waited for a quiet moment when he might casually mention it, but the quiet moments were so precious with his new wife, and they invariably became, or immediately followed, passionate moments.

He sought for a pause in the activities in the stables when he might casually pass along some relevant asides, but how to frame such a problem as this?

"By the way, I'll be plunging us into scandal and penury, attempting to gain custody of my niece."

"Don't take this amiss, but I'll be wrecking the peace of our union by litigating a family issue in public."

Almighty God in heaven, he had to tell her and soon, before some well-meaning gossip—or Windham family member—decided to see to the matter. If his marriage was to enjoy one-tenth of the potential he sensed it had, then he must find a way to make Eve understand Georgie's situation, and soon.

Deene climbed into his coach, equally preoccupied with the thought of joining his wife for dinner and the notion that he ought to pay a call on Dolan and make one last offer to settle Georgie's future like… civilized men.

"Gentleman" being too far a stretch for such a one as Deene's brother-in-law.

"Was this meeting any more successful than its predecessors?"

Anthony lounged against the squabs, looking as if he'd had nothing better to do than catch a nap in the middle of the afternoon.

"You've taken to lurking in coaches, Cousin?" Deene settled beside him on the forward-facing seat.

"Discretion seemed the better part of valor, and no,

I didn't plan on this. Rather than loiter in the street, I appropriated a bit of privacy. I didn't know you'd be in Town today."

"I did not particularly want to be in Town, but the pleadings in Georgie's case are finally drafted."

Anthony smiled faintly. "So holy matrimony is agreeing with you?"

"Quite."

His cousin's smile became wolfish. "And your marchioness, is she similarly pleased with the institution?"

The question rankled. "It is my pleasure and duty to ensure she is."

Anthony's smile faltered. "Quaint, Deene. I give it two years or one healthy son, whichever shall first occur, and you'll be living separately."

"I believe we've had this discussion. How goes the planting in Kent?"

Deene managed to keep the conversation oriented toward innocuous matters until they reached the Mayfair townhouse. The footmen were waiting outside the coach, the steps in place, when it occurred to Deene that marriage had put an option in his hands he needed to exercise.

"Eve and I will be spending more time in Town as time goes on, Anthony."

"Is it wise to be showing her off when the rumors are still circulating at a great rate?"

"I want her to show me off, you idiot. The wedding should have the rumors scotched quite neatly."

Now Anthony looked pained.

"Spit it out, Cousin. I was going to say I'd understand if you wanted your own establishment in Town, since dwelling with a pair of newlyweds might not be to your taste."

Anthony's brows rose. "My own...? You think I'd desert the cause now, when just last night some jackass had the temerity to intimate your situation with Georgina might be comparable to Byron's with his half sister?"

Rage welled at Anthony's quiet question. Rage and a determination to see Jonathan Dolan ruined. Byron was rumored to be the father of his half sister's third child, though proving such a thing was impossible.

"Who said that?"

"I will *not* tell you. The man was far into his cups, and his fellows shut him up immediately with apologies and excuses all around. I did not want you to know, because now you'll challenge Dolan and you a newlywed and it all just being talk and a duel being no better for Georgina's situation than outright murder."

"Talk that vicious is going to ruin Georgina's life, Anthony. Dolan has to be stopped."

But why *now*? Why must this issue be coming to *point non plus* now, when all Deene wanted was to spend time with his wife?

Very likely because Dolan had planned it that way.

"If I need a second, Anthony, will you serve?"

"Of course. Is there anybody else you'd like me to speak to?" The reply was gratifyingly swift and certain.

"Not yet. Even asking such a thing will fuel the rumors."

"Then I shall keep my counsel and wait for further orders from you. My regards to my new cousin, the marchioness."

Anthony climbed out, and when Deene wanted to head directly for Surrey, he instead followed his cousin into the town house, wrote several notes to be delivered by messenger, and only then allowed himself to turn his direction toward home.

❧

"My love, I grow concerned."

Kesmore's expression suggested he wasn't quite teasing, though in the course of their marriage, he teased his lady wife a great deal.

"Then I am concerned as well," Louisa replied. She had to stifle a yawn as she spoke though, since his lordship's version of a late-afternoon nap could leave even a stalwart wife more drowsy than refreshed.

"Such loyalty." Kesmore rolled to blanket her naked body with his own. "I should kiss you for it." He did, a lovely, thoughtful coda to the beautiful composition that was Joseph Carrington in an amorous mood.

When Louisa could form coherent sentences again, she seized the moment. "What's bothering you, Joseph?" Whatever it was, it could not be of too great moment, given that her husband's body was indicating a notion to add another *movement* to his most recent marital sonata.

He nuzzled her neck. "I got a note from Deene this morning, delivered out from Town by private messenger."

No man had ever used his nose to such great advantage in the course of marital relations. Louisa's husband had a way of breathing her in, canvassing her features with his proboscis, gathering her scents the way other husbands might gather up compliments to toss back at their wives.

"That tickles, Husband."

"Tickling is a fine thing, you might consider—given the magnitude of your devotion to my ever-precarious well-being—reciprocating. How well do you know Deene?"

Louisa did not tickle her husband. If the man wanted tickling, he was going to have to beg for it. She did, however, meet his gaze and saw his question was serious.

"Very well. He's a lifelong neighbor, he served with Bart and St. Just, he's of the same political persuasion as Papa most of the time, and he was always underfoot as a boy because he had neither male siblings nor much family with whom to associate."

"And he served with me, and now he is family in fact. A situation is brewing, and while I do not know the exact extent of it, I believe Deene and his lady need our help."

Louisa loved her husband for any number of reasons: because he was a wonderful father, because he made her feel like the loveliest woman on earth, because he was protective of those he cared for right down to the smallest runt piglet ever to squeal its way into their keeping.

At that moment, she loved him because he had neither charged off to Deene's aid without confiding in her, nor had he even considered such a notion. To be married to Joseph Carrington was to have not just an adoring and passionate husband, but to have a friend, a best, most loyal, devoted friend, and—almost as wonderful—to be that sort of friend to him as well.

Louisa brushed his hair back from his brow,

wrapped her legs around his flanks, and kissed him on the mouth. "Tell me what's to be done, Husband. If there's something amiss with Deene, then it's amiss with our Evie too, and that we cannot allow."

It took another half hour, but when they did get around to discussing the matter further, they were—as usual regarding anything of consequence—of one mind about it.

❧

"You see how Aelfreth looks down and to the left?"

Deene saw no such thing. He saw the way his wife never took her eyes off the combination of Aelfreth and King William as they circled the practice arena. She had the same focus in bed sometimes, even when her eyes were dreamy with heat and desire.

"And the significance of this?"

"It's a matter of attention, Deene. Aelfreth signals the horse to pay attention in the same direction just by where he looks."

"For God's sake, Eve, the horse can't see where the man on his back is looking."

A particular dimple flashed on the left side of Eve's mouth. Deene had only recently discovered this dimple, and it fascinated him.

"When I'm… sitting on you, Deene, straddling your lap, and your eyes are closed, can you tell where I'm looking?"

"Of course."

"Tell Aelfreth to lift his eyes up, then, unless you want William thinking the only interesting things in the arena are on the ground to the left of him. He'll eventually go crooked like that if you don't break Aelfreth's habit now."

"This is just a schooling session, Evie, a little variety in the routine. When they're on course, Aelfreth will be looking from jump to jump, from straightaway to turn."

She folded her arms, looking as prim as a governess. "Every time we're around King William, we're teaching him something, Deene. I have explained this to you."

She had, and her little lectures and homilies were charming—also very insightful, and in just the two weeks his marchioness had been in residence, Deene could see a difference in the way his equine youngsters and their lads were going on.

He bellowed at Aelfreth that the marchioness said to look the hell where he was going, which provoked a sheepish grin from the jockey—and immediate compliance such as Deene's command alone would likely not have merited.

"You've made slaves of my lads, Wife. The horses are no better."

"Such flattery. Are we to drive out today?"

If the weather was fine, they'd taken to picnicking at various secluded spots on the property. Sometimes Deene made love to his wife in the lazy afternoon sunshine, sometimes he dozed with his head in her lap, and sometimes—the times he suspected they both liked the most—they mostly talked.

"I had something else in mind today."

Her expression became... guarded. "Husband, we got a late start this morning because you had something else in mind, and while I always enjoy what you have in mind—"

"As I enjoy what you occasionally have in mind, Wife, but this is not that kind of something else."

And still she was wary. When it came to love-making, Eve took a little—a very little—convincing to try new things. Whether it was a new position, a new location, a new variation on something he'd shown her previously, she always hesitated:

"Lucas, this cannot be decent…"

"Husband, I am not at all sure…"

"Deene, are you quite certain *things* can go that way…?"

She was not shy, exactly, so much as she lacked confidence in her responses—or confidence in her entitlement to enjoy the God-given passion of her own nature.

And yet, she always gathered her courage and met him halfway, something he loved about her almost as much as he loved the way she gave him small touches and caresses throughout the day.

"Where are you taking me, Deene?"

He laced his fingers with hers and drew her in the direction of the unused foaling stalls. "This is a surprise, Evie. I wanted to give you this surprise the morning after our wedding."

"You did give me a surprise, as I recall."

He'd awakened her with an introduction to the pleasures of making sweet, sleepy love spooned around each other amid the warmth of the covers.

"One can't offer his new wife too many pleasant surprises."

"Is this a pleasant surprise then?"

Always, the wariness. "I hope and pray you find it so." At the serious note in his voice, Eve paused to peer over at him. He could not back out now, and maybe because of that, the vague anxiety in his chest gathered into a tighter knot. "If you don't like this surprise, you don't have to keep it. I can send it back."

She resumed their progress, moving into the mostly empty barn. "This is a gift then?"

"Customarily, a husband presents his wife with a token of his esteem following consummation of the nuptials."

"You are being sentimental, then. I love it when you dote on me, Deene, but I understand we must be mindful of the economies, and I'd have you freed from any—"

She stopped dead outside a roomy stall bedded in fresh, deep straw.

"Lucas, what have you done? Good God... what have you done?"

❧

Eve could not draw breath. She could only stare and cling to her husband's hand.

"I am going to faint."

"You shall not." Deene moved behind her and wrapped his arms around her, a bulwark against the roaring in her ears and the constriction in her chest. "Breathe, Evie. It's just one more horse."

Oh, but not just any horse. Eve knew those gorgeous brown eyes, the deep chest, the little snip of pink skin on the end of the mare's big, velvety nose.

"She's white now, no longer gray. This is my Sweetness, isn't it? Tell me this is my dearest... oh, Husband. *What have you done?*"

"I can send her back, if you'd rather not... I didn't want to upset you, Evie. But you'd asked, and I thought perhaps you'd worried..."

"Hush." She turned in his arms to put her hand over his mouth, but then craned her neck to keep the mare in her sight. "Oh, hush. She will never leave my care again, never. You must *promise* me, Lucas. Right now, swear to me she is mine to keep."

"She is yours to keep, always. I swear it, vow it, and promise it. It's in the settlements, it's in the bill of sale, it's in my last will and testament. She will always be yours to keep."

That he would do such a thing and do it so thoroughly... Eve could not hold to her husband tightly enough, could not take her eyes from the mare even when tears made the horse's image blurry.

And while Deene stroked Eve's back and held her upright on her shaking knees, Eve did breathe. She breathed in, she breathed out, and she made a tremendous discovery. The emotion welling up from her soul made her lungs feel too small and her heart beat hard in her chest. It affected her perceptions, slowed down her senses of sound and vision, made her sense of scent more acute. In many particulars, her body was mistaking the moment for one of anxiety approaching panic.

Except... except her husband held her securely, and her mind understood now—seven years later—that the other casualty of Eve's great fall was well and happy.

The mare was content, in good weight. Sweetness's eyes bore the same steady, clear gaze Eve had long associated with her, and her coat was blooming with good health and proper nutrition.

Eve's physical symptoms might resemble panic, but the emotions flooding her were gratitude, relief, and overarching all others, what she felt was soaring, unbounded, bottomless joy.

Eight

DEENE DID NOT RUSH HER, SO EVE KNEW NOT HOW long she stood suffused with happiness outside the mare's stall. The lightness in her body was... celestial, like flying over a whole course of jumps in perfect footing, from perfect spots, in perfect rhythm, to perfect landings.

Like riding this very mare.

When Eve had thoroughly abused Deene's handkerchief and probably her husband's poor nerves as well, she managed a question. "Is she sound?"

She felt the tension ease out of him, as if all through her weeping he'd been holding his breath. "Dead sound. She rides to hounds, Evie, and the squire who parted with her said she's his best afternoon horse."

Sound, indeed. "All this time, all these *years*, I've wondered, but I haven't known how to ask. I haven't known whom to ask. I have prayed for this horse nightly, prayed she was not suffering a painful life, longing for her misery to end, or worse..."

He gently pushed Eve's head to his chest. "She has been in the care of a hounds-and-horses fellow by the name of Belmont, farther south of us. He gave her a year off then bred her twice. Her first foal has been under saddle for a year, which is probably the only reason he allowed me to buy her. Her progeny—both fillies—show every sign of having their dam's good sense and heart."

"Then St. Just chose very well for her. I must thank him."

"There's something else you have to do, Evie."

Sheltered against Deene's body, Eve knew exactly what he intended to say. It should provoke all the panic she hadn't felt at the sight of the mare. It should have her ears roaring again and her hands going cold.

"You want me to ride her."

"No." He held her so gently. "What I want does not matter. I hope you believe that. What matters—the only thing that matters at all—is what you want, and what you want at this moment, Eve Denning, more than anything in the world, maybe more than you've *ever* wanted anything, is to be up on your mare again."

There was... a tremendous gift in being known and understood like this. A relief from loneliness at a fundamental level. There was healing in it, and more joy, and also... *truth*. While Eve remained in her husband's embrace, letting that truth seep through her mind and heart, Deene went on speaking.

"I'll take you up with me—the mare is in quite good condition, she'll tolerate it for a bit—I'll put you on a leading line or a longe. I'll mount up on Beast and stay right at your stirrup, if you prefer. I'll walk by your boot. I'll lead her where no one else can see us, but, Eve, you want to get back on that horse."

Eve felt tears pricking her eyes again, tears that had something to do with the horse but more to do with the man who'd brought the horse back into Eve's life.

She held on tightly to her husband even while she figuratively grabbed her courage with both hands. "I think astride will do for a start."

She'd surprised him. When she glanced up, he was smiling down at her with more tenderness than she'd beheld in his eyes even under intimate circumstances.

"Astride makes perfect sense. The lads are under orders to stay clear of the loafing paddock, and I bought the mare's saddle and bridle when I purchased her."

He'd thought of everything, bless him. And when Eve said she wanted to saddle up her own horse, Deene dutifully took himself off to fetch her a pair of boys' breeches.

"And, Deene, bring Beast along too. We can go for a ramble down to the stream."

His smile at this pronouncement would have lit up the entire world—and it scotched any second thoughts Eve had about the wisdom of her decision. As Eve took down the headstall and lead rope hanging outside the horse's loose box, her smile was quieter but no less joyous.

❧

War changed a man, Deene reflected, and not often for the better. He watched his wife knotting Aelfreth's signature red kerchief around the boy's head, and realized marriage was changing him too.

A soldier knew to be only guardedly protective of his fellows. The man sharing a bottle over the evening campfire might be taken prisoner by the French while bathing in a river the next morning.

The promising young lieutenant reciting ribald poetry at breakfast might be shot dead by noon.

When Deene had stopped recently to make a list—something he hadn't done in the years since Waterloo—he'd realized that, save for St. Just, Wellington himself, Kesmore, and several others, few of Deene's comrades-in-arms had survived the war.

This made the protectiveness he felt toward his wife somewhat easier to tolerate, but it did nothing to explain the shift Deene had felt toward everything from the weather, to his properties, to the children Anthony claimed to be raising on a tidy manor only several miles away.

Eve patted Aelfreth's arm and gave him some last-minute instructions before approaching her husband. "My lord, it's going to rain. Do we remain here or repair to the books?"

She was smiling at him—he had a whole catalogue of her smiles by now, both with and without her dimple—and she was ready to accommodate whatever his pleasure might be.

"We tend to the books." He could have her to himself that way, and she made even something as tedious as ledgers more bearable. "Aelfreth and Willy can go for a mud gallop while we stay warm and dry."

"I was hoping you'd say that." She slipped an arm around his waist and wandered with him toward the house. "I've had a note from Louisa. She and Kesmore will be calling on us soon, and then I suppose the floodgates will open."

"Must they?"

He liked her family, liked them a great deal, but he'd loved these weeks to get to know his wife and her smiles. He was developing some sense of her silences too, though, so he settled his arm around Eve's shoulders. "Tell me, Wife."

"I should not resent it when my sisters observe the civilities, but, Deene, I do. I am jealous of my time with you."

"How gratifying to know."

She punched him in the ribs. "Rotten man. You're supposed to say you feel the same way."

Of course he felt the same way. He did not admit this. Instead, as soon as they had gained the library, he closed the door behind them and locked it. At the one small, additional click of the latch, Eve looked up from where she stood by the fire.

"We're to attend our ledgers, Lucas Denning."

"Quite. I've consulted my accounts and found it has been more than twelve hours since I've enjoyed my wife's considerable intimate charms. Almost eighteen hours, in fact, which deficit must be immediately rectified if I'm to concentrate on anything so prosaic as ledgers."

"And what of luncheon? What of being conscientious about one's duties? What of—oof."

He lifted her bodily onto a corner of the estate desk and stepped closer. "I am being conscientious about my duty to the succession."

"No one could ask more of you in this regard, Husband, but it's the middle of the—"

As if they hadn't made love at practically every hour

of the day and night. He'd worried at first about asking too much of her, and he still did. Eve never refused him, but neither did she initiate lovemaking.

Not yet.

"Kiss me, my lady. If you kiss me long enough, it will no longer be the middle of the day."

She looped her arms around his neck. "You have made a wanton of me, Deene."

"You worry about this?" Something a little forlorn in her voice had him lifting his face from the soft, fragrant juncture of her shoulder and neck to peer into her eyes. "You do. You worry that a perfectly lovely passion for your new husband is something untoward. What am I to do with you?"

She didn't contradict him. Didn't tease or flirt. She regarded him steadily out of green eyes shadowed by doubt. "I know I shouldn't fret over such a thing. We're newly wed, after all."

He had the sense she recited that fact to herself in more moments of self-doubt than he'd perceived. Far more than she should. Was this why she never approached him with amatory intent?

Rather than increase her sense of self-consciousness, Deene started frothing her skirts up at her waist. "Tell me something, Lady Deene. Are you ogling the footmen hereabouts? There's one fellow in particular, the blond with the cheeky smile, with a nice set of shoulders on him."

"Godfrey. He's sweet on the tweeney. Why would I ogle him?"

Deene set aside a moment's consternation that Eve knew the man's name and the name of his current interest. "Because he's devilish handsome, and I suspect some sort of relation to me on the wrong side of the blankets."

"He's a boy. I do not ogle—Deene, what are you doing?"

"Removing these wildly embroidered silk drawers. Your sister Jenny should have a shop for gentlemen to patronize, where they might buy such underthings for their *chères amies*."

"She'd die of mortification first. Stop looking at me."

Deene loved to look at his wife. In intimate places, her hair had a reddish tint to the gold, and her skin had a luminous quality. "Lie back, Evie, but tell me: If you are such a wanton, do you ever think of what it would be like to make love to, say, my cousin Anthony?"

She did not lie back. She glared at Deene as if he'd stolen her last bite of cherry tart. "Are you mad? Anthony is a nice enough man, and he bears a pale resemblance to you, but—I cannot think when you touch me like that."

Like *that* was with just his thumb, ruffling her curls and glancing over the little bud at the apex of her sex. "You never think of anybody but me in these intimate circumstances, do you, Wife?"

"I cannot think—You're still looking at me."

He intended to look a good deal closer, too. Had been thinking about it ever since he'd assisted her at her bath just a couple of hours earlier in the day. "A truly wanton woman would be seeing every man as an opportunity to copulate, Evie. She'd be restraining herself from flirting with everything in breeches, and on occasion, with other women too. She'd be eyeing the lads, the footmen, her husband, as if plagued by a hunger that knew no satiety."

Deene kissed her, mostly to get her to lie back on the desk, but when he opened his eyes, Eve was studying him.

"And you, Deene. Do you find yourself interested in other women?"

He straightened and ambled over to the couch to retrieve two pillows. One he tossed to the floor for his knees—he intended to be kneeling for some little while—the other he placed in the middle of the desk blotter. This was a delaying tactic to allow him to choose his words carefully.

A man wanted to say the right thing, to be honest, but not more honest than he had to be.

"I desire only you, Eve Denning, and cannot foresee a time when I will desire anybody else but you. I desire you right now, in fact, and in less than five minutes, I will desire you even more than I do at this moment. My fervent wish is that your inclinations are similar with regard to the person of your husband. That you enjoy his attentions—and his attentions only, I might point out—makes you a devoted wife and the farthest thing from a wanton."

She wasn't fooled. He could tell by the exact, curious angle of her head that she understood his words were only a limited reply. As Deene sank to his knees between her legs and breathed in the clean scent of his wife's intimate person, he realized he was not going to tell her he loved her until he'd also been honest about how far he was willing to go to achieve his ends where Georgie was concerned.

"Deene?" Eve's hand landed in his hair. "Lucas, what on earth are you—?"

He settled his mouth on the seat of her pleasure, and for long moments thereafter, the only sounds in the library were the cozy hiss and pop of the fire, and Eve's sighs of pleasure.

When he'd introduced his wife to one more avenue of sexual pleasure, Deene let her bring him off with her hand—something she had a positive genius for—then set their clothing to rights, unlocked the door, and ordered luncheon from the footman in the corridor.

Married life worked up a man's appetite.

"I do wonder, you know." Even though she wasn't quite as prim and tidy as she had been thirty minutes earlier, Eve still managed to project an air of domestic calm.

"What do you wonder about?"

"Are all new couples as… enthusiastic about their marital duties as we are?"

Her question was fraught with insecurity, making Deene regret his earlier reference to the damned succession. "Ask your sisters, why don't you? I'm sure they're dying to hear what you think of marriage and of my efforts as a husband and lover."

Her brows rose. "One doesn't think to discuss such things, even with sisters."

"Yes, one does. I trust your reports will be flattering, so you can't accuse yourself of breaching any kind of marital loyalty." He frowned at her. "Your reports will be flattering, won't they?"

She beamed at him. "They will be adoring, Deene. Gushing, breathless, and quite appreciative as well.

Also lengthy—quite lengthy and fulsome. And you're right: Sindal, Hazelton, and Kesmore all needed either an heir or a spare. I'm sure my sisters will want to compare notes."

Which wasn't at all what he'd meant. His muttered, "Hang the blooming succession," however was obscured by a stout knock on the door. "Our staff knows not to knock softly when we're behind a closed door. That ought to tell you something, Wife."

They spent the afternoon together in the library on the sofa, Eve with the household books, Deene trying to focus on the racing-meet schedule for the upcoming season.

While he mostly studied his pretty wife.

"I'll be going into Town tomorrow, my lady. Is there any errand I can run for you?"

She glanced up, a pair of his reading glasses perched on her nose. "You do not enjoy these visits to Town, Husband. Shall I go with you?"

He reached over to remove her spectacles. "Not this time. If you want a shopping outing, I am happy to plan one of those and trot about at your heels like an obedient swain."

For an instant, he thought she was going to pry, but for what he had to say to Dolan, he could not have an audience, much less one as tenderhearted as his marchioness. "Will you have time to ride out with me before you go, Deene?"

"Of course." He folded the glasses and passed them back to her. "Was it hard for you to ask that of me?"

She nodded. "I should just take the lads, make it a hack in company, but I feel... more comfortable when you're up on Beast. I think Sweetness has a fondness for your gelding."

"My gelding has a fondness for you. Every creature on this property is in your thrall, Wife, including me."

He'd meant it as a tease, but in her grave smile, he saw she'd heard the truth of it too.

"I worry, Lucas Denning." She climbed across a cushion and tucked herself against his side. It wasn't a sexual overture, but it was an overture, and he treasured it as such.

"About?"

"I have not been this happy… ever. Not ever. I thought I was once, as a girl, but I was a fool. You know I got into some difficulties earlier, before my come out?"

Instinct told Deene that with no warning whatsoever, the moment had become fraught. He knew very well there had been difficulties, but he had not hoped she'd confide the nature of those difficulties to him quite so early in their marriage. Deene considered distracting her with kisses, but instead wrapped his arms around her.

"Your brothers mentioned some menial who'd gotten ideas far above his station. I understood it came to naught."

He let the words hang between them while he nuzzled her temple and waited.

"I made a complete, bleating fool of myself, Deene. I jeopardized everything and everybody I loved. No young lady was ever as stupid as I, or so lucky to escape the worst consequences of her folly."

"You were very young, as I understand it. I cannot begin to tell you the idiocies I committed when I was very young. I should be dead several times over, of drink, of stupidity, of excess."

In his arms, he felt her relax fractionally. He might not have said the exact right thing, but neither had he said the wrong thing.

"You are such a comfort to me, Husband. I should tell you this more often."

Deene propped his chin on her crown. "You are a comfort to me as well, Evie. I used to abhor rainy days, for example, and now I enjoy them even though you keep me preoccupied with things like ledgers, accounts, and other inescapable duties."

She extricated herself from his arms. "Duties? Duties only, Deene?"

He nodded, his expression solemn—until she hit him with a pillow and started tickling him.

❧

Eve endured a kiss to her cheek, and then a slow, thorough perusal from her brother-in-law, Joseph, Lord Kesmore. He sat beside his wife for two cups of tea, and then bowed to Eve in parting, muttering something about having to see to the horses.

"Louisa, did you or did you not somehow just give your spouse permission to withdraw?"

Louisa paused in the middle of chewing on a tea cake. "Give Kesmore permission? You must joking. He does as he pleases, and I am happy to have it so, that I might enjoy the same license. What shall I report to Their Graces regarding your situation here, Evie? Is Deene acquitting himself adequately?"

Oh, the reports. No doubt Anna had made one,

and soon Sophie and her baron would be dropping by, followed by Maggie and the entire world.

"You may tell all and sundry that I thrive in my husband's care." This was nothing less than the truth. Eve glanced at the door, which Kesmore had closed upon his departure. "Louisa, might I ask you something?"

"Of course. Excellent cakes, by the way."

Which were fast disappearing. "Does Kesmore... study you?"

"Study me?"

"Study your person? Examine you in detail?" When Louisa looked blank, Eve shifted her gaze to the fire crackling in the hearth. "Does he acquaint himself with the details of you... with the candles lit?"

There was no hiding Eve's blush, but neither was there any disguising Louisa's grin. "Oh, to be sure, though when I take a notion to study him, the curtains are drawn back, there being a deal of Kesmore to study, him being such a handsome specimen."

Louisa and... Kesmore.

Studying each other.

"Merciful heavens."

"Maggie sometimes has to tie Benjamin to the bed, for he's not inclined to be docile about it when it's his turn to be studied. I expect Sindal is a more obedient sort of husband. Somehow asking Sophie directly is beyond me, but she has that rosy, well-examined look about her sometimes. Makes a lady feel wickedly special when her husband takes such an interest."

Wickedly special. Louisa had the right of it. Not just wicked, but wickedly *special*. "Deene says he is making a science of being my husband."

"Good for Deene, and good for you, Evie Denning. We worried for you."

For just an instant, Louisa's teasing smile slipped, and Eve had to wonder exactly how much her sisters suspected regarding her past. "You need not worry. I am happily married, and I daresay my husband is too."

"Usually works that way. Where is this husband of yours, by the way? I think Kesmore was looking forward to interrogating him."

"I expect him back from Town momentarily. Deene is ferociously determined to gain control of the marquessate's finances, and this requires much in the way of meetings with his cousin Anthony and what I gather are armies of solicitors, merchants, and factors. He's offered to take me shopping."

Why she felt she had to add this, Eve did not know.

"He wants to show you off, then, but mind you, he'll also be spying." Louisa spoke with great confidence.

"Spying? On me?" That did not sound promising at all. "Why?"

"He'll lurk in the corner of the shop and watch as you make your selections. He'll see what you linger over, what you almost purchase, what you consider giving to someone else as a gift but not for yourself. Next thing you know, there will be a little box beside your bed one night or at your place when you come down for breakfast."

"*Kesmore* indulges in such activities?"

"Joseph is the most generous man I know. I'm hard put to keep up with him when it comes to the doting and spoiling, but one contrives lest a husband get to feeling smug."

To think of Louisa—managing, competent, brisk Louisa—being doted upon and spoiled... it warmed Evie's heart toward her taciturn, unsmiling brother-in-law, and toward Louisa too.

And while she was about it, such thoughts warmed her heart toward Deene as well.

"Come with me, Louisa. I must show you what Deene found for me not two weeks past. It is the best thing ever, though it would not fit in a box to place by my bed."

Evie rose and took her sister's arm, steering Louisa toward the door.

"Eve Denning, is that a divided skirt you're wearing? I haven't seen you in such a costume since Jenny made one for you years ago."

"This is the one Jenny made for me, and before you ask, yes. I ride out regularly, provided Deene is with me. That's part of the surprise."

Louisa stopped just inside the parlor door. "Did I hear you aright? You're riding out? Not just driving out? Climbing aboard a horse and trotting around?"

"And cantering, and the day before yesterday, we galloped and even hopped two logs. Why?"

"Bless this wonderful, wonderful day. Westhaven said I was being a ninnyhammer, and for once I cannot mind that he was right. At long last, my baby sister once again rides out."

Standing right there in the parlor, in full view of the footman across the corridor, Louisa, the Countess of Kesmore, threw her arms around Eve's neck and burst into tears.

❧

"If our wives have been weeping when next we see them, you must not remark it." Kesmore kept his voice down, but the man's characteristic diffidence was nowhere in his tone.

"Whyever would they weep?" The thought of Eve weeping was alarming, though Deene kept his expression calm as they ambled up the barn aisle.

"I have reason to suspect my wife is with child, and no less personages than Westhaven himself, seconded by Sindal, St. Just, Hazelton, Lord Valentine Windham, *and* His Grace have assured me a penchant for lachrymosity is to be expected even in such a bastion of sense as my estimable Louisa."

"Is there a married fellow whom you have not canvassed on the matter?"

"You, for obvious reasons."

"Eve doesn't cry much." Except sometimes, deep in the night, when they'd made a particularly tender kind of love, and then she clung and wanted to be held securely until she dropped off to sleep in Deene's embrace.

And he wanted to hold her.

Kesmore glanced over sharply. "Your wife had best not be crying on your worthless account, Deene. My lady would take it amiss, and you do not want such a thing on your conscience, presuming you survived the thrashing I would be bound to mete out."

"Marriage has made you quite ferocious, Kesmore."

Kesmore paused outside a roomy foaling stall. "On behalf of a woman I care about, I will always be capable of ferocity. See that you recall this should you ever be inclined toward the wrong sort of weak moment. This mare is new, but what is she doing in a foaling stall when she's neither gravid nor boasting a foal at her side?"

Kesmore was not a charming man, something Deene was coming to like about his brother-in-law more and more. "This is Eve's mare, and she will always merit the very best care we have to offer."

"This is a mature animal." Kesmore was a former cavalry officer, gone for a country gentleman sort of earl who rode regularly to hounds. He extended a gloved hand toward the mare, who sniffed delicately at his knuckles. "She's in good condition—I suppose she's come off a winter hunting?"

"She is, and Eve takes her out almost daily. So what have you heard in the clubs about your new brother-in-law's licentious nature?"

"Not one word, if you must know. I have swilled indifferent wine by the hour, read every page of every newspaper, and all but lurked at keyholes, and I have heard not one thing to your detriment, save that you are unfashionably enamored of your new wife. The suppositions are that you are tending to the succession and dodging all the disappointed debutantes. I saw no reason to disabuse anybody of such notions."

The mare went back to her hay. "I am enamored of my new wife."

"I am in transports to hear it. Likely she is as well."

Deene turned and hooked his elbows over the mare's half door. "I wasn't aware a man bruited such sentiments about, or is this another aspect of domestic life about which I am too newly married to be knowledgeable?"

Kesmore looked like he might be considering parting with a smile in a few weeks time, provided the weather held fair. "You'll learn. They teach us, no matter we're slow to absorb the lesson. Make the first time count, though."

"The first time?"

"For God's sake, man, the first time you tell her you love her. Make it count. Even His Grace knew that much."

"Of course I love her." Who could not love such a courageous, generous, fierce, passionate... The words trailed off in Deene's mind, disappearing into a mist of surprise, wonder, and joy. He was at risk for babbling and laughing out loud, for doing something outrageous, like kissing Kesmore on the cheeks. "*Of course I love my wife.*"

The feeling settled around Deene's heart, warm, substantial, and right. He loved his Evie; he would always love her. The certainty was his both to keep and his to share with her when the moment was right.

"Of course you love your wife. Is this the mare Lady Eve came a cropper on?"

"How did you know?"

"Louisa has described her to me in detail. She said Eve used to have dreams or nightmares about this horse. Well done, Deene, to retrieve the lady's familiar. I had my doubts about you, but this is quite encouraging."

"Glad to oblige."

Kesmore's expression suggested another dry rejoinder was about to be served up, but the man went still, his eyes becoming watchful. "Our ladies approach. I'll keep my vigil in the clubs, at least when we're in

Town, but so far, Deene, your marriage seems to have worked its magic with the gossips and with your lady wife both. See that you don't muck it up."

Deene smiled, walked forward to take Eve's hand, and bestowed a kiss on her knuckles while Kesmore's warning faded from his ears.

Nine

EVE WAS TO RECALL A SMALL MOMENT FROM THE balance of the day, the first moment when she felt well and truly married. Her husband had taken her hand upon greeting her, kissed her knuckles, and then tucked her against his side as they saw Louisa and Kesmore into their coach.

As the conveyance rattled away with Louisa's handkerchief waving cheerily out a window, Deene sighed gustily. "I am displeased with myself."

The sentiment sounded at least partly genuine. "Why would you be displeased with yourself, Husband? After a day with the solicitors, my father is usually airing his best vocabulary to regale Her Grace with his displeasure with his factors."

Deene smiled down at her and began to escort her toward the house. "His best vocabulary?"

"You know." Eve waved her free hand. "Damned, befouling, toadying, parasitical, blighted, bloated... There, I've cheered you up."

"You could cheer me up further, except I've gone and invited Anthony to dine with us tonight."

Their first dinner guest, and Eve had to like that Deene assumed she'd welcome his cousin without any fuss—for she surely would. "I will cheer you up when we retire."

"This thought will console me as I reflect upon a confidence Kesmore let slip."

"Kesmore is not a confidence-slipping sort of fellow." They slowed as they approached the house. Deene would disappear to their rooms to change; Eve would have to let the kitchen know they were having company for dinner. She'd missed her husband the livelong day and considered helping him undress, attending him at his bath, and then notifying the kitchen, except dinner would be served at midnight if she adopted that course, which did not comport with an early bedtime.

"Kesmore is... He suspects his wife to be in expectation of an interesting event, but he has not confronted her."

"And he did not swear you into the familial brotherhood of secrecy over this," Eve pointed out. "He must be rattled, indeed. Louisa suspects she is carrying, but she doesn't want to burden him with such a hope until she's certain. They are very... considerate of each other. Surprisingly so, given how brusque each can be individually."

Deene stopped on the back terrace, wrapped Eve in his arms, and propped his chin on her crown. "Evie? I should not say it, because they've scarce been married longer than we have, but I am jealous of this secret they're keeping from each other."

Eve leaned into her husband and reveled in the

simple closeness of the moment. Because she and Deene were a couple—a unit of marital trust—they knew something about Louisa and Kesmore's union that the parties to that union had not yet shared openly with each other.

This was what it meant to be married, to have a husband, to no longer stand alone in the world. This was what it meant to love and be cared for in return.

When Deene stepped back, Eve smiled at him, blew him a kiss, and at the foot of the main staircase, sent him off to his bath while she went in search of the cook.

The kitchen took the news of a dinner guest very well, almost as if they too had been waiting to demonstrate their willingness to put their best, most gracious foot forward. The housekeeper sent maids to ready a guest chamber, "just in the event the gentlemen get to lingering over their port," and dispatched a maid to cut flowers for fresh bouquets.

Leaving Eve free to be preyed upon by the odd worry: If the gentlemen got to drinking their port in the library, would there be a lone pillow peeking out from under a table skirt to betray some of the marital activities pursued yesterday in that same library?

Would all the writing implements still be pushed off to the side of the blotter…?

Merciful heavens, might there still be a certain pink, brocade pillow *on* the blotter?

Eve was in the library without willing her steps to take her there. No pillows lurked in questionable locations, not a slipper peeked out from beneath the sofa, not an inkwell betrayed the many occasions when the desk had served some purpose other than the composition of correspondence.

Three days ago, however, Deene had stuffed a handkerchief into one of the desk drawers. Eve dreaded to think of Anthony searching for sealing wax and coming across such a thing. She sat in Deene's high-backed chair and began opening drawers one a time, only to find the very handkerchief—crumpled, but otherwise inoffensive—in a drawer that also sported two bundles of paper, one tied with a red ribbon, the other with gold.

Was this also something Anthony should not happen upon? Deene was very sensitive to the need to avoid slighting Anthony's feelings, for though he held a courtesy title, the man was essentially the senior steward over the entire marquessate holdings, Deene's heir, and family into the bargain.

Eve and her husband were a unit of marital trust. She'd coined the term not an hour earlier, and that meant she was bound to protect her husband's confidences even before such confidences could be bestowed.

In this spirit of protectiveness, she tucked her husband's linen into a pocket and unrolled the document tied with a red ribbon. By the time she'd rolled up and retied the one with a gold ribbon, three quarters of an hour later, her focus had shifted.

She was feeling protective not of her husband, though she would at least allow him a chance to explain himself in private—but once again of her own heart.

❧

Something was off with Deene's wife. He sensed this without knowing how, sensed it as a certainty all through dinner. Eve was gracious and charming to Anthony, who looked a little dazed to be on the receiving end of such smiles and warmth.

Prior to the meal, when Deene would normally have been helping his wife to dress and perhaps helping himself to a small taste of marital pleasure as well, their timing had been off. Deene had been quick to bathe, while Eve had lingered at her ablutions, the dressing room door closed "to prevent a draft."

She'd brushed out her own hair, she hadn't asked his opinion regarding her choice of gown, and most telling of all, she'd worn very plain undergarments. No embroidery, no lace.

As the fruit and cheeses were finally brought out, it struck Deene that his wife was perhaps getting her courses. This little insight was warming in the extreme, an intimacy such as a husband might guess without being told, such as he might intuit before the lady herself realized she was leaving her devoted spouse any clues.

"Wife, if you'd like to retire early, Anthony and I can take ourselves to the library. I'm sure your day has been long, and I would not tire you unnecessarily." He added a small, smoldering look, one that had Anthony studying the cheese tray.

"Thank you, gentlemen." Eve got to her feet and aimed a wide smile at Anthony. "Cousin, you must make our home your home as well for the duration of your stay. Husband, good night."

She withdrew before Deene could offer to light her way upstairs, before he could do more than bow her from the room and hope Anthony wasn't going to want to linger over the damned port.

"The library has the best selection of libation," Deene said. He turned to the waiting footman. "Bring the fruit and cheese along, if you please. Anthony, shall we?"

"Sounds just the thing to settle a wonderful meal. Having spent some time with your marchioness, Deene, I can see why you're keeping her all to your-self out here in the shires. It fuels the talk, I'm sure, but what's one more rumor?"

Damn Anthony, anyway. Deene waited until they were in the library, the door closed, drinks in hand, before he inquired further. "What are you hearing now?"

"Just more of the same, and that you're ruralizing with your wife to make sure your firstborn is truly yours. The usual innuendo and nastiness. How did the interview with Dolan go?"

Deene turned to study the fire. "The stage lost a considerable thespian talent when Dolan decided to keep his dirty hands in trade. He was angry to think I'd invite him to my wedding, then turn around and accuse him of spreading vile gossip regarding the nature of the union. Shocked and livid."

But quiet with it, not reeling with melodramatic outrage, which was puzzling.

"Did you tell him about the lawsuit?"

"In no uncertain terms. Suffice it to say an amicable settlement is not in the offing."

A soft rustling in the shadows near the door suggested the fruit and cheese had been brought along.

"You're married now," Anthony said, coming up on Deene's elbow. "Eve's dowry can finance the lawsuit, her respectability will lend your petition impeccable credibility, and if you can knock her up posthaste—I assume you're giving that a decent go as well—then you'll be a parent yourself by the time anything reaches a public courtroom. Well done, Deene. Too bad the rest of our family business doesn't come as neatly to hand as your litigation strategies have. And from the look of the lady, you're even enjoying the duties the union has imposed on you, while she believes this whole marriage to have been at least half her idea."

Deene was forming some snappish, off-putting rejoinder in the ensuing silence—he did not care in the least for Anthony's tone—when a cultured female voice spoke from the door.

"I'll put the food on the desk, gentlemen, and once again bid you good night."

Eve had turned her back before Deene could utter a word, while Anthony reached out and plucked a succulent bunch of grapes off the tray, and the door clicked quietly closed.

"She even waits on you hand and foot, Deene. Very well done of you. Well done, indeed." Anthony popped a grape into his mouth, his smile conspiratorial.

Eve's voice had been calm and more than civil. She'd spoken with a terrible, *ducal* cordiality Deene found as unnerving as the prospect of charging into a French artillery barrage.

"You will excuse me, Anthony, and if you ever make such cavalier comments again about the nature of my marriage, my motives for marrying, or my regard for my wife, I will disinherit you, call you out, and aim to at least terminate your reproductive abilities."

Deene stalked toward to the door, only to be stopped by Anthony's hand on his arm.

"You are not going to fly into high dudgeon and act the besotted spouse on me, are you?"

"I *am* in high dudgeon, and I *am* a besotted spouse, but more to the point, Eve has every right to be in high dudgeon." She had every right to go home to her parents, to eviscerate Deene in his sleep, to bar Anthony from the house... Deene recalled Anthony's words phrase by phrase, and aimed a thunderous scowl at his cousin.

"If she's truly that sensitive, Deene, then give her a few moments to compose herself. She'll want her guns at the ready before you wrestle her into *coitus forgiveness*, and believe me, I know of what I speak in this regard."

He popped another grape into his mouth, the picture of a man undisturbed by what could be the end of Deene's domestic bliss. Deene's determination to join his wife wavered in the face of such sangfroid. "You will apologize to her at breakfast, Anthony. You will apologize on your knees and mean it."

And still, Anthony merely smiled. "But of course. Now, you've been pestering me these weeks for a discussion of the profits to be had from the estates in Kent. Pull up that decanter and prepare to listen."

Now, *now* when Deene wanted nothing so much as to crawl into his wife's bedroom and explain that his only adult relation was an insensitive oaf with execrable timing, Anthony started spouting facts and figures at a great rate. The very information Deene had been seeking for weeks, provided in an orderly, articulate fashion.

He listened, he asked questions, he asked more questions, and even though he nearly glared a hole in the door and paced a rut in the carpet, Deene did not join his wife above stairs until it was quite late indeed.

❧

Eve did not cry. Not this time, perhaps not ever again. She wasn't going to give the situation that much effort.

She'd been a fool, again, believing herself cared for and valued, when what had been sought was her wealth, her position, her standing, her status.

Perhaps even her body—her womb—but not her heart. *Again*, she'd tossed the best part of herself at an undeserving, scheming, handsome man, and found her greatest treasure of no value whatsoever.

And where was her husband now? Munching grapes and swilling brandy one floor and several universes of arrogance away. Well, so what? His cavalier behavior gave Eve time to marshal her composure, to recall that if she had given her heart into Deene's keeping, she could just as well snatch it back without him being the wiser. She'd made no declarations; she'd let no impassioned endearments slip even in their most intimate moments.

Her pride was intact, and she intended to keep it that way.

In the dark, the door to the dressing room eased open. Eve knew exactly the way it creaked, the top hinge being the culprit. She'd purposely not had the thing oiled, because she liked knowing Deene was coming to bed.

"Evie?"

"I'm awake." A war started up inside Eve's chest. Part of her wanted to throw herself into Deene's arms and make him tell her he'd blistered Anthony's ears for his disrespect of their marriage, and another part of her wanted to order her husband from the room.

"I didn't mean for you to wait up."

What was that supposed to mean? "Do you need assistance undressing?"

"No, thank you." She felt him sit on the bed, heard first one boot then the other hit the floor. "I suppose you have some questions?"

So civilized. The offer was tired, almost casual—not the least wary or apologetic. "About?"

"You overheard Anthony mentioning litigation strategy."

"You are suing Mr. Dolan for custody of your niece."

A silence, while Eve flattered herself she'd surprised him.

"How do you know?"

Eve manufactured a yawn while she cast around for a reply. "I use the estate desk too, Deene. The papers were all but in plain view."

In the darkness, she felt him measuring her words, trying to decide how long she'd known. "You're not upset?"

"Lawsuits between family members are the very essence of scandal, Deene, but I am merely a wife. If you are determined on this course, I cannot stop you."

She had intended to plead with him not to file his damned lawsuit. His niece's entire future would be blighted, and even Jenny's remaining Seasons would feel the taint. Their Graces would be disappointed, and the idea that Eve's parents would have to weather one more scandal on her account was enough to make her throat constrict with unshed tears.

"I cannot tell you, Eve, how relieved I am to find what a sensible woman I've married. Wresting Georgie from her father's grasp means a great deal to me."

He did not sound relieved. He sounded wary, which suited Eve nicely, even as it made her sad. She heard more sounds signaling his end-of-day routine. His cravat pin, cuff links, and signet ring dropping into the tray on his bureau. The doors to his wardrobe opening and closing. Wash water dripping into the basin as Deene wrung out a flannel, then the faint scents of lavender and cedar wafting through the air.

He was coming to bed, just as if Eve hadn't been served up the miserable truth of her marriage a few hours before. In her idiot, grasping, scheming husband's mind, nothing was to change.

Seven years ago, Eve had been a victim, little more than a child, and left unable to even walk to the close stool without assistance.

She was Marchioness of Deene now, a grown woman, and not without resources or the resolve to use them.

Deene slid under the covers, a clean, warm, devastatingly skilled specimen of a husband, toward whom—despite all—Eve still felt a damnable quantity of attraction. She rolled up to her side, presenting him with her back, but the lunatic man slid an arm around her waist and spooned his body around hers.

"I am sorry you overheard Anthony's unfortunate sentiments, Eve. They do not reflect my own."

"Deene?"

"Hmm?" His cheek rested on her hair.

"I'm afraid I'm at risk for a slight headache tonight. I'm sure you understand?"

She *felt* the understanding go through him physically. He went still, even to a pause in his breathing. Then his hand settled on her shoulder and began to gently knead her muscles.

"Sleep, then. The last thing I want is to impose on you when you might be suffering."

She waited, waited for that hand of his to slide around and stroke over her belly or her breast, waited for his lips to presume to touch her nape, waited for him to hitch himself closer so the burgeoning length of his erection pressed against her buttocks.

She waited until his hand slowed then stilled on her shoulder, until his breathing evened out and became measured.

She waited until she was sure he'd well and truly dropped off to sleep, until, with her husband's arm around her and his body pressed close in the darkness, it was at last safe to cry.

❦

Deene found himself in the middle of a wrestling match, though it was as if he were doing battle with his own shadow. He could not anticipate his opponent's moves, could not divine the rules, could not study the combat long enough to find patterns.

At breakfast, Eve was again all cordial smiles, and Anthony charmed by those smiles.

"Deene says you overheard my plain speaking last

evening, my lady, and that I must apologize for such blunt speech over the port."

"Nonsense, Anthony." Eve didn't pause as she topped up her teacup. "Deene and I have a sensible union. I understand he did not marry me out of any excesses of sentiment, nor I him, though we are of course fond of each other. Would you like an orange?"

Eve had fired some sort of shot across Deene's bow with that offhand observation, but Deene was at a loss to know from which cannon it had been launched or at what particular target. She peeled Deene an orange, the same as she did every morning, and put most of it on his plate.

He watched while she munched one of the three sections she'd kept for herself. "I note you are not dressed for the stables this morning, my lady. Might I inquire as to your health?"

"I did not sleep as well as I might have liked. More tea, Anthony?"

She'd slept well enough. He'd been the one to lie there feigning sleep, arms around her, listening to her tears and wondering how many times he was supposed to apologize—except he had the sense his efforts in that direction had only made the situation worse.

"I'll accompany you to the stables, Deene," Anthony said. "I've been hearing a great deal about your stud colt, and he's beginning to show up on the book at White's."

Deene glanced up in time to see the interest in Eve's eyes and the way she masked it behind a sudden need to rearrange the eggs on her plate. "People are placing bets on King William?"

"A few," Anthony replied. "That he'll win by so many lengths if rematched against Islington's colt. That Dolan's colt would beat him on the flat but not over fences."

"Dolan's colt didn't run all last year," Deene said. "Word is he's retired to stud."

"Would that we all…" Anthony had the grace to leave the sentiment uncompleted. One had to wonder if the lady in Surrey missed Anthony's company at her table if such was Anthony's conversation.

"I didn't know Mr. Dolan had a racing stable," Eve said. For a woman who'd fended off a headache and slept badly, she was putting away a substantial breakfast.

"He has any accoutrement that would proclaim him a gentleman," Deene said, "except the right to call himself one. Anthony, pass the teapot."

Anthony obliged, his expression the usual bland mask mention of Dolan provoked.

"Empty." Deene passed the pot to a footman. "I will miss you in the stables, Eve. Will you ride out with me later?"

She arranged her cutlery. She folded her serviette on her lap. Deene had the satisfaction of seeing she was at least torn.

"It's a lovely day," Anthony said. "I'll be toddling on back to Kent, there to deal with lame plough horses and feuding tenants. Join your husband on his ride, Lady Deene. All too soon he'll be absorbed in the race meets, and you'll hardly see him."

Anthony was trying to help, but Deene resented his cousin's assistance, implying as it did that Anthony would be working shoulder to the plough, while

Deene drank and gambled and frolicked. If Anthony had kept his big mouth shut…

While Aelfreth put William through his paces an hour later, it occurred to Deene that if Eve hadn't overheard Anthony, Deene would still be left trying to puzzle out a way to explain the custody suit to her. The papers had sat in the desk drawer for days, with Deene making up a new excuse each day for why he did not give the solicitors leave to prime their barristers and fire off the first true scandal of the Season.

"Yon colt is pouting." Bannister's tone was lugubrious. "He wants the lady to watch him go."

"Lady Deene is a trifle indisposed."

"Then the colt will be indisposed too. Your horse has fallen in love, and though you breed him to half the shire, he'll not try his heart out until her ladyship is on that rail, watching him go."

"For God's sake, Bannister, he's a horse. He can't fall in love."

Bannister snorted and fell silent, leaving Deene to watch as his prized stallion put in a lackluster performance for no apparent reason.

"He wants her ladyship," Aelfreth said when the horse was making desultory circles on the rail. "He kept looking at her spot, and she's not there."

Even Deene had seen that much. It was pathetic, how a dumb animal…

"Keep walking him, Aelfreth. My wife has taken me into dislike, but she's as smitten with the damned horse as ever, or I very much mistake the matter. Bannister, have my saddle put on the mare."

When Deene reached the house, he was relieved to

find Eve in one of her divided skirts, her hair neatly arranged into a bun pinned snugly at her nape.

"You're feeling better." He made the observation cautiously, no longer certain of anything except that where his marriage ought to be, a battleground was forming.

"Somewhat. I will try a quiet hack on Sweetness, mostly because I think you and I need a chance to speak privately, Deene."

This did not bode well. If she was going to tell him she wanted her own bedroom, he'd fight her. If she wanted to visit her parents, he'd go with her. If she was going to try to talk him out of trying to gain custody of Georgie...

He'd listen. He wouldn't make any promises, but he would listen.

"A hack is exactly what I had in mind." He took her by the hand and led her to the stables, almost as if he were afraid she'd go marching off somewhere else did he turn loose of her.

When they reached the stables, Eve stopped in her tracks and dropped his hand. "My lord, what is your saddle doing my mare?"

"A change of pace, so to speak. Willy was stale this morning. I was thinking you could hack him out, and I'd take your mare."

Ah, the reaction was satisfying. Eve came to an abrupt halt, blinked, and then... she smiled. A slow, sweet curving of her lips, a genuine expression of pleasure that had nothing to do with firing shots or joining battles.

Until she cocked her head. "Are you trying to bribe me, Deene?"

"I am not—unless you want me to bribe you?" *Though bribe her in what regard?*

"Bribe me." She put her hands on her hips and glared at him, as if...

"Oh. As in, you will not suffer any more headaches if I put you up on Willy?" Crudely put, but he'd apparently gotten the right of it. "This has not crossed my mind. The horse was dull this morning, not mentally engaged in his work, and I think having you up on him will address what ails him. And as for the rest of it..." He glanced around and saw the lads were all giving them a wide berth. "I need an heir, Evie, and you are my wife."

He'd kept his voice down, but where such idiot words had come from, he did not know. They were the truth, of course, and no insult to anybody, but they'd come out of his mouth like so much ammunition, when what he'd wanted to say was something else entirely. Something to do with needing her in his arms and in his life.

Eve tugged on her riding gloves, looking damnably composed. "Shall we mount up?"

He tossed her onto Willy's back—such a little thing, his wife, and so full of dignity—then swung onto the mare. Willy was a gentleman and Sweetness not given to coming into season at the first sight of a stallion, else the ride would have been a disaster, though Deene privately considered Bannister was right: as long as Willy had Eve's attention, the horse would have nothing to do with mares or work or anything else.

Rather like his owner.

When the horses had cantered and trotted and hopped logs and otherwise had a good little romp— with Eve and Willy looking like they'd been hacking out together for years—Deene brought the mare back to the walk.

"If we're to have a private discussion, Wife, then we have exactly one more mile in which to have it before every lad on the property will overhear us."

She readjusted her reins then petted her horse. "Can you be dissuaded from filing this suit, Deene?"

"I don't think so." He spoke slowly, wondering where even the smallest doubt might come from. "Dolan was not my sister's choice, and as far as I'm concerned, he cost her her life."

Eve grimaced. "How does a husband cost his wife her life?"

"He forces children on her when she has already shown that her constitution is not suited to child-bearing. I can only think what my sister suffered…"

He fell silent and disciplined himself not to tighten his hands on the reins. "She begged me with her dying breath to look out for her family, Eve. I cannot abandon the child now."

"You've tried being a doting uncle?"

"Dolan won't have it."

"Here is what I will not have, Deene. I will not have you spending us into the poorhouse to create scandal, when in a few years, I am likely the one who will be responsible for presenting Georgie to Polite Society. I can prevail on Mr. Dolan to see reason in this regard if you'll allow it."

The mare came to a halt without Deene consciously

cueing his mount. "It's ten years until her come out, Evie. I cannot wait ten years to keep a promise to my sister, not when Dolan can betroth the girl wherever he pleases at any point, and have the contracts be binding on all parties. He can ship her to Switzerland, or France, to her relations in Boston or Baltimore, for God's sake... Marie wanted her daughter raised here, in the style befitting..."

Eve regarded him steadily, Willy standing as still as a statue beneath her. "You need an heir, Deene, and I am happy to give you as many heirs as the Lord sees fit to bless us with, but I will not bring down more scandal on my family, much less allow you to use my good name, my standing, and my entire dowry to do it. Find another way to keep your promise to your sister, or until I do present your niece to the sovereign ten years hence, I'm afraid—should you file those papers—I will be besieged by an entire, possibly never-ending plague of headaches."

She touched her heels to Willy's sides, and the colt bounded off, a flat chestnut streak against the undulating spring grass, the woman on his back completing a picture of grace, beauty, and strength as she rode him home.

Ten

EVE REALIZED AFTER ABOUT A WEEK THAT HER STRATEGY wasn't working. Part of the problem was that other than preventing Deene from starting his lawsuit, she wasn't entirely sure what her aim had been.

To keep him at arm's length?

That wasn't happening. Each night, he made deeper inroads on her attempts to separate their routine: he brushed her hair, he attended her baths, he helped her into and out of her clothing, and he asked for her assistance with his.

The staff was colluding with him, telling him when she ordered a bath, when she'd asked not to be disturbed in the middle of an afternoon. It was maddening, really, to find such a pleasant, considerate husband where Eve needed to find a calculating, underhanded, self-interested opponent.

And if she'd intended to keep him from her bed?

That wasn't happening either. Each night he tended to his ablutions, then climbed between the sheets and took her in his arms. If she turned her back to him, he rubbed her back or her neck and shoulders. His attentions were unselfish, pleasurable, and in no way could Eve consider them intimate advances.

And for all Eve had been denying her husband—and herself—marital congress, the damnable papers were still in the drawer in the library. That was beyond maddening. He'd *said* he needed an heir. She'd *said* she'd oblige him as long as suit was not joined. What was the damned man waiting for?

"I do not understand you men." Eve announced this to her brother when Westhaven stopped by ostensibly to offer good wishes to the newlyweds. Deene was out spying on some promising three-year-old colt, which meant Eve had her brother's company to herself.

"We often don't understand ourselves, much less you women. You are looking a trifle fatigued, Eve. Do I tell Her Grace married life agrees with you or make up some other fabrication?"

He spoke quietly—Westhaven was not given to dramatics—but Eve was relieved at his insight.

"Deene and I are quarreling."

Westhaven picked up a sandwich and demolished it in about two bites. "I can't very well call him out for you, love—he's your husband now, and I was under the impression this marriage was motivated at least in part by your desire to see the man remain above ground."

"You are no help."

He studied her for a moment over his tea. In the opinion of his sisters, marriage was maturing Westhaven from being merely handsome into a sort of breathtaking elegance. He was going to make a marvelous duke—though this did not mean he lacked for shortcomings as a brother. "Anna and I went through a ninnyhammer stage, though we were fortunate to tend to it before the nuptials, for the most part. Even if I don't call Deene out, I can talk to the man if you want me to."

"What would you say?" Eve rose, wondering if her sisters had brought their marital troubles to Westhaven, and whether his prospective role as head of the family meant they had the right to do so.

"I would say that time, honesty, and kindness can see two people in love through almost any difficulty."

"My husband is not in love with me." She realized immediately what she'd admitted. "We are not in love with each other."

A silence, a damnable, knowing silence from her brother had Eve wanting to cry. She crossed her arms over her middle and pretended to be watching the flowers bob in the breeze, when what she was really doing was looking for her husband to come in from the stables.

"Evie?" Westhaven had risen as well to stand by her elbow. "What is the problem?"

There was such concern in his eyes, Eve had to swallow three times before she could trust her voice. "He wants to sue Georgie's father for custody, and I have forbidden it."

"Forbidden it?" An ominous note of puzzlement laced Westhaven's voice.

"I have… intimated that my favors would be withheld did Deene pursue this course, and not just because I want to avoid the scandal, Westhaven."

"You have forbidden your new husband to keep a deathbed promise to his only sibling?"

"You don't understand." And that Deene had explained the situation to Westhaven was disconcerting. "He married me to finance the lawsuit—I saw the estimated costs, projected out over five to eight years, Westhaven. The costs of litigation exceed even the settlements I brought to the marriage, plus interest."

"A man doesn't typically expect to lose money when he marries a duke's daughter."

This was not sympathy she was hearing from her brother. Normally, his misplaced capacity for common sense would provoke Eve to railing at him or smacking his meaty shoulder.

She felt instead a need to make him—to make somebody who cared about her—see the entire mess her marriage was becoming from her perspective.

"In addition to the money, Deene wanted my consequence as a proper wife, and he wanted to be able to present himself as a doting father by the time the suit reached the courtroom. He has been diligent in assuring this aim."

"For God's sake, Evie, he's a man newly married. Anna and I were so diligent in the first few months of our marriage we were out of our clothes more than we were in them. Ask any of our siblings, they'll say the same, *and so would our parents.*"

Were the circumstances different, this revelation would have fascinated Eve—and warmed her heart in some way not possible prior to her marriage.

"You love your countess, Westhaven, and she loves you. It makes a difference."

"And Deene is merely a convenience to you?"

"I am a convenience to him."

Westhaven ran a hand through his hair, a gesture Eve associated with the few times he found himself at a loss. "You ride out with this merely convenient husband of yours, Evie. I'm told you ride his prized stallion."

"I weigh no more than a jockey, and we only hack."

"You are being deliberately obtuse, Sister. That horse has the potential to earn Deene as much coin as all his acres in Kent put together."

This set Eve to pacing the room, because she hadn't realized King William's financial promise was of such magnitude. "He's a wonderful horse, but even there…" She trailed off, while Westhaven watched her tack around the room.

He was damnably patient, was Westhaven.

"I'm back in the saddle, Gayle, but my riding is… off. There's something missing. I have the skills, and I enjoy it tremendously, and I love… I enjoy the time I spend with the horses, but it isn't what I thought it would be."

Maybe this was why Westhaven cultivated silence so assiduously, because it inspired people to make confessions to him they hadn't even realized they were about to make. That something was missing in Eve's riding had lurked just below her awareness, an inchoate grief she feared had something to do with her marriage or with parts of herself she was never going to recover.

"I'm going to send Anna to you," Westhaven said. "She is a very good listener and can offer you sympathy where I can offer you only sense. From my limited, admittedly male perspective, you've forced your husband to choose between his vows to you at the altar—which contemplate his duty to the succession—and his vows to his sister. I do not see how you've left him an honorable course, Eve, so it remains to you to find the compromise."

He fell silent, looking unhappy with his own pronouncements, and then he surprised Eve by taking her in his arms. "And I think, Evie, part of you wanted this reckoning from your new husband, for reasons you have not examined very closely yourself, valid reasons though they must seem to be."

He spoke quietly—his worst insights were always delivered quietly—and then he kissed her cheek, swiped a last tea cake from the tray, and left her alone to… resume watching the flowers bob in the breeze.

❧

"I will write you a glowing character, of course."

Dolan strolled along through his perfectly manicured gardens, telling himself the young woman at his side would see the sense in his offer. Miss Ingraham had been hired in part because she was sensible enough to earn coin at honest work rather than starve or accept just any proposal of marriage to come her way.

"Let me understand you, Mr. Dolan. You are warning me that Georgie is about to become the object of a contested lawsuit, in which her uncle, the Marquis of Deene, seeks to take her from your care and keeping."

"He'll try his damn—I beg your pardon. He'll try very hard. The situation will become unsavory, Miss Ingraham. Your character will likely come under scrutiny, as will every aspect of my own. Every time you've scolded Georgina in public, every time you've seen me be short-tempered with her, every time I've stayed out all night…"

He trailed off, though the exact measure of the indignities looming close at hand had kept him up many an hour since Deene's last visit. Staying out all night, however, was invariably the result of a protracted negotiation rather than of time spent with a mistress of tireless charms.

Dolan could not explain such a thing to his daughter's governess, of course.

"Sir, may we sit?"

"For God's sake, woman. You don't ask me such a thing."

She cocked her head, a smile lurking at the corners of her full mouth. "You are my employer, Mr. Dolan. It is for me to ask you."

"On your day off, you were not so prickly, Amy Ingraham."

His use of her first name visibly surprised her, though he was intrigued to see it did not displease her. When he took the place beside her on the bench, she spoke easily, as if maybe this were another day off.

"I am under the impression, sir, that lawsuits take years to come to a hearing, so many years that Georgina might well reach her majority before you have a decision in the matter."

"Then Deene will modify his petition to become her guardian rather than her custodian, or guardian of her property. He will not give up on this, though I'm not sure what exactly drives him. I have taken some steps to try to flush out his motivation, but they have been unavailing."

Miss Ingraham studied her hands in her lap. "You have thought this matter through? You're not inclined to make any concessions to his lordship?"

If there was anybody—anybody on the face of the entire earth—who might understand his position, it was the woman beside him. This realization was a little sad, but also heartening.

He would miss her, the quiet Miss Ingraham of the fine gray eyes and wonderfully pleasing figure. Georgina would miss her too, and that... gave him a pang.

"I'm not inclined to make any concessions at this point, but there will ensue some period of bargaining—I'm not sure how long. Deene hasn't filed the papers yet, though he gave me to understand I'm to be served notice any day, likely in an intentionally public manner. You have some time to find other employment before the scandal actually breaks, though as to that..."

He fell silent. If he offered to pension her off, she'd take it amiss. Late at night after a few too many brandies, Dolan had contemplated learning the exact shape of Miss Amy Ingraham's feminine form, and he had not censored himself for such imaginings. He was... male, single, in good health, and she was an attractive woman near at hand.

He did not admit to himself they were both lonely, but the realization was there. *He* was certainly lonely—if she was, she hid it well.

But a gentleman did not bother the help.

"I have been in your employ for several years now, Mr. Dolan."

Dolan mentally prepared himself for a pretty little farewell speech, though the part of him still comfortable with a stonemason's tools wanted to hit something with his bare, callused fists.

"I will give you the highest possible recommendation, Miss Ingraham, and do all in my power to see you properly placed and well compensated in your next position."

"Will you?" She arched an eyebrow, her tone so dry and starchy Dolan risked meeting her gaze. "I am touched. Also puzzled."

"Regarding?"

"Do you intend to win this lawsuit, or lose it? For if you intend to win it, then surely you will want to curry my favor, Mr. Dolan. I am the only party who can credibly testify that you have never in any manner neglected your daughter's upbringing, that you are a doting—no, a loving and devoted—papa, that you would cheerfully die a thousand painful deaths for this one little girl, and yet you seek to disengage my services. This is quite, quite puzzling."

She said nothing more, but left Dolan there beside her on the bench, rearranging the chess pieces he'd put on the board between himself and Deene.

"Miss Ingraham... *Amy*. I cannot allow you to be involved in... I have connections in Dublin, York, Edinburgh, Paris, even Boston, if you'd..." He fell silent, wondering how much she guessed, how much she knew, and if Deene had already tried to bribe her.

"What's it to be, Jonathan Dolan? Will you win or lose, and don't think to dissemble with me. I've seen you with your daughter."

It took him long silent minutes to understand that he was being offered a sort of conditional friendship, a cooperation on a level he had not anticipated, from an ally he could never have approached directly, not about this.

He considered prevarications, outright lies, and near-truths, but...

Amy Ingraham had called him Jonathan. His mother had called him Jonathan, and his dear departed wife had—at least toward the end of their marriage—and now this quiet, sensible woman had used his given name and asked him for the truth. He closed his eyes, and when he opened them, she'd linked her arm with his there on the bench.

"The truth, sir. I'll know if you're lying—just ask Georgina."

To his very great surprise, and even greater relief, he did indeed tell her the truth.

❧

"If you could define the problem, I might know better how to advise you to solve it." Kesmore passed his guest a drink but doubted Deene was even aware of the glass in his hand.

"I'm mucking up my marriage, or my... something."

"Most of us do, eventually. Unmucking it can be a cheerful undertaking."

Deene's incredulous expression suggested he could not envision his host being cheerful in any circumstances, but then, a lack of imagination plagued most new husbands when on the outs with their wives.

"Sit, Deene, and do not ignore your drink."

Deene tossed back his brandy and dropped onto a sofa like a load of bricks. "Evie and I are civil, but she has it in her head I'm not to hold Dolan to account where Georgie is concerned. Lawsuits, particularly between family, are scandalous to my wife's way of thinking."

"They are scandalous to any sane person's way of thinking, also tedious, uncomfortable, and expensive. Litigation has always struck me rather like tuning a fine watch with a stonemason's hammer." Kesmore appropriated a cushion from a wing chair and took a seat on the raised hearth, the better for the fire to cook some relief into the aching muscles of his back and leg. "I've yet to meet the Windham who flinched in the face of scandal, though, including most especially Their Graces. The lawsuit itself is not the entire problem."

Deene scowled. "It took me a week to figure that out, though the lawsuit is certainly part of it. Evie will not countenance such a protracted and public scandal."

"You endured a week during which, if I might be delicate, you did not enjoy the occasion of connubial bliss in the arms of your bride."

Deene made a noise a lady would have described as a grunt and another man would have understood as unhappy assent.

"Who is holding out on whom, Deene?"

Deene studied his empty glass. "I'm not sure. I don't make advances beyond the perfunctory, which she does not rebuff, but she doesn't make advances either."

"And a good time is had by all."

This brought Deene's head up, a battle light in the man's blue eyes. "And when the fair Louisa takes you into disfavor, Kesmore, do you go charging forth into the bedroom, saber at the ready, risking all, only to have her freeze you with a look or a word?"

Kesmore pretended to fuss the pillow under his arse rather than smile openly at Deene's misery. "It might surprise you to know, young Deene, that the fair Louisa, *particularly* on those rare and mistaken occasions when she has taken me into disfavor, generally *wants* me to come charging in with my saber at the ready. She is not a woman who finds a propensity for pretty talk a winning quality in her swain, and I am not a swain to disappoint my lady."

"If I do ask Evie what she wants of me," Deene said, glowering at the fire, "she will say, if I have to ask her, then I don't understand what the problem is, or some such rot. Women speak in riddles when you most need them to be clear and direct."

"Why do you need to be anything? Many a considerate husband goes for a week without pestering his wife, Deene. The ladies become indisposed, they get preoccupied, they… need their rest."

Deene blinked. "I'm thinking of entering William in the June meet at Epsom."

"Ah. A show of preoccupation. Brilliant strategy, one heartily endorsed by the most proud and unsatisfied husbands the world over. Why don't you instead find a cozy, private moment between the sheets and ask your wife not about lawsuits or scandals, but if she'd like you to make love to her? Tell her you miss her more than you'd miss the beating heart torn from your chest, and nothing would bring you as much gratification as seeing to her pleasure."

"What if she says no?"

"I didn't say you should necessarily ask her with words—or expect her to see to your pleasure while you're about it."

Deene's brows shot up. He was off the couch in the next moment and heading for the door. "Thanks for the libation. My regards to Lady Louisa."

❧

Deene had not filed his blasted lawsuit. Eve knew the papers yet resided in the estate desk, just as she knew with uncomfortable clarity that Westhaven had put his finger on a part of the real problem: Eve had married an honorable man, one who could not simply walk away from an obligation to his niece.

And yet, Eve could not merely accept that another man—however outwardly honorable—had taken her measure, seen how she could be exploited financially and socially, and used his intimate charms to achieve her complicity in his selfish ends.

Then too, she could not countenance Georgie growing into young womanhood amid a cloud of whispers and gossip, dodging the smirks and knowing glances of the other girls, sent invitations not out of graciousness but out of spite. This Eve truly, genuinely could not have endured, and she was certain it was an outcome Deene had not figured into his strategy.

The front door slammed, and Eve glanced at the clock. The hour was late enough that Deene might go straight above stairs, where she might have been waiting for him, but for having lost track of the time completely.

"Belt said you were nesting in here."

Eve's husband stood in the library doorway, looking windblown and tired—and devastatingly attractive. Also hesitant.

The hesitance tore at her spirit, and yet she understood it, too. "Deene." She rose and crossed the room, holding out her arms so he would know they hadn't yet descended to nodding at each other in greeting. "I thought perhaps you might stay the night in Town."

His arms came around her, bringing with them the scents of horse, rain, and husband. "A little dirty weather is to be expected in spring." He hugged her to him, making Eve wonder if he meant to imbue his observation with comforting symbolism. "Shall we have a nightcap? I've rung for a tray to be brought in here."

They were to stay on neutral territory for a bit, which was a relief. "A biscuit or two and some tea wouldn't go amiss."

He walked with her to the sofa before the hearth, where Eve had indeed been nesting. Pillows and blankets marked her preferred end of the couch, and a novel lay on the side table.

"I do not expect you to wait up for me, Evie, but I appreciate that you did."

He was being conciliatory or simply polite. In either case, Eve did not want to fight with him, not silently, not politely, not in any way.

"William was in good form today. Bannister let me take him over some proper jumps."

Deene came down beside her on the sofa. "Which might have scared me witless, had I watched. Bad enough I let you and that colt hop logs and ditches and streams all over the shire."

"William is a horse in a million, isn't he?"

Something flickered across Deene's tired features. "For you, he is. Kesmore sends his regards."

"And Westhaven his."

"They are spies, the lot of them. What did you tell your brother, Evie?"

She picked up Deene's arm and put it around her shoulders, where it lay unmoving for a moment. When she put her head on his shoulder, that arm curled a little, so the side of his thumb could stroke her neck.

"I told him we've hit a rough patch, and it's tearing at me awfully. He said I must find a way to compromise." To say this out loud was to take a risk; but with a flash of insight, Eve realized that to keep it inside, to pretend there was no problem worth mentioning, was a worse risk yet.

Deene blew out a sigh. "I said much the same thing to Kesmore, who gave me much the same advice. And I want to, Evie… I want to find a way through this, but Georgie…"

Eve put a finger over his lips. "I want to as well, and perhaps that's as much progress as we can hope for in one day."

They ate mostly in silence, exchanging just a few safe comments about the horses, until Deene took Eve by the hand and helped her to her feet.

"Something about this room is different." He was

peering at her as he spoke, the room being mostly in shadows.

"I've not been exactly tidy." Eve kept her gaze away from the far wall, where something was very different indeed. Deene studied her, then took a candle from the mantel, and as if he'd divined her thoughts, he took the candle across the room.

"I had forgotten this portrait entirely."

Eve's feet took her to stand beside her husband, when her flagging courage ought to have had her making her good nights. "You were handsome even as a boy."

"And Marie was pretty. She looks like a child, though, and this was painted right before her wedding."

"She was a child, Deene. Sixteen? Seventeen? Certainly not a woman grown at that point."

"And yet…"

The look he gave Eve was inscrutable, and she wished she could just ask him if hanging the portrait served as a peace offering or an irritant. She'd meant it as a peace offering, but now, hours later…

"We can take it down if you think it doesn't suit."

"It suits." He leaned in and kissed her cheek, then winged his free arm at her. "It suits exactly."

A tension in Eve's middle eased, though not entirely. She was coming to expect a subtle dyspepsia to plague her throughout the day, a symptom of a marriage in trouble and a wife who knew not what to do about it.

Deene must have felt the same way, for he was particularly solicitous as they prepared for bed. He did not undress in the dressing room, but remained where Eve could see him and feast her eyes on his nakedness.

Had he lost weight? Were his ribs and the bones of his hips a trifle more in evidence?

"Will you be going to Town tomorrow, Deene?"

"After I watch William go, very likely. Would you like to come with me?"

He hadn't extended such an invitation in more than week. "Perhaps I shall."

He shrugged into a forget-me-not blue dressing gown that made his eyes look positively electric, and shifted to stand behind where Eve sat at her vanity.

"Have I told you lately, Wife, what beautiful hair you have? The feel of it…" He closed his eyes and let her gathered hair run through his hands. "I have missed the feel of your hair." He brought a lock to his nose. "The scent of it, the warmth of it tickling my chin when I hold you."

He might have whispered these things in her ear two weeks ago. Now he had merely to recite them, and Eve's insides started churning.

"It wants braiding, Deene."

He opened his eyes, and in the vanity mirror, Eve saw him smile. There was a hint of mischief in that smile—also a touch of sadness. He braided her hair with brisk efficiency and then laid his dressing gown across the foot of the bed. "I'll get the candles, Wife."

So she watched him move naked around the room, watched the play of firelight on his lean flanks when he knelt to bank the coals, watched him stretch up to blow out the candles on the mantel, watched him stalk over to the bed and climb in with no ceremony whatsoever.

"You will keep those cold feet to yourself, Deene."

"Cold feet?"

Oh, what an opening she'd handed him, and without meaning to. Entirely without meaning to—he had her that rattled.

"You run them up my calves, and then we're both shivering."

"I am not shivering, Evie." He scooped her up and arranged her on her side, so the warmth of his chest blanketed her back. His hairy, muscular legs snugged up to her bottom, and his arm came around her middle.

She loved it when he held her like this, loved the way it made her feel safe and cherished and toasty all over. The only thing that might have made it better would be if she had thought to take off her nightgown so she might be as naked as he.

"You will tell me if there's anything else I can do to make you more comfortable, Wife."

His lips grazed her nape. A casual caress, one he'd indulged in many times before, and each time, Eve felt the impact of it in low, wonderful places. She wanted him to do it again.

And he did, more lingeringly, more tenderly.

Never in their marriage had he made her ask for his attentions, and Eve was not about to start now—no matter how badly she needed the reassurance, no matter how passionately she wanted… him.

And yet… she needed to find the compromise that would allow them to move ahead, and Deene had not filed his lawsuit.

She shifted so they were facing each other on the mattress. "Do you think to get me with child and then file your lawsuit, Deene?"

He looked for a moment as if he'd rise up from the bed and not come back, but then his features composed themselves. "And if you had a girl child, Evie, would you then expect me to wait to file the petition until you were carrying a second child? To withdraw the suit until we had a son, and then file yet again? And what of a spare? Anthony does not want to marry, and the burden of the succession is ours."

He was so angry.

And so hurt. They were both hurt, and even as Eve despaired, she also recognized that any common ground was better than none.

"Please make love to me, Lucas. I need you to make love to me."

He was on her in an instant, poised over her, one arm under her neck, the other on her hip, pushing her nightgown up. "We cannot go on like this, Wife, but if I tell you I will not file that damned lawsuit, will you agree not to take any rash measures yourself?"

Rash measures? With her husband's weight pressing her into the mattress, Eve tried to fathom his meaning.

Women could prevent conception, or try to. They could take herbs to make it less likely a child quickened. She'd had reason to learn these terrible things seven years ago.

"I will not betray the vows I took at the altar, Deene."

"For God's sake, call me Lucas. At least here, at least when we're like this…"

He fell silent, and Eve closed her eyes, feeling the hot length of his engorged manhood against her belly. "Lucas, please… I want… I need…"

He slid into her, a slow, hot glory that had her body

fisting tightly around him in a welcome that should
have been ecstatic. He loved her slowly, thoroughly,
ravishing her with physical pleasure until she understood that until that night, he'd been holding back
with her.

He'd been her husband and her lover but had denied
them both the greatest depth of his passion. When at
long last he allowed himself to spend in her body,
when Eve had lost awareness of anything save the
pleasure he showered upon her, she lay beneath him,
sheltered in his arms and saddened beyond measure.

Deene had made his point: if they did not find a
way through their current difficulties, Eve would be
giving up not just her husband's expert lovemaking,
not just passion and pleasure and companionship of the
deepest order, she would also be giving up the only
man she would ever love.

Eleven

"THE MARQUIS OF DEENE, SIR. HE CALLS UPON you alone."

Deene pushed past the butler—a stuffy old fellow who smelled of camphor—and found Dolan in his shirtsleeves at a massive desk much like the one in Deene's own library.

"We're family, Brampton. I hardly think I need be announced."

Dolan did not rise, which showed exactly the kind of animal cunning Deene expected from his brother-in-law.

"That will be all, Brampton, though have the kitchen send up a tray. Marriage has apparently put his lordship off his feed." Dolan waited until the butler had withdrawn before turning an expression with a lot of teeth—and no welcome whatsoever—on his guest. "How is it you know my butler's name?"

"They all know one another's names, Dolan. It's what we overpay them for."

Dolan did not roll down his shirtsleeves, though Deene had the sense it wasn't an intentional rudeness;

it was instead a function of having been caught off guard by an opponent.

"How's Georgie?"

Dolan's brows rose. "Still protesting her French lessons, though she has an aptitude for them. You may use that against me in court: I force her to learn French by withholding my granny's Irish lullabies from her."

"You had a granny? I am astonished to find you were not whelped by some creature sporting scales and breathing fire."

Dolan fiddled with a gleaming silver penknife. "Insult my sainted mother, Deene, and a lawsuit will be the least of your problems."

"My apologies. I meant only to insult you."

Except he hadn't, exactly. Antagonize, of course, but not quite insult. If Evie would not countenance a lawsuit, she'd certainly not countenance a duel.

Dolan brushed his thumb over the blade of the penknife. "I was under the impression a gentleman—using the term as loosely as present company necessitates—plotting to do murder on the field of honor generally slapped a sweaty riding glove across his opponent's chin before witnesses of similar rank."

"I cannot challenge you to a duel, Dolan, though every day you draw breath offends me."

"Oh, of course. Because I married your dear sister, whose hems I was not fit to kiss, though I certainly paid enough to have them trimmed in lace. You'll not be seeing your niece very frequently if this is the tack you take, Deene. A bit more charm is wanted or some lordly attempts at groveling—one's in-laws ought to be a source of amusement at least."

"I don't see Georgie at all as it is, Dolan. I have nothing to lose."

This point must have struck Dolan as valid. He rose from his desk, his expression thoughtful. It remained that way until a lavish silver tray fit for the highest tea before the highest sticklers was brought in and set on the desk.

"You will please pour," Dolan said. "I haven't the knack."

This was not said with any particular sneer or smirk, and it set the tone for an oddly civilized session of tea, crumpets, sandwiches, cakes, fruit, and cheese.

"There is an issue between us," Deene said when the tray had been decimated. "You made my sister miserable, and you are not the best resource to have the raising of her daughter."

"You are so confident of your facts, Deene. One would envy you this, except the quality is an inherited reflex of inbred aristocracy and not a function of any particular wit or study on your part."

Dolan had a way with irony—the Irish did; the Scots did as well.

"You are telling me Marie went into your loving arms at the altar and never once looked back? You are telling me she consented to marry you of her own free will? You are telling me she was happy and well cared for married to you?"

"She was a minor at the time of the wedding. Her consent was neither needed nor binding, and I have been patient with your rudeness long enough. You may either leave or state your reasons for imposing on my fast-dwindling and unlikely-to-be-repeated hospitality."

The moment became delicate, all the more so for having to seem otherwise.

"I am prepared to leave here and go directly to White's, where I will place the following wager in the book in legible script: I propose a match race, my colt against yours, the stakes to be as follows."

Dolan listened, then sat back and rubbed his chin.

"You would make these terms public, Deene?"

This was the crucial moment, when Dolan's shrewdness and social ambition had to blend and balance so the choice Deene wanted Dolan to make became the choice Dolan grasped as his own device.

"You would not trust my word any farther than you could throw me, Dolan." Deene shot his cuffs and fiddled with a sapphire-encrusted sleeve button.

"Would you trust mine?"

Deene wrinkled his nose. "Marie accused you of many things, but dishonesty was not among them. Your reputation, plebeian though it is, is one for veracity."

"Such flattery, Deene... I can only return the compliment. You are a pompous, arrogant, overstuffed exponent of your most useless and only occasionally decorative class, but if you give me your word you'll abide by the terms laid out here today, then I will give you my word as well. Neither of us would be served by visiting notoriety on Georgina's situation."

Deene thrust out a hand. "Done. On the terms stated."

Dolan had a firm handshake, and somewhere along the way, somebody had explained to him that the gentleman's handshake was not an exercise in breaking finger bones.

"When shall we do this, Deene, and where?"

"There's a practice course not two miles from Epsom, and I'm thinking the week before the June meet. Much later, and the heat can be oppressive."

He should have been more casual, should have kept his cards closer to his chest, but to let the matter linger was going to wear on Eve and see the horse overconditioned.

"Last week in May, then, with the social crowd still preoccupied in Town. The alternative would be July, when the house parties start up, or after the grouse moors open in August."

Dolan was watching him, no doubt gauging from Deene's reaction just what the state of King William's conditioning was.

"Suit yourself, Dolan. I was going to enter William at Epsom—anybody with ears has heard that much in the clubs."

"May, then. I'll be having a look at this course before I agree to turn my pony loose on it, Deene. Dirty footing or rotten timber serves no one."

"Now you do attempt to insult me, Dolan. I thought Greymoor might head the ground jury."

"A ground jury? This isn't exactly a Jockey Club match, Deene."

"Nor is it merely a lark between two gentlemen."

Dolan appeared to consider the point. "Greymoor and two fellows of his choosing, one from your set, one from mine."

"Fair enough."

"And, Deene? This match will be conducted as if it were a lark between two gentlemen. I want a damned crowd to see you go down to defeat, a big, not entirely inebriated crowd, the titled half of which is going to line my pockets every bit as much as you are."

"But of course." Deene had the sense this boasting was where the real posturing had begun. "We'll make it the usual holiday, and see who goes down to defeat before whom."

Dolan smiled again, but this time, the expression reached the man's eyes. It struck Deene that had he wished to, Jonathan Dolan might have been a charming man, even handsome in his way.

"I'll see myself out, Dolan, and wish you best of luck."

"Oh, and the same to you, Deene. You'll need it."

A beat of silence went by, during which Deene suspected he was to ask again after his niece, perhaps even ask to see her. He did not ask; Dolan did not offer.

Deene took his leave, trying to formulate how he'd convey this development—some acceptable version of this development—to his wife.

❧

"What is this?" Eve looked at the shreds of paper in her lap, and the red string among them.

"That is my promise to you, Eve."

Deene stood over her where she sat at breakfast. Since they'd last made love a week ago, it was as close as he'd come to her, even in bed.

"Your promise?" Eve glanced up and noticed that the footman typically assigned to tend the sideboard was nowhere to be seen. "What promise is this?"

"We're at a stalemate, Wife." Deene moved off and closed the door to the breakfast parlor. "You cannot countenance a lawsuit. I cannot abandon a promise made to my sister. I am promising you I will not now, I will not ever, resort to litigation to keep my promise to Marie."

He looked very fierce but also guarded. The guardedness kept Eve from throwing her arms around his neck in relief.

"I am very pleased to hear this, Deene. Can we discuss this?"

"What is there to discuss?"

He took the seat at the head of the table, which was at Eve's right elbow. The way he snapped his serviette across his lap only confirmed Eve's sense that their problem was intensifying, not resolving.

"How will you keep your promise to Marie when Mr. Dolan does not allow you to be a proper uncle to our niece?"

Our niece. Deene speared Eve with a look at her word choice, a look laden with incredulity and maybe even—*God help them*—resentment.

"Are you sure you want me to answer your question, Eve? If I do answer, you might like it even less than you liked the idea of a perfectly legal civil suit brought by legal intermediaries and resolved by a judge according to rules of evidence, statute, and case law."

The tea Eve had begun her day with started rebelling in her belly. "I do want you to answer the question, Deene."

But Eve wondered what he could say that she'd want to hear? That he'd decided his niece meant nothing to him? That his niece meant less than his wife? Was this what Westhaven had been intimating all those days ago? Was Eve angling for some assurance of her place as foremost in her husband's affections?

Was she still that insecure? Still that much afraid her past controlled her future?

"There is to be a friendly little match race between Dolan's colt and King William. A sum of money has been wagered, all quite symbolic and good-natured."

She studied him as he poured a cup of tea for her, then one for himself. The pleasant scent of Darjeeling wafted to her nose, and steam curled up from their cups as Deene set the cream and sugar by Eve's plate.

"You have wagered my dowry, haven't you?"

He spooned sugar into her cup. "I have made a gentleman's wager with Dolan. It will not be reflected on any betting books. The amount remains between Dolan and myself, and even he understands that to bruit it about would only redound to our mutual discredit."

Deene poured cream into Eve's cup and gave her tea a stir. So attentive, her husband, so considerate.

What had she done?

"I was given to understand our finances are tentative, Deene."

"By whom?"

"Anthony, for one. He was apologizing for the household allowance at Denning Hall before he last took his leave of us, but I honestly cannot agree with his assessment of matters."

Deene stirred his own tea. "In what regard?"

"The allowance is ample, at least based on what I know so far. Her Grace and Westhaven have been on something of a campaign in recent months to make sure Jenny and I understand and can manage our own funds. It isn't complicated."

Deene blew out a breath. "It should not be, but add properties all over the realm, throw in a sorry lot of bankers, allow a few solicitors onto your dole, and fairly soon, it's all Anthony can do to keep the picture up to date, much less make improvements upon it."

His words, tired, quiet, and laced with despair tore at Eve even as they enraged her. "So why in God's name would you wager money we cannot afford on a stupid race that's run for pride's sake?"

It was the worst thing she could have said. She knew it as the words left her mouth, and yet... Deene's attempt at a compromise was scaring her more than any lawsuit might have.

"My pride is indeed a stupid thing, Wife, and yet I cannot seem to misplace it long enough to please you."

He lifted his tea halfway to his mouth, then put it down untasted. If Eve could not find something to say—the right something to say—this was the moment one of them would stalk out of the room, and tonight, for the first time, they would sleep in separate beds.

"Deene, I don't want to quarrel with you. I should not have said what I did just now, but I don't understand... I cannot understand how I am to accept this."

"And I cannot understand how you expect me to do nothing, Eve, while I watch my niece grow up from a distance, as if I'm some sort of monster, a leper because of my title and standing, because of things I cannot change. Marie loathed the notion of marriage to that man, and Georgie is the only good thing to come of the entire tragedy. I cannot abandon her. I cannot."

Eve nodded. His reasoning, stated thus, made a kind of sense.

But so did hers: if she'd wanted proof that her marriage ranked below this claim the past held on Deene, her husband had just handed it to her. He was wagering at least the sum of her dowry on the outcome of a single race, money they could not afford, money he'd garnered solely by marrying Eve.

She sipped her tea in silence, wondering what else her husband had tossed to the winds of chance along with their financial well-being, and any hope their marriage had of thriving.

❦

The decision to withhold the entirety of Deene's bet with Dolan sat uneasily, but less uneasily than it had several days ago.

Deene understood clearly that his wife disapproved of the match race, disapproved of the stakes as she knew them, and disapproved of the notion that Deene had concocted the entire scheme without consulting her.

And as to that last, Deene could only reason that had he discussed it with her, she would have somehow prevented him from challenging Dolan. She would have turned her big green eyes on him, let him see her disappointment, and that would have been that.

"He's getting a sense of purpose about him," Eve said from her perch on the rail. "He's growing up, and none too soon."

Deene followed his wife's gaze out across the prac-tice field, where Aelfreth and William were tearing around a course of three-foot jumps.

"He's getting stronger," Deene allowed. "He still isn't where I'd want him to be, though he's trying his heart out."

Eve sighed and glanced over at him, suggesting to Deene that yet again, he'd said something that could be taken on different levels. Their marriage had become a chess tournament played out on several boards at once, and over it all lay a compulsion to apprise Eve of what exactly hung in the balance with this race.

"The difficulty is that Aelfreth has not settled into his role." Eve climbed down from the fence, nimble as a monkey in a pair of boy's breeches and old tall boots. "When they approach the jumps, they're still in discussions about whose job it is to pick the take-off spot. They should be well past that by now."

"What do you mean?"

"Between horse and rider, one of the two has the better eye for choosing the best distance for the take-off spot, and often it's the horse. A sensible rider will trust the horse and intervene only if he thinks the horse's choice will be lacking."

Deene watched as in the distance horse and rider cleared the last hedge from a place just a hair too close to the jump to be in perfect rhythm. "Aelfreth is a good jockey."

"He is good, but he's on a young horse with a lot of speed, power, and discernment. Unless Aelfreth knows something the horse does not—the ground is not as solid as it looks, the land slopes away immediately following the jump, there's a hard turn into the next obstacle— then he's better off letting William build up confidence in his own judgment over the next two weeks."

"So William learns that if Aelfreth makes a suggestion, there's good reason for it," Deene concluded. "Can the horse learn that in two weeks?"

Eve's expression was doubtful. "He can learn it in a single outing with the right rider, but Aelfreth keeps changing the game. For this jump, he makes a suggestion, for that jump, he sits back until the last stride and then tries to make a correction. For the next two jumps, he battles the horse for the decision, and so on. They cannot go on like this."

Another phrase laden with double meaning.

"Can you explain this to Aelfreth?"

"She has." Bannister spoke up from several feet away. "But when the lad's flying at a four-foot hedge at a dead gallop, it's a different proposition than in the schooling ring."

Deene resisted the urge to punch his senior trainer. "I rode dispatch, need I remind you, Bannister, behind enemy lines in all manner of conditions. I comprehend the difficulties."

Eve's gaze remained on the horse and rider trotting over the field several hundred yards away. "I have wondered, Deene, if you would not be the better rider for this race."

"She has a point." Bannister's tone was that carefully neutral inflection observed when an employee cannot raise his voice to an employer, or speak the words "I told you so."

"I weigh twice what Aelfreth weighs, I've never done more than hack the colt or school him in the arena, and it's too late in the game to make such a change in any case."

And there again, his words were fraught with meaning. Whatever the ramifications of this race for Deene's marriage, it was far too late to back out of his wagers. Word had gone out in the clubs, the side betting was heating up, the course had been rented, the stewards chosen, and the plans laid. Bannister had managed to get a spy to Dolan's stables, and if anything, Goblin's year of rest and conditioning had put the stallion in fine form.

What else had Deene expected? That Dolan would risk everything he held dear on some broken-down nag?

"I find I am peckish." Eve looped her arm through Deene's. "Will you accompany me up to the house?"

"Of course." But he could not help one last glance at Aelfreth, a glance Eve had to note.

"You cannot lecture him now, Deene. You must show confidence in Aelfreth, so he will show confidence in himself and in the horse."

"How is it you understand this? I've probably spent a great deal more time on a horse than you have, and yet I cannot find the words to explain what makes perfect sense when it comes out of your mouth."

She smiled, a tired, sad version of her usual good cheer, and Deene wanted to howl with frustration.

"I understand because I have crawled, Husband, and been proud of myself for even that accomplishment."

"We all start out crawling—"

She shifted her grip, so they were holding hands, something they hadn't done in days. "Come sit with me."

A vague uneasiness took hold of Deene's insides. They needed to talk, to come to some understandings, to start over… but the wrong talk, the wrong under-standings, and he had every confidence Eve would be off to visit her siblings indefinitely. When Deene was in Town, Eve would be in the country. If he went north shooting in the autumn, she'd depart for Portugal within days of his return. His parents had managed for decades with such arrangements, and Eve had made no secret that she'd originally wanted a white marriage.

He sat beside his wife, despair crowding him more closely than the small woman immediately to his right.

"Do you recall that I once suffered a bad fall, Deene?"

Deene, Deene, Deene. She no longer called him Husband, much less Lucas.

"Quite some years ago, yes. I am pleased to note you don't seem bothered by it now."

"Every time I get on a horse, I'm bothered by it, but not the way I thought I would be."

This was a confidence, a precious, unlooked-for break in the marital clouds. "What do you mean, Evie?"

"I could not walk, you know. I did something, something to my… hip, my back, I'm not sure what, but it hurt like blazes just to breathe. There were times…" She stared hard at a bed of roses coming into bloom, while beside her, Deene did not dare move. "There were times I wanted to die. I could not get to the chamber pot without assistance, Deene. My life became a balancing act, to eat and drink enough to sustain me, but not one bit more, because everything one takes in… you understand?"

He nodded, not wanting to understand, but comprehending the extent of her indignities clearly.

"I could not walk, I could not use crutches, even, but one day I realized I could not bear for my mother and sisters, much less the servants, to see me in such a condition. I could not… I could not walk, so I started crawling. I crawled first on my elbows and one knee. This is not dignified, but it will serve with some practice. Louisa came upon me once thus, crawling back to my bed. She became Cerberus at the gates of my personal hell, ensuring that if I said I did not want to be disturbed, by God, nothing disturbed me."

"Evie…" He covered her hand with his own. "I did not know."

"Nobody knew the real extent of my incapacity, not even Louisa, though she likely guessed. I crawled for weeks, then I hopped, then I used canes, and I learned something, something you learned riding dispatch."

"I learned nothing riding dispatch save to choose the best mount I could find, say my prayers, and ride like hell." He could not have let go of her hand in that moment to save his own soul.

"You learned that you could not worry over the whole ride. You could not face covering twenty miles by a setting quarter moon behind the lines with no provisions and a tired mount. You could face only the terrain between your present location and the stream across the valley, or between the woods where you caught your breath and the next church steeple. You lurched, dashed, slunk, and crawled if you had to, from one shadow to the other."

She'd described it exactly, the race against the dawn, the darting from shadow to shadow, the soul-deep weariness that made the senses sharper, not more dull.

"You're saying we're riding dispatch?"

"With this race, Deene, your lads, your jockeys, Bannister, even the damned horse look to you for their confidence. I could not allow you to lecture Aelfreth just now when what he needed was a smile, a whack on the back, and some ribald remark unfit for ladies' ears."

Such remarks abounded, there being endless parallels between riding horses and a man's sexual endeavors. "You're saying I have to get us all to the next steeple in safety."

"I should not presume." She was still staring at the roses. "Your people would ride to hell for you, but I feel I have by my actions contributed to the household's sense of—"

He put his arm around her shoulders and squeezed. "Hush. We'll manage. We are managing." Barely.

She turned her face into his shoulder, not bothering to argue.

"Evie, will you stay with me?" He nearly whispered the question, so much did he dread the answer. His heart started a slow pounding in his chest when she did not immediately offer him reassurances. "Evie?"

She drew back a little. "We will get through this race, Deene. Until that finish line is crossed, other obstacles are just going to have to wait, aren't they?"

He did not experience this as a reprieve, not even when Eve led him up to their rooms and undressed him to his skin, not even when she tugged him toward the bed then let him watch while she removed every stitch of her own clothing.

She was making some statement having to do with

confidence—her confidence, perhaps, and it did not reassure Deene in the least. They hadn't coupled since Deene had last made advances to his wife, but this time—for the first time—Eve made all the advances.

She straddled him, the tail end of her braid tickling Deene's groin in a peculiar little dance she could not possibly have planned. While she feathered her thumbs over his nipples, Deene tried to memorize the angle of her brows, knit in concentration while she studied the effect of her touch on his flesh.

"We are similar in this regard," she announced, studying his puckered nipples.

"And similar in the pleasure it gives us."

She leaned forward and stroked her tongue over one of his nipples, then pinched him lightly with her teeth. "I like it when you do that to me. Do you like it when I do it to you?"

He could not find the words. He cradled the back of her head with his palm and silently asked her for more of the same attentions. Before she was done with him, she'd put her mouth to his cock, tasting and teasing him as if he were something served up on special occasions at Gunter's, making the muscles in his groin and belly ache with the force of his arousal.

And yet, he did not ask her to have done with him, to slip her hot, wet flesh over his and put them both out of their misery.

Evie, will you stay with me?

Maybe this was her answer; maybe she would make damned sure she conceived an heir for him, and their obligations to each other would be at an end.

It was not fair, that she'd be so obstinate, that she'd

make such demands on him, that his best efforts to keep all the promises he owed should come at such a cost.

It was not fair to him; *it was not fair to her.* The solution Deene had envisioned, a gentleman's agreement undertaken with ungentlemanly determination, began to waver before his eyes. Eve shifted, and then her mouth was gone, leaving a need to join with her that came from Deene's very soul.

When she would have mounted him—a novel boldness, coming from her—Deene rolled with her, so she was beneath him—so she could not get away.

Before he was done loving her, her cries of pleasure were swallowed in his kisses, her fingernails scored his back and buttocks, and her tears wet his chest.

And yet, he could not ask her again: *Evie, will you stay with me?*

∽⁂∾

A race meet was an oddly democratic event, with there being no ability to keep any particular segment of society off the premises—and no incentive for doing so. The crowds segregated themselves such that the festivities might be enjoyed in a station-appropriate manner, with half-pay officers and their doxies enjoying indifferent ale, cards, and one another's company in one pavilion, while in another, the shopkeepers on holiday could bring their ladies for an outing, and in a third, the cream of society would lounge about with servants tending to every comfort.

Eve envisioned it all through new if tired eyes as she and her husband scanned the scene the day before King William was to meet Goblin.

"The place will be thronged by this time tomorrow."

Deene did not sound happy about this, but unless he was in the stables bantering with his lads or in conversation with the horse, he hadn't sounded happy about much of anything lately. He sat on his gelding, his frown conveying displeasure at all and sundry.

"William has run before crowds in the past, Deene. He seems happy enough to be here."

Aelfreth had hacked over earlier in the day at a leisurely pace, with Deene escorting on Beast, and Bannister on another gelding.

"He's happy because he had his audience with you, Evie. He was about to start weaving in his stall until he caught sight of you on your mare."

"He was pleased to see the mare."

This earned her a smile from her husband. Not a blinding display of teeth and mischief, but a grin that acknowledged a shift in their private dealings.

Eve could not keep her hands off her husband, and the situation was *vexing*. Having once initiated marital intimacies with him, she found it impossible not to take advantage of a wife's privileges in the company of a generous, creative, and lusty husband. If Deene's attentions had pleased her before, they left her positively witless now, a situation she suspected he exploited to further confuse her priorities in matters outside the bedroom.

Which they discussed not at all. Eve leaned forward and patted her mare.

"Let's ride the course, Deene. All the rain is likely to have affected the footing."

His smile faded as his gaze swung out over the rolling green terrain around them. "Goddamn rain."

"William is not a delicate flower. He and Aelfreth have been galloping in all sorts of weather and managing more than adequately."

"Dolan's arriving."

Eve followed her husband's line of sight, where two grooms were leading a big, restive gray down past a row of stalls.

"A handsome animal."

"The horse or his owner?"

"I meant the horse. Mr. Dolan's looks are a matter of indifference to me."

Deene's mouth flattened, making Eve wish she'd kept the last comment to herself. There was never a right thing to say, but there were so many wrong things to say. Marriage like this was wearying and fraught, and though she tried to tell herself otherwise, the quagmire they found themselves in wasn't simply a function of facing the financial consequences of the bet Deene had made with Dolan.

Eve waited until their horses were ambling along toward the scythed swatch of grass before the first jump, a fairly low stile meant to get the race off to a safe and uneventful start, to inform the horses that it wasn't to be a test of pure speed on the flat.

"Will you tell me the rest of your wager with Dolan?"

Now Deene petted his horse. "What makes you think there's more to it than the small fortune already hanging in the balance?"

Not a small fortune, a very great fortune by most people's standards. "That fortune is more or less a windfall in the form of my settlements. You didn't have it two months ago, and you'll likely manage if you don't have it two months hence. Such a wager should not be costing you your sleep night after night."

"Why are we discussing this now, Evie?"

She fiddled with her reins. "You are hedging, which confirms my sense you have not been entirely honest with me." To give her husband time to consider his answer, she urged her mare into a canter—one rarely trotted in a blasted sidesaddle—and headed for the second jump.

It was at some distance, to allow the horses to gather speed early in the race—to tempt them to gather too much speed—and set on the top of a small rise, which would also encourage the jockeys to ask for a tad too much effort, given that the land sloped away sharply on the back side of the jump.

"What else do you think I've wagered, Wife?"

A question for a question. Eve was not encouraged.

"Something you are hesitant to tell me because you think I won't understand."

"It isn't that you won't understand." Deene frowned at the jump. "At least the footing on this one will be solid."

It would, because the jump was on a rise, but the footing at the top and bottom of the rise would be mushy, perhaps dangerously so at speed—all the more reason not to rush the fence, and why did everything—every blasted thing—seem like a comment on Eve's marriage?

"So tell me, Deene. I will not pitch a tantrum here on my horse. You know me at least that well."

He glanced over at her and sent his horse toward the third jump, a brush fence, the first of three such on the course. This was a straightforward effort, but it lay in the shade of a line of trees, and therein lay the challenge. A horse's eyes would not adjust for changes in lighting as quickly as the rider's would, and thus a jump in shadow might or might not be as evident to the mount as it was to the jockey. A smart jockey would give the animal time to sight in on the obstacle. An overeager jockey would consider the jump to be one of the easier on the course and rush the fence.

"I hate this kind of question," Deene observed, scowling at the jump. "We should have practiced such efforts more consistently with William."

"We vary the timing of his workouts throughout the day, so the shadows lie in different places and at different angles. Do you think I cannot understand the concept of honor, Deene? I know you and Dolan are at daggers drawn over your niece's situation."

"You called her our niece when last this issue arose." His tone was devoid of heat—carefully so.

They did not argue, which meant they also did not discuss, which meant Eve felt her marriage slipping from her grasp. She cantered on toward the next fence, a big, stout oxer—a jump with both height and spread—in the form of a sort of tabletop stile. The wood was dark, solid looking, and the jump was meant to intimidate, though there was nothing in the approach, takeoff, or landing that would challenge a fit horse—provided the jockey's confidence didn't waver.

"The trick fence," Deene said. "The fourteenth fence is the same. Perfectly straightforward but sitting at the end of a long approach, looking massive and daunting. I hate trick fences."

"Every fence can be a trick fence. The next obstacle is the water, which might be the worst thing about the course."

When he met her gaze, Eve found concern in her husband's eyes. "You're worried about the footing, aren't you, Wife? You always worry about the footing."

"Footing is how I came a cropper all those years ago. It's how my mare bowed two front tendons. It's how I ended up crawling to the chamber pot." She blew out a breath while her husband merely looked at her. "This race is upsetting me, Deene, but not because you may have wagered more than we can afford—or not just that. I question why we'd put a good animal at risk, why we'd put Aelfreth at risk. I know this isn't a lark for you, but…"

"Eve, I assure you, we can afford the money riding on this race. I know what Anthony has told you, but on many of these outings to Town, I've been meeting with my bankers and their clerks and my men of business. Anthony has reasons for presenting the situation conservatively, and I will brace him on those reasons, but trust me when I say we are not in difficulties."

He would tell her that even if they were in the worst difficulties imaginable—wouldn't he? His Grace was a poor manager of finances. Her Grace would never admit such a thing, but it had become evident to Eve when she observed the lengths to which Westhaven had gone to secure management of the family's resources.

A gentleman could be deeply, deeply in debt and still maintain appearances, and the gentleman's family would have no notion of the problem. If he were a titled gentleman, then he could not be thrown into the hulks for his indebtedness, and the situation could get very bad indeed.

Eve caught up with her husband at the rushing brook bisecting the racecourse. He rode Beast right up to the bank. "The ground is still more or less solid, but if we get more rain tonight…"

"I hate mud, and I hate muddy water." Eve's tone was grimmer than she'd intended. "If I were riding William, I'd cue him to jump the entire blessed thing, to overjump it, so he lands well away and runs no risk of having to scramble on either bank."

"You will tell him this when you tuck him in tonight."

Deene was perfectly serious. He believed Eve could communicate with the horse on some level known only to horsemen and horsewomen, though Eve herself didn't give the horse—or herself—that much credit.

"I will tell Aelfreth, and we'll send somebody out to inspect before the stewards close the course tomorrow morning."

They rode the remainder of the course, though they already knew each jump, had inspected each jump for loose nails, bad footing, rotting timber, and subtle shifts brought about by weather, the passage of time, the time of day, and even changes in the wind.

At the last fence, where the horses turned for home and had a long, level stretch to use up whatever speed remained to them, Eve paused.

"There will be flags tomorrow on the pavilions and at the finish line."

"What of it?" Deene was still glowering, and he'd

still not told Eve the rest of his wager, which left her with an ominous, queasy feeling.

"If there's a stout breeze, the horses will come around the last turn and be able to hear the pennants whipping in the breeze. They'll see the flags snapping and the flag ropes slapping against the poles."

"A detail, surely. These horses are bred to run, Eve, and they'll know they're headed for the finish."

There was no such thing as a detail in a contest like this, but Eve and her spouse had run out of race-course. "Husband, won't you tell me, please? It isn't that I don't…"

She fell silent. The word *trust* was too explosive, a Congreve rocket of issues lay therein, and not all on Deene's side of the marriage. She thought back to their wedding night, when she'd had every opportunity to trust her husband, and had yet held her silence.

If a horse refused a jump for no apparent reason, a competent rider reconnoitered, then turned around, aimed the beast right back at it, and cleared the thing smartly, brooking no excuses.

"I want to know what hangs in the balance with this race, Lucas, because I do not want you carrying the burden of this wager all on your own shoulders. You've allowed me to contribute to William's training, and that means a great deal to me. Allow me to contribute something as a wife as well."

He fell silent, his expression grave. The unease inside Eve grew greater as she concluded that whatever he was about to tell her, it might yet not be the full extent of what he was risking with this race.

"I've wagered William. If I lose, William becomes

Dolan's possession. If Dolan loses, I get Goblin—and the money. Mustn't forget the money. Shall we return to the stables?"

He'd wagered a one-in-a-million horse, a horse to whom Eve was quite attached, and a fortune into the bargain. Eve said not one word. She turned her mare for the stables and cantered along at her husband's side, trying not to cry.

For herself, for the horse, and for the man whose honor—or whose wife—had compelled him to engage in such a wager.

❧

Deene sat among blankets on a pile of straw, his back against the wall, his arms around his drowsy wife.

He should have told her the whole of it earlier in the day, but her expression had gone so bleak when he'd admitted they might lose William. He'd not been able to say another word. And yet... silence was not serving them either.

"I should have told Anthony to send the coach back for you."

She stirred in his arms. "If you're staying, I'm staying. The child hasn't been born to the English countryside who hasn't snatched at least a nap in some obliging hayloft."

Below them, Beast shifted in his stall, giving a little wuffle at the sound of Eve's voice.

"I can understand your willingness to pass a night up here with me, Evie, but how is it you come to know so very much about how to ride a course like the one out there on the downs?"

When he'd reflected back on their most recent ride over the course, he'd realized Eve saw the entire challenge like Wellington saw a potential battleground, anticipating moves, choosing options, and analyzing the exercise on a level Deene himself had been oblivious to.

"I used to talk to Devlin and Bart endlessly about their cavalry exercises, about how a battle could turn on horsemanship. Boggy ground played a role in the French defeat at Waterloo, and Devlin is convinced Wellington knew it would when he put his artillery up along the ridge."

"A grim thought." The feel of Eve's hair tickling his nose was not grim. It was dear and precious and soothing.

"When I was a little girl I'd talk to Papa about the hunt meets and his cavalry days. It was one of few ways to gain his notice when I had so many older siblings competing for it. I would interrogate him at every turn about the good gallops and the bad falls."

Deene kissed her temple, an image of a very young, diminutive Eve on the fringes of the loud, busy circle of otherwise tall and robust Windham family members coming to mind. "And then you fell and lost more than just the ability to waltz with every swain in the shire."

He was holding her close to his body, so he felt something go through her. A shudder, a shiver, something. She'd come close on at least two recent occasions to telling him more about her fall, but he hadn't known how to encourage her confidences when he wasn't being entirely honest with his own.

"I must go for a walk." She tried to rise. He prevented it by virtue of kissing her cheek.

"Not without me."

"Yes, without you. Sometimes a lady needs a little privacy, but I won't go far, and I'll look in on William."

She was going to find a convenient spot in some clump of bushes, racetrack facilities being next to nonexistent.

"Don't be gone long. We'll be up well before first light."

"Which assumes we sleep at all."

He let her have the last word, let her disappear silently down the ladder, and felt the prayers start up again in his mind:

Please give this marriage the chance it deserves.

Let no harm come to horses or riders tomorrow.

Let there be a harmless explanation for the horrific and false disarray in which Anthony presented the Denning family finances.

Let there be an end to the mess between Deene and Dolan, and let it be an end that didn't cost him his niece, his wife, and his honor, much less his available coin and his prize stallion.

The litany grew longer before Deene spied Eve's blond head coming up the steps in the weak slats of moonlight making patterns through the barn siding.

She tucked herself in very close, and from the feel of her—from the heat and the tension in her—Deene knew immediately something was afoot.

"Evie? What's amiss?"

"Husband…" She was breathing rapidly and trying to whisper. "Husband, we must hurry. Somebody is going to drug poor William, perhaps with a quantity of somnifera, and I fear they've already done Aelfreth a bad turn."

God damn Jonathan Dolan.

"You stay here."

"No." She clutched at him with desperate strength. "There were four of them. They went off to fetch the drug, all quite merry with their mischief. I do not think them completely sober, but neither are they so drunk they could not do you an injury."

"Eve, I cannot allow Dolan's henchmen to drug William."

Her head came up, and she peered at him closely in the moonlight then leaned in and whispered into his ear.

He went still. She leaned in again, but he framed her face in his hands, kissed her soundly on the mouth, and pronounced her brilliant. They could solve the problem of Aelfreth's hangover in the morning, but for now, time was of the essence.

By the time they were back in their hayloft, Eve once again bundled into her husband's arms, Deene wasn't feeling quite so sanguine.

"We've thwarted this plan, Wife, but it still leaves us with a considerable handicap tomorrow if Aelfreth is in no condition to ride." *We.* It felt good to use that word when solving problems. Eve snuggled in more closely, giving Deene the sense she felt the same.

"You could ride him, Lucas. You know that course inside and out, you know your colt, and you're every bit as skilled as Aelfreth."

She was loyal. She'd not suggested Bannister or one of the other lads; she hadn't hesitated to put her faith entirely in her husband. She hadn't mentioned that Deene was far more weight than any jockey would be, and she hadn't once considered the most logical choice to get the beast around the course safely.

"We have another option, Evie."

"Bannister isn't in fighting shape, Deene, and he's been focusing more on Aelfreth than on the horse, and furthermore—"

Deene kissed his wife. Kissed her soundly enough to get her attention, almost soundly enough to lose his focus on the matter at hand. "Not Bannister, Eve Denning. The best chance that horse has of making it around the course in record time is the woman I'm holding in my arms right this minute."

He spent another hour arguing with his wife, his marchioness, his lady, and his love, and in the end, she agreed to trust his judgment. In this, Deene reflected— though perhaps in little else—she was going to trust him, and he was not going to let her down.

❧

"The steward is coming to look over the horse," Kesmore reported. "For God's sake, get her hair stuffed under that handkerchief."

Kesmore was looking thunderous but said nothing more, which was fortunate, because otherwise, Deene looked like he was going to indulge in a bout of fisti-cuffs with his brother-in-law. Aelfreth, sick as a dog, had handed over his silks without a word of protest, right down to his signature red, black, and white handkerchief. Bannister was muttering profanities as he saw to William, Beast was contentedly napping amid the commotion, and Eve was...

In love with her husband.

How could she have doubted him? How could she have put some silly fear about scandal and ruin ahead of the kind of faith she saw in Deene's eyes every time he looked at her? She still had the sense he wasn't being entirely forthcoming about his situation with Dolan—and didn't Mr. Dolan also have a great deal to answer for on this fine day?—but nothing else seemed to matter beside the magnitude of Deene's faith in her.

"You don't seem nervous," Kesmore observed while Deene led William from his stall.

"I cannot disappoint my husband, Joseph. He has placed all of his trust in me, and this… this is reassuring."

Kesmore draped a heavy arm around Eve's shoulders, and she realized—because the man could not be seen exactly hugging Deene's jockey—this was a show of support from the earl. "How is it, my dear, Deene asks you to risk your fool neck in a goddamned idiot horse race over wet grass and greasy mud, and this earns him your undying devotion?"

She didn't understand it entirely herself, and had considered that Deene had asked her to ride merely as a show of loyalty, while he fully intended to ride himself; but no, they'd argued about which of the two of them should ride the colt—they'd finally argued, in heated whispers and long silences, and even a few pointed fingers and waved hands, and now Eve was going to do the unthinkable and ride William in a match race.

The steward watched while William was trotted straightaway, turned, and trotted back. The horse went sound—of course he did—and with no evidence of any drugging.

"To the starting line, then," the steward said. "Greymoor wants a clean race." This last was directed at Eve where she stood beside Kesmore. "No bad conduct, no allegations of bad conduct, not even muttering into your ale next week about bad conduct—not with the riding crops, not with the horses, not with anything, or Greymoor will declare the match a dead heat, see if he doesn't."

Eve tugged the brim of her cap even lower with an acknowledging nod, then breathed a sigh of relief to see the steward hustle off toward the starting line.

"Thank God there's no handicapping, so we don't have to weigh you in. The finish will be tricky as it is," Kesmore said, keeping his voice down while Deene went about saddling William up. "You dismount at the first opportunity, and we'll put Bannister or one of the lads up to walk the horse out. You off, Bannister on, and then out of these silks, my lady. Louisa will assist you."

Eve nodded again, accepting that the subterfuge was unavoidable. She hardly wanted her family knowing she'd indulged in such a flight, much less the world at large—why, it would cause a scandal—

She watched Deene snugging up the girth on the horse and wondered why this hadn't occurred to her earlier. If it was discovered Deene had let his wife ride even in a private match race, there would be such awful talk, about him, about her... Dolan would exploit that talk and use it mercilessly.

Her knees went weak at the magnitude of the risk Deene was taking. She moved a little closer to Kesmore. "You will keep an eye on Deene, please.

He's been under a tremendous strain, and I fear he isn't thinking clearly."

"He isn't, and I will. Do not take off those goggles if you value my sanity, madam, not until you're out of your silks and in a very private situation."

He took a flask out of his pocket and held it out to Eve, who declined with a shake of her head. Kesmore blinked, as if realizing he'd just offered strong spirits to a lady, then took a nip and put the flask away. "The whole damned Windham family is mad. I have reason to know this. Even Lady Ophelia, who is the soul of kindness and discretion, has agreed with me on this."

Kesmore muttering about his prize market sow was not soothing Eve's nerves. She caught Deene's eye and realized the moment had come to leave the safety of the stable block.

Deene smiled at her, a private, challenging smile. A smile that said, "You can do this," and even, "I know you can do this."

He'd hatched up a daring plan, a crazy plan—and a plan that could work.

"Come, Aelfreth." Deene's voice was raised a little, to carry over the bustle in the barn. "Your horse and your adoring public await you."

Eve checked the chinstrap on her cap and tried to swagger out to the yard like a jockey. Deene tossed her up on the little racing saddle, then climbed aboard a very sleepy Beast. Kesmore, on his black, came up on William's other side, and they moved off toward the noise of the crowds at the starting line.

William was on a fine edge, bursting with the need to compete but still mindful of the rider on his back.

"Don't override," Kesmore muttered as they moved off, "but don't underride either, lest the horse start taking matters into his own hands, except a horse hasn't any hands."

He sighed gustily and took another quick nip from his flask. "I've married into a family of lunatics, and now the Denning line must strengthen this deplorable tendency. I'm not having any children, and what children I do have aren't going to be given any ponies. They shall ride pigs, see if they don't."

"Joseph." Deene's tone held banked humor. "You are excused. Find Louisa and try not to lose your composure entirely."

"Louisa awaits us on the rise, the better to plan my commitment to Bedlam as this race unfolds." He kneed his horse off to the right, leaving Eve riding beside her husband to the line that would mark the start of the race.

Dolan's gray was dancing around beneath his jockey, looking barely sane, gorgeous, and quite put out with the idiot holding onto his bridle.

"Evie?" Deene halted Beast, who seemed content to come to a bleary-eyed stop amid all the mayhem and tension of the impending race.

"They're waiting for us, Deene."

"Let them. Turn William as if you're letting him study the flags and pennants. Let him see the crowd as he'll see it when he roars up to the finish."

Not a detail. Eve had lectured herself at length not to forget this at the last minute, and here she'd gone…

"Listen to me, dearest, most precious wife, but pat the horse while you do, because Dolan is looking this way."

Eve thumped William soundly on the neck, as a male jockey might.

"You will win this race not because we have money riding on the outcome. I assure you we can afford the loss, and we don't honestly need the coin if we win. I promise you this. You will win this race not because it means we keep William—he's already covered every mare I could possibly put him to. I promise you this as well."

He wasn't finished. Eve gathered up her reins just as Goblin started to prop in earnest, and the stewards started motioning her closer to the starting line.

"There is more I would say, my dear." Deene reached over and stroked a hand down her shoulder, and Eve felt all manner of tension dissipating at just his touch. "You will win this race because it is yours to win, because this horse is yours to command. I have every faith in you, every faith. But if you don't win, that hardly matters. I will love you for the rest of my days and beyond, because when I asked for your trust, you gave it to me."

Another pat to her shoulder, and then he gathered up his reins and signaled to the steward that the horse and rider wearing the Denning colors were ready for the start.

Eve nudged William over to the starting line—the start was a dangerous, tricky moment—gathered up her reins, and crouched low over William's glossy neck. Lucas Denning had just told her he loved her, he trusted her, and he would love her for all the rest of his days.

He believed she could win. He believed she *would* win. Eve tried to believe it too.

"Dolan is headed this way on a showy buckskin." Kesmore passed his flask to Lady Louisa, who took a delicate sip and offered it to Deene.

"No, thank you." Not for one instant would Deene take his eyes off the horses sprinting forward from the start. The start was a critical moment in any race—a dangerous moment—but Eve had taken up a position off Goblin's left shoulder. She could pace Dolan's stallion from there without being at risk for getting kicked or—inadvertently or otherwise—thwacked by the riding crop Goblin's jockey held in his right hand.

Kesmore put his flask away and kept his voice down. "One hesitates to point out the obvious, Deene, but by every Jockey Club rule book in the known world, a female jockey's ride will be disqualified."

"One comprehends this."

Lady Louisa's horse shifted, as if Eve's sister might not have been aware of this fact.

"Then why in blazes," Kesmore went on in a rasped whisper, "would you put your wife at risk for injury or worse, much less scandal, if no matter how well she rides, the results cannot inure to your benefit?"

"Yes," Louisa echoed, her tone truculent. "Why in blazes?"

The horses cleared the first fence almost as a unit, clipping along at a terrific pace.

"On this course, on that horse, my wife is as safe as Lady Louisa is perched on that pretty, docile mare. And as for the rest of it, I know exactly what hangs in the balance. There will be some talk, of course, but weathering a bit of gossip is almost a Windham marital tradition."

He fell silent, lest he part with a few other things he knew.

For example, because he knew his horse and jockey so well, Deene saw Eve subtly check William as they approached the shadowed jump. The horse did not slow, but rather focused his attention more carefully on the upcoming obstacle. They cleared it a half stride behind Goblin—who'd chipped, taking a short, ungainly stride for his takeoff—and landed in perfect rhythm.

"Whatever else is true," Kesmore said quietly, "that is one hell of a rider on your colt."

One hell of a rider, indeed, and one hell of a colt. Aware of Dolan approaching on his showy mount, Deene did not share what else he knew of that rider, which included the fact that in all the weeks of their marriage, she had not been burdened with the female indisposition even once.

෴

Three strides away from the start, Eve had known she wasn't on some flighty two-year-old. William knew his job, relished his job, and intended to see to the matter of trouncing Goblin without a great deal of interference from Eve.

She had been tempted to use the first fence to disabuse the colt of his arrogant notions, to use a safe, easy fence to insist on a little submission from three-quarter ton of muscle and speed—except William's pacing was perfect, his takeoff flawless, and his landing so light Eve merely murmured some encouragement to him.

Where an argument might have started, she instead

complimented the horse, and so when she had to point out to him that a fence lay in the upcoming shadows, he was attentive to her aids and cleared the thing in the same perfect rhythm.

Goblin's jockey hadn't fared quite as well, the big gray being more intent on maintaining the lead than listening to his rider. Because of their bickering, they took off too close to the jump again, while Eve kept William a few feet off Goblin's shoulder and snugged herself down to the colt's back. The brush fence was coming up, and brush had been known to reach up and pluck an unwary rider from the saddle merely by getting tangled between boots, stirrup leathers, horse, and rider.

❧

"Lady Kesmore, Kesmore." Dolan spoke from the back of his golden gelding. "Deene. Your colt is giving a good account of himself."

Deene nodded, not trusting himself to speak to a man who would stoop to drugging either horse or jockey, much less both.

The crowd roared as the horses, neck and neck, thundered up to the water... the goddamned water, with the goddamned mud that scared Evie so.

"Holy Christ." Dolan's oath underscored Deene's own prayers. Whether William had taken the initiative or Eve had cued the horse, the colt soared high over the water, jumping bank to bank in a mighty, heaving leap, landing clear on the other side but losing ground to the other horse merely by spending so much time in the air.

"Your colt is a formidable jumper," Dolan said, frowning. "Though perhaps not in the hands of the most prudent rider."

❧

"Good boy." Eve didn't risk patting William again, but the horse flicked his ears as if listening for her voice. Their decision at the water had been justified when Goblin had landed closer to the far bank and had to scramble for footing. The instant's loss of forward momentum by the gray had William surging forward, claiming the lead. The horse would have widened the gap even farther, except Eve countermanded his wishes. Too much of the race lay ahead to be using up reserves of speed that would be needed for the long straightaway at the end, and much could happen between one jump and the next.

❧

"I hate this fence."

Deene didn't realize he'd spoken aloud until Dolan nodded. "It sits up there on that small rise, an oasis amid boggy ground, tempting the unwary to over-jump, and all manner of mayhem can ensue when the horses are running this closely."

As Eve and William galloped headlong toward the fourteenth fence, Deene was aware of resentment that, of all the thousands of people gathered around the racecourse that morning, he and Dolan were sharing a particular bond exclusive to the two of them. Maybe it was what he'd sought—some acknowledgement of their familial connection—but watching Eve put herself on the line, jump after jump, it was hard not to hate Georgie's father.

"God help them." Kesmore went on to swear viciously as Eve's horse cleared the big oxer only to land in bad footing.

Deene was already spurring Beast forward, when Dolan's hand shot out and grabbed the reins. Deene brought his crop down hard on Dolan's wrist and was prepared to use it on Kesmore's restraining hand as well when Lady Louisa spoke.

"You can't do a thing to help, Deene. Not now."

~

The fence Deene had dreaded, the fourteenth, was coming up quickly. For no other reason than that Goblin had dropped back almost even with William's quarters, Eve gave her horse the suggestion of a check on the reins. *Look up, focus, beware.*

William cleared the jump in excellent style, knees under his chin, back rounded in perfect form, and all going swimmingly—until the landing.

With the clarity of one in the midst of a pitched battle, Eve realized as the horse's shoulder slipped from beneath her that the top of the oxer had not been quite level, and rain had drained off to puddle closer to one back corner of the jump—the corner nearest where William landed. In the soft footing, the colt slipped, and when he slipped, Eve's world nearly came to an end.

This horror had befallen her seven years ago, a horse galloping along one moment, and in the next instant, heading for a disaster that could be fatal to horse and rider both.

As William pitched forward and fought for balance, instinct screamed at Eve to yank up on the reins, to try to haul the horse to his feet on main strength, to defy gravity itself.

She defied instinct; she defied every primitive imperative of self-preservation and relied instead on hard-won wisdom and experience. As William thrashed to keep his feet under him, Eve's arms shot forward, giving the colt as much slack in the reins as she could without actually dropping the leather from her grip.

He used the leeway she created to throw the great weight of his head and neck up, and in one tremendous surge, got himself organized and moving forward again. The magnitude of his effort was so great, Eve was nearly unseated as leap followed bound followed leap, until stride by stride, they reunited their efforts and took off after the gray, who'd already opened up a gap of several yards.

❧

"Bloody game pair you've got there," Dolan muttered. "Begging the lady's pardon for my language."

Deene said nothing. How Eve had managed to avoid disaster eluded him. Sheer grit, luck, skill... or her husband's unceasing prayers. One more fence, and it would come down to a grueling test of stamina—a test where Dolan's more experienced jockey and bigger horse might hold all the advantages.

❧

"You can do this," Eve whispered. "*We* can do this. Catch him, William. Catch him and show him who owns the bloody course."

She didn't need to shout. William's ears swiveled, proof he was listening for her voice. In Eve's mind, she heard her father's voice, though, imparting a piece of advice she'd never understood until that moment.

"In any fair contest, the horse with a sense of rhythm will beat the larger, stronger mount who lacks rhythm. Rhythm is what makes the beast efficient, so he's not working against himself, his rider, or his job. Let your horse develop his own rhythm, and then time the aids to his cadence. It's like dancing, my girl. Just like dancing."

They cleared the second-to-last fence flawlessly, William's strides to the fence perfect, his move off a graceful bound.

"Well done, Your Highness. One more, and we'll be bound for home."

They were closing the distance to Dolan's stallion too, stride by stride. Eve resisted the urge to check William's increasing speed. The colt had yet to mistime a fence, yet to misjudge a single distance. She crouched lower over his neck and gave the reins forward a hair.

"Go, William. Get us home."

He tackled the last fence from an impossibly long distance, his leap flat and efficient enough to gain half a stride and bring him up to Goblin's quarters. The gray was breathing in great, heaving bellows as the jockeys turned their horses into the straightaway toward the finish.

William galloped on, his stride, if anything, lengthening, while beside them, Goblin threw up his head. His jockey cursed over the thundering of the hooves and screaming of the crowd, and Eve knew a moment's sympathy.

Had Deene not insisted she show William that final stretch, the waving flags, the shifting crowd, that might be William registering a protest at having to gallop on into what could appear to a horse to be absolute mayhem.

But it wasn't William. Deene had recalled this detail, and so Eve gave the reins forward another hair.

"It's your race, William. God bless you, it's your race."

∽✦∾

"Deene, congratulations are in order." Dolan stuck out a hand, which Deene merely glared at.

"The stewards have yet to render a decision." Deene nudged Beast forward, intent only on getting to Evie and William, on holding his wife in his arms and taking her somewhere safe and private where he'd never, ever let her go, nor even sit on a horse again.

"Deene." Kesmore trotted his black up along beside Beast. "Greymoor will stay with her, you needn't hurry."

"Shut up, Joseph. When Greymoor finds out my jockey is a woman, there will be hell and a half to pay, and I don't want Evie dealing with that alone."

The stewards would keep any horse crossing the finish line in sight at all times until they'd confirmed the horse was the same one that began the race, and this would very likely result in Eve's gender becoming common knowledge. Greymoor was a gentleman, but he'd resent like hell that his race had been tainted by a breach of the rules.

Kesmore kept pace even when Deene moved up to the canter. "Given what Dolan attempted, I'm not sure you need worry so very much for your jockey."

"Two scandals for the price of one. I'm counting on it."

"You're counting on *both* horses being disqualified?"

"Aelfreth will swear he was drugged—the man's still barely able to stand, and you saw the condition Beast was in this morning."

Eve was up in her irons, hand-galloping William in a great sweeping arc while Greymoor on his black paced her a few lengths back. As she brought William down to the canter, then the trot, Greymoor closed the distance, reaching William only a moment before Deene did.

"Well ridden," Greymoor pronounced. "Deene, it appears congratulations are in order, though my official decision will wait until I've conferred with my subordinates." They trotted on another moment, until Goblin's owner joined them on his golden horse. "Dolan, good morning."

"Greymoor."

Bannister came bustling up, tossing a cooler over William's sweaty quarters while another groom put a hand on the reins.

"Off you go, lad. Well done." Bannister peered up meaningfully at Eve, who had made no move to take off her cap or goggles, thank God.

"Right. Off I go."

Beneath the mud and grime flecking her cheeks, she was pale as a ghost. Deene felt his heart turn over in his chest as Eve swayed a bit on William's back. William, still bristling with energy from his victory, began to dance, and Eve almost toppled from the saddle.

Deene was off his horse and dragging Eve against his chest just as Greymoor reached for her as well.

"Husband." Eve's voice was distant, a fading whisper that had Greymoor's dark eyebrows pitching upward and Kesmore swearing under his breath. Greymoor reached over and gently removed Eve's goggles.

"Lord Deene," Greymoor said quietly. "A word with you and Mr. Dolan."

"You may have your word," Deene said, "in a moment. Kesmore, where is your lady?"

"I'm here," Louisa said as her husband assisted her to dismount.

Eve's eyes fluttered open. "Lucas, did we win?"

Such hope shone from her eyes, such trust. "You won, Eve." Never had Deene been more grateful for his command of English. "You crossed the finish line first, you put in the best race, you rode like hell, and you won."

She reached up and laid her hand against his cheek. "*We* won."

"Deene." Louisa was glaring at him, Greymoor's expression wasn't exactly friendly, and Dolan was looking amused.

"Off with you now," Deene said, passing Eve into Kesmore's arms. "I could not be more proud of you, Wife, or more impressed. Well done."

Greymoor at least waited until Kesmore had moved out of earshot. "Well done, but you must know any horse and rider combination where the jockey is not of the male gender…"

Dolan spoke up, his brogue thicker than Deene had ever heard it.

"If your great, pontificating lordship would cease nattering for a moment, my brother-in-law and I will be havin' a wee discussion yonder, like the gentlemen we are."

"An odd pronouncement, Dolan," Deene replied, "considering you tried to drug my horse and succeeded in drugging my jockey."

"Enough," Greymoor hissed. "I will meet you both at the stable block, once I have conferred with the other stewards, and you will behave yourselves until then." He stalked off, swung up on his black, and cantered away, leaving Deene resisting the urge to plant a fist in Dolan's handsome face.

"You might have gotten my wife killed today, drugging King William. I hope the knowledge chokes you to death, Dolan."

"I did not drug your damned horse, Deene, and if you want to live to see another sunrise, you will stop implying to the contrary."

Rage at the man's indifference threatened the edges of Deene's vision. "Eve heard your minions plotting last night, Dolan. We switched Beast for William, else you might have succeeded in fixing the race. Do you know what your fate would be if word got out you'd tried to fix this race?"

"Listen to me, Deene." Dolan swaggered in close and planted his fists on his hips. "I did not fix the bloody race. Until I rose from my bed this very morning, I had every intention of losing the damned race—why would I drug your colt if I wanted to lose to him?"

"You *wanted* to lose?"

"For God's sake, I wanted my daughter raised in the household of a bloody benighted damned lord of the realm. I wanted every advantage for her. I wanted her auntie, the marchioness, firing her off in a few years. I wanted..." Dolan's hands dropped from his hips. He scrubbed a palm over his chin then dragged his fingers through his hair. "I wanted what was best for my daughter."

"Then why...?"

Deene took a step back, measuring the man before him. The man who'd fought Deene's every effort to be an uncle to Georgie.

"My lord?" A woman's voice. Deene turned his head and vaguely recognized a willowy blond with serious gray eyes.

"Amy, this is none of your affair." Dolan's tone had a gruff note in it, a warning note, and something else—something beseeching.

"Hush, sir. Inasmuch as I love Georgina too, this is my affair."

Of all people, the Earl of Westhaven shouldered through the circle of curious onlookers forming around Dolan and Deene. "Might I suggest we take this discussion back to the privacy of the stable block?"

Others appeared at Westhaven's elbow: Lord Valentine Windham, the Baron Sindal, the Earl of Hazelton, and bringing up the rear, no less personage than the Duke of Moreland himself.

Dolan sighed, smiling faintly. "Your wife has an honor guard, Deene. It seems we're to repair to the stables. Amy, you will walk with us."

※

Jonathan Dolan was not much given to prayer, but walking along through the thick spring grass on a pretty day, he prayed the gamble he was about to take might pay off.

For Georgina. For him it might be a flat loss, except it would expiate some of the guilt left by Marie's death.

"Dolan, we haven't much time." Deene spoke softly as his relations-by-marriage hovered near, making it plain they weren't about to let his lordship deal with Greymoor without a show of support.

"I intended to lose, Deene, it's as simple as that. Georgina would go into your keeping, I'd be labeled an arrogant Irish fool, and you would allow me ample visitation with my daughter. Amy would keep an eye on the girl, you'd dote upon Georgina and spoil her rotten, and she'd have her pick of the lordlings when the time came."

Deene scowled at him. "Does this have anything to do with a promise you might have made to my sister?"

Dolan blew out a breath, feeling a reluctant pang of admiration. "Oh, of course. I was to keep an eye on you, to help you deal with your idiot father, and so on."

"Then why the hell…?" Deene stopped and lowered his voice when one of the Moreland lordlings glanced over. "Why the hell did you give me such a hard time when I wanted to see Georgie?"

"Because you are a lord of the realm," Dolan said. "Everything comes easily to you, on every hand. You value only what's denied you, and so I denied you your niece, and you came to value her greatly."

"You are an idiot, Dolan. A bona fide, blazing, certifiable…" Deene fell silent again.

"I am an idiot, but until I started limiting your access to Georgina, you were intent on haring off in all directions. Cairo one moment, Baltimore the next, which is exactly what your sister did not want to see happen."

Deene glanced over again, his expression considering. "I was supposed to keep an eye on you as well, but I soon gave up on that. If looking after Georgie was the only way I could keep a promise to my sister, then look after Georgie was what I would do."

It must be galling to the younger man, to know his sister had set them both up like this. A few more years of marriage, and his perspective would shift, if Dolan's estimation of the marchioness was on the mark.

"I suppose all's well, then," Dolan pointed out. "You won the race. You get the prize."

"I did not win the race," Deene said, his voice low but forceful. "My jockey will be disqualified, and if you didn't try to drug my horse, then I'd like to know who did?"

Dolan took Miss Amy Ingraham's arm and caught Moreland's eldest noting the gesture.

"Amy has something to tell you, something she managed to tell me only after we'd saddled up and wrestled Goblin up to the starting line. Tell him, Miss Ingraham, and make it quick, because Greymoor will not spare us a moment's more privacy than he has to."

"I know who drugged your horse, my lord. At first I thought it was you, so closely does the man resemble you. Then I realized he's older than you, a little less broad through the shoulders, and so forth."

"The man's name?"

Dolan gave Deene credit for asking civilly. Amy seemed to shrink against Dolan's side, and her pace slowed as they approached the Denning stable block.

"I am familiar with *Debrett's*, Lord Deene. The man I overheard congratulating his minions for drugging your horse is Lord Andermere. I believe he's a cousin of some sort to you."

"Amy, would you excuse us for just a moment?" Dolan tried for a conciliatory tone but wasn't quite successful.

"Jonathan, you promised."

"I know, my dear, and I shall keep my promises. All of my promises."

She looked like she wanted to say more, but went up on her toes and kissed Dolan's cheek right there before the Moreland horde, with Deene looking on, Kesmore glowering at all and sundry from the stables, and the Earl of Greymoor standing around smacking his boots with his riding crop.

That one small kiss on the cheek gave Dolan the resolve he needed to explain to Marie's brother what should have been made plain to the man long since.

That Dolan had been in awe of his pretty, oh-so-proper wife, and would have paid five times the fortune he had to make her his own.

That he'd fallen in love with Marie despite every intention to the contrary.

That he'd waited a year after their vows for her permission to consummate the union, and that, when it was obvious more children might be the end of her, he'd still been nonetheless helpless to deny his wife anything, including the babies she'd begged for.

A decision he'd regretted every single day of his widowerhood.

⁂

"Be patient, my lord, please. They've needed to talk for years, and a few more minutes won't make a difference."

Eve wasn't about to beg—Greymoor was in charge of a simple horse race, for pity's sake. He wasn't Lord High Admiral of anything; nor was his own family history so free of scandal that Eve feared the man would stir up trouble for the pure mischief of it. He looked like he might be formulating some polite rejoinder when Eve heard a familiar voice.

"Eve Windham… Denning."

Her Grace approached at a pace a bit less decorous than the duchess usually displayed in public, while Greymoor bowed slightly and called out to one of his subordinates.

"Mama."

The duchess appeared composed, until Eve caught Louisa's eye. Louisa looked fretful, which suggested she might be scanning the surrounds for His Grace, which suggested in turn that Mama was not as calm as she appeared.

"You… You…" Her Grace stared at Eve, and while Eve braced herself for a lecture that would trump any scene the menfolk might be brewing, her mother's eyes filled with tears. "I am so *proud* of you."

It was the last thing Eve expected her mother to say, much less in a public location. "Proud of me?"

"Oh, you rode like a Windham. I wish Bartholomew had been alive to see his baby sister out there, soaring over one fence after another. I wish St. Just had been here to brag on you properly. I wish... oh, I wish..."

She reached for Eve and enfolded her daughter in a fierce, tight hug. "You showed them, Eve. You showed us all. Deene will be wroth with you for such a stunt, but he'll get over it. A man in love forgives a great deal. Just ask your father."

Her Grace whispered this between hugs, tighter hugs, and teary smiles.

"Mama, Deene is the one who said I ought to ride. I would never have had the..."

The *courage*. The *faith* in herself. The *determination*... All the things she'd called upon time after time in the past seven years, her own strengths, and she'd been blind to them.

"I could not have ridden that race without my husband's blessing and support, Mama."

"But you did ride it," Her Grace said, pulling Eve in for another hug. "I about fainted when you had that bad moment. Your father had to watch the last fences for me, but then the finish... You were a flat streak, you and that horse. I've no doubt he'd jump the Channel for you did you ask it. Oh, Eve... You must promise me never to do such a thing again, though. I could not bear it. Your father nearly had another heart seizure."

"I did no such thing, and I will ask you, Duchess, to keep your voice down if you're going to slander my excellent health in such a manner."

His Grace was capable of bellowing, of shouting

down the rafters, of letting every servant on three floors know at once of his frequent displeasures, but the duke was not using ducal volume as he approached his wife and youngest daughter.

He was using his husband-voice, his volume respectful, even if his tone was a trifle testy.

"Papa."

Eve pulled back from her mother's embrace to meet her father's blue-eyed gaze. Mama might be willing to make allowances, but His Grace was another matter entirely.

"Evie." He glanced from daughter to mother. "You've upset your mother, my girl. Gave her a nasty moment there at that oxer."

She was to be scolded? That was perhaps inevitable, given that His Grace—

Her father pulled her into his arms. "But what's one bad moment, if it means you're finally back on the horse, though, eh? I particularly liked how you took the water—that showed style and heart. And that last fence… quite a race you rode, Daughter. I could not be more proud of you."

He extended an arm to the duchess, who joined the embrace with a whispered, "Oh, Percival…"

So it came about that, for the first time in seven years, Eve's proud parents saw her cry—and it was a good thing for them all, and for Eve's brothers and sisters too. A very good thing, indeed.

~⁂~

"I think she's all right," Greymoor said, his glance anxious as he took in Eve and her parents farther down the barn aisle. "One doesn't want to ask a duke and a duchess to shove off so one can decide which scandal should be propounded regarding the simple match race one was supposed to supervise, so perhaps you'd best intervene."

Deene did not care for Greymoor's irritable tone, but he cared even less for the prospect of Eve's parents browbeating her for overcoming years of self-doubt in spectacular fashion.

"Evie?" He kept his tone casual and sauntered up to his wife. "Accepting some additional congratulations?"

He draped an arm over her shoulders and shot a challenging look at His Grace.

To Deene's surprise, the duke was beaming at his youngest daughter. "Indeed she was, Deene. And there will be a proper celebration going on in our private pavilion once you get Greymoor set to rights."

The duke offered his wife his arm, but Deene noticed they did not withdraw very far.

"Greymoor is about to explode, Wife. Shall we go take our medicine?"

Eve looped her arm through his. "William is faring well?"

"He's still cooling out, but yes. He's going sound, he knows he won, and he's quite pleased with himself."

"Papa and Mama were proud of me, Husband."

She nearly whispered this, her tone one of awe. Deene stopped and wrapped her in a tight hug. "Of course they were. *I* am proud of you. William is proud of you. You need to know that, Eve, regardless of what Greymoor does with the race results."

"I do know it. Louisa told me I'm to be disqualified."

He stepped back just far enough to meet her gaze. "That doesn't matter. You know it doesn't matter?"

She nodded, her smile a thing of such joy and beauty, Deene's heart began to hammer hard against his ribs.

"Deene." Greymoor motioned them over to where Dolan stood beside the earl. "I am prepared to render a result in this race, and then—meaning no disrespect to her ladyship here—I am going to go home, get roaring drunk, and swear off stewarding private matches for at least ten years."

Eve spoke up. "It's all right, your lordship. I understand you cannot let my ride stand."

Greymoor looked relieved, but Dolan didn't let his lordship reply.

"I don't see as that's the necessary result."

Deene appreciated the gesture, but rules were rules. "Dolan, there isn't a jockey club on any continent that would allow a female jockey's ride to stand. I know this. I knew it. I did not intend to keep Eve's gender a secret."

Dolan's gaze was measuring. "I am a man of my word, Greymoor. It's often the only grudging, honest compliment I garner from those of greater rank, but they must concede that much. At no time in our discussions did we stipulate that Jockey Club rules would apply. We did not run a standard distance, we did not use a standard steeplechase course, and we did not use a standard flat track. We ran a race designed to show off our two colts for the athletes they are, and we accomplished that aim. I say the first horse past the post should stand as the winner."

"Mr. Dolan—" Greymoor's brows knitted, and he

slapped his crop against his boots once. "I understand this race to have entailed wagers between you and Lord Deene. If I decide the race in favor of Deene, what of the wagers?"

Dolan's eyes went flat, his face expressionless. "I am prepared to abide by my word."

"Lucas?" Eve cocked her head. "What does he mean?"

"I mean," Dolan answered, "that I will surrender into Deene's legal keeping my daughter Georgina, along with a sum certain in the tens of thousands of pounds, and that stallion known as Goblin, and further described as a gray standing seventeen one hands unshod, bearing no other—"

Deene cut him off. "I am not taking your daughter from you. That was never my aim, and I won't be held responsible for doing so because your damned pride insists on it."

"You wagered your daughter?" Eve asked.

"I wagered her future, which is better served if she's raised by her uncle and by yourself, Lady Deene."

This discussion was not going the way Deene had intended.

"I can declare Lady Eve the loser," Greymoor volunteered, which earned him a scathing glance from Eve.

"Hush, my lord. This is a family matter. Mr. Dolan needs a moment to see the wisdom of my husband's reasoning."

"Lady Deene," Dolan began, "I lost. I had considered losing apurpose, truth be known, and have had some time to accommodate myself to this outcome. I'm sure Deene will allow me ample visitation. We agreed on that for the loser as well."

His gaze, when he raised his eyes to Deene, was... pleading. How long had Deene waited to see Jonathan Dolan brought to this, only to be unable to stand the sight of the man's importuning.

"Lucas, we cannot. Georgina loves her father, and while I will happily do all in my power to see the girl launched, please don't do this. You'll see eventually..." She started to tear up, and so Deene kissed her to stop the flow of words, then speared the earl with a glare.

"Greymoor, *I forfeit the race.* I forfeit the race, the wager, everything. Declare Dolan the winner before my wife starts crying. I'll get my visits with my niece, and Eve will sponsor her come out, which is all I ever truly wanted from this whole match."

"Fine," Greymoor sputtered. "The race is for—"

"Not a forfeit, for God's sake," Dolan expostulated. "Declare him the damned winner, and I'll keep my daughter, but the money and the colt will be... wedding presents. Goddamned wedding presents, with the horse going into her ladyship's keeping."

Deene most assuredly did not want such a large sum of money from another family member, much less another horse for his wife to fall in love with, but before he could take up the argument, Eve had stuck out a small hand.

"You have a deal, Mr. Dolan." She shook, she kissed the man's cheek, and she looked like she'd hug the sorry bastard while Greymoor cracked a smile and the sound of applause filled Deene's ears.

Eve's family stood around them, Their Graces, her brothers, her sisters, their spouses, all beaming like idiots. The race, it appeared, had been decided.

Westhaven leaned in. "You will not, I hope, choose this moment to indulge in any ninnyhammer behavior, Deene. Shake the man's hand, and get my sister the hell home before she faints again."

Again?

Deene shook Dolan's hand, endured the moment when Greymoor declared victory for King William, then got Eve the hell home. While she did not faint "again," she did fall asleep in Deene's arms, such that he had to carry her over the threshold and up to their chambers thereafter.

❦

Eve awoke deep in the night to find her husband blanketing her. In one instant, she went from a sweet, sleepy awareness of his body draped over hers, to a focused yearning for intimacy with him.

"I wasn't sure you'd awaken." His voice held a note of humor in the darkness, also concern.

She wrapped her arms and legs around him, got one hand anchored on his muscular buttocks and the other in his hair. "I'm awake."

The day had been long, with her family celebrating at great and noisy length, until Valentine had started singing, Westhaven had joined in, then Sophie with her lovely voice, and Her Grace had all but wept to see her brood engaged in such a display of good spirits.

They'd fallen into telling stories next, with every other tale seeming to center around "Remember the time Evie went steeplechasing on Meteor," or "Recall that it was Evie who wanted to see if the beasts really did speak on Christmas Eve…"

And Deene had waited patiently through it all, occasionally toasting his marchioness, but mostly keeping her by his side while the Windham family recovered from having one of its members in seven years of self-imposed exile.

When Deene had bundled Eve into the coach, she'd fallen asleep on his shoulder, then later had fallen asleep at her bath, literally, and needed her husband's assistance to get from the tub to the bed.

He hadn't bothered to put her in a nightgown, a decision she had to approve of as he kissed his way across her collarbones.

"These bones could have been broken at that bloody oxer."

"They weren't. My husband had faith in me."

He shifted up, to rest his chin on her crown. "I have never been so goddamned scared in my life, Evie. I have faith in you, and you rode one hell of a race, but please—I beg you—develop no aspirations involving a career as a jockey. There aren't enough prayers in me or in all of Christendom for that."

"I won't."

He sighed a big, husbandly sigh, proof positive he'd truly been concerned about this. And if she'd started spouting plans to work Goblin into better condition, no doubt he would have learned to pray harder and faster.

"Lucas?"

"Beloved?"

"Can we talk later?"

"We will talk later."

He settled in then to love her. She already knew

this about him after only a few months of marriage, knew when he was teasing and testing, knew when he was serious. He was very serious.

He was usually careful to insinuate himself into her body in easy, almost-pleasant stages, but this time, he seated himself at her opening, took her mouth in a voracious kiss, and drove home in one hot, sweet thrust that inspired her body into fisting around him in abrupt, clutching spasms of pleasure.

Eve gathered, as she lay panting beneath him, that her husband was making some sort of point. He waited a few minutes before resuming his diatribe, this time using slow, measured thrusts with a relentless quality to them that made Eve dig her nails into his backside and moan against his throat.

The third time he started up, she realized he was riding some sort of race of his own, an obstacle course of pleasure and persistence, in which she had no choice—in which she had no wish—except to submit and be amazed. When he finally allowed himself to cross his own finish line, she held him tightly, for long, long moments, until she understood what her next obstacle was going to be.

It was time to talk.

She smoothed her hand down the elegant length of Deene's spine, down to the lovely contour of his buttocks. He sighed and lifted half an inch away.

"I have imposed on you," he said, biting her earlobe. "You must scold me, Eve."

"I am too well pleasured to scold anybody for anything. Shall I fetch a cloth?"

"Somebody ought to."

He would have heaved himself away, except Eve clutched him a little tighter for a moment—for courage. Deene waited, then climbed out of the bed and crossed the room to the washbasin. Eve watched while he rinsed off by the glowing embers of the fire, then accepted the cool cloth from him and felt his gaze on her while she did likewise.

"Being married to you is very intimate, Lucas."

He accepted the cloth from her and tossed it in the general direction of the hearth. "Are you complaining?"

A guarded note in his voice betrayed the sincerity of his question.

"I am rejoicing. Also a trifle chilled, so please get under these covers and stay awake for a bit longer."

She caught one corner of his mouth tipping up slightly before he scooted under the covers and moved to spoon himself around her.

"Not like that." Eve wrestled him about, so he was over her. "What are we to do about Anthony?"

"Anthony has taken ship for Boston, his consort and children with him. I expect he also has at least a small fortune in coin packed among his bags, which I will choose to regard as compensation for his years of service."

"He stole from you, Lucas."

"Not as much as you'd think. He skimmed liberally, but as best I can reason, he liked more the sense of being the one who held the power and the purse strings. He didn't want me discovering his schemes, but more to the point, he didn't want me to figure out that he was merely a well-paid cipher, not the linchpin of some convoluted, ailing financial empire."

"A lying, well-paid cipher."

Deene nuzzled her ear, which tickled. "We ought to be grateful all Anthony's talk of rumors was mostly exaggeration of his own efforts to slander me, and that nobody has been paying the least mind to us or to my misspent youth."

Misspent youth. The term reminded Eve of the topic she had yet to broach. "I have something difficult to say to you, Husband."

"I do hope that white marriage business isn't going to come up, Eve Denning."

He snuggled his body in closer, as if to admit that the white marriage business had been lurking somewhere in his male brain, creating havoc these weeks past, and to further clarify that he'd have no part of it.

"God love you, Husband, a white marriage is the last thing I could contemplate with you. I would be devastated…"

He left off nuzzling her neck. "Go on."

This wasn't at all the tack she wanted to take. She wanted to be brisk, informative, and unsentimental. To pass along a few minor facts in the interests of easing her conscience and showing the same faith in him he'd shown in her.

A marriage needed to be based on mutual respect, after all.

"There are things I've needed to tell you, Lucas, but haven't found quite the right moment. Things that want privacy."

"I'm listening, and this is as much privacy as we're likely to get anywhere."

His reply was not at all helpful, but he stroked a

hand over her hair then repeated the caress, and that…
It reminded Eve of the way he'd patted her shoulder
before the race. The way he'd stayed near her all day,
the way he'd carried her over the threshold.

"My courses are late, Husband."

This merited her a sigh and a kiss to her cheek.

Her *cheek*?

"Being the sort of intimate husband I am—and
being married to the lusty sort of wife you are—one
noticed this."

She liked that he thought she was lusty… But
he'd *noticed*?

What else had he noticed?

"Did you notice that I was scared to death on that
horse today?"

"Of course. The more frightened you are, the
calmer you get. Usually." Another kiss to her other
cheek. "Though you were not particularly calm on
our wedding night."

Oh, he would bring *that* up. Eve had wanted to ease
into the topic, to whisk right over it, to drop hints and
let him draw conclusions.

Subtlety was wanted for the disclosure she had
in mind.

"I was not chaste."

God help her, she'd spoken those words aloud. Deene's
chin brushed over her right eyebrow then her left; his
arms cradled her a little more closely. "You were chaste."

"No, I was not. I had given my virtue… Lucas, are
you listening to me?"

"I always listen to you. You did not give your
virtue to anyone. It was taken from you by a cad and

a bounder who'd no more right to it than he did to wear the crown jewels."

Eve's husband spoke in low, fierce tones, even as the hand he smoothed over her hair was gentle.

"How did you know?" *He'd known? All this time he'd known and said nothing?*

"I thought at first you were simply nervous as any bride would be nervous of her first encounter with her husband, but then I realized you were not nervous, you were frightened. Of me, of what I would think of you. As if…"

He rolled with her so she was sprawled on his chest and his arms were wrapped around her. By the limited light in the room, Eve met his gaze.

"Your brother Bartholomew caught up with the fool man first, and the idiot was so stupid as to brag of the gift you'd bestowed on him. He was further lunatic enough to brag about the remittance his silence would cost your family. He bragged on his cleverness, duplicity, bad faith, and utter lack of honor to your own brother."

"Bart never said… Devlin never breathed a word."

"I don't think Devlin knew. By the time Devlin arrived on the scene, Bart had beaten the man near to death and summoned a press gang. I know of this only because I happened to share a bottle—a few bottles—with Lord Bart the night before we broke the siege at Ciudad Rodrigo. He regretted the harm to you. He regretted not avenging your honor unto the death. He regretted a great deal, but not that you'd survived your ordeal and had some chance to eventually be happy."

"You have always known, and you have never breathed a word."

"I have always known, and I have done no differently than any other gentleman would do when a lady has been wronged. You are the one who has kept your silence, Evie, even from your own husband."

He was not accusing her of any sin; he was expressing his sorrow for her. Eve tucked herself tightly against him, mashed her nose against his throat, and felt relief, grief, and an odd sort of joy course through her.

"All these years I thought I was alone with what had befallen me, but I had a friend in you, didn't I?"

"I haven't always been a friend to you, Evie. When a man finds himself damnably attracted to a woman who has suffered enough at the hands of…"

She shut him up with a kiss, a soft, helpful kiss such as a wife bestows on a husband inclined to temporize when he ought to be listening.

"I love you, Lucas. I love you for the faith you have in me, for your patience, for your honor, for so many reasons. I love you and I trust you and I love you."

He heaved the biggest sigh ever. "And you won't feel compelled to ride in any more races to demonstrate these lovely sentiments you hold toward me?"

"Not on horseback."

Though she did spend much of the remaining night—as well as most of the ensuing decades—demonstrating those same sentiments in myriad other ways.

Author's Note

The history of horse racing in England goes back at least to the Crusades, when returning knights brought the quick, intelligent, and hardy desert horses back to breed with local stock. The last Thoroughbred foundation sire was born in 1724, and by the 1800s, the Thoroughbred stud book traced the lineage of every horse racing officially in England back to the three foundation sires.

In the 1750s, the Jockey Club arose as an elite social club centered on the sport of racing. As part of its mission, the club propounded racing rules that were soon adopted by all of the major competitive courses. Women did not ride in these officially sanctioned races, though in informal meets, they did ride in Lady's Cup races. In some of those races, women participated as owners; in others they rode their mounts, resulting in contests where male jockeys competed in fields that included lady riders.

To this day, even at the Olympic level, women compete against men in the equestrian sports—and often emerge as the victors.

I'm indebted to author Emery Lee (*The Highest Stakes, Fortune's Son*) for providing background regarding British racing history. Though her books are works of fiction, they include myriad marvelous details that will fascinate the true aficionado of "the sport of kings."

READ ON FOR A SNEAK PREVIEW OF
GRACE BURROWES'S

Lady Maggie's Secret Scandal

NOW AVAILABLE
FROM SOURCEBOOKS CASABLANCA

"THE BLIGHTED, BENIGHTED, BLASTED, PERISHING thing has to be here somewhere." Maggie Windham flopped the bed skirt back down and glared at her wardrobe. "You look in there, Evie, and I'll take the dressing room."

"We've looked in the dressing room," Eve Windham said. "If we don't leave soon, we'll be late for Mama's weekly tea, and Her Grace cannot abide tardiness."

"Except in His Grace," Maggie replied, sitting on her bed. "She'll want to know why we're late and give me one of those oh-Maggie looks."

"They're no worse than her oh-Evie, oh-Jenny, or oh-Louisa looks."

"They're worse, believe me," Maggie said, blowing out a breath. "I am the eldest. I should know better; I should think before I act; I am to set a good example. It's endless."

Eve gave her a smile. "I like the example you set. You do as you please; you come and go as you please; you have your own household and your own funds. You're in charge of your own life."

Maggie did not quite return the smile. "I am a disgrace, but a happy one for the most part. Let's be on our way, and I can turn my rooms upside down when I get home."

Evie took her arm, and as they passed from Maggie's bedroom, they crossed before the full-length mirror.

A study in contrasts, Maggie thought. They were the bookends of the Windham daughters, the eldest and the youngest. No one in his right mind would conclude they had a father in common. Maggie was tall, with flaming red hair and the sturdy proportions of her mother's agrarian Celtic antecedents, while Evie was petite, blonde, and delicate. By happenstance, they both had the green eyes common to every Windham sibling and to Esther, Duchess of Moreland.

"Is this to be a full parade muster?" Maggie asked as she and Evie settled into her town coach.

"A hen party. Our sisters ran out of megrims, sprained ankles, bellyaches, and monthlies, and Mama will be dragging the lot of us off to Almack's directly. Sophie is lucky to be rusticating with her baron."

"I don't envy you Almack's." Maggie did, however, envy Sophie her recently acquired marital bliss. Envied it intensely and silently.

"You had your turn in the ballrooms, Maggie, though how you dodged holy matrimony with both Her Grace and His Grace lining up the Eligibles is beyond me."

"Sheer determination. You refuse the proposals one by one, and honestly, Evie, Papa isn't as anxious to see us wed as Her Grace is. Nobody is good enough for his girls."

"Then Sophie had to go and ruin things by marrying her baron."

Their eyes met, and they broke into giggles. Still, Maggie saw the faint anxiety in Evie's pretty green eyes and knew a moment's gratitude that she herself was so firmly on the shelf. There had been long, fraught years when she'd had to dodge every spotty boy and widowed knight in the realm, and then finally she'd reached the halcyon age of thirty.

By then, even Papa had been willing to concede not defeat—he still occasionally got in his digs—but truce. Maggie had been allowed to set up her own establishment, and the time since had seen significant improvement in her peace of mind.

There were tariffs and tolls, of course. She was expected to show up at Her Grace's weekly teas from time to time. Not every week, not even every other, but often enough. She stood up with her brothers when they deigned to grace the ballrooms, which was thankfully rare of late. She occasionally joined her sisters for a respite at Morelands, the seat of the duchy in Kent.

But mostly, she hid.

They reached the ducal mansion, an imposing edifice set well back from its landscaped square. The place was both family home and the logistical seat of the Duke of Moreland's various parliamentary stratagems. He loved his politics, did His Grace.

And his duchess.

One of his meetings must have been letting out when the hour for Her Grace's tea grew near, because the soaring foyer of the mansion was a beehive of servants, departing gentlemen, and arriving ladies.

Footmen were handing out gloves, hats, and walking sticks to the gentlemen, while taking gloves, bonnets, and wraps from the ladies.

Maggie sidled around to the wall, found a mirror, and unpinned her lace mantilla from her hair. She flipped the lace up and off her shoulders, but it snagged on something.

A tug did nothing to dislodge the lace, though someone behind her let out a muttered curse.

Damn it? Being a lady in company, Maggie decided she'd heard "drat it" and used the mirror to study the situation.

Oh, no.

Of all the men in all the mansions in all of Mayfair, why *him*?

"If you'll hold still," he said, "I'll have us disentangled."

Her beautiful, lacy green shawl had caught on the flower attached to his lapel, a hot pink little damask rose, full of thorns and likely to ruin her mantilla. Maggie half turned, horrified to feel a tug on her hair as she did.

A stray pin came sliding down into her vision, dangling on a fat red curl.

"Gracious." She reached up to extract the pin, but her hand caught in the shawl, now stretched between her and the gentleman's lapel. Another tug, another curl came down.

"Allow me." It wasn't a request. The gentleman's hands were bare and his fingers nimble as he reached up and removed several more pins from Maggie's hair. The entire flaming mass of it listed to the left then slid down over her shoulders in complete disarray.

His dark eyebrows rose, and for one instant, Maggie had the satisfaction of seeing Mr. Benjamin Hazlit at a loss. Then he was handing her several hairpins amid the billows of her mantilla, which were still entangled with the longer skeins of her hair. While Maggie held her mantilla before her, Hazlit got the blasted flower extracted from the lace and held it out to her, as if he'd just plucked it from a bush for her delectation.

"My apologies, my lady. The fault is entirely mine."

And he was laughing at her. The great, dark brute found it amusing that Maggie Windham, illegitimate daughter of the Duke of Moreland, was completely undone before the servants, her sisters, and half her father's cronies from the Lords.

She wanted to smack him.

Maggie instead stepped in closer to Hazlit, took the fragrant little flower, and withdrew the jeweled pin from its stem.

"If you'll just hold still a moment, Mr. Hazlit, I'll have you put to rights in no time." He was tall enough that she had to look up at him—another unforgivable fault, for Maggie liked to look down on men—so she beamed a toothy smile at him when she jabbed the little pin through layers of fabric to prick his arrogant, manly skin.

"Beg pardon," she said, giving his cravat a pat. "The fault is entirely mine."

The humor in his eyes shifted to something not the least funny, though Maggie's spirits were significantly restored.

"Your gloves, sir?" A footman hovered, looking uncertain and very pointedly not noticing Maggie's hair rioting down to her hips. Maggie took the gloves and held them out to Hazlit.

"Can you manage, Mr. Hazlit, or shall I assist you further?" She turned one glove and held it open, as if he were three years old and unable to sort the thing out for himself.

"My thanks." He took the glove and tugged it on, then followed suit with the second.

Except his hand brushed Maggie's while she held out his glove. She didn't think it was intentional, because his expression abruptly shuttered further. He tapped his hat onto his head and was perhaps contemplating a parting bow when Maggie beat him to the exit.

She rose from her curtsy, her hair tumbling forward, and murmured a quiet "Good day," before turning her back on him deliberately. To the casual observer, it wouldn't have been rude.

She hoped Hazlit took it for the slight it was intended to be.

"Oh, Mags." Evie bustled up to her side. "Let's get you upstairs before Mama sees this." She lifted a long, curling hank of hair. "Turn loose of that mantilla before you permanently wrinkle it—and whatever happened to put you in such a state?"

Acknowledgments

I didn't aspire to start my writing career with an eight-book series, but here we are, at the end of the seventh Windham family story, and Lady Jenny's story already in the works. The people who've contributed to and supported this accomplishment are too numerous to mention. How about I try anyway, because saying thanks is one of the best parts of being published.

Big thanks:

To my editor, Deb Werksman, who knows just how to buff the shine on the good ones, and how to send the not-yet-good-enough ones back to me for more work.

To my production editor, Skye, who has the gene for catching what everybody else misses, and is so nice about it.

To Susie, who is the goddess of the calendar, among many other unsung duties, and always so pleasant to deal with.

To Cat, another friend to every book I've written, and more of the glue holding both good spirits and successful production together.

To Danielle, the standard-bearer who truly believes in the books and authors fortunate enough to have her as their publicist.

To Gail, my copy editor, who probably goes to sleep at night praying to The Almighty that Grace Burrowes will please stop abusing the word nor.

To the rest of the team, in marketing, bookmaking, accounting, and every other Sourcebooks department. I have never met a nicer, more hard working, professional group of people.

To my agents, Steve and Kevan, who are always just a phone call away, no matter what obscure question I'm obsessing over.

And also to my publisher, Dominique Raccah. I don't know of any other tadpole author who can turn in a manuscript secure in the knowledge that if the rest of us can't figure out quite what's amiss with the book, the publisher herself will stay up late some night and pore over the story page by page. To have this much support is a blessing of significant magnitude, and bodes wonderfully for all the sequels, spin-offs, and prequels we have planned for the Windham family and their friends.

Waking Up with a Rake

Connie Mason and Mia Marlowe

The fate of England's monarchy is in the hands of three notorious rakes.

To prevent three royal dukes from marrying their way onto the throne, heroic, selfless agents for the crown will be dispatched…to seduce the dukes' intended brides. These wickedly debauched rakes will rumple sheets and cause a scandal. But they just might fall into their own trap…

After he's blamed for a botched assignment during the war, former cavalry officer Rhys Warrick turns his back on "honor." He spends his nights in brothels doing his best to live down to the expectations of his disapproving family. But one last mission could restore the reputation he's so thoroughly sullied. All he has to do is seduce and ruin Miss Olivia Symon and his military record will be cleared. For a man with Rhys' reputation, ravishing the delectably innocent miss should be easy. But Olivia's honesty and bold curiosity stir more than Rhys' desire. Suddenly the heart he thought he left on the battlefield is about to surrender…

For more Connie Mason and Mia Marlow, visit

www.sourcebooks.com

Checkmate, My Lord

by Tracey Devlyn

❧

The stakes are high, the players in position...

Catherine Ashcroft leads a quiet life caring for her precocious seven-year-old daughter, until a late-night visitor delivers a startling ultimatum. She will match wits with the enigmatic Earl of Somerton, and it's not just her heart that's in danger.

Let the games begin...

Spymaster Sebastian Danvers, Earl of Somerton, is famous for his cunning. Few can outwit him and even fewer dare challenge him—until now. After returning to his country estate, his no-nonsense neighbor turns her seductive wiles on him—but why would a respectable widow like Catherine risk scandal for a few passionate nights in his bed?

❧

Praise for *A Lady's Revenge*:

"Devlyn makes a unique mark on the genre with her powerful prose and gripping theme."—RT Book Reviews, *4 Stars*

"Devlyn reveals the darkness of the spy game and entices readers with a talented and determined heroine."—Publishers Weekly

For more Tracey Devlyn, visit:

www.sourcebooks.com

Once Again a Bride

by Jane Ashford

❧

She couldn't be more alone

Widowhood has freed Charlotte Wylde from a demoralizing and miserable marriage. But when her husband's intriguing nephew and heir arrives to take over the estate, Charlotte discovers she's unsafe in her own home...

He could be her only hope...or her next victim

Alec Wylde was shocked by his uncle's untimely death, and even more shocked to encounter his uncle's beautiful young widow. Now clouds of suspicion are gathering, and charges of murder hover over Charlotte's head.

Alec and Charlotte's initial distrust of each other intensifies as they uncover devastating family secrets, and hovering underneath it all is a mutual attraction that could lead them to disaster...

❧

Readers and reviewers are charmed by Jane Ashford:

"Charm, intrigue, humor, and just the right touch of danger."—RT Book Reviews

For more Jane Ashford, visit:

www.sourcebooks.com

About the Author

New York Times and *USA Today* bestselling author Grace Burrowes hit the bestseller lists with her debut, *The Heir,* followed by *The Soldier* and *Lady Maggie's Secret Scandal. The Heir* was also named a *Publishers Weekly* Best Book of 2010, *The Soldier* was named a *Publishers Weekly* Best Spring Romance of 2011, and *Lady Sophie's Christmas Wish* was named Best Historical Romance of the Year in 2011 by RT Reviewers' Choice Awards. All of her Regency romances have received extensive praise, including starred reviews from *Publishers Weekly* and *Booklist.* Grace is also branching out into short stories and Scotland-set Victorian romance with Sourcebooks.

Grace is a practicing attorney specializing in family law and lives in rural Maryland. She loves to hear from her readers and can be reached through her website at graceburrowes.com.